Review Copy
Not for Resale

Jack Jaeger was born in 1943, the son of a Durham miner. He joined the army at fifteen. Three years later passed the selection for The Special Air Service, serving two years in Borneo through the insurgency and then onto Aden in the Radfan, Somalia and South America. Briefly in the Oman and Beirut. After six years with the Regiment and married five times life didn't get any easier when he was recruited into MI 6.

To Sandra – my wife who taught me how to 'move-on' and leave anger behind. To the other two loves of my life, my two wonderful cats: Princess 'Piggy-Wiggy' who sits at my computer most of the day in an advisory capacity and to 'Tommy-Tuck-Box' who loves me to death just for the cost of a tickle behind his ears… occasionally.

And to my good friend Deborah Boyd who was the very first to read my manuscript and insisted that I try to have it published. Thank you.

Jack Jaeger

The Stone Killers-Saga

AUSTIN MACAULEY
PUBLISHERS LTD.

Copyright © James Jaeger (2016)

The right of James Jaeger to be identified as author of this work has been asserted by him in accordance with section 77 and 78 of the Copyright, Designs and Patents Act 1988.

All rights reserved. No part of this publication may be reproduced, stored in a retrieval system, or transmitted in any form or by any means, electronic, mechanical, photocopying, recording, or otherwise, without the prior permission of the publishers.

Any person who commits any unauthorized act in relation to this publication may be liable to criminal prosecution and civil claims for damages.

A CIP catalogue record for this title is available from the British Library.

ISBN 9781786120359 (Paperback)
ISBN 9781786120366 (Hardback)
ISBN 9781786120373 (E-Book)

www.austinmacauley.com

First Published (2016)
Austin Macauley Publishers Ltd.
25 Canada Square
Canary Wharf
London
E14 5LQ

Prologue

Slowly, she pushed the wheelchair to the stern of the big motor yacht and, easing it against the furthest guard rail of the transom, carefully applied the brakes, very aware now of the spray and the drizzly rain making the deck so slippery. From here she knew he could look out into the vastness of the Atlantic Ocean and watch the great round topped waves rolling in from the west.

Antonia Vargas had carried out the same routine with him for the past twelve years on exactly the same day, each year and still really had no idea of exactly why he performed this annual ritual. She had asked on several occasions, but had never received a satisfactory reply, just a series of grunts and mumbled mutterings that she could never fully understand or comprehend but was content to dutifully go along with it, anyway.

"Is that good for you here, corino?" She tucked the heavy blanket tighter around his lifeless legs and made sure that his scarf was fully covering his chest under the big coat. 'Corino' was the Galician word for 'darling', and it was all she ever called him.

The old man smiled, thinly and nodded his head in thanks. On his lap he cradled a bouquet of giant white lilies, which had been carefully wrapped in bright red paper, the bouquet was interspersed with red 'floribunda' roses and an occasional delicately fragrant orchid. The florist in La

Coruna had specially made them up for him, as she had over the past years. Slowly he reached a bony white hand to his face and wiped the tears from his eyes and cheeks, sobbing quietly.

"We're right on the spot of the coordinates you gave me, sir." The Captain stood behind him, dressed in an immaculate white uniform with gold buttons and smartly braided epaulettes; deferentially he touched the peak of his hat in a salute. "Are you sure you are alright, sir, it's bitterly cold out here, should I bring you another blanket?"

The old man raised a feeble hand and attempted a smile again, but said nothing, just shaking his head, his eyes focused on the turgid waters gently rocking the stationary motor yacht.

Antonia Vargas, touched the Captain's arm and thanked him, steadying herself against the lurch of the yacht as a particularly large wave made it pitch and roll a little more violently than normal sending a deluge of spray and bubbling foam across the quarter deck as it hit the hull. She knew the captain was right though, the wind was bitterly cold and biting through her own coat as if she was standing here naked.

Gently she laid her hand on the old man's shoulder and kissed his cheek watching nervously as he slowly lifted the bouquet to the rail trying tentatively to drop them over the side. His eyes were fixed only on the bouquet, but the wind snatched it from his hands and threw them violently into the water... as if angry with him, spiting him and yet the waves seemed to sympathise, 'cradling' them easily into the deep troughs, gently lifting them over each wave as if they were being guided by an unseen hand. For a brief moment they drifted back and touched the side of the yacht and the old man leaned far over the rail, his tears mixing with the salt spray.

"I'm sorry..." He whispered, trying to reach down to touch them for one last time, but Antonia held him back, her hands on his shoulders fearing he might topple over and eased him gently back into the wheelchair touching his cheek tenderly with her fingers.

"It's done, corino... it is done... now I must get you back inside, or the cold will touch on you."

Antonia Vargas had been born in the village of Dante in the far northwest of Spain in the province of Galicia where the tip of rocky outcrops of land touched the rage of the North Atlantic Sea... a buttress against the waves that had travelled, unobstructed for four thousand miles, only to vent their immense anger and rage on the rocky cliffs to meet their own destruction.

The Galician people had always been a hardy, self-reliant race of people and Antonia was no exception. She was not a beautiful woman... perhaps not even pretty... to some eyes... more of a robust, rosy-cheeked, country woman and she held the honest 'no-nonsense' values of her Galician forebears. Her bright, ruddy complexion and sparkling blue eyes... gave off a radiance of reliability and 'natural' honesty, masking the torture she had kept hidden within her own soul for so many years.

She touched the old man's cheek again rubbing them gently trying to build some warmth into the almost transparent, veined skin. She had been his nurse for the past twenty-five years and still knew almost nothing about him, only that he was an Englishman and that he had been brought into her hospital, very close to death after a terrible accident. Twelve years ago, they had married and she had relinquished her position at the hospital so that she could nurse him back to health.

From the outset she had known that because of his terrible injuries the marriage could never be consummated... and that he would be bound to a wheelchair for the rest of his days, but that had suited her own personality, anyway. The need for an intimate, sexual companionship had never been something she had ever craved or wanted.

As a child from the age of nine she had been repeatedly raped on many, many occasions by her stepfather, the eventual, fateful outcome was that at the age of fourteen she had become pregnant by him. Initially everyone in her village, including her own mother had looked on her as a 'Puti'... a whore... a girl of loose morals, a woman to be shunned and avoided. Consequently she had suffered gravely, all of it in absolute silence, fearing the wrath and retaliation of her stepfather so much that she never spoke of him as the father of her child. 'His' own guilt had eventually saved her, with his suicide soon after the birth. He had left a note explaining the 'torture' he had inflicted on the girl and how he himself had suffered the ignominy of self-hate and shame and of disgracing himself and his family, begging them for their forgiveness. But the damage had already been done.

When the baby was born it had been taken away from her immediately and offered for adoption and Antonia had never been allowed to see the child. Many times she had wondered where that young man was now... and what he was now doing.

In the warmth of the cabin she removed her hat and coat and laid them neatly on the bed and then took the old man's hat, folding it and laid it with her coat and gently touched his cheeks with her fingers rubbing his cold hands. Antonia smiled at him; although the face was now wrinkled and the hair had receded, his bright green, sparkling eyes still shone with a radiance of life... it was the very first thing she had noticed about him when she first walked into his intensive care room at the hospital.

"It is done now, corino, we will go home and I will make you some hot soup... maybe lenteja, no? You like that very much."

The old man strained his neck to look up at her and smiled, he touched her hand and patted it gently and nodded. Silently hoping that he wouldn't be here... next year to endure the same torture...

Chapter 1
August 20th 1979
Twenty-Five Years Earlier

"That's all of them then." The tall young man fidgeted nervously, shuffling from one foot to the other. He glanced cautiously for the 'umpteenth' time towards the locked door that led through into the main staircase of the bank. His dark grey, immaculate suit showed patches of perspiration around the armpits and the collar of his shirt. Earlier, he had removed the cumbersome tie that was choking him and had stuffed it into his pocket out of the way, just to be free of it.

This would be his third and last trip to the basement car park where his car was parked, and he was extremely glad about that. Unused to manual labour, his soft white hands were already showing signs of blistering, and his thin, wiry leg muscles were aching. More than anything Daniel wished that he was anywhere but here at this moment; even now there were a million and one things that might go wrong. "Shall I go, do you think?" He wiped the sweat from his face with a clean handkerchief, inadvertently glancing at the door again... "What about them..." He nodded at the two men and a woman, bound to the office chairs with grey duct tape, but he couldn't look at them as they seemed to be in such terrible discomfort and pain.

"Daniel, just go..." Kristianna van Ouden spoke softly to him and gently touched his cheek with her fingertips. Daniel stood at a shade over six feet, and she was almost as tall. "I'll take care of everything here, just stick to the plan." Due to his incompetence in parking the car, they were already fifteen minutes behind her planned schedule.

How she hated men, their weaknesses... and their stupidity never ceased to amaze her; she considered that most of them weren't worth the skin they stood up in. Of course there were times, like now, when they were needed, to lift and carry and fetch. She would have been just as happy living in a world where men were reduced to being 'sperm bank donors' to provide the necessary 'productive juices' for those women who felt the need to breed... and just to keep the human population of the planet reinforced. "Calm down, Daniel, it is nearly over." She touched his lips with her own, wanting to dissipate his fear. "All you have to do is get those cases to the yacht. In four or five hours we will be in international waters, heading for a different country. Do you understand that?" she added, firmly.

Daniel nodded. His blonde, lank hair was dishevelled and soaked with sweat. "But if someone finds them in the next couple of hours, then we are done for... aren't we? They will know who we are... and hunt us down." He spoke with a heavy American accent.

"Daniel..." Her voice was sharper and she wanted to slap him, but restrained herself, fearing that he might crumple into a heap on the floor and start crying... or something. She squeezed his arm, reassuringly and spoke calmly to him and then brushed a blonde lock of damp hair from his eyes. They could easily have been taken for siblings, her eyes were the same soft blue, but her blonde hair was shorter cropped and tucked neatly behind her ears. "Just stick to the plan; we have been through this countless times. Get to the yacht and then your job is finished. You can sit down and relax with a very large whisky. I'll be there in about two hours... Now go." She nodded towards the door. "... and, Daniel." He looked back at her. "... don't speed... stick to the speed limit, there is no hurry now..."

Kristianna watched as he closed the door behind him and felt more relaxed... it was done... just these few 'loose ends' to take care of. In a way it had been a shame to bring him into the 'operation' at all, he was completely unsuitable for anything that took him away from his desk, but it had been necessary. The 'process' of convincing him had taken months of 'intimate persuasion', at times allowing herself to become his 'subservient whore'... almost. She had needed him because he was the Junior Executive Director of Met. Corps, in the financial section of the company they both worked for and had just successfully robbed... Daniel was the only other key holder able to unlock the stairwell doors to the garages.

She felt a little tingle at the nape of her neck, just thinking about what they... what she... had just achieved, it gave her a heightened sense of excitement and had been three long, arduous years in the planning. Three years of subservience, tolerance and obedience... but now... it had all been worth it... It had been worth all the times she had had to degrade herself to people she knew were not her equal, or ever would be, all those times she had smiled and agreed with them... Now it was her turn.

Kristianna sat on the desk, one foot on the floor to steady herself, facing her 'captives' and slowly removed the tiny automatic pistol from her shoulder holster and cocked it. The action causing consternation to the three bound and gagged captives. The larger, heavily overweight man was the security guard. He sweated profusely, the duct tape had bitten into the skin around his blooded mouth and cheeks, and a tiny trickle of blood had stained his blue, company shirt. He seemed to be having problems breathing and had wet himself, so much so that the urine formed in small puddles on the floor beneath his chair.

The second man was much older and she knew him well, he was her uncle... Drogda van Ouden was her father's brother and she hated him with a vengeance that almost bordered on insanity. Kristianna always blamed him for her father's untimely death, ten years ago, but she had never allowed him to see her hatred... ever, or given him the slightest indications of her feelings towards him other than pleasantries or courtesy. If he had known, or had even felt her resentment towards him, it would have spelled her own demise... very quickly. Two years ago she had even allowed him, under the 'pretence of innocence', to 'rape' her... late one evening in his office. Even now there were times she could taste and feel his sweaty, fat, nauseous body in her nostrils... She shuddered, involuntarily.

The bound woman sobbed hysterically, but there were no tears left, her face was contorted by the tightness of the duct tape and her bloodstained eyes bulged from her head in fear. She was thin and gaunt and breathed heavily through a very large, pointed nose. Kristianna knew her only slightly, as one of the junior accountants who worked for Met Corps, and wondered what terrible hand of fate had chosen her to assist Drogda this Saturday morning...

"Well, Drogda, we have a parting of the ways, it seems..." She slowly screwed the suppressor onto the end of the barrel and checked the load, balancing the pistol lightly in her hand. It had been custom-made for her in South Africa, her birthplace, by a master craftsman and presented to her by her father on her thirteenth birthday. The 1.75mm caliber was minute. In the hands of an amateur the pistol would have been no better than a child's 'toy', but in the hands of an expert like Kristianna... it was as lethal as any cannon.

Her father had specifically asked for the gun to be made with such a small caliber. "It will breed 'accuracy' and confidence my dear." He had said. "...any fool can hit a target with a big .45, and make an awful lot of noise and mess at the same time. But proficiency with a weapon such as this will make you untouchable... invincible! And, it can be hidden almost anywhere on the body, even in the very intimate places where no one will ever search..." He had been right so many times...

She smoothed the front of her charcoal grey slacks and raised the pistol, and with one fluid movement, fired just once. The recoil for such a small gun was out of proportion to its size, but she had made and packed the shells herself, early this morning whilst everyone slept and had overloaded each shell with double the amount of powder.

The bullet struck the security guard just above his right eyebrow and threw his head backwards, his body writhing and thrashing so much that his leg tore through part of the tape. Kristianna cursed herself, the target had been his eye and she had missed... She re-aimed holding the pistol with both hands and waited for the man's head to come upright and fired, this time hitting the 'mark' she had originally aimed for. She considered that from twelve feet, it wasn't a bad shot...

The hapless woman's screams although muffled by her gag became louder and louder, her head frantically shaking from side-to-side, her eyes begging Kristianna to spare her. Her fruitless attempts to free herself served only to ravage her arms and legs where the tape had dug into her flesh. The first shot hit her low in the throat just nicking the jugular but causing the blood to spurt from her in great, pulsed bursts. Kristianna cursed her for struggling so and fired again, the second shot entering her cheekbone, killing her instantly as the bullet tore through brain tissue and bone...

"And now for the 'Grand Finale', Drogda..."

With a massive effort the old man forced himself upwards, still bound to the chair and lunged headlong at her, his eyes bloodshot with hate. But it was a clumsy attempt and Kristianna stepped to one side as he crashed into the table and then back to the floor. She fired twice in quick succession, both shots hitting him at the back of the head.

"It's done..." She unscrewed the suppressor and returned it to her clutch bag. Lovingly she cleaned the pistol and reloaded it and returned it to the bag. A tiny patch of blood had splattered onto her slacks, so she removed a tissue from the holder on the desk, and wetting it with her spittle, rubbed at the patch of blood, but it just made it look worse. "Later..." she said out loud as if they could still hear her. As she closed the door behind her, she smiled... Everything... she thought ...has gone to plan, as I knew it would...

Chapter 2

The door of the old Astra van was sticking again and squeaked as he leaned on it to close it, reminding him again that he needed to get some oil on the hinges. "...on the list." He mumbled to himself, kicking the ground with his old, paint covered boots.

He'd had the van from new, but that was nine years ago and it was starting to show signs of age, it didn't help that he hardly ever washed it, or cleaned out the inside. But then there was more to life than cleaning 'damned' cars, and anyway life over the past three or four months hadn't been so easy for him, that's when the divorce papers had come through his door and it had seemed to start off a 'chain-reaction' of other 'minor disasters' around him, such as living in 'digs'. After eighteen years of marriage, evicted by the courts out of the home he had virtually built from scratch, and then to be 'literally chucked out' on the streets was the final straw.

He leaned on the van and took out his old beaten up 'baccy pouch' from the inside pocket of his bomber jacket and rolled a cigarette. "That's another thing I need to cut down on." He mumbled again, stuffing the lighter back into his jeans and drawing deeply, inhaling the smoke for too long so that it made him cough. "... and I'm bloody forty... Jesus, I don't feel 'forty'." Webbley Pendleton was almost six feet tall, hard-boned with a shock of dark brown hair and other than a few missing wisdom teeth... they were all his own... "Where the bloody hell did all those years go..?" It was a mystery how the time had passed so quickly since he had been invalided out of the army in '69. "Christ! Nearly ten years ago... Feels like yesterday." He missed the army, badly. Next to being a carpenter; it was one of the few things he had excelled at. More than anything he missed the companionship of his 'mates'. Friendship in the army was so different than in 'Civvy Street', he thought. In there a 'mate' would give you the shirt off his back and not complain. "I can't be forty..." He felt the hardness of his muscles along his biceps and forearm and the tight, flat tummy. "That's not the body of a 'forty-year-old', Christ no." But then he knew his job as a carpenter kept his body fit, lumping heavy, fire-check doors up flights of stairs and bulky timbers onto roofs all day, had kept him pretty fit. Sometimes he wondered how long he could keep the job up... maybe another ten years... and then what... "Bench work, I suppose." But compared to some of the younger 'chippies' he could still hold his own and produce more work and at a higher quality and in a shorter time than most of the younger carpenters, half his age...

He rubbed his sore head and spat out a grain of tobacco that had stuck to his tongue. Last night had been his birthday so he'd gone to the local for 'a few', which had ended in 'many'. Consequently this morning, he had overslept and had left his digs an hour late and... without breakfast. His stomach churned. He re-lit the 'roll-up' and returned the lighter to the pocket of his jeans and looked along the lay-by to the mobile burger stand at the end; even from here he could smell it. It wasn't the sort of place he would normally have eaten at, but this morning it was a case of 'needs must'.

"What's it to be, matey?" The almost toothless grin of the 'greasy Joe' behind the long counter asked as soon as

Webb was in earshot. "Slack today, normally Saturdays is quite busy."

"Burger... no, make that a cheeseburger." Webb stood back as the man threw a burger onto the scalding hot plate, sending globules of hot fat everywhere. "Whoa, Christ, easy... man."

"Sorry, matey, bit clumsy there. Did any of that git yer?" He gave a toothless grin and flipped the burger over, depositing a ready cut slice of cheese on top of it.

Web shook his head. Already he was missing Mrs. Sumpter's breakfast. But she had made it clear from the outset that breakfast was from seven-thirty to eight-thirty. "If you're late, you don't get none," she'd said, scornfully, when he had first booked into her bed and breakfast, making her rules clear. "I does this all me self, ya know, ten guests most days, bed linen once a week... ironing, washing... everything by me self. I ain't got time fer no enjoyment even."

But he knew she was a good sort really and he had been lucky to find her. The house was always spotless and the rooms kept nicely up together. There had been multiple times she had helped him out, kept his dinner in the oven when he'd phoned to say he was going to be late, or doing the odd bit of shopping for him.

"Onions?"

'Greasy's' voice brought him back. "Mmm, just a few though, don't swamp it..." The damp weather had brought on that nagging, aching pain in his leg again... and the 'booze' hadn't helped it, either.

A crashing of gears and screeching tyres made them both look towards the roundabout, where the driver of a big black Volvo was having trouble controlling his car as it sped towards them, the gears crunched again, sounding like they were tearing the bottom end of his engine out. Webb jumped out of the way as the Volvo entered the lay-by too fast and came to a dubious halt, two feet from the back doors of his van...

"'E nearly 'ad you then, matey, and yor motor..." Greasy giggled, already pleased with the day's events, things were starting to look up already. "Good place this, 'ere. I see's that sort of fing, a dozen times a week 'ere. There ya go, 'two an' six'." He wrapped the bun partly in a tissue, but the grease broke through almost immediately. "No, sorry... twenty-five pence. I still ain't used to this decimal crap yet. Can't get me bleedin' 'ead round it, don't know why they gotta mess about wiv stuff like that, aye?"

"Jesus!" Webb gave him the correct money, not wanting to take anything else out of the hands of this man that wore a dirty overall and barely had a tooth in his head, for fear he might catch something. He decided to eat it in the van, but on the way there, made the mistake of biting into it. The cheese burnt his lip and the rancid taste of stale fat in his mouth made him wretch. "Christ!" He spat out what he had already partially chewed and threw the remainder into the ditch and then vigorously rubbed his teeth with the tissue, but it still didn't take away the taste of grease.

"You know anything about cars, buddy..?" A tall blonde man smiled and popped his head out from under the raised bonnet of the Volvo, wiping the oil from his fingers onto a rag. His dark grey suit was smudged with oily stains across the lapel and the waist band of his trousers.

"Sounds like your cam belt, mate. It's a garage job," Webb mumbled, not wanting to be embroiled in conversation with him, he was late enough already.

"Could you fix it, d'ya think?" The American smiled affably. "I'd be happy to pay you."

Webb fanned the smoke away from beneath the bonnet and peered in. "I told you, it's a garage job. Sounds like you ripped out the bottom end of your engine when you came through the roundabout. You need to phone the A.A., or whoever you're with."

The American looked bewildered. "I'm not sure if I'm with anyone, it's a company car..."

"Oh, well get them to pick it up, because you won't fix that here, mate." Webb walked to his driver's door and turned the key in the lock.

"Hey, buddy... look, I'm in real trouble here, I need to get to Birdham Marina straight away." The American followed him to the side of the van and shrugged his shoulders nervously and made a face. "D'ya think you could give me a lift there, I'd pay you?"

Webb shook his head. "Sorry, I can't... I'm already late for work, if I'm not there in another thirty minutes, I won't have a job to go to... and anyway, it's in the opposite direction to where I'm going." It was a white lie really as he was self-employed, he'd meant to say that his customer would be really pissed with him and boot him off the job... but that was starting to get too involved and anyway, his head throbbed and the grease that had finally reached his stomach was starting to 'act-up'.

"I'll pay you, that's not a problem... wait a sec. ..." The American rushed around to the passenger door of his car and returned holding a sealed, see-through plastic envelope, wrapped around the front of it was a band that read '£1,000 Sterling'. "Here..." He stuffed the envelope into Webb's hands. "You get me there in under an hour, and I'll put another one of those up for you... is that fair?"

"Christ that's too much, man," he said, half-heartedly. The money represented almost five weeks' hard work to him. He tapped the package against his hand... fretting... he didn't get breaks like this... ever. Webb looked at the child like pleading in the man's eyes and weakened.

"Another when we get there... or do you want it now?"

The offer was too tempting to turn down. "No... No, that's alright... aagh fuck it. Get in." Webb tucked the plastic envelope into the inside pocket of his bomber jacket.

"I just need my things... my cases." The American rushed around to the boot and started unloading the suitcases, six in all and dumped them, unceremoniously at the back of Webb's van. "You load 'em, I'll stack them...Yeah?"

The inside of the van, as usual was a mess, he pushed a half opened bag of cement to one side and stacked the timber on top of it. His huge toolbox was a problem so he laid it flat, and piled the cases on top. "Damn, that's a lot of cases... you going on holiday, or something?"

The American pushed passed him and threw in another case. A length of sharp, aluminium that Webb was about to clear, tore through the bottom of the beautiful red leather, tearing a strip from it. "Whoa, easy, look what you just did." He pointed at the tear, but the American didn't seem to hear him. "Hey... let me do it, you just bring them over." It worked far better with Webb stacking them neatly. He slammed the door on the last case and walked around to his driver's seat, quickly brushing off the old crisp packets and pasty wrappers from the passenger seat. He'd meant to clear them out a couple of days ago and felt desperately embarrassed as his passenger squashed himself in, cradling his briefcase on his lap, his legs jammed against the dashboard.

"If you jump out for a second, I can push some of that crap out of the way and move your seat back," Webb said, by way of an apology.

"No... No worries, it's only about thirty minutes from here, anyway." He fidgeted in the tight seat and found the safety belt and secured it. "Right, let's go, buddy..."

For the first ten minutes or so as he drove, they sat in silence, neither one, seemingly wanting to know anything about the other... "You got a boat down there, Birdham I mean?" Webb asked, just to ease the silence.

"What? Oh yeah... motor yacht."

The rain had started again and Webb cursed it under his breath, the rubber on his windscreen wiper was slightly torn and when it swept the glass it left a trail of water at eye level and squeaked. It was 'another' job on his long list of 'jobs to do'. He tapped the package in his pocket and smiled. Maybe he'd get four new tyres as well, he thought.

The silence was interrupted by a ringing sound that to Webb sounded like a telephone. He watched out of the corner of his eye as his passenger scrambled to open the briefcase in the tight confines of his seat and produced a large, bulky mobile phone. To Webb it looked like one of his army field phones...

"Yes... yes I know, honey... Mmm. I'll be there in..." He looked at Webb.

"Twenty minutes..." Webb half whispered.

"Ten minutes... I know, damn it. I broke down... this kind chap is giving me a lift." The 'half conversation' seemed stinted. "For God's sake, Kristianna... ten minutes... damn it! I already said that."

"That the misses?" Webb smiled as the American replaced the mobile and relocked the briefcase. "...you in the shit, or something?"

Daniel nodded. "No, she's my... boss." It wasn't strictly true of course but sufficed as an explanation. "She's 'super-efficient' and I always seem to be messing things up, when I'm around her." He shrugged his shoulders, feeling a little depressed. "Anyway, we'll be there soon..." His voice was flat. "I'm Daniel by the way, you a builder or something?" He pointed backwards with his thumb to the tools and timber, now almost buried under six large, red suitcases.

"No, a 'Chippy'." Webb dropped a gear as he negotiated the roundabout that would lead them onto the Whiterings and eventually Birdham Marina.

"'Chippy'?"

"Carpenter... ya know... chip, chip, chip." He did a small 'demonstration', chopping at the steering wheel with the heel of his hand. "'Chippy...' Webb." He glanced across, briefly. "Webbley Pendleton..."

"Oh..." For a brief second it brought a smile to Daniel's face and he seemed to relax a little. "Gotcha. Is that a 'nickname' or something?"

"No, it's real, the old man was a bit of a comic... or so he thought... he worked for the Webbley Arms Company for about fifty years, although sometimes it sounded like 'five hundred years'. He was there until they were taken over by B.S.A. It was a sort of 'thank you gesture of gratitude' to the company... my name, I mean."

"Well, Webbley, I'm real grateful for the lift, you kind'a saved my bacon. More than you'll ever know. Kristianna..." He indicated towards the mobile. "She's one of the most beautiful women I have ever met... but hell, she can be such a bitch at times."

An uncomfortable silence ensued for a short time until... "You always been a... 'chippy'?" A faint smile touched his lips. In the 'States', he thought, a 'chippy' would be thought of as a 'chipmunk' or a 'whore'.

"No, I did nine years in the army, that was pretty good... really enjoyed my time in there." Webb had seen the smirk on the other man's face but didn't really care... he had a thousand pounds in his pocket and was about to collect another thousand, the 'Yank' could smile all he wanted. He just wished the 'trip' was over; the 'friendly American banter' was starting to irritate.

He eased the gear into fifth, his cruising gear, as he drove along the only straight stretch of road in the whole trip but he remembered the sharp right-hand bend a mile or so ahead, the sign indicating the bend was normally partially obscured by the overgrown branches of trees, that the council never seemed to find time to cut back, so he dropped it back a gear. The bend always caught 'the unwary' off guard; more than once he had seen an overturned car in the ditch. Years ago, when the kids had been a lot younger, he'd had his own little boat at Birdham Pool, in the days before the 'yuppies' and the wealthy had bumped the price up so high that 'ordinary' people like him had to find their berths on the mudflats. Now Birdham Pool was a massive and very expensive marina complex, landlocked at low water but still the exclusive preserve of the super wealthy.

He had travelled this route every weekend on a Friday night and then back home Sunday after a weekend's sailing... times had been a little clearer then. Webb glanced at his wing mirror, a long way back he could see a big white car approaching fast... too fast, so he eased his foot from the accelerator pedal and dropped down to third.

"That's one of those new mobiles then." He nodded at the briefcase, occasionally flicking his eyes at the wing mirror; the big car seemed not to be slowing. "...They any good?"

"Brilliant, the coverage is sometimes a little patchy but that's 'cos they only have four or five satellites up there at the moment, next year they're launching another six... man, that will be something else." Daniel had suddenly 'come alive' talking about his mobile.

"Too bloody expensive though... I looked into it at one time... more than I could afford." He was starting to worry about the speed of the big car approaching from behind him now.

"Agh... that's now, one day everyone will have one, every kid in junior school will own one."

"Not in my lifetime," Webb scoffed.

"Sure in your lifetime... in less than ten years... and..." His enthusiasm seemed to overtake him, his face sparkled and his whole bodily actions seemed enthused. "They'll be half... no... a tenth the size of that one and the facilities available on them will be unlimited, absolutely unlimited. It will cause another industrial revolution."

"Mmm, can't see it me self, really." Too late Webb caught a glimpse of the big white Mercedes as it clipped his rear right wing scraping along the side of his van forcing it towards the ditch and then as his wheels hit the muddy curb the impact swung it back into the Mercedes. He fought to control the van as it veered again and became entangled, dragged along by the bigger car. Webb heard Daniel scream but didn't look to see what the problem was, concentrating only on avoiding the ditch to his left and trying to separate his van from the screeching, tearing metal as the Mercedes ploughed into the side of the van ripping his wing mirror off...and then, in less time that it took to blink, was gone. Speeding away in front of them... Webb hit the brakes and pulled the van over to the edge of the road... his hands shaking violently.

"Jesus, fuck me." He took a deep breath to control his panicked breathing. "What the fuck was that about?" He leapt out to inspect the damage. The side of the van was badly dented, part of the bodywork and the wheel arches were torn up and the wing mirror hung limply upside down, held only by a tiny piece of plastic. He kicked the side of the van and looked down the road; the white Mercedes was nowhere to be seen. "Well, that's fucked that up." He leaned his hands onto edge of the roof and hung his head. "Nobody gets nothing for nothing." He quoted his father's words and touched the bulge of the £1,000 envelope in his inside pocket. "Fuck it..." he tore off the damaged wing mirror and threw it over the van into the ditch.

"Webbley... please, we have to go... please." Daniel's voice was pathetically weak and very frightened.

"Fuck off! Go where? I need to find a call box and call the cops, that bastard's not getting away with that." He flopped down into his driver's seat and slammed the door. "No... Better still, call them on that mobile." He started the car and slowly drove down towards the village. The 'squeaks' in the van seemed to be much worse now.

"No!" Daniel's voice had raised several octaves. "We can't do that..." He had lowered himself down into the seat and was holding the briefcase tightly against his chest, absolute fear on his face.

"What. Why for fuck's sake?" He watched the fear grow on Daniel's face. "Don't talk like a prat... I have to... Jesus Christ!" A sudden realisation hit him. "Hey! Don't tell me... that was something to do with you... was it?" He took his eyes off the road for a second, but an oncoming car made him swerve back onto his side of the road. "Is it, you bastard?"

"No... No... Of course not. How could it be?" He shook his head vigorously.

"It fucking is... I can see it in your eyes... you bastard." He slammed his left hand into Daniel's chest, angrily. "Well, I'll tell you what, matey." He spat the words out. "You're going as far as the village and then you can get your fucking arse, and you're fucking cases out of here... and piss off."

Webb was still fuming as he approached the traffic lights and cruised to a stop as the lights turned red. Fifty yards away on the other side of the road he spotted a garage. "That's where you are getting out, mate..." He pointed to the garage. "This..." He banged the side of the van door. "... Is the only bloody transport I've got... without it I'm fucked. Do you understand that, you jumped up ponce?" Webb tried to wind his window up but it was stuck halfway and wouldn't budge. He turned on his passenger, ready to strike him again but the low-pitched, deep-throated throbbing of a big engine very close made him turn... too late.

He felt the hand around his throat, strangling him, pulling him against the restraint of his seat belt, trying to drag him out through the half closed window. Through his panic he could see the white Mercedes parked alongside his van, the deep, ragged scratches clearly visible. Desperately he fought against the hand on his throat, somehow using both hands he managed to break the grip and turn it away from him. Just as he thought he had succeeded, the man pushed an automatic through the window. Webb forced his head forwards as the gun exploded, barely a foot from his ear. He felt the terrible pain of the blast shatter his eardrum and a deep, burning pain across his shoulders... and then a second shot... That, through the fug of his brain seemed to come from a different direction.

"Drive... for God's sake drive..."

Webb looked around him, dazed, his eyes were blurred and the pain in his ear and shoulder felt unbearable. He rubbed his hands across his face and gently touched his ear, but the pain was too much. In a fuzz of confusion he glanced at Daniel, watching his lips move but couldn't hear what he was saying... nothing seemed to make any sense. The fear on Daniel's face was evident and his hand frantically pointing out at the Mercedes, but it seemed to make no sense... any of it.

"Drive, you bastard... drive!" Daniel screamed at the top of his lungs.

Some of the words registered, but it was the fear in Daniel's face that made Webb slam the car into gear and hit the accelerator, more than the understanding of what was said, his primordial 'fight or flight' instinct kicked him into gear. From the corner of his eye he could see the driver of the Mercedes, rushing around the front of his car to stop him, but he couldn't see the first man. He released the clutch too quickly and the van jumped forwards, knocking the Mercedes driver off his feet... and stalled... Desperately he restarted the engine, eased the clutch and shot across the road, barely missing a car crossing at right angles to him. He accelerated quickly, looking into his mirror to see if he was being followed... but the wing mirror was no longer there and the rearview mirror was blocked by the stacked suitcases.

He wasn't sure how long, or how far he had driven before he realised he was in the countryside again, with green trees and woodland replacing the multitude of houses and shops of Birdham village. He slowed the car, trying desperately to sort out his thoughts and regain a little of his reasoning powers again... More than anything, he needed time to stop and think. Ahead he noticed an old, overgrown farm track and turned into it. It was muddy from the recent rain and the van had difficulty negotiating the incline, and the deeply rutted potholes, but eventually, reaching the top of the rise he drove it into a small grove of tightly woven saplings... and turned the engine off. At first the silence hurt his ears more that the gunshots had, but at least the panic was leaving him. He leaned his head on the steering wheel and regulated his breathing... until...

"Right, you bastard..." He turned to face Daniel but the pain in his shoulder stopped him. "Jesus!" He touched the back of his neck and his fingers came away bloody. "The bastard shot me... he fucking shot me." Webb traced the gash with just his fingertips, realising that it was just a flesh wound and that the bullet hadn't actually entered, just skimmed across his shoulder. "Lucky bugger..." He felt a strange relief.

"I don't think I was quite that lucky, Webbley..." Daniel's face was ashen white, with hardly a red vein showing.

Webb released his safety belt and swivelled in his seat. In Daniel's hand, resting in his lap was a large .45 Automatic pistol, his finger was on the trigger and the safety catch was still off... "Here... let me take that..." Webb pointed the barrel away from him and eased the gun cautiously from his fingers and applied the safety and then laid it down in the well of the driver's seat. Above Daniel's right breast was a huge patch of deep red, oozing blood. "Jesus, man..." He lifted Daniel's shirt away from the wound and saw the bullet hole, still pumping blood. He had seen wounds like this before when he was in the army and knew that the survival rate, without immediate medical attention would be minimal.

Webb leaned over his seat and with some difficulty found the roll of industrial tissue paper, and unrolling a huge handful stuffed it between Daniel's shirt and the wound. "Try to hold that on there." He gently lifted Daniel's hand and placed it over the wound. "I got to get you to a hospital, or you're going to be a dead man." He went to start the engine, but Daniel groaned.

"No, Webbley... you... can't do that, they would kill you on sight..." He coughed, trickles of blood dribbling down the sides of his mouth. "'Phone Kris... Kristianna... she'll know what to do... please."

"Don't be bloody stupid, man, you can't..."

"Please... if you go anywhere near a hospital... they will kill you... I can promise you that. They'll kill you."

"Who will? Bollocks... this is bloody England, not the fuckin' States for Christ sakes. We don't go around shooting each other here." But at the back of his mind he somehow knew Daniel was right. Those men in the Mercedes hadn't wanted to talk, or ask questions... just 'kill'. "So, they are after what is in the cases, yeah?"

Daniel nodded and tried to smile. "Yes, it belongs to them...'Phone Kristianna... please." He made an attempt to open the briefcase, but the pain was too great and he slumped back into his seat. "Open it... please open it." He pleaded.

"This is bullshit... bullshit." But he opened the case anyway. The briefcase was stacked with rows of the same see-through, plastic envelopes Daniel had given him. Webb thought there must be at least a hundred or more packets in the case. "Christ!" Attached to the lid of the case, in a neat, tailor-made holster was another automatic... and three magazines of ammunition.

"Look in the front of the journal, her number is there..."

"This is just bloody crazy... you know it is." He was starting to panic again, but dialled the number anyway and waited for the ringtones to stop.

"Daniel!" The voice was female, it seemed angry and sharp. "Where in God's name are you, you imbecile. The tide is out in another hour, if you are not here by then... we are stuck here for another twelve hours."

"It's... not Daniel... miss..."

For a long time, there was utter silence. "Who... is this, please?"

Webb could hear another female voice in the background. "We've had an... accident. Well no, we didn't have an accident at all; we were shot up by some chaps in a big Mercedes..."

Again the silence... "Where are you now, mister...?"

"... About two miles from you, if you're still at Birdham."

"Good, I'll come and get you, where are you exactly?"

"Do you want to ask how your feller is, or you're not interested in why I'm phoning instead of him?" Webb was starting to feel irritated; the female voice had a slight accent that he couldn't quite place.

"Oh dear yes, is he there, perhaps I can speak to him, please."

"He's unconscious at the moment, but he's been shot pretty bad through the upper chest." He looked at Daniel, his breathing was getting shallower and more blood was coming from his mouth. "If I don't get him to a hospital soon he's going to die. Do you understand that?"

"Yes... yes I do, but you mustn't do that, please don't do that." The voice seemed unconcerned, flat and controlled. "They will kill you the second they see you... do you understand?"

"Who are 'they', for Christ's sake?" He touched Daniel's neck and could still feel a faint pulse. "Look, I'm going to take all of this crap to the cops, they can sort it out. I just..."

"No!" The voice screamed down the line. "The police are in with this as well, you can't go to them... Look, mister... What 'is' your name?"

"We..." He stopped himself. "That's not important, what is important is that we get this chap into the hands of a doctor straight away..."

"I can do that, please let me help you." Kristianna was becoming desperate, she knew that the yacht had to be moved soon, or it might well spell the death of all of them. "Tell me where you are, I can come to you straight away, with a doctor."

The hairs on the back of his neck started to tingle; he knew something here was just not fitting right. "No..." He said flatly. "Not sure that I like that idea very much...makes me too vulnerable. In fact every bit of it stinks. What makes you so sure that the cops are mixed up with this?"

"In Daniel's briefcase there is a leather bound journal... it's just one of four, he has." She wished so much now that she had kept them in her possession at least that would have given her a small bargaining tool. Now she had nothing.

"Read through the journal, you will see that there are a great many policemen involved here... Please, please tell me where you are... I promise you, we can resolve this amicably."

Daniel forced himself upright and stared with bloodshot, vacant eyes at Webb for a second and then with a great heave of breath fell back into the seat. Webb pressed his fingers to Daniel's neck but could not locate his pulse. "Fuck it..." Quickly he put the mobile onto the dashboard and eased Daniel away from the seat so that he could see his back. The hole through Daniel's back was enormous where the bullet had exited, and his seat was covered with chunks of bone and large pieces of flesh. Webb eased the body back into the seat. In the background through the speaker of the mobile Webb could hear Kristianna's frantic voice asking him what was going on.

"Well yer man's dead, I'm afraid, so you don't have to worry about him... now what?"

Desperately Kristianna repeated her plea for him to allow her to come out to him. "We can make an arrangement to suit us both; you could be a very rich man, sir..."

He noticed she showed little or no remorse about the death of her 'friend' and her voice seemed cold and demanding. To her, he was dead, so that was the end of that part of the 'saga'. "No, I don't think so... there's something about your voice that just spooks me, well it frightens the crap out of me actually. I need some time to think this crazy business out..."

"Listen please... sir. If you walk away from us now we are both dead... my sister and I... I promise you, they will find us and they will kill us." The tone of her voice had softened, she actually sounded frightened. "Please I'm begging you... don't sentence us to a terrible death... please."

Webb stepped outside of the van and sat on the bonnet, pondering her words, his shoulder and ear still hurt badly but it was the turmoil in his mind that troubled him more. "Look... I need to get some things sorted out in my head first, but I 'will' call you back..." As he pressed the 'off' button he heard her scream, but wasn't sure what she had said.

Chapter 3

"What did he say, Kristianna, who is he?" Gabriella van Ouden asked her sister. She was frantic and in a complete state of panic. In her hands was her third, large glass of red wine.

Kristianna slammed the handset back into its cradle as she passed the lounge of the big super yacht. For the first time in her twenty-eight years of life, she felt panicked... and afraid. "I... I don't know. Somehow that idiot Daniel broke down and this man, whoever he is gave him a lift... I don't... understand it... how could this happen? He had a simple job to do, all he had to do was drive twenty miles to the yacht, how could that go so wrong?"

"What about Daniel, is he alright?" In times of stress, Gabriella drank a lot, normally it would make her light-headed and happy and relieve the tension, this time, however, it was having little effect on her circumstances. She was two years younger than her sister, slightly shorter and of a more 'robust', fuller figure, but she could always 'force' herself into a size twelve, psychologically it made her feel much better. At no stretch of the imagination would they ever be taken as sisters. Kristianna was tall and her hair was blonde and short cropped and her eyes were a bright 'bluish-green'. Gabrielle as with almost every feature was different, with long dark hair, hazel eyes and a tendency to put on weight, very quickly if she over ate or overindulged at all and she was two inches shorter at around five feet eight.

"He's dead..." Kristianna said, acidly.

For a moment the comment didn't register, but when it did Gabriella was devastated. The glass of wine slipped from her fingers, shattering its contents across the pristine carpet. She held her hands across her mouth and screamed... until Kristianna slapped her hard across her face and held her hands, shaking her violently...

"Get hold of yourself, you stupid child... this isn't a game, you knew the consequences of failure, so did Daniel." She shook her again, more violently and threw her onto the couch, still sobbing. "If for some reason he doesn't phone back, our life expectancy will be monitored in mere days... think about that if you need something to cry about..." She was trying to think on her feet and Gabriella's hysterics had interrupted that flow... "We need to get the yacht moved from here... now." She checked the time with her watch. "We have barely an hour before low tide..." She picked up the internal phone and spoke quickly to the captain; he wanted to know their destination. "I don't know... get us into deep water, in the channel and I'll decide then..."

She felt trapped by someone she didn't even know or had ever had contact with. "Will he go to the police?" She spoke out loud, but to herself. "No... I don't think so... He's probably frightened... what would I do in his position?" But she put that thought from her mind... she knew exactly what she would do. "There..." She pointed to a position on the huge chart, mounted on the bulkhead. "You stay with the yacht. Tell the captain to moor up in The Queen Charlotte Marina; in Southampton... he can be there in..." She fanned her fingers across the chart. "Less than three hours... I'll meet you there." She dragged her sister from the couch and shook her. "Do you understand... do you?"

Gabriella nodded.

It had been over an hour since the phone call; in that time he had smoked too many cigarettes and read through a small part of the journals. The realisation that he actually knew of some of the names, shocked him. Some were prominent politicians, one was even a cabinet minister, and others were senior police officers, two from The Met, whom he had seen several times on the television investigating high profile cases.

He had managed to come to several conclusions, namely that whichever way he went from now on, he was in grave danger of losing his life and, secondly, that he needed a safe place to 'hide-up' until a satisfactory solution could be found and to that end it would mean first and foremost that he needed new 'transport' to get him out of here... the white van with a ladder on the roof rack would be spotted instantly.

Fortunately he knew Hayling Island well and knew also that the island was far too small to hide in, it was almost like a large village and anything out of the normal routine would be picked up, instantly. More than anything he would need to devise a safe way of get across the narrow causeway, the only single way on and off of the island without being spotted or worse still, apprehended. His mind was much clearer now, it would need to be planned out in a military fashion for it to succeed... and would have to be done quickly before the authorities or whoever those men were that had already tried to kill him could organise themselves and prevent his exit from the island; but first the car.

He took another eight packs of the bank notes from the briefcase and added them to his own after tearing off the plastic wrappers. He found his 'man-bag' and stuffed them into the wallet section, checking that everything was in place. He tore up more of the bracken and a few small branches and covered the back of the van with them just as added security.

Since he had moved into his digs, he'd been forced to carry most of his important documentation with him; including his passport, drivers' license and rent book, for fear that someone might break into his room whilst he was out. He spent another thirty minutes or so camouflaging the van with branches and saplings that he cut down from the surrounding tree, it would take a good eye to spot the van now... he checked himself over as best as he could in the undamaged wing mirror making sure that no one of the blood stains were visible and then set off at a brisk pace for the main road, hoping that the garage he was heading for didn't close early on a Saturday... He knew one of the main problems with buying a new/second hand car would be that he would have to give his own name, at the moment there was little or nothing he could do about that, so he cast it to the back of his mind, there were other, more pressing problems to worry about at the moment... one thing at a time. He reasoned that until the van was found his name would not be connected with the shootings...

He had rinsed the blood from his hands with his container of paraffin that he always used to clean the paintbrushes. It smelt a bit but did the job even though the smell of the blood still seemed to be in his nostrils. He found an old scarf and wrapped it around his neck to hide the drying blood on his shoulder, it was rough and ready and looked a little scruffy... but, what the hell, it would have to do for now.

He remembered the car dealership just this side of the town and hoped it hadn't closed down or changed location. The money in his bag would easily be sufficient to buy him his transport out of here, anything at this stage would do as long as it was big enough to take the cases. He wondered about all of his tools, some he'd owned for most of his adult life, but pushed the thought to one side... they would have to stay where they were, at least until he could clear his name and feel safe again...

It was two o'clock before he reached the dealership and was a little 'winded', there had been a time when he had run full marathons... but that was a long time ago. Slowly he walked onto the forecourt, breathing heavily, but controlling it, heading straight towards a cream-coloured B.M.W. 5 series estate. The window sticker read. 'One owner from new − Pristine condition −Full five-year service history. 1978 £8,500'.

"Nice car, sir, I sold it to the original owner." An 'overdressed' man in a 'loud' sports jacket and grey slacks had popped smartly out of the office as soon as he had seen Webb. He fiddled with the flowery cravat tucked into the neck of his shirt and smiled broadly.

The voice startled him. "Yeah, I saw it on the way to work this morning, nice-looking motor." A car drove down the road towards the village and stopped at the crossing before turning onto the main road. Webb waved as the car passed, as if he knew the driver. "We'd better make a deal, mate..." He smiled at the salesman. "I told my mate to just drop me off... can I try it?"

"Sure, jump in..." The salesman opened the door for him and Web sat into the driver's seat. "I think you'll like it..." It didn't seem to worry the salesman that Webb's clothes were hardly appropriate for the immaculate condition of the car. "Leave the plastic covers on though..."

It was probably the fastest sale the man had ever made, but to make it seem a little more 'authentic' Webb 'haggled' him down to £8,250. Compared to driving his van it was like sitting in the drivers set of a Rolls Royce Phantom... and he had never owned a B.M.W. or any 'real swanky' car before, especially one that was as new as this.

Webb checked his watch as he drove back to the spot where he had hidden the van, already it was four-thirty, in another hour it would be fully dark, but he needed to be at the entrance of the track just before dark, switching on his lights up there in the woods would only cause concern and enquiry from anyone who saw them... on the road it would make little or no difference. He parked as close as he could to the old van and loaded the last of the cases into the B.M.W. and then covered them over with the 'comfort blanket' that had been left in the car. The briefcase he kept with him on the passenger seat.

He nodded at Daniel, talking to him as if he were still alive. "Well, old chap... I'm sorry you ended up like this, but far better you than me that's for sure." He collected the automatic from the seat well and wrapped it in a rag and then tucked it under the driver's seat of the B.M.W. "I would far sooner have collected my two grand and gone about my business..." He slammed the door of the van and without looking back started the engine of the B.M.W. and drove steadily away... content that everything he could do had 'been' done.

It was almost dark by the time he reached the main road again and took some comfort from that, in another three or four miles he would be off the island and back onto the main A27 heading for where ever he wanted to go. So far, he hadn't managed to formulate a definite plan only that it was important to get as far away from here and this damned, isolated island as possible. Beyond the small valley he could already clearly see the lights that always illuminated the causeway, the last obstacle before he could really feel free... once across that he was out of it. As he rounded the blind bend before the bridge, he was dazzled by the flashing lights and an array of handheld torches in front of him waving him to the side of the road. He cursed as he dropped the car down a gear and obeyed the policeman in front... it should have been obvious, any fool would have expected a road block but his mind had been so 'cranked' and disrupted that he hadn't given it a thought.

Webb wound the window down slowly, his heart racing. "Evening, officer... trouble?"

"Is this your car, sir?" The officer stood close to the drivers' door, shining his torch around the interior. "Could you tell me where you've just come from... and your license please, sir...?"

Webb tapped his inside pocket. "Yeah, the car's mine but I only bought it this morning. Christ, I don't think I've even got anything on me, officer... I'm just moving my mother from the Whiterings to Petersfield, everything's been a bit of a panic today. I didn't even think of bringing any I.D." He knew it sounded 'thin', but nothing else came to mind. His panicked mind working on the basis that the police would still be looking for two men in a white van. "I only bought the car a couple of hours ago... I'm coming back here in a couple of hours, I could pick up my driver's license on the way back, if that would help." He repeated the fact that he had only just bought the car, just in case the officer hadn't understood him the first time.

He watched as the second policeman approached and handed a slip of paper to the first officer, before returning to his own car that was forming one side of the chicane.

"The car is registered to the Beridge Garage Group, sir..." The officer did another sweep of the interior of the car. "... and you're going where?"

Webb gave him the address of the only place in Petersfield he had worked in... which seemed to satisfy the officer. He removed a booklet from his pocket and copied the details of the car registration and then handed the ticket to Webb.

"You need to report to any local police station within the next three days, sir, and produce your documents." And then called over to his colleague to open the chicane... two other cars came in behind Webb and stopped as the policeman held his hand up.

Webb was fearful that the officer might see the panic on his face and the pounding in his chest felt like a massive pump... inflating and deflating his jacket... surely he could see that? Thank God it was dark.

Driving over the causeway bridge, he stuck to the thirty mile an hour speed limit, even though every fibre in his body wanted him to jamb his foot to the floor and get away as soon as he could. Eventually, after what seemed like an age, he reached the last roundabout and signalled left onto the old A27 and headed in the direction of Alton, fifty miles away... better to head for somewhere he knew well, he reasoned.

After driving for about forty-five minutes until he recognised the road sign for the Travel Lodge Motel as it came into view and cautiously turned into the car park, stopping outside of the office with the flashing, neon 'Reception' sign above the door. Years ago he... 'They'... had brought the kids here because it had an outside play facilities for kids with slides and a roundabout and swings. 'They'd' had a snack lunch but would never have been able to have afforded to stay here overnight.

He stretched his legs and arms as he opened the door to the reception and walked in. The drive had been easy enough, with the exception of the police road block that is, but other than that, the car had been an absolute dream to drive... Now he was far enough away from the shooting to feel a 'little safer'. He'd travelled all the way up the Meon Valley almost to Alton, hoping that at least for now, the distance would be sufficient for him to 'hide'... just for a few days at least.

A pretty blonde girl behind the desk smiled, greeting him and said 'good evening'. "How can I help you, sir?"

Her forehead wrinkled a little when she looked at his dirty bomber coat and scruffy jeans, but the smile didn't alter.

"Hiya." He smiled at her. "Have you got any of the chalets available?" He smiled, feeling a little self-conscious, in his work clothes.

"Two, sir, but... they are... um... the five-star suites." She made a face, as if apologising. "They are a little... expensive, I'm afraid."

He smiled at her. "Yeah fine... I'll take it, for a week, I think." He pointed out of the window. "Can I have the one right at the top of the drive; is that one available?"

She said it was. "But it's £150 for the week, sir." She wrinkled her nose again and smiled nervously, eyeing his clothes again.

"Don't worry, I don't always dress like this, it's just that the car had a puncture and... Well, there ya go." It annoyed him a little that he was 'justifying' himself to her.

She smiled again, her eyes telling him that she wasn't really convinced. "It's the one in the far corner?" She pointed out of the window, but he couldn't make it out in the dark. "Shall I book you for a week, sir?"

He nodded, noticing for the first time another girl seated behind a computer in the far corner of the reception, she had a flock of unruly, auburn hair. "A week... yes please."

"...Cash or credit card, sir?"

"Cash..." He counted out the money below the level of the counter and handed it to her. "What time is dinner?"

Her smile looked awkward, but it hadn't changed at all. "Normally from six until about ten-thirty... should I book a table for you?"

"Mmm, please... about eight." He smiled at her; there was something about her face that he liked... a lot. She was a little 'overweight', but was tall enough to carry it off and she had a 'carefree, pleasant attitude'. As he opened the door he turned back to face her and smiling broadly asked if she would like to join him. "I don't really like eating alone."

"Thank you so much, sir. But the management really do frown on staff, 'fraternizing' with the clients. But thank you anyway."

Seemingly, an age later after she had taken his details and handed him the receipt and key he was seated on the bed in his chalet. The cases stacked on the carpeted floor, still unopened. She had offered him a porter but he'd said not to bother, figuring the least amount of people who saw the cases, the better.

He rolled a cigarette and lay back on the bed, suddenly feeling absolutely exhausted, overwhelmed by the events of the day. As he felt his eyes close, he forced himself to sit up, rubbing the tiredness from his face and finished his cigarette. Now was no time to sleep, more than anything he needed a shower and something to eat, other than a bite of a disgusting burger, he hadn't eaten all day...

He roused himself and staggered off into the bathroom, looking back guardedly at the cases wanting to open them now but a little frightened at what he might find in them. He knew they must contain something pretty important to kill a man for, but he put it off needing to freshen up and feel a little more 'human' again before he opened them.

The water of the shower stung the wound on his back but revived him. A close inspection told him that the wound was just superficial, barely a scratch even, he'd had worse accidents on the building sites... far worse, but he found a plaster in the small first aid kit and with some difficulty stuck two over the wound. He dabbed at it with the towel making sure the wound was clean, and wrapped the towel around his waist and then shaved.

"Now let's see what all the fuss is about..." Before opening the first case he rolled another cigarette and lit it and then nervously with shaking hands, flipped the lid of the first case open... "Jesus fuck!" He stared in disbelief at the contents. "Fuck me."

The case was stacked to the very top of the rim with English sterling bank notes, neatly wrapped in plastic see-through bags, as the others were, the same as Daniel had given him, all with the amount boldly printed on the front of the wrappers.

"Fuck... fuck... fuck..." He stood up quickly and leapt over to the curtains, checking again that they were drawn properly and then looked back at the case. "Jesus... you're in deep shit here, boy... deep shit." He flipped open the second case with his toe, not wanting to touch it with his fingers. Inside was a repeat of the first case but in German Marks. He turned his head away, but made himself open the remainder of the cases and looked down in horror at their contents...

The third case held Daniel's clothes all neatly stacked with three pairs of beautiful leather shoes, pristinely secured to the lid in separate pockets, next to another automatic pistol in a holster with the 'body harness,' and loaded clips of ammunition, eight in all. No wonder the damn thing was so heavy, he thought. Webb hadn't seen so many guns since he had been out of the army...

The next case was a repeat of the first, but the fifth case held, what looked to Webb like 'certificates'. Each were beautifully written with fancy decoratively scrolled boarders, on them was clearly written the names of companies or corporations, at the head of each was the words 'Bearer Bond' and attached to it was a certificate that said, 'Users Certificate'... The sums inscribed across the fronts were vast, some as high as fifty million dollars. Next to the bearer bond certificates was an internal case with separate compartments containing diamonds and jewellery, necklaces, and rings. The exception was the sixth and last case which was half stacked with Bank of England notes, but the remainder held small bags of white powder... Webb had never seen a bag of 'cocaine', but knew that's what it must be...

For a long time he sat on the edge of the bed, his hands shaking and cold sweat forming around his body... just staring at the open cases, occasionally he shook his head, amazed at the sight in front of him. A crack of thunder made him jump and brought his reverie to an abrupt end as the rain pounded on the windows. What could anyone do with that amount of money? How much is actually there? He thought, but he couldn't bring himself to count it, just looking at it scared him enough...

Slowly, methodically he closed the lid and slid each one under the bed, with the exception of the case holding Daniel's clothes which he unpacked and neatly hung in the wardrobe. Never had he felt clothes of this quality, the three suits seemed to be made of silk but the labels said 'British Wool' and held the name of a tailor in central London that he had never heard of. The shoes were the softest, handmade leather, he tried one on and it fitted almost perfectly, it felt like wearing a pair of 'slippers', he thought... His tummy rumbled again, there was another hour or so to go before he could eat but he needed a drink... something to null the throbbing of his 'overloaded brain'. But he felt an uncontrollable need to 'talk', to know why he was in possession of six red suitcases with millions in them...

"Kristianna... it's... me." He was using the mobile rather than the house telephone of the hotel, unsure whether the main line could be traced, not sure of the bulky mobile either but it seemed less likely.

"Thank God! You phoned back... thank you..." Her heart pumped blood rapidly to her brain... now she knew... 'she had him'... "I'm driving at the moment, please; just give me a second to pull over..." some moments later. "Thank you for telephoning back... It means you may have saved our lives, thank you... so very much."

Webbley noticed the softening in her voice and liked the sound of it now. "You made quite an impression, that's for sure... I wouldn't want to be the cause of anyone's... demise. Tell me something about all of this."

"We... can't really talk on the telephone. Could we... um... meet somewhere, tonight possibly. Do you still have the... 'packages'?"

"Yes... yes I do. They are with me now." He looked under the bed, just to make sure.

Her heart jumped and her fingers shook, but she was in complete control of her voice. "That is such a relief... Where are you, could I come out to you now... I don't even know your name..."

Webbley hesitated for a second. 'Did it make any difference if she knew his name? Soon half of the damn country would probably know it.' "Webbley Pendleton..." He volunteered. "... and no, I don't want to meet you this evening, in fact I don't think I want to meet with anyone right now... today has not exactly been the best day of my life, my head's pretty badly screwed up at the moment and I need time to think."

"I understand... really I do, it must have been quite traumatic for you." She took a pack of Sobrani from her bag and lit one; it always calmed her.

Her words surprised him. He thought she was going to oppose almost anything he said or be as demanding as she was earlier. "Look, we'll meet tomorrow... but somewhere safe." He wracked his brain for a location. Most of this area he knew like the back of his hand having lived and worked here for years. "How well do you know Alton and the Meon valley road?" He gave her instructions to where he would meet her and got her to repeat it so that she wouldn't make any mistakes. "So, I'll see you tomorrow at one o'clock... and please come alone. Oh... I've seen a lot of firearms today... I hope not to see any tomorrow..." He rung off. There were still other problems that bothered him, problems he hoped she might help him sort out... such as his car... as soon as the van was found the police would put out a warrant for him... and then what?

Slowly Kristianna folded the long aerial on the mobile and placed it on the passenger seat and then stubbed out her cigarette, smiling. She'd had her 'death sentence' commuted to life imprisonment... in one telephone call... she would now need to change that sentence to 'wealth and freedom' and as quickly as possible if the 'death sentence' wasn't to be reinstated on her, the fact that 'he' had called her, meant everything, now it was 'she' who would control the situation from now on... once they met she knew it would be just a simple matter of time before she could wind her web around him and the money would be back in her possession again.

She quickly dialled the number she needed and waited until the flat, dull voice answered. "Mr. Tanner... I need some equipment. Yes, straight away. Please."

Chapter 4

He selected the light grey suit and a black silk shirt with button down collars and a soft pair of black brogues and then looked at himself in the mirror... It had been an awful long time since he had looked anything like that... and then... No... he thought, 'you've never looked as good as that... ever...' He felt pretty pleased with himself.

A muffled ringing sound brought his thought back. "Damn, I thought I'd switched that off..." He debated whether to answer it, but knew that he had too... wondering what she wanted this time...

"...Yeah?"

A polite, educated, male voice answered. "Please hold for a moment, sir..." He spoke quietly to a third party at his end. "...your call, sir."

"Good evening... I don't have the advantage of knowing your name, yet, sir." The voice was cold and unemotional and flat.

"Who's this?" He had expected Kristianna again

"My name is Alexander de Los Santos... and you must be this 'builder chap', everyone is looking for." There was just the hint of an accent at the back of his perfect English. "I believe you have something that belongs to me..."

Webb was stuck for words for a moment; he sat back onto the bed, feeling frightened and apprehensive. Nervously he looked around the room and then rushed over to the curtains opening one just a tiny bit, his eyes scanning through the darkness along the length of the car park. The raindrops reduced his visibility but he could see nothing untowards. Quickly he drew the curtains again, making sure they were tightly together. "Yes... I do. Look..."

"Could you tell me your name, sir... please do me that courtesy." The voice interrupted him.

"No, I would prefer not to do that... I feel pretty vulnerable enough anyway." He sat back onto the bed, his hands shaking, feeling deflated.

"Fine... it won't be long before I know it, I can assure you..." The voice had lost its soft tone, replaced by something sharper, more threatening. "We need to resolve this problem; I think you will at least agree with that."

"What would you suggest, Mr. Los Santos..." His fear had made him forget the man's name already.

"Talk to me... I'm a business man, sir. At this moment you have the trump hand, tell me what you want." Alexander de Los Santos's voice had returned to its softer tone.

"Look, I just got into this purely by accident... I gave a feller a lift when his car broke down, that's all." Webb felt some of his confidence returning and his hands had stopped shaking. He desperately wanted a cigarette but the mobile was too bulky to put between his ear and shoulder. A terrible thought occurred to him that they might be tracing the call... he wondered if that was possible with these new-fangled mobiles.

"I know and I understand that... what is that you want, please tell me?" Alexander drummed his fingers on the table and waited, he wasn't a man noted for his patience.

"I... want my life back, simple as that really, but I can't see how that is going to happen." He laid the mobile on the top of the bedside locker and knelt in front of it so that he could still hear it whilst he rolled his cigarette and when complete, lit up and drew heavily, feeling better already he put the telephone back to his ear. "If your men had just stopped me in the village and just 'talked', none of this would have happened, they could have just taken the damn stuff. I was just about ready to dump that bloke anyway, but instead they came straight in... shooting, it's a wonder both of us weren't killed."

"So Daniel is dead then?" Alexander quietly signalled to Paul Kyso to sit as he came into the office and then replaced the handset and turned it over to 'voice' mode.

"Yes... yes, he is. Why did they do that, I don't understand? If you say it was your property why didn't you just call the police?" He wished he'd rolled two while he was on the floor.

"Yes, they were wrong and one of them paid the ultimate price... unfortunately. But it was a normal response after you killed three of my people at the bank." His tone had become bitter again. "Why the young lady accountant, she has three young children, why did you kill her?"

"Oie... hang about, Christ man, I didn't kill anyone. I told you, that feller... Daniel... broke down and I gave him a lift, that's all...Christ, I'm just a bloody carpenter." He bit his lip. That was stupid, he thought, now they know what I do.'

"Now we are getting somewhere. I will accept your story; tell me now what you want from us to return the situation back to how it was."

He didn't know... what could he possibly say? What could he ask for without getting... killed in the process? "He was carrying about a hundred grand in the briefcase, what do you say to me keeping that and we call it quits?

You get all the rest back. Let's face it, as soon as the police find my van they are going to be all over me... don't you think?"

"I would say that is very fair, 'Mr. Carpenter', you are obviously not a greedy man. Let me give you a number that you can reach me on." He flicked his finger and thumb for his secretary to write down the number and then repeated it to Webb.

The mobile sounded three 'bleeps' and a tiny red light indicated the batteries were low. "Give me a second to find a pen... damn, this phones going to die on me any minute." He found a pen in the draw of the bedside locker and scribbled the number down quickly. "I'll phone you tomorrow..." But the line was already dead.

***

Before he left the room he pulled the bedcover down to the carpet to cover the cases fully and for the 'umpteenth' time, checked the curtains. He was glad to have made the call to Kristianna, but worried about the conversation with Alexander de Los Santos, he would need to think that through, carefully, but not on an empty stomach.

The deal he had made with Alexander sound a little too 'amicable' and simple... and very, very dangerous. Why wouldn't they just take the cases from him and still kill him, what would they have to lose anyway? If he arranged for them to pick them up in his absence, they could still find him... and what about his family. How safe were they?

He knew that he was still in grave danger. His mind wondered back to what Kristianna had said about how dangerous these people were, for a second thinking about the softness of her voice... what was she really like? There was just something about her that disturbed him he would sooner trust the devil than her. Daniel had said 'she' was his 'boss'... had she organised all of this... surely not just the two of them... but then he distinctly heard another woman's voice in the background of the first call... and this man Alejandro... hadn't he said that three people including a young mother had been murdered in the robbery? What chance then, would he have of safely handing back the cases without dying in the process? "Agh, it's no good trying to beat myself up, I need some food, a couple of drinks and night's sleep... I'll sort it out in the morning, can't bloody well think straight at the moment. Tomorrow will have to do."

He made his way over to reception, following the veranda's all the way around so that he wouldn't get wet. "Hiya... again". He startled the young receptionist making her jump as he entered.

At first she didn't answer, even though her mouth was open. He could see the 'cogs' turning inside her head looking for recognition. "Mr. Adams..." Her 'country smile' lit up her face. "My word, I didn't recognise you, sir."

He'd thought it wise to 'change' his name when he booked in. "Sorry, I made you jump." The girl with the frizzy auburn hair looked up from her computer and smiled. "I'm going through for a drink." He smiled at her as he placed the bunch of keys on the reception desk top as he walked away... "...The offer still stands if you fancy dinner."

"Claire, darlin', take him up on his offer." The auburn-haired girl spoke with a heavy Belfast accent, as she watched him walking down the hallway to the bar and restaurant. "He's a cocky bogger, that one... but very good-looking. Go on, oil stand in fer ya..."

"No..." Claire smiled back and slapped her friend's hand playfully. "Don't embarrass me," she whispered. "He might have heard you, silly. But he does 'scrub up well though'."

***

The bar was an unimpressive mixture of old and modern. It was registered as five stars, but he couldn't see much evidence of it. The bar itself had been beautifully constructed in solid oak and looked the part but the imitation plastic ceiling beams and posts let it down badly. He flopped down at the nearest bar stool as most of the tables were occupied and ordered a large gin and tonic. The 'customers' seemed to be an 'odd' mixture of people ranging from the two 'brassy blondes' sat at the table nearest to him to an older-looking couple that seemed more intent on watching the television than talking to each other. He wondered how they could hear it as the volume had been turned down so much... Most of the others seemed to be a mixture of travelling salesmen and women and middle-aged couples... He hoped the receptionist had booked him a separate table, not really wanting to sit with anyone in here.

The sitting position of the bar stool was irritating the wound on his shoulder and the only other table available was a little too close to the two 'brassy' women, but for the sake of comfort, he risked it and chose the comfortable-looking armchair opposite them. He finished his drink and signalled for a refill... The gin was having the desired effect and the ice was cooling the pain in his shoulder...

What must she be like? His mind wondered to Daniel's 'girlfriend... boss', or whatever she was to him. Sounded pretty hard, determined sort of a woman and yet Daniel had said that she was the most beautiful woman he had ever seen. It didn't seem to fit somehow, and who were these people who they had robbed... could he somehow make a deal with them? He would be perfectly happy with the money in the small briefcase; there must be at least a hundred grand in there. Jesus! 'A hundred grand' what couldn't he do with that right now... he could buy that little farm in Wales he had always dreamed of, or... He stopped himself, none of it belonged to him... and anyway... how could you spend all that money... in cash...?

The waiter brought his drink over and replenished the ashtray, Webb handed him a fifty pound note and told him to tuck it into his pocket. "That's for you, just keep me topped up..." The smile on the barman's face was worth the gesture. He took out his old paint stained tobacco pouch but hid it under the table as he rolled a cigarette feeling strangely 'self-conscious' in his 'million dollar suit' and an old 'baccy pouch'. Instead of putting the pouch on the table as he would normally do, he tucked it away into the inside breast pocket of his suit.

"Excuse me; are you here for the annual general...?" The croaky, 'Sybil Thorndike' voice came from one of the 'brassy blondes' behind him.

He turned slightly towards them, wincing a little as the pain of his shoulder bit into him. "Oh... no... No, I'm not. I do... um... a bit of property." It was the only thing he could think of on the spur of the moment, knowing that if he was 'quizzed', it was, at least a subject he was familiar with.

"It's just that Carole thought you might be... with the meeting, I mean..." the other lady added.

Up closer, they didn't look 'too' bad, the make-up, for his taste was a little too heavy... but 'passable'. Although, he thought that Carole really should have found herself a bigger 'blouse', the one she was wearing at the moment couldn't possibly 'contain' all of her...

"We are you see... with the 'General...'" 'Carole' smiled pleasantly and giggled. "We're with Avon; this is our annual general meeting, all the other girls will be here tomorrow. It's always brilliant on these 'do's', no worries about the 'men folk' walking in..."

"Oh right." He laughed with them, feeling the pain in his neck again. "Ding-dong... aye." They laughed with him at his attempt at the 'Avon signature tune'.

"Would you like to join us?" Carole asked, a little unsure of herself now.

"I'd love to, ladies, but I'm waiting for my... um... wife." He smiled kindly. If it hadn't been for the 'special circumstances' he was in at the moment, he would happily have taken them up on their offer.

Their faces fell a little, but they smiled and sank back into their own conversation. Webb turned back to his drink, easing the pain in his shoulder.

"You're a fast worker..." The soft country voice behind him said.

Webb stood quickly and smiled at the pretty receptionist and took her hand. "What a nice surprise." He spoke quietly and then in a whisper. "You've just saved me from two of the Stygian Witches. I'm so pleased you changed your mind, it's quite made my day..."

She sat in the chair next to him and leaned forward to whisper. "I swapped shifts with my friend Jonti, the Irish girl you met in reception, she'll cover for me. I hope that was alright... it's a little forward I suppose... especially for me. But you... seemed to be a gentleman." She laughed, a little nervously, holding her hand across her mouth.

The evening turned out to be the best he'd had in years. Her name was Claire, she was twenty and was born in London and had recently finished a university degree in hotel management. He had felt slightly guilty when she asked him his age and he'd skirted around it, eventually, after she had 'badgered' him he'd mumbled something about 'late thirties' and was pleased when she said he looked more like 'early thirties'...

She said she liked Champagne, so he ordered her a bottle, not necessarily to 'impress' but because he really liked her. She was light-hearted and a little frivolous and had a beautiful smile. Through the evening they covered most subjects... including his 'marital status', but he felt that she hadn't really believed him.

His 'social life' over the past for months, after the divorce had been 'nonexistent'... in fact it was nonexistent 'before' the divorce. Their sixteen-year marriage had had dissolved into a sort of 'liberal anarchy' of spite and eventually a mutual hatred for each other, resulting in him being 'evicted' from the marital home by order of the courts. Those had been desperate times, without a doubt. In the end he stopped fighting it and just surrendered everything, just to get some peace from it all...

Later as they walked through to the reception, she slipped her hand through his arm and leaned her head on his shoulder. "I've really enjoyed tonight, thank you. You seem to be a nice man. It makes such a change to meet a man who doesn't talk all evening about himself, or football. How I hate that game." She smiled cheekily.

"Did you enjoy yourself, 'moddom?" Jonti's cheeky smile greeted them from behind the reception desk.

"Oh you..." Claire laughed with her friend. "This is my friend Jonti, she's incorrigible. It was her that put me up to it." She leaned across the counter and hugged her.

"Ah... well it's you that I have to thank then..." Webb laughed with them and shook Jonti's hand. She was a little younger than Claire and much shorter, with a mass of freckles and a huge mop of crazy, flaming red hair that seemed to have a mind of its own. The heavily drawn accent seemed to add to her personality and character. "I should think that's a Banger accent isn't it?"

"Jesus, Mary and Joseph... yor mon's a psychic, so he is." she 'chimed', a little dumbstruck. "How did you know that?"

Webb laughed but avoided the question, telling her that it was very nice to have met her. "... and thank you again for the introduction..."

Outside the entrance to the foyer, he kissed Claire lightly on the mouth and tickled the back of her neck with his fingers. "Hey you want to come over for a nightcap?"

She hid her head against his chest and wrapped her arms around his waist. "I've had a really nice time tonight Webb, thank you." She lifted her face to his and kissed him on the mouth again, touching his cheek gently with her fingertips. "I have to be up so early in the morning... I start at eight... maybe we could do something in the afternoon, I get off at two... Oh, sorry, I expect you have loads to do tomorrow, anyway..."

"Mmm, maybe. It just depends if everything goes to plan. I have to see some people and I'm not sure how long that will take." For a second his mind drifted off, thinking about the uncertainties of what tomorrow might bring... out of choice, he would far sooner stay here, with her and the peace and tranquillity of this moment. Being with her tonight had settled him down... "I'll phone you when I get back, or just pop into the reception, but like I say... I'm not sure when that will be."

She told him she lived in one of the smaller chalets at the rear of the complex, but to leave a message at reception on his return. They would get the message over to her or find her.

He kissed her on the lips again, holding her to him. "Sure you don't want a nightcap?"

For a second she hesitated, unsure of herself. Unsure of him... She liked him, that was for sure, he had been great company, in fact one of the few of his gender, that actually seemed interested in 'her' life, rather than, as most men did... just talk about how 'wonderful' they were... He'd said that he was divorced, but she wasn't sure about that either...

not sure whether she believed him or not... "I can't... really"

He kissed her again and said his good nights and as he walked away she wondered if she had done the right thing, and waved at him as he entered his chalet.

"What are you doin' here, pray?" Jonti asked as Claire came back into the reception. "Well, girl... you have more willpower than me... with a big handsome hunk like that, I'd have him buried up in my thighs by now... so I would."

"Jonti, that's disgusting." Claire laughed out loud feeling a little embarrassed. She pretended to hit her but instead threw her arms around her friend and hugged her. "Oh... he's so nice though. Really nice..."

They hugged each other... Jonti wanted to know all about the evening and what they had talked about and what he did and... everything really. Finally, exhausted Claire 'begged off' and returned to her own chalet. On the way, she noticed that Webb's light was still on and was tempted to knock at his door, but held back. We'll see... see what happens in the next few days... he's booked in for a week, that should be enough time to get to know him, she thought.

Chapter 5

Sunday morning 10 am.

The roads were quite as he drove into Alton town centre and headed for the rail terminal at the far end. The rain had started again but he didn't mind, it would 'keep people's heads down'. Earlier he had telephoned the station office to make sure they were open and enquired about their baggage storage. After talking to the very polite, very efficient baggage handling department they assured him that even thought they were a small substation they were up to date with the most modern facilities.

"...and for valuables we even have a lockable vault that is controlled by a time lock system." The baggage manager had assured him proudly, not wanting to appear 'rural'.

It sounded perfect. Originally he had thought about the main line station at Southampton, but reasoned that the police presence would be far more conspicuous there, especially after the recent spate of I.R.A. bombings. No, far better with a provincial line... not too many eyes there.

He drove as close to the entrance to the station as possible and after unloading the four cases, called for a porter.

Webb found the procedure more nerve-wracking than going through the police road block yesterday, and was very glad when everything was finished with and locked away in the secure storage area.

In a way, it settled his mind... now... at least they wouldn't just 'kill' him, not without the suitcases. It was a small 'consolation', but at least he felt as if he was making 'some' progress.

Kristianna selected a light, cream jacket and matching skirt, cut just above her knees. She hoped it would look 'soft and feminine', but not too provocative or overly sexual... beneath the jacket she had selected a simple white, button fronted blouse, and decided not to wear anything beneath it. After some thought she unfastened another button of the blouse, it wouldn't be overtly sexual... just a tiny glimpse of 'the possible'.

She watched her reflection in the mirror and flicked a loose strand of hair back over her ear... satisfied that she had accomplished the desired effect... sensually evocative, but not demonstratively obvious. Normally she would not wear make-up at all, but today was the exception to her rule, just a slight touch to her eyes to cover up her lack of sleep last night and the merest touch of lipstick. In fact, last night had been one of the worst night's sleep since her father's death.

Above all else, Kristianna 'knew men'. They had always been like toys to her, to play with and then to discard when not needed... she had never been fishing in her life, but by the way men talked of the sport...it would certainly make her 'a fisher of men'. Most were so, actively stupid and desperately easy to manipulate, that sometimes it even ceased to be fun, anymore. Most of the time... and this 'strange little man' with the even stranger West Country accent would be no different.

She smoothed the imaginary creases from her skirt and slipped her hand inside the double-fronted pleat to touch the tiny Metlinger pistol in its special 'panty' holster, positioned just above her groin. Her fingers released the safety holding strap and slid the weapon out, smoothly, quickly and very easily... she cocked it, putting a round into the chamber and applied the safety catch before replacing it.

Last night her life had changed completely after his call. It had dissipated the despair she had felt and lifted her spirits somewhat. Before the call she had almost given up hope of ever hearing from him, or of seeing the money again or of living longer than a mere couple of days, the consequences of failure terrified her beyond belief, 'failure' was a concept unknown to her. She knew whom she had stolen from and had known the outcome of failure from the start... but had been satisfied in the knowledge that she 'never failed'...

"Webbley... what a ridiculous name," she spoke out loud as she applied a little moisturiser to her lips. At least now there was every chance of regaining the initiative... but what ever happened... now she would have 'her' money back, of that she was very sure.

"I'm coming with you..." Gabriella stood at the entrance to the doorway. In her own right she was an exceptionally beautiful woman, but palled into insignificance when standing next to her older sister.

"Like that?" Kristianna stormed. The discussion of whether to allow her to come or not had raged for the last hour. "I don't think so, put something 'decent' on, you certainly can't go in that."

Gabriella pouted. "I don't care, I'm coming." She smoothed the front of the tiny mini frock and pouted again. "Anyway, I want to know what happened to Daniel and you won't tell me... I don't care about the money." She was wearing a bright yellow, button fronted mini frock the hem line of which was almost halfway up her thighs. The plunging neckline was how she liked it, showing what she considered as... 'her very best assets'. Daniel had been her friend, and for a time... her lover and he had always loved her breasts.

"Damn it, Gabriella." Kristianna capitulated; there were far too many things on her mind at this moment to fight her anymore... and far too many things that even at this stage could go wrong. "You are to say nothing... nothing." She wagged her finger, threateningly. "If anything goes wrong with this... then... you know the consequences. Say nothing... I warn you." She felt a shudder wrack her body. "Come on, I want to be there early, just in case this fool's directions are wrong."

"Ha..." Gabriella pouted again. "'He's' the fool... but he has all of the money... he must be one of those 'smart fools', then."

Webb hid amongst the trees and leaned his back on the big oak tree for support. The slight rise enabled him to see both sides of the dual carriageway in both directions. Each three lane section was separated by five miles of continuous Armco barrier down the centre. He had parked his own car twenty yards in front of him, in a lay-by if anything went wrong the Armco would shield his exit as they would be facing in the wrong direction... and on the opposite side of the barrier. His instructions to her would have her parked in the opposite lay-by.

He watched the old Ford Consul through the binoculars; they were one of the most useful finds in Daniel's cases. The Ford slowed, and then stopped in the exact position he had designated for Kristianna, the lay-by was almost fifty yards away but he could clearly make out the driver and passengers and knew instantly that it couldn't be her. Almost before the car had stopped, two teenage boys leapt from the car and rushed into the woods, followed by the driver, they reappeared some minutes later, the driver still attending to his fly zip. But the car didn't move off...

He glanced at his watch... or rather Daniel's beautiful Rolex Sea Oyster watch. There was barely five minutes before she arrived. He cursed the occupants of the family car. Christ... he thought, what if they stay for lunch? Then what would he do?

Eventually, in their own good time, the car moved off and he watched it until it had disappeared around the far bend... From the corner of his eye he saw the black Mercedes Sports car enter the lay-by and stop, following it carefully with the binoculars, knowing instinctively that this time it 'was' her...

He watched as the driver slowly, methodically open her door and stand by it, in her hand she held a long cigarette. The tall, blonde woman stepped around to the back of the car and leaned against the boot, almost facing him and pushed her sunglasses to her forehead cupping her eyes with her hand, scanning the woods on his side of the Armco and then confidently walked around to the passenger door casually leaning against the bodywork, her hand on her hip, leg bent slightly forwards as if she was posing for a 'photoshot'.

Webb took a deep breath, realising that it must have been the first breath since she had stepped from the car. Daniel had been right, she was stunningly beautiful. Fanning the glasses over her, he could see that she was tall, probably almost as tall as him at almost six feet... he thought she must be about twenty... something... twenty six... or eight and she looked confident, almost arrogant. He watched her closely, resting her elbow on her folded arm as she smoked. It seemed that nothing in the world could shake her. Bugger... he thought, if she shoots me it ain't going to matter too much, how tall she is...'

Now that the time had come to meet her, he felt desperately nervous, not really wanting to meet her... at all, wishing this nightmare to be over and done with as quickly as possible. He held his right hand with his left to stop it shaking but it didn't seem to work very well. The trouble, he decide was his tummy, even though he'd eaten a good breakfast, it was still rumbling. Damn... Slowly he controlled his breathing until his nerves felt steadier. I really don't want to go over there and make a complete prat of myself...

He removed the pistol from its shoulder holster under his left arm and checked the load making sure that there was a round in 'the spout' and that the safety was on and then replacing it, took a deep breath and walked out from his position and across the Armco to where she stood...

Kristianna watched him carefully as he emerged from the woods and crossed the Armco barrier and approached her, meeting him as he stepped onto the lay-by and smiled at him, her smile soft and seductive. Behind her he could see another person in the passenger seat. Quickly he tucked his hand under his coat and felt for the butt of the pistol. "I said come alone..."

"It's alright, Webbley..." She held her hands out to her front, almost defensively. "She is my sister, she's involved with this also... Gabrielle, get out of the car... Please." She spoke calmly, without taking her eyes from his.

He was startled at the contrast in the two women. They could never have come from the same womb, surely. "Go around the other side of the car, please... both of you." He indicated with his fingers. "I hope that's the only surprise you have for me... Kristianna."

"I'm sorry, but she insisted on coming. This is Gabriella." Her smile seemed genuine. "Did you bring the cases?"

"No... Of course I didn't," he said curtly, watching her eyes, trying to fathom her. Gabriella nodded at him, pouted but said nothing, her fingers fiddled with the hem of her frock like a child would... "You people play a bit too rough for a simple feller like me. I'm just an ordinary old carpenter; normally the only injury I take is when one of my chisels bites back. This game's a bit different." He hadn't taken his hand out from under his coat yet.

Kristianna knew immediately that there was something different about this man, he seemed confident and overly caution, she felt it straight away... he showed too much 'caution'... too much 'professionalism' to be just a 'carpenter'. She recognised the 'stance' he was taking... one leg forwards to steady himself... his body relaxed, ready to 'act', instantly. But the muscles in his face were taught and his eyes fixed on hers... like a lion watching its prey. She knew he must have been in 'similar situations' as this, before...

"I'm going to need some assurance that you are not bugged, or carrying anything." The words didn't come out quite as he had intended.

"You want to search us?" Gabriella almost spat the words at him. She placed her hands on her hips and cranked a knee towards him, making a face. "What would you imagine we could hide under this...?" She quickly raised the hem of her frock above her waist, displaying her tiny, white lacy panties and then she pirouetted for him, her bottom barely covered by the almost nonexistent 'string backed' panties.

"Jesus!" He looked away, without thinking... a little embarrassed. "Alright... alright, you've made your point." He waved his hand at her to cover herself.

"Gabriella!" Kristianna stormed at her, knocking the hem of her frock down. She winked at her sister; silently blessing her for her act of 'stupidity'... she knew he wouldn't want to search 'her' now.

"Did... Daniel... suffer very much?" Gabriella's spoke softly her eyes' looked only at the floor, her face a little flushed now.

"Daniel, no..." He lied, not wanting to cause her any more grief than she seemed to be suffering at the moment. "It was pretty quick..." He wanted to apologise... but not sure exactly for what... "I didn't want anything to do with any of this, I was just going about my business, and if your chap hadn't asked me for a lift... it would have been some other poor bugger." He shrugged, made a face and relaxed a little. "I was all for going to the cops but Daniel insisted I phone you... and of course when I read through the journals, I knew he was right." He checked his watch gain, almost one fifteen.

"That's Daniel's watch... and... Oh God... you're wearing his clothes." Gabriella touched her mouth with her hands, fretting.

A car sped past them going far too fast, the 'slipstream' blowing Gabriella's flimsy frock around... the two male occupants hooting wildly as they saw Gabriella and Kristianna.

"I'm sorry... but I didn't have anything else to wear. Most of my clothes were ruined and I only had working clothes with me anyway. What else could I do, go back to my place and pick up my own clothes? That would not have been very smart... would it?" The weather had turned warmer and he felt a little 'overdressed' in Daniel's thick leather bomber jacket and his jeans... "Look, there's a pub a couple of miles up the road, we can talk there. I just get this itchy bad feeling stood here that someone's going to shoot at me again... We'd better go in mine." He pointed across the road to his car. "I don't think we're going to get all of us in that..."

"Good lord, is that what you want us to ride in?" Gabriella showed her disgust as he opened his car door to them. He felt annoyed with her comment as she grudgingly took the rear passenger seat. He was annoyed because it was the best car he had ever owned in his life and certainly the best to drive, most of his life he'd just owned vans. Kristianna sat in front, her knees towards him. As he started the car and turned his head to check the road she dropped her clutch bag into the passenger well... accidently... and as she bent to retrieve it placed a tiny magnetic electrical 'sender' under the dash board...

It was still a little early for the Sunday 'rush' to start, in the pub, which he was pleased about. Later it would probably be filled to capacity.

All eyes, especially the 'male' eyes turned towards them as they entered. Some were discreet; other's blatantly obvious, almost drooling. In a way he felt a great feeling of 'satisfaction' at their awe, as if these two 'beauties' actually were 'with him'...

The pub was not impressive in the least. The 'pseudo oldie-worldie' plastic beams and cheap linen table cloths did nothing to set it up as 'the place to eat'... but for now, it would do.

"Oh dear..." Gabriella scoffed, as he held her seat out for her. "This must be where all the 'poor people' congregate to eat. Soon it will be like a trough in here. I'm sure there will be scruffy, spotty children crawling out of the woodwork... too."

Webb bit his lip and said nothing, but signalled for the waitress. "What can I get you?" he asked as the waitress came over. He'd asked them both, not really carry whether they drank or not, but for him he needed a couple of very large gin and tonics. Under 'normal' circumstances he wouldn't dream of drinking in the daytime and knew that later he would have a screaming headache and just want to sleep... but for now. He ordered his drink and raised his eyebrows, enquiringly of the two women.

"I'll have a glass of champagne," Gabriella demanded, her eyes still angry with him.

"We only do it by the bottle or half bottle, madam..." the already nervous waitress said.

"Well then... I'll have a bottle." She crossed her legs and took out a silver cigarette case from her bag and a 'Courtier' lighter and lit a cigarette, directing the exhaled smoke directly into the face of the waitress.

"Water please, Evian if you have it." Kristianna scolded Gabriella with her eyes. "Thank you."

The waitress fled back to the bar...

"Settle down." He pointed a threatening finger at Gabriella," wondering now, if he shouldn't have just sorted something out himself and just kept all the money, but last night in the restaurant he had noticed a tiny, almost insignificant incident when he had paid for the meal, the head waiter had scrutinised each of the fifty pound notes with a blue light to verify their authenticity... how then would he get rid of 'several millions' of them, without being caught out... No, it needed someone better than him, someone who understood finance to shift that much cash. Maybe these two have the answer to that... maybe not.

"Right... Let's get down to business," he said curtly, wanting to be out of this 'meeting' quickly. It hadn't gone unnoticed that Kristianna had made a point of sitting next to him. "...how do we sort this out?"

"You give us back our money and we pay you a 'finder's fee'... simple." Gabriella was the first to answer.

Kristianna shushed her and explained the whole of her plan to him. "We could still be out of the country tonight, Webbley... free," she finalised.

"No, I don't like that... not one bit." He shook his head; it had all the makings of a trap. "I get on that boat with all the cases and I guarantee I don't get off alive at the other end... no."

"We want our money back... it's as easy as that..." Gabriella spoke too loudly and heads turned in their direction.

He waited until the waitress had served the drinks and thanked her. "You are a fucking rude little cow... dy'a know that," he said in a hoarse whisper, leaning forwards into Gabriella's face. "For a kick-off, it's not your money any more than it's mine. If you haven't got anything constructive to say, keep you big, fat mouth closed... or... I'll just fuck off and leave you to your executioners... how does that sound?"

She was stunned by the brutality of his voice... and lowered her eyes away from his venomous gaze.

"Please, we need to be civilised." Kristianna touched his arm. "...Gabriella, that is enough."

"Why?" She wouldn't let go.

Kristianna grabbed Gabriella's hand and squeezed it hard, making her wince. "... Because you are making a fool of yourself," and then to Webb. "Please, do go on."

He took a long swallow of his drink, feeling it burning his stomach, but signalled for another. His outburst had taken both of the women by surprise... but unabashed, he continued. "I told you... I'm a simple bloke. I wanted nothing to do with this, but I got dragged into it. If there was some way I could just give it all back and then go on as if nothing had happened... I would..." He pondered that thought for a second... knowing 'now'... he 'wouldn't' give it 'all' back, not now that he'd gotten used to the power and luxury of what this sort of wealth could bring... He liked the feel of Daniel's beautiful clothes and his soft shoes, most of all his beautiful Rolex watch.

"It was you two." He continued in the same vein. "...that fucked it all up, you and your 'wanker' boyfriend... Give me an answer and I'll go along with it happily, but don't expect me to step on a boat with you two... Christ... do I really look that bloody stupid?"

For a second they were silent until Kristianna spoke. "You are right..." She turned in towards him and touched his hand on the table, hating him for the power he held over them... at this moment. His hands were calloused and rough and it excited her... they were the hands of her father, the same rough skin and broken fingernails. "We have a stalemate, but please realise we are not your enemies, some quirk of fate has thrown us together into this situation and we all need to find a way out of it...Webbley."

Gabriella mumbled something, but they took no notice of her.

He felt the warmth of her hand and the unbelievable softness of her skin and felt himself weaken. His temper subsided, slightly but he felt his loins hardening, softening of his reserves... That was the second time she had used his name. He remembered watching a David Attenborough, wildlife program, years ago... on the television about the mating habits of Tarantulas... the female spread her sex gland fluids around the nest to tempt the male... and then when he had mated with her... she ate him. "Poor bastard..." He inadvertently spoke out loud.

"Excuse me?" The female tarantula asked, rubbing her hands around his...

"What did you say, Webbley? She was feeling a little nervous now, he wasn't responding as he should have.

"…Mmm? Oh nothing, just running something through my head." He eased his hand away from hers and leaned back in his chair. "Who are these people then... this Met Corps, are they like the Mafia, or something?"

They both smiled nervously and Gabriella shook her head. "...they give orders to the Mafia, Webbley... almost none of the larger organised crime syndicates do anything without the say-so of Met Corps" Kristianna added, "They provide the muscle and the brains and the intelligence, worldwide. Above all, they dominate the policy for all of the other crime organisations."

"How in God's name did you expect to get away with this then?" He pulled his hands away from her and rolled a cigarette.

For a second Kristianna panicked... inwardly, her mind a little confused, he wasn't responding at all to her... she knew and understood her own power over men and yet from this 'animal', this... this... uneducated oaf, for some reason she could not get an acceptable response... Two days ago, instead of being sat with him, holding his hand... she would have had him forcibly thrown out onto the streets like the dog that he was... and beaten up for his impudence to her but now... he held the keys to their very survival... the key to whether they survived or not... lay entirely with him. She fought for an answer and knew that it still lay in her 'sexuality, if she could just get him alone... just for a short time... things would be so much different. "They can't find ghosts..." she said simply, adding nothing. "But you are right... yes; I can see that now..." She humbled her tone. "I can see how you would feel insecure..."

"Insecure... let's face it, I would have to be off my head, wouldn't I... to get on a boat with all that money... gimme a break..."

"Well, how do we know we can trust you?" Gabriella added.

"You don't."

"Well then..." She wouldn't let go.

Kristianna reached across the table and touched her sister's hand, caressing it. "If you leave us now, Webbley, we are dead, without the shadow of a doubt, both of us... are dead." She forced a tear into her outer eye and looked into his face, helpless...

"I've messed things up, haven't I.'" Gabriella started to cry and dabbed at her face with a tissue... "It's my fault and I'm sorry..."

"... Jesus... what a bloody mess." He was starting to feel sorry for them now and knew that he would have to do something, wishing that he hadn't been so rough on her. "I just want to get back to my shitty 'messed-up life' really. He touched Gabriella's hand and apologised. "I'll phone you this evening, we'll work something out and I promise you I won't leave you in the lurch. It's your turn to trust me. I know you don't know me or anything about me... you don't know me at all, but if you did you would know that I am a straight feller... I'll phone you later with my proposal."

Kristianna protested and begged him not to leave them, but at the back of her mind she didn't care... in another two or three hours she would know exactly where he was and where the cases were... the transponder would give her all of that information.

As they left Webb diverted to the bar to pay and touched the waitress on the arm. "I'm sorry about the little cow I'm with, she's not normally that rude and I apologise for her behaviour." And then he tucked a fifty pound note into her pocket.

"We have very little time, Webbley." Kristianna sat closer to his seat as they drove, her hand massaging his thigh. "These people are super-efficient and they will stop at nothing to get their money back and they have the power."

"Just out of morbid curiosity, how much is there?"

She looked across cautiously at her sister. "About six hundred million, if you include the bonds... and the diamonds."

For a second his hand slipped from the wheel and he had to make a dramatic correction to keep the car on the road. "What!" The sum staggered him. Six hundred... Jesus Christ!"

"I just hope you left it somewhere safe." She moved her hand onto his thigh and gently manoeuvred it across the tops of his thighs. "We need to pay for the yacht, Webbley, at the moment it is just held with a deposit. Fifty thousand would cover everything, could you arrange that for me?"

He chuckled to himself, wondering what sort of life these people lived? His normal 'yearly' earnings would be less than a quarter of that... On the return journey he purposely took a longer circuitous route so that before returning to the same place from which he had started before pulling into the lay-by. "Is that car registered in your name?" He pointed across the Armco at the beautiful black Mercedes Sports car.

"I don't understand, darling..." Kristianna smiled.

"Is that car registered in your name?" He said it more slowly.

"No..." Her eyebrows wrinkled a little. "It's... well... registered with my personal accountant's office."

"Good... I need a clean car... I'll take that one... you can have this." He handed her his keys and took hers from her hand.

"No!" She screamed after him but he just waved at them and smiled, casually he jumped over the Armco and strolled back across the road to her car...

Chapter 6

SUNDAY 12:30 pm. Alejandro de Los Santos sat at the head of the huge boardroom table, glaring down the length of it at his board members. Other than a cordial, nervous greeting, none had spoken since they had entered... all knew that it was no time for idle banter or frivolous conversation. Every member understood the gravity of the situation...

"Gentlemen, we have a situation, which by now I'm sure you have been briefed on." Alejandro spoke softly as was his usual way... but this time with greater impact. Less than an hour ago he had landed at Heathrow Airport after an eight-hour flight from New York... he was tired and irritable and needed to be home in bed. He was eighty-two years old and had been the Chairman of Met Corps for almost fifty years. He had wanted to retire ten years ago but a 'suitable' replacement was almost impossible to find... no one knew the Met Corps Corporation as he did. He removed a long Cuban cigar from the box in front of him, snipped the end and lit it... His doctors had insisted... or tried to insist, that for the sake of his failing health, he should stop smoking completely. 'What do they know...?' He drew heavily and coughed, the restricted space left in his lungs already filled with greasy, black tar, but at his age... he didn't care, in fact the only thing he really cared for was his grandchildren... especially his granddaughter Anastasia. Ah... Anastasia... For a second he could forget all of the problems, she was the greatest joy of his entire life. He had chosen her name, taken from the greatest Russian Princess, the birthplace of his own mother. But Anastasia was 'his' *princess*... intelligent... beautiful... tactile and beguiling. She was the one thing that made him feel young again... His eyes watched the deep rich smoke spiralling towards the ceiling, before they settled on his head of security... Paul Kyso.

"Sir... everything that can be done, is being done. We do at least know that he is a carpenter. My men are going through the names of every carpenter in the area with a white Vauxhall van that would fit the description... we will have his name, very soon." He held Alejandro's gaze steadying his voice, confidently. "At the moment I am at a loss for the reason how this could have happened... but I will find out." Inside his guts turned to jelly, if this wasn't resolved... and quickly, his head would be the first to roll.

Paul Kyso was sixty-two, overweight and balding. The glass on his spectacles was as thick as the base of a Coca Cola bottle and he sweated profusely... especially when he was in a situation such as this. He had worked for the Met Corps for eighteen years and before being recruited by Alejandro, had been a section chef with the C.I.A. for over twenty years... in all that time his record had been spotless... he prided himself on being a perfectionist at everything he did.

"You are the head of my security, Paul, you ought to know."

"Yes, I am, sir." He passed his hand nervously over his head, wishing to be anywhere but here, at this moment. "I've diverted every available person that I have onto this, Alejandro, and I've asked for more people from the northern divisions. They should be here in a day or so."

"A 'day-or-so' is not good enough... you should have brought them down straight away... why didn't you do that?" Alejandro's tone was harder, nastier now. "I want these people found... now and when you find them I want them executed and their entire families... is that clear...Paul?"

"Yes, it is, Alejandro. I have fifteen of my men in the immediate area... they will..."

"They are 'my men'..." Alejandro stormed, smashing his old fist onto the table, his face turned red and then into a light purple. He breathed deeply; controlling his temper... everyone in the room at some stage had felt his wrath... but never quite like this. "The shipment arrives on Friday... I don't need to remind anyone here the importance of what has been stolen... or the consequences of not being able to pay for the shipment... It is the only reason so much money was placed in our trust."

No one looked at Alejandro, most fiddled with their fingers or held their hands on their laps or just bowed their heads... with the exception of Alexander and Paul Kyso... none spoke.

"Yes, sir..." Paul felt the sweat break out on the back of his neck, soaking his shirt, hoping that no one would notice. He glanced around the table at the sixteen other members of the board and smiled inwardly... none would help him, he knew that but didn't care, he held files on every single one of them... and they knew it. The files documented the 'weaknesses' of their nasty little habits... sexual... specific perversions... and habits. In fact he knew more about them than their 'partner's' did... He also knew that each and every one of them would delight in his downfall. 'Oh yes... they would sympathise with him and pretend great sincerity and pat him on the back... and tell him they were fully with him on this... but he knew different.

"Have I made myself clear on that, Paul?" Alexander didn't alter his vicious stare. "Take the members through what you 'do' know, and what has happened... to date. Please."

Paul stood and spread his notes across the table in front of him. He explained that all six suitcases, which were to pay for the shipment, had been stolen from the vault. "If it hadn't been for a bright young security guard the robbery would not have been discovered until Monday morning. "We have assembled, in the lower offices, every member of Met Corps staff, all one hundred and fifty... they are being interviewed at this moment."

"Who knew of the cases, other than Drogda?" the Chief Executive Officer asked. He was a tall, wiry man with glasses almost as thick as Paul's. "I knew nothing of them..." He looked around the table for support but each member shook their heads.

"Only Paul and I, and Drogda and two of our people who delivered the cases knew." Alejandro intervened. "We thought it better that way... obviously we were wrong."

"...there are eight people missing from the staff at this moment, five we can account for. The three unaccounted for are the two Ouden sisters and Daniel Ousterhousen. Ousterhousen, we believe was shot by one of my men who was also shot and killed in the incident." There was a plausible intake of breath from around the table.

"I've known that boy since he was a child... why would he turn on us?" Alejandro was perplexed.

"He was having an affair with both of the Ouden sisters. But it seems the plan went awry when his car broke down and was given a lift by a builder or carpenter, in his van. A street vender selling dubious hot dogs and burgers was quite happy to talk to my... our men. I believe with what I have to date is that the organiser was the older girl, Kristianna who was also..." He held his breath, ready to deliver the 'bombshell'. "... Having an affair with... Drogda. That is how they gained his confidence and entry."

Alejandro shook his head... it was such a different world now... he thought. "Do we know anything about this builder?"

"Not at the moment... but we soon will. There is only one way on and off of Hayling Island and our men are absolutely certain that a white van of that description didn't re-cross the causeway, so he must have 'acquired' another vehicle. We are checking ever garage for new sales, every report of a stolen car and every track throughout the island, he won't get far... not with that amount of 'luggage'."

"What was Drogda doing in the vaults on a Saturday?" A minor executive at the far end of the table asked.

"It was Drogda's practice to go into the vault every Saturday morning, but from what I understood, no one ever knew the exact time he would go there, normally he would vary his times. That must have been where Kristianna van Ouden came in."

"Why weren't extra security guards laid on for his visits? I don't understand that?" The C.F.O. deliberately drove the 'knife' deeper into Paul Kyso's throat. He had hated him for years.

Every eye was on him now...

"Hindsight is such a wonderful thing, isn't it?" Paul didn't look up from his notes, it wasn't said in a 'cocky', offhanded way... just a statement of fact. "Drogda was a law unto his own, Alejandro, you know that," he added simply.

Alejandro de los Santos scowled...

"Seems very odd to me..." The C.F.O. looked at Alejandro for confirmation.

"Order a 'termination order' on the builder, and a twenty thousand dollar reward for the first to find him, it will give everyone a greater incentive to find him. Start with his immediate family and put Preston on it. This case calls for his form of brutality..."

Paul was shocked, they hadn't used Adrian Preston in years, 'because' of his extreme brutality. "It's too soon for an order of that magnitude, Alejandro ... surely?" he asked, tentatively.

A 'termination order' was normally issued only in the most extreme circumstances and would mean the complete annihilation of the holder and his entire family... and his friends.

Alejandro looked at Paul, cuttingly and said nothing... he hadn't needed to.

"Sir..." Paul Kyso knew he was putting himself in jeopardy. "Let me talk to this man first, before we bring Preston in."

"Why, why delay the inevitable...?"

"Because, sir, there may be an easier way around this... it's worth a try, surely?" Kyso looked directly at Alejandro.

"... and you will handle it with the same efficiency that you have already handled this?" Alejandro cut him down.

"It's too soon, Alejandro, far too soon..."

The meeting lasted for another hour. In the executive wash room Paul stripped of his wet shirt and showered and replaced the shirt with a clean one before leaving for his office. His hands still shaking, in the years he had worked for Alejandro there had never been a situation like this before. What ever happened, he needed to find the 'builder' or the white van... or both? His own life may depend on it...

Chapter 7

Two women were standing outside of Webb's chalet door as he drove back into the motel car park, both intently staring at the 'do not disturb' sign he had hung on the handle. "Ladies..." He closed the car door behind him and approached them. "Is there a problem?"

"Oh, no, sir, we wus just wondering when we could clean through, thas all." The older of the two answered, she looked a little embarrassed.

"Leave it for today, luv, please..." He needed to be in the chalet when they cleaned as the two remaining suitcases were still under the bed and what ever happened he couldn't afford to have them nosing around.

After he had closed and locked the door behind him he counted out the money Kristianna had asked for and put it into the briefcase... then showered and changed. It was already four-thirty, so he called her.

"Hi, Kristianna, it's Webb, I've got what you want, where do I deliver it? Just give me the direction and I'll pop it over..."

She seemed pleased to hear from him, but hesitant. "Oh dear... I'm not on the yacht at the moment, darling... just give me a second..." She covered the receiver with her hand

and addressed the gaunt, pale man sitting at the desk next to her. "I need to talk..." She said simple.

The grey, ashen-faced man rose from his seat, without comment. The office was his, but he knew his place, he nodded... smoothed the wrinkles from the trousers of his suit and left the office. Herbert Tanner was 'The Undertaker'. Not in the 'literal' sense of the word but only in the grey, murky, deep 'underground world' he moved in. He was a professional 'fixer'... an assassin... and had worked for this particular 'client' on a number of occasions, she always paid exceptionally well and seemed 'satisfied' with his work. His grey, facial parlour was not that Mr. Tanner never saw the sun or light of day... his condition was due to a pigment defect at birth... it could have been rectified when he was a child but his mother thought the colour suited him...

Webb noticed that it was the second time she had called him that, but she seemed a little flustered, then her 'confident' voice returned. "Gabriella is there, shall I call her to tell her you are coming over? Yes... yes I will." She answered her own question. "She would be so pleased to see you... anyway, I know she regretted her outburst, it's not like her at all to be so rude." Kristianna thought rapidly... 'I hope to God she's sober...' She gave him the directions and the name of the yacht.

"Sorry about the car, Kristi... hope you got rid of it okay. It's too dangerous to be driving around in; they'll pick it up pretty soon..." He felt strangely disappointed that he wouldn't be able to see her...she was pretty good to look at. Instead he would have to put up with that 'snotty-nosed', bigoted little bitch. 'Ah well... he'd just drop it off and come back to see Claire.

She told him she had rid herself of the car, but that it had caused her a lot of problems and she did love her little 'sports car'... He knew that was 'bullshit'... if everything had gone to her plan she would not have needed a car until they reached Brazil... or wherever it was she was going...

After his call she quickly telephoned Gabriella and explained the situation. "He'll be there in under an hour, I should think. ...And, Gabriella, for God's sake, don't upset him, whatever you do. You know how important this is to us." She pleaded.

"Yes, I do, Kristianna... I am not totally stupid you know." She heavily emphasised her sister's name, pointedly. "Shall I sleep with him, do you think? Is that what you want me to do? Or shall I just lock him in the bathroom until you get home?"

"I don't care what you do or don't do with him, as long as you keep him sweet. Is that clear?"

"Yes." She pouted. "... or perhaps he would prefer to sleep with you... most of them do..."

"I don't have time for your stupidity at the moment, Gabriella. Just do whatever is needed to keep him happy, when our money is returned to us you can be as rude and stupid as you like." After she had replaced the receiver she began to worry... 'Damn her sister and everyone else...' A glance at her watch convinced her that she couldn't get back to the yacht for at least another three or four hours before her 'business' was complete... she had little or no choice but to leave him in Gabriella's hands.

***

He arrived at the yacht by six, after some difficulty entering the 'Private Owners' car park and walked up the pasarelle and tapped at the glass doors of the yacht. The yacht itself was not difficult to spot; it dwarfed everything else around it... and was lit up like a Christmas tree.

Before leaving the motel he had found an old 'Tesco's' carrier bag and transferred the money into that, chuckling to himself as he filled it, liking the fact that it would not appeal to that 'snotty-nosed' Gabriella at all, to accept anything in such a bag. He was still smirking when she slid the patio doors of the yacht open... and greeted him with a smile.

"Oh, Mr. Pendleton, you came earlier than I expected, do come in." Her smile was open and friendly. Her hair wrapped in a towel, turban style, draped across her shoulders and she wore a silk, knee-length dressing gown held around the waist by a thin, silk cord. "I've hardly had time to change, but please, do come in."

He handed her the Tesco's bag and turned to go. "No, I won't stop... just came to drop this in to you...as promised, it's the money Kristianna asked for. I hope that's enough, thanks." He could smell her very delicate perfume and felt a little uncomfortable being so close to her.

"Please... don't be silly... come in. Kristianna would be very angry if she knew that you had left without me offering you a drink... or something. Please." She held his hand and urged him in.

"Wow! What a boat." The interior was huge and some of the best work he had ever seen. Hardly a detail was not to the highest standard. "Can I just suggest that you knock out some of your lights, I don't really think you want to be advertising your presence, quite so much?"

"I'm not sure how I do that..." She looked bewildered.

He walked through to the cockpit, opened the electrical panel door and switched most of the lights out just leaving a few interior lights on.

"Oh, that's very romantic..." She giggled. "I wish I'd thought of that."

He noticed the half empty bottle of red wine on the table and the empty glass besides it.

"What shall I get you... you drank gin and tonic earlier, is that your drink?" She smiled again and threw the carrier bag onto the bar as if it contained last night's rubbish. "Please... sit..."

"Mmm yes, thank you." He felt even more uncomfortable now.

"... In a tall, glass with ice and lemon?" She called over from the bar at the far end of the main saloon. "Is that right...?"

"Yes, thanks." He thought how pretty she looked when she smiled rather than scowling all the time, as she had for most of the morning, especially in the pub. The couch was comfortable and he leaned against the arm and took off his street shoes, not wanting to scratch the teak flooring.

"I am... sorry about this morning." She handed him his drink and then sat opposite, curling her legs under her. "I was so... well, you know... upset about poor Daniel. He was so kind and gentle, I wish Kristianna hadn't brought him in on this damned job... in the first place, he was completely unsuitable for it... the poor dear." She clicked her teeth, speaking as if she had been his 'mother' rather than his... what?

"Mmm, I was pretty upset myself... came as a bit of a shock being suddenly thrown into all of this." He tried to avert his eyes from her lower body, but found it difficult... The dressing gown had ridden up her thighs and she seemed to be wearing nothing beneath it and the neckline had slipped open too, but she seemed to be totally unaware of the effect it was having on him.

"The weather's a lot better now that the storm's blown over." He thought how pathetic it sounded, the minute the words had left his mouth. "How did you get into all this?" That sounded even worse, so he hid his face behind the gin and tonic as he sipped...

She shrugged her shoulders. "It was Kristianna's idea... we all became entangled with it..."

"... and you both worked for this 'Met Corps'?"

"I did for a short time but Kristianna was an executive, with her own office... very 'posh'." She sneered.

"If they are so powerful, whatever possessed you to do it?" He fidgeted but couldn't find a comfortable position to 'settle' his rising passion, so he held the glass in his lap.

She shrugged and made a face. "Kristianna..." She added, simply. "She convinced both of us."

"...and you and Daniel just went along?"

"Yes... when I think of it now I realise how stupid we were to think that we could get away with it."

He noticed the sadness in her eyes, like those of a little child and wondered what she would do if he just went over and sat next to her and kissed her...

He couldn't remember the last time he had been this close to a woman or felt the warmth of a woman lying next to him, and certainly not a woman that looked like 'her'. She was so... beautiful... elegant and... in a way, delicate.

He placed his glass on the table, making sure it didn't touch the beautiful lacquered wood and loosely crossed his legs, there were 'things' going on in his groin that he was embarrassed for her to see... "It's hot in here..." The conversation seemed to have run dry for the moment.

"Let me take your coat... silly of me." She dumped her glass, roughly on the table and sprang from the sofa, holding her hand out to take his coat, seemingly oblivious of her dressing gown opening, flaying around her thighs. "That's me I'm afraid, such a cold mite... Oh." The holster and gun frightened her as he removed his coat. "Was that Daniel's also?"

He nodded and removed the holster, laying it neatly on the sofa, besides him. "Yeah..."

She stepped back, a little frightened. The tie of her dressing gown had loosened, but she showed no outward signs of noticing that most of her body was exposed to his gaze... or making the tie tighter. "Have you ever carried one of those before?" She pointed at the automatic. "They frighten me so much."

"... Mmm, a long time ago." He answered her question, his eyes fascinated watching the slow, revealing progress of her dressing gown as her nakedness unfolded in front of him.

"Silly me..." She held her hands across her waist, smiling, and re-tied the cord. "Have you ever... used one?"

He nodded again. "I was in the army, nine... ten years ago..." 'Jesus...' His mind screamed at her to step back a little, she was far too close and her perfume and sexuality was overwhelming. But he looked away and took up his glass and leaned his elbows on his knees to hide his embarrassment. "I can't believe you are Kristianna's sister, there is no resemblance at all." He finished his drink quickly and offered it to her for a refill. As soon as she turned her back, he sat up and readjusted himself...

"No... I think in truth, we had different fathers. I asked Momma about it once and she just smiled." she 'tip-toed' back over to him, her tiny feet patting on the teak flooring, and handed him his drink and then sat down next to him, her knees touching his leg.

"Oh..." he said, simply.

"Yes... Kristianna is the beautiful one though... everyone tells her that." She pouted a little.

Webb looked at her full, voluptuous body... preferring it to that of Kristianna's 'plastic'... perfect body. "I think you are far prettier..." he said, honestly.

Gabriella made a face and scoffed. "Really? I don't think so."

"I think you are…" He just couldn't remember how 'this' went… the 'courtship routine'… the 'dating thing', it had been so long since he had done anything like this and felt embarrassed at his 'stumbling' effort.

"No Kristianna really 'is' beautiful…" She was searching for compliments and enjoying herself now.

"Too skinny… I prefer someone with…"

"Someone 'fatter' like me, with a very big butt?" She interrupted him, watching him coyly, smiling inside at his awkwardness.

"No… no, not at all just, well…" He stumbled again, trying to stop himself making a complete chump out of himself again. "Just… better 'proportioned' really. Like a 'real woman' ought to look, not like some 'stick insect' out of the pages of Vogue, that's all."

"You read Vogue, Webbley?" She teased him.

"No… but, well my ex. Used to, I know what they look like." He fidgeted again nervously.

"Well, I thank you anyway for saying it, 'kind sir'… even though it might not be true, I will accept it as a compliment."

Webb took a long sip… there was a time when he had been 'good' at this sort of thing.

"Was it awful?"

"Was what awful?" He turned slightly so that he could face her, wishing that she had returned to her own seat and not sat quite so close to him.

Gabriella nodded towards the automatic between them. "Being in the army and that…"

Webb shrugged his shoulders. "It was just part of the job… then." He cocked his head to one side and cautiously looked down the long hallway. "Is there someone else on board?" He'd definitely heard a sound.

"Yes, Sui Yan... the cook and her husband." She touched his arm, reassuringly. "It's alright; they have been with the family for years. Don't worry..." She patted his arm again and giggled. "I'll protect you... Oh... would you like something to eat, I'm such a bad host I should have asked you." She was getting excited now, sitting this close to him.

At this moment, he could have eaten a horse, wrapped in two haystacks but he shook his head and thanked her for the offer... but no... He couldn't possibly concentrate on 'food'... not at this moment anyway... not with ten million hormones racing through his body.

"Should I show you through the boat, would you like to see it?" Her face was excited with a wonderful, broad smile. She seemed completely unaware of his 'condition', laying her hands on his thighs as the tie of her gown worked itself loose again...

"I'd love to..." He turned his back on her as he rose to readjust himself again. Daniel's tiny little boxer shorts were not what he was used to.

Gabriella took his hand and led him along the companionway. "Do you like boats?" She teased him, walking closer like the feeling of his rough hands on hers.

"Love 'em." He was stunned at the quality of finish as they wondered through the yacht and the sheer size of everything.

"This is the kitchen..." She waved at the tiny Chinese lady, chopping salad at the far end.

"Galley..." He corrected her, but she didn't hear him.

The galley was huge. Sui Yan barely looked up as they entered, hardly looking at them and mumbled something. He nodded at her, his eyes on the stray prawn that had slipped to the edge of the plate and was tempted to 'rescue' it, but stopped as her inscrutable eyes predicted his intentions and flicked the prawn back onto the plate with the ten-inch knife in her hand...

"I was never much into motor yachts, just sail boats. Nothing compared to this size though. Christ, I just can't get over how big everything is." He couldn't take his eyes away from the fabulous timberwork.

"Well the cabins are quite small though... look, this is mine." She pushed the door open into an enormous double cabin.

Webb looked at the huge cabin and smiled. His tiny boat could have been left on the after deck and used as a life raft, compared to this huge boat. "Yeah..." He chuckled, changing the automatic and holster from his right to his left hand, to ease the weight. "... I can imagine how uncomfortable 'this' would be... I don't know how you manage..."

Gabriella tapped his arm. "You're just teasing me now, aren't you, well look, the cupboards are so small; there just isn't anywhere to put anything."

He looked at the massive array of lockers and the integral dressing table built into the bulkhead and the huge, full size double bed. "You couldn't possibly fill all those, surely, could you?"

"Of course, look..." She opened the first draw and then the other wardrobe doors, each compartment and every hanging rail was filled to capacity with clothes and shoes of every description... every teak fronted draw was full to the very top.

This is not the world that I live in, he thought. "Yeah... it's a hard old life... I could see how you would struggle with this."

"You see..." But she realised he was joking and slapped his arm playfully, leaving her hand there for a long time. "Oh you... you're teasing me again... you bad man."

She felt the muscular arms and rough 'peasant hands' and felt her own excitement rising. As she closed the door to the wardrobe her dressing gown caught on the handle and opened it all the way down the front. This time she didn't attempt to redo the tie but turned to face him. "I'm always having 'accidents'... like that, silly me." She purred, closing the gap between them and resting her head on his chest, controlling her own breathing and felt his rough hands surround her shoulders pulling her to him, lifting her dressing gown away from her she allowed it to fall to the floor...

She fought, not against him but with him, tearing at his clothes, desperate to feel his flesh against hers... melting into his body, already feeling her moisture building.

"I'm not sure if I remember how to do this..." he mumbled, almost incoherently as he eased her backwards onto the bed...

She moaned deeply, feeling the wetness between her own thighs. "I do..." She panted, tearing at the last of his clothing. "I remember."

Chapter 8

It was ten-thirty by the time he returned to the Motel complex and the damp air of the evening already felt cold. He'd called into reception to collect his keys, Jonti smiled and handed him an envelope. Opening it in his room, he saw that it was from Claire and had been left at the reception at eleven o'clock this morning. It simply said that she would be free from two and hoped to see him this afternoon if he was free. Her telephone number was scribbled at the bottom.

He locked the door behind him and put the automatic and holster into the bedside cabinet and then flopped onto the bed, tired but happy. It was the first time in... As long as he could remember... that he actually did 'feel' happy. His 'existence' since the divorce had been thoroughly miserable.

He smiled and put his hands behind his head... I like this life, he thought, it really wouldn't be too difficult to get used to it... not at all. But he knew it was just a dream... a simple, temporary loss of sanity on his part... he knew also that it would have to end, sooner or later the walls would come crashing in and he would be lucky to come out of it... alive.

But what if..? At least his mind was working now. There had been times in the army when he should have died... lots of times. He touched the old scars around his groin, feeling the sharpness of the skin where the bullets had entered. Sitting up he put his feet back onto the carpet and rolled a cigarette, wondering about the people who had 'lost' all this money... was it really theirs? Didn't they just 'steal' it from someone else? Why then... couldn't he 'share' in their ill gotten gains? What if they couldn't find him... ever? He had read somewhere that most criminals who escape from prison are caught within seven days because they always returned to the same environment and area that they had committed their crimes... But no one knows me... or anything about me... why couldn't I just disappear... for ever... I could that... couldn't I?

The idea was already gaining substance in his mind, even the information he had gleaned from Gabriella, after their lovemaking would be invaluable. Now he had a much better idea of what he was up against. The Met Corps were a massive multi-million dollar, international organisation who, on the face of it were a legal, respected company, but they were still dealing in class one drugs and prostitution and the 'trade' in 'human flesh'... whether that was in the form of international prostitution, or the smuggling of young girls and boys for the sex trade, and on a massive scale. She estimated that they controlled forty percent of the money obtained from organised crime... worldwide... is it sensible to go up against something like that... really?

His instincts told him that he could trust Gabriella she was so much different from her older sister, seemingly more honest. But that was not the same feelings he had about Kristianna. She was a 'fox'... Her car had been in the marina car park when he had left the yacht, but he hadn't seen her... 'I wonder where the crafty bitch went'.

He felt excited...

In the shower, his mind was still working. Plan it like any military operation. Prioritise the dangers and the benefits... who are the enemy... what are their strengths... weaknesses... above all... stay alive.

As he towelled himself down he could still smell Gabriella's perfume, but hoped that it was just his imagination. Dear God... months and months without the touch of a woman... any woman and then to be made love to by that little 'demon'... A thought occurred to him. He wrapped the towel around his waist and went back into the bedroom and sorted through his shoulder bag until he found an old, dog-eared business card. It read simply... Global Securities... with an artist's impression of the world in a very 'arty' design. In the bottom right-hand corner in bold type was the name... Peter Copping, 'Managing Executive Director'...

Webb smiled... It would be worth a call, at least. Peter Copping had been in 'The Regiment' with him as a fellow sergeant and had been on the same patrol in Borneo when they were ambushed resulting in two men dead and Webb shot in the groin. The card had been 'forced' on him, primarily to remind him of the Regimental Reunion held every year around Christmas time. He'd attended one meeting only... it just wasn't his sort of 'scene' Just a group of old 'farts', talking about even older experiences... most of them 'bullshit' anyway...

A gentle 'tap-tap' on his chalet door broke through his thoughts and startled him, he quickly took the automatic from its holster, only replacing it when he heard Claire's whispered calls. Damn... It wasn't that he didn't want to see her, on the contrary... it was just that there was so much to do and he needed to get some sleep...

"Hay..." he whispered as he opened the door to her, not sure exactly why he was whispering... only that she had. "I've only just got back in... Bit of a heavy day..." He 'pecked' her on the cheek and closed the door behind her, realising that he was still just wearing the towel.

"I know... I saw you drive in." She seemed a little 'flat'. "I managed to get off early tonight I... wondered if you would like to... do something." Her eyes glanced at his towel for a second but quickly diverted.

"Well I'm starving; I haven't had a bite since breakfast... just no time." The 'lies'; were already stacking up and he felt a little guilty. "I suppose the kitchen's closed is it?"

"I could have a word with chef... if you..." She rubbed her finger and thumb together in the universal sign of 'money'...

"Yeah, I don't mind that at all... you want a drink?"

"We ought to leave it until were in the bar really, those mini bars are so expensive." She noticed the raw scar across his shoulder. "Oh dear... what's that from?"

He told her it was when the car had broken down and he'd caught it on the underside... another lie.

He made himself a drink and poured her a small whiskey with ice and water. "Bugger the expense..." As he handed her the drink she seemed to pull away from him. Damn it... she knows, he thought, women have this, 'six sense'... especially when it comes to other women.

"Do you want me to have a look at that..." She pointed at his shoulder.

Webb shrugged. "I think it's pretty well dried up now. The restaurant sounds pretty good to me though. Have you eaten?"

She said she'd had a snack earlier, but that dinner sounded nice...

"That's for me then..." He wanted to hold her. Gabriella had started his 'appetite' off, and he was 'ravenous'.

"Should I ask him... the chef?" She smiled.

"That'd be great..."

He wondered if there was something 'different' about her or whether he was just getting paranoid about everything... the last day or so had not been exactly... normal. Then he started to worry... about her and her 'involvement' with him. She seemed such a decent, honest sort of person... not like the other two he was dealing with. She just seemed so 'straight', and his life at the moment was 'complicated' and in a mess, to say the least. He wondered if he should allow her to get involved... with him, it wouldn't exactly be fair on her. But then what could he say? 'Look sorry, I'm mixed up with a load of gangsters that want to kill me and a couple of 'floozies' that I met yesterday and I've just stolen about six hundred million pounds... she'd believe that...wouldn't she?'

"Are you upset with me, or it's something else?"

"No... Well yes, I suppose so..."

"What, not about today? I did say that I had a lot to do, darlin', didn't I? It just went on a lot longer than I thought it would." He tried to keep his tone light so that she wouldn't pick up on his lies.

She shook her head. "I'm... well, just a little worried, Webb..." She sipped her whiskey.

"About...?"

For a second she caught his eye and then quickly diverted her eyes to the carpet. "Are you sure you're... not married..."

So that was it! He knew there was something wrong. He smiled and touched her chin, lifting her head up, then bent and 'pecked' her on the cheek. "Now somewhere, in amongst all this crap that I carry." He placed his drink on the bedside table and rifled through his bag. "...There should be... ah... there..." He pulled out a scruffy, dog-eared sheet of paper that had been folded for too long, badly worn at the creases and handed it to her... It was his 'Decree Absolute' and dated six months ago.

"Okay?" He touched her cheek, gently. "Come on... let's go and get 'rat-arsed'... I'm in the mood for it now."

She laughed with him, a little shyly at his crudity, feeling desperately guilty. "I'll go over and grab a table and have a word with chef. It won't be too busy at this time of the night anyway..." She stood and kissed him on the mouth her arm around his waist, welcoming the touch of his bare skin. "I'm sorry... my treat tonight..."

When she left he dressed, putting on the same shoes he had worn all day, loving the feel of them, and then a clean shirt and chinos, feeling like a million dollars. Good old Daniel... nothing but the best...you poor bastard.

Chapter 9

Paul Kyso crossed over to his desk throwing the pile of buff-coloured envelopes into the in tray and nodded for his deputy to close the door. "Grab a seat, Dick." Glancing out of the window he could see the continuous lights of late night traffic, party goers… late night worker… who gives a shit, he knew it would be a long time before he could see the insides of his own eye lids. "We've got a shit storm raging here, and until we can come up with something concrete… the shit is going to hit us all."

"Why didn't that stupid old bugger Drogda ask for coverage?" Dick Condon had been Paul's deputy for eight years and he loved his job, it virtually gave him the freedom to do what he pleased.

"Because he thought he was 'untouchable'. Damn him." He flopped down into his comfortable swivel chair and lit a long Cuban cigar. "Yeah, it would have been the easiest thing in the world for me to cover him.

"… Now what?"

"That's up to you and your guy's on the ground, but I tell you… we need some answers and quick." Paul fiddled with the cigar holding it between his finger and thumb relishing the delicate taste and the pungent aroma. "I can't get hold of that damned Preston, he's not answering his house phone and his mobile must be switched off. I need you to track him down and tell him to hold off, at least until such times as I can talk to this goddamned carpenter."

"But the termination was put on by Alejandro, Paul," Dick Cordon showed his concern.

"I know... but I run security in this company. Call him off."

"Damn, I don't like it you know. What if Alejandro finds out."

"It's just a temporary measure that's all. Just make sure everything comes through me first." He knew he was playing a dangerous game countermanding Alejandro's direct instructions could lead to his own demise... very quickly. His impeccable 'time served' with Met Corps would count for nothing if he messed up on this. "The carpenter has Daniel's mobile, I've tried it half-a-dozen times but he's not answering the damned thing. I should think Alejandro has frightened the shit out of him."

"Why did Alejandro use Preston? I thought we'd stopped using him years ago." Dick was thinking laterally.

Paul shrugged his shoulders. "God knows, there are far better, far 'cleaner' operatives than him. He's just an out and out animal. Never did like the man... an animal."

Dick smiled, he had been to some of Adrian Preston's parties on several occasions and they were always a 'blast', he always brought in the very best 'talent' and boasted that whatever your 'preference' was, whether it was young boys, young girls or even animals... that he could cater for it. ...Yeah, he thought, no one could throw a party like that man.

"You know his haunts, Dick, get after him, just tell him to hold off... just for a couple of days. That's all until I can get a handle on all of this."

Chapter 10

"Hiya..." Webb kissed her gently on the mouth, feeling the softness of her lips against his. She had chosen a table at the rear of the restaurant, almost hidden from sight in a tiny alcove, and they were the only customers. "This is nice... was the chef okay about it?" He sat opposite her but close. She had dressed in a cotton, pleated black frock with a halter neck and had tied her hair back with a simple ribbon. "You look exquisite... absolutely beautiful."

She thanked him and smiled. Touching his hand she lifted it to her lips and kissed it. "I do feel good, especially with you..."

They ordered drinks and when the waiter had been and gone, she said softly. "Tell me something more about yourself and this business that keeps you out 'til all hours of the night." It was not said with malice or suspicion, more an interested, female curiosity. She was desperate to know more about this... stranger that she had met just hours ago and now had such deep feelings for. It was not like her at all, to allow her emotions to be exposed so easily, but there was just something about him that intrigued and fascinated her and he was so easy to talk to. It had been such a long time since she had allowed this to happen to her. The last relationship she'd had was over a year ago and had ended in heart rendering disaster for her and she had sworn that she hated all men and that it would be 'forever' before she allowed it to happen again.

Webb rolled a cigarette and lit it, placing his old Zippo lighter on top of his pouch, watching the softness of her childlike eyes. She had a kind, homely face. Not beautiful like the other two but a face that any man would be happy to wake up next too... for the rest of his days.

"Could I try one of those?" She giggled excitedly, with that little 'twinkle of a laugh' he liked about her.

"I didn't realise you smoked..."

"Sometimes I do... when I'm happy and in nice company."

He rolled another and handed it to her. She coughed heartily as the acrid smoke hit her lungs. It was slightly easier on the second draw. "Strong..." She coughed again, fanning the smoke away from her face with her hand. "Now you see... that's one of the things I can't understand about you. You can obviously afford to smoke anything you wish, and yet you choose to smoke these awful things..."

"A poverty-stricken upbringing, I guess." He laughed with her.

"What were you like when you were a teenager, Webb? Tell me something about 'you'."

He smiled. "A bad bugger really, I suppose, always in trouble, especially at school. I was the one always standing outside of the headmaster's office waiting to get the cane."

"Oh..." She put her hand over her mouth and giggled. "... What for?"

"Scrapping mainly... ya know, fighting." He shrugged. "I couldn't read and write until I went into the army at sixteen, so everyone thought I was a bit of a 'Dumbo'... and they were always taking the piss out of me, so I had to beat the shit out of them... hence the headmaster."

"... and yet now, you seem so gentle."

He shrugged again. "What about you...?"

She told him she was twenty-four and had spent most of her life in the tiny village of West Hampnet, thirty miles away and that she had gone to university in Exeter but that she hadn't been as clever as she had thought she was and flunked her exams in mathematics and science, but that she had been drawn into the business of hotel management. It was just something that interested her a lot.

He had a fillet steak Diane and she had a lobster salad which she seemed to just push around the plate rather than eat it...

"You're not hungry?"

She shook her head. "Sorry... I've got myself a little, overexcited and... a bit anxious."

"Anxious... why that?"

"Just... this, I suppose." She touched his hand, looking into his bright green eyes. "It's all a bit... new... I suppose."

"Mmmm... and me really."

"Has it been... a long time for you... since you had a last date?"

He nodded, not wanting to include Gabriella that was... just something else. "Six months... probably longer."

"I always swore I would never have another... entanglement, not after the last one. That was far too painful."

"I'm sorry..." He was already starting to feel bad about this.

As the evening passed they talked easily and he found that he really liked her... a lot. She laughed at his stories of when he was in the army and the antics of the building trade. But he felt a deep sense of guilt when he told her of his life... now, most of which were complete lies. He shrugged his shoulders inadvertently... wondering if it mattered anyway... in a couple of days, this might all 'fizzle out'... so why worry about it? Let the future take care of its self...

She yawned, holding her hands across her mouth. "Oh dear... I'm sorry. I didn't realise how late it was, I was enjoying myself so much."

"Mmm. I think we better go." He glanced at his watch, it was two-thirty. "These poor sods have probably got to be up at the crack of sparrows. He rose and eased her chair for her and kissed her lightly on the mouth. "I'll get this..." He picked up the bill, amazed that it was so expensive. The head waiter thanked him for the huge fifty pound tip, the largest he'd ever had from a single table. "... and that's for the lads in the kitchen." Webb handed him another two, hoping that it would reach the chefs.

At the juncture where they would part, along the long veranda, he pulled her to him and gently kissed her lips, feeling the warmth of her body through the thin frock amalgamating with his own.

She held him tightly, her feelings in turmoil, uncertain of herself. Wondering what she should do.

"Right, 'Cinderella'." He touched her cheeks with the tips of her fingers and brushed her lips with his. "I'll call you in the morning, as soon as I'm up... although I'm not sure what time that will be. But we'll definitely do something tomorrow, as soon as I get back..."

She pressed her head to his chest, not wanting to let him go. "Aren't you..." She hesitated, feeling embarrassed. "...going to ask me in for a... nightcap?" She stumbled with her words.

He lifted her face to his and kissed her again. "Um... well, yes I'd like that... are you sure."

Sometime through the night, he had woken up in a sweat of cold fear... shouting and thrashing his arms around and she had held him, calming him down, cuddling closely into his body, her hands soothing his face against the nightmare...

"Are you alright, Webbley... what was it?"

"Agh, nothing... it's just... too damned dark in here." And he had gotten up from their bed and opened the curtains a touch, just to let some of the light from the yard in.

"Do you get those very often?"

He had shaken his head but his hands were still trembling. "Faces... that's all... sometimes... I hate the dark, that's when the faces come..." But he couldn't finish.

***

After such a bad night's sleep, it was ten o'clock before he eventually woke. A stream of sunlight broke through the tiny gap in the curtains, casting a beam across the bed. He watched the tiny sparkles of dust along the beam creating a miasma of life, and followed the light with his eyes along the whole length of the beam terminating on the carpet.

Claire was lying on her tummy, the quilt just covering the lower half of her body. He leaned over and touched the nape of her neck with his tongue and gently ran it down her spine. Slowly she stirred and turned to face him, pulling the quilt up to her neck. "Mmm, what a lovely way to be woken up..." She purred. "Good morning... stranger," and touched his lips gently with her fingertips. "What time is it?"

He told her and said that it was the best 'half-night's' sleep he had ever had and nuzzled his face into her neck.

"Mmm..." She stretched her arms above her head, yielding to his petting. "Do you have to go out today, darling?" Her arms surrounded his head and onto his back, her right hand touched his belly and then down, wandered onto his groin, feeling as excited as she had last night. "Can't I tempt you to stay?" her fingers gently playing with him, feeling his arousal.

"No, you little devil, as much as I want to... I can't... although..." He opened his legs wider for her. "I'm almost tempted to phone the buggers up and cancel everything... just tell them to sod off..."

"Let's do that!" She wriggled out from his arms and pushed him onto his back and then laid across his chest, feeling him responding to her fingers. "Let's just be decadent today, stay in bed all day and have the food sent in. Why don't we do that?" Touching him was arousing her again.

"Don't tempt me, or I might just do that... and you would probably get the sack." He turned her, easing her gently onto her back... back into the pillows and lay across her, taking his weight with his elbows... gently tickling her neck with his tongue.

"You don't want me, now that you've used me... I suppose." She smiled, making a face teasing him, wrapping her legs around his buttocks, wanting him to be deep inside her again, as he was last night. It had been her 'first'... not the first time she had been made love to but the 'first time she had been made love to... 'Like that'.

She felt his fingers gently seeking her out and responded to him, as he touched her, probing gently inside her body. She released her ankles from behind his back and placed her feet firmly on the bed forcing her body up into his thighs. Her head already spinning out of control as she felt him enter her, the words in her mouth gurgling, animal like sounds of passion.

For a moment she felt her body freeze not wanting to move her position, lest she spoil the ecstatic moment and break the spell. Everything of him was deep inside her body now, boiling her blood and her passion as if in a vice as his fingers touched her, gently caressing her into a hard pinnacle of ecstatic, of unbearable pleasure, as he entered her deeper. Her buttocks pounded upwards into his groin, her arms around his body not wanting to break the bond of flesh. As her passion built she felt her body freeze again and tried to hold the impossible moment as her juices exploded from her, onto him, around them, her thighs gyrating with his rhythm, feeling the hardness of him deep inside her body, she screamed, long and desperate, like a child in pain. Like a small doe caught in a trap, calling for its mother...

Seconds after her own explosion, she felt the hardness of his 'volcano' as it erupted his hot juices into her, around her and gushing from her. The terrible, wonderful ecstatic 'pain', pleasure... love... slowly left her body to be replaced by just the closeness of their bodies. But she fought against it, not wanting him to withdraw, to separate... ever!

And then she cried... as she had last night. Uncontrollable, sad tears of happiness and joy... of fear and doubt and misgivings and longings... and every emotion in between...

"Hey..." He kissed the tears from her face and gently with his fingers, brushed the hair from her forehead and kissed her lips...

She laughed and sobbed... both at the same time, returning his kisses, passionately, still unable to understand exactly what had just happened to her... again! "I love you so much..." she whispered, almost to herself... so that the world would not hear her.

He kissed her again, tenderly, but said nothing and held her tightly to his chest, fighting his own, inner demons. Eventually the turmoil; of his mind would ease and the guilt of the lies he had already told her would subside... but for now he would have to live with it... there was just so much to do.

She felt his distance, immediately and told him that she felt sad that he had to leave and that she 'really' wanted to be with him... today. She relaxed herself and wiped the tears from her face, her mind begging him just to say the words she wanted to hear. The words that would make her 'whole' and 'complete' again... but they never came from his lips...

Eventually, they lay back, each with their own thoughts. Some of her thoughts terrified her... she had made love... twice to a 'total stranger' that she knew little or nothing about... and had... fallen in love with him... how could that have happened?

Webb leaned into her and kissed her lips, then rested his head on her breasts watching the tiny, almost invisible, 'silk hairs' of her upper lip move as she breathed. "I'm not sure what is happening at the moment..." He fought for the right words. "But that was... the... most wonderful thing that has ever happened to me..." He lifted his head and kissed her again.

Her mind fought the words he had just spoken, trying to 'decode' them. Did he just say that he loved her? Or that she was just... a great lay? Her mind begged him to tell her... she mouthed the words silently... but no sound left her lips... 'For God's sake...just say it'. The words screamed through her brain.

She hid the 'pleading' in her voice. "What... time do you have to leave?"

"An hour ago..." He kissed her again, wishing that he 'could' stay.

"Can... Can I come with you...?"

He shook his head. "Not today... today is very important." He said it as nicely as he could.

"It's another woman... isn't it?" She found the courage to joke with him.

"It is..." He smiled. "Two actually..."

"You beast..." She laughed with him and leaping to her knees pummelled him with the pillow and straddled him, her buttocks on his belly... her heat already rising again... still unable to understand what was happening to her... and her body.

He felt for her inner thighs and she responded immediately, arching her back and opening herself to his touch. Throwing the pillow to the floor, she lay full-length along his body, kissing his face... his mouth... wanting him inside her again... as he was last night.

"Hey... hey, you little vampire..." He tickled her around the ribs but it seemed to make her more sensual. He forced himself to a sitting position, taking her with him and held to his chest, he could feel her hand seeking him behind her back. Rolling her over gently onto her back, he held her at arm's length. "I really... really have to go, love," and softly kissed her on the mouth. "...later... I promise you we will continue this later..."

She pouted but released him... not caring if he 'loved' her or not... she did... No she did not! "Damn... are they very beautiful?"

"...Who?"

She hit him with the pillow again. "The two women you are meeting... and probably going to have sex with..."

"Well..." He rolled from the bed and stood in front of her. "Do you remember reading about the three Stygian Witches... When shall we three meet again... blah, blah, blah?" He contorted his face "... come hail or rain... blah... blah... etc. Well, this is two of them..."

"Good God! What's that..?" She pointed at the three huge indentations, one each side of his groin and the other just below his lower belly. The skin around them was deeply indented as if a small pebble had been dropped into water and frozen before the water could refill the hole.

He looked at the scars, his fingers gently touching each one, most of the time he could forget they were even there. "I got shot... in Borneo, when I was in the army..."

"Oh..." She laid her finger on the scar closest to her, but he screamed and jumped away from her, frightening her... and then, burst out laughing, hopping from one foot to the other.

"Gotcha..."

She threw the pillow at him, pouting. "You made me jump, you silly man. I thought I'd really hurt you..."

He laughed again, teasing her. "Right... I need a quick shower and get dressed and out of here or I'm in trouble..." He rushed for the bathroom. "... I need to sort some clothes out..."

"I'll do it... can I do that for you?" she asked, enthusiastically.

"What?" he called back.

"Can I pick out your clothes... just for today... you have such beautiful clothes?" She picked up the bath towel from the floor and wrapped it loosely around her waist.

Webb popped his head around the bathroom door and nodded. It was the first time he had seen her naked, standing up and liked what he saw. As the water hit his body, his mind kept tempting him to stay... how could he leave her like that... just dressed in a towel... maybe he could leave his business until tomorrow... No! Get it done... He needed to think of a way to divert her so that he could retrieve the automatic from the bedside locker... If she saw that she would freak out... for sure.

"What do you think?" She seemed pleased with her selection. She had smoothed out the quilt and laid his clothes neatly on top.

"Brilliant. It's what I would have chosen." She had picked his favourite shoes, and the brown leather bomber jacket and a pair of chinos. The light pink, Armani shirt he wasn't too sure about...

"... and I just love these..." She held up the tiny boxer shorts and passed them across her face like an Arab veil. "I've never seen anything like them... very sexy..."

It didn't take him long to dress, rejecting only the tie she had picked out. He couldn't remember the last time he had worn one, probably at his brother's wedding, twenty years ago. "Could you pop over and get me some fags, love... please. I don't want to smoke those 'roll-ups' today; the company is a bit 'posh'..."

"Like this..." She laughed and pirouetted in the towel, her hands cupping her breasts.

"Mmm, seems a shame to cover such a beautiful body."

"... Beautiful... my eye." She suddenly became very conscious of her nudity and held her hands across her breasts. "Look at the size of my hips and bum... Lummi... I'm fat." She patted the 'puppy fat' of her bottom.

"Not for me... I like to see a woman with a 'proper body', not a stick insect." He said it sincerely, meaning it. "... fags..." He reminded her and rushed over and patted her on the bottom.

She smiled and dressed quickly, not bothering with her panties or bra... maybe it would tempt him to stay.

After she had left, he quickly packed the automatic and holster into the briefcase. He knew she would be bound to 'hug' him before he left so he would find somewhere quiet later to put the holster on.

Chapter 11

Monday 10:30 am.

"I need to speak to Peter Copping... please."

"Good morning, sir. Can I ask whose calling?" The voice was curt and professional.

"It's Quillion, and just tell him that he's a big, ugly, black bastard..." Webb chuckled to himself.

"I think you had probably better do that yourself, sir... I'm just putting you through..."

Some minutes later... The deep, rich African/Caribbean voice boomed over the telephone line, "... you old bastard. What are you doing with yourself? Why didn't you come to the last reunion... you shit, where are you?"

"Whoa! Hang about, slow down a bit... but yeah, I'm good." It was good to hear him again. They had been two years together in 2 Para as recruits and then gone on together for the 'Selection trials' for the Special Air Service, both passing first time. Peter had initially been posted to The Radfan and him to Borneo... a year later they met up again in Borneo.

"What's up then... I was pissed you didn't come though... mate." The voice was interested and curious.

"What sort of security set-up have you got?" he asked, simply.

"That's a bit of an odd question, mate, but yeah it's pretty big now, very efficient... well you know what I'm like for doing things right, everything has to be 'tickety-boo', business is booming, what with all the troubles going on at the moment, and of course we're International now. Hang about, mate, you're not thinking of asking me for a job are you? No... Come on, you're kidding me, yeah? You're too old for this game, mate..." He'd assumed Webb wanted a job.

"I wouldn't work for you... you cunt. Fuck me no... you'd be the last lunatic 'I'd' work for." He said it light heartedly. "But I need some help... I... need some close protection stuff..."

"...For who, you?" Peter remembered the last time he had seen Webb at the reunion... he'd looked a little bit... 'down on his luck'.

"That's pretty expensive, Quill, you know it is." He felt even more 'confused' at the request.

"I know, what sort of money we looking at." He tried to make it sound 'casual', but worried that he hadn't succeeded.

To Peter, the conversation seemed a little 'academic' and pointless. "... Two fifty a day, each... plus expenses. Probably work out more like three-fifty a day... overall, but that's not quite the point though, is it, Quill... I'd need to know what you want them for, you're a bit of a mad bastard, you probably want to rob a bleeding bank or something, Yeah?"

"Fuck off... I was no 'madder' than you were, in those days. Anyway, have you got any available now... I need two, immediately, from today?" He was feeling a little easier now.

"And this is for you, you in some sort of trouble, boy?"

"Up to my armpits, mate..."

"Shit... how did that... never mind. If you're really serious I could do you deal, but it won't be much cheaper. Call it three hundred each, and that'll including expenses. Yeah?"

"Look, get me two of your best and I'll pay five hundred a day each, plus the expenses and..." He was thinking out the plan he had worked through last night. "If any of them get seriously hurt I'll put in half-a-mill extra..."

"Jesus... I'll come down and do it myself for that sort of 'dosh'. Where'd you get that sort of... forget that question, it's nothing to do with me. But I need to ask... is this legal?"

"Almost..." Webb laughed. "They'll just be looking after me, nothing more. I have to be out of the country in a week or so anyway, so it will only be until then... There's a hundred grand bonus for each of them if they complete the two weeks..."

Peter was silent...

"Peter...You still there?" Webb shouted down the line. "Or have you dozed off again, like you used to when you were supposed to be on watch..."

"Fuck off... Where are you?"

"... Just outside of Alton."

"We're in Guildford, hour and a half away. Do you want to meet now... I'm intrigued?" Peter tapped his desk with his pencil.

"Sounds good to me, mate." Webb gave him directions to the pub he had taken Kristianna and Gabriella to. He knew the layout now and felt more comfortable there.

"One o'clock... and, Quill... this better not be a wind-up... or I'll be well pissed. I don't have the time to fuck about."

Webb looked at his watch eleven-thirty... half an hour to get to the pub... and half an hour to be early. "Don't worry about the money, Peter; I'll pay you a week up front. Make sure you bring those people with you... and, Peter, no bull shitters... I want 'seriously' hard buggers... fellers that can take care of themselves in a scrap."

"I might just have the perfect two for you, they got back from Bosnia two weeks ago and are on leave, but they must be getting seriously pissed with family life by now. I'll see if I can't bring them along. But, Quill, like I said I don't run a charity, mate or no mate; it still comes down to pound, shillings and pence at the end of the day."

"Yeah, yeah, yeah. Don't worry I'm good for it, don't worry, man. Oh, Peter, one other point, can a mobile be traced?"

"Mmm, sure it can, but it costs... man it really costs, you've got to be pretty serious about wanting to trace one. If you're worried, don't talk for too long on it, two maybe three minutes tops, no more."

After he had replaced the receiver Webb wondered whether the decision he'd made to keep the cases wasn't just a little foolhardy... at first he'd thought of keeping just the briefcase, as was agreed with Alexander de Los Santos, but decided that 'for his troubles', that wasn't enough. Yes, a hundred thousand was an awful lot of money... but with properties in Wales going sky-high he would get very little for his money and still with the same amount of danger lurking behind him... and then he had counted out, roughly what was in the suitcase under his bed and it had come to about twenty million pounds... that sounded far more like it. With that he could go back to Malaya and buy an island or some other paradise... he would never have to worry ever again about finance, or working, or where the next penny was coming from, reasoning that if two women could do it... then so could he.

Chapter 12

Monday 10:45

Kristianna sipped her coffee; it was quiet now as she sat in the main saloon of the yacht. The rain had stopped, leaving the smell of freshly mown grass in the air; it permeated the whole of the marina and the interior of the yacht. But she hardly noticed it; her mind was elsewhere and far too preoccupied on other things...

Earlier she had scolded the chaps with the mowers to go and cut the 'damned' grass somewhere else, for now... she just couldn't think for the noise. She was worrying again, things just 'had' to be moved on and quickly. Today was the second day, there was perhaps tomorrow or possibly Wednesday and then they 'would' be discovered, even if she kept the yacht moving, they needed to be out of the country. Once into Africa, they would be safe. She knew the Met Corps well enough to know they would eventually find them here, and knew the efficiency of Paul Kyso and his team, they were like bloodhounds on the trail of blood. She shuddered at the thought of the consequences.

There was nothing else she could do, that hadn't already been done. Most of it was out of her control anyway, and she hated that more than anything. Earlier she had called Daniel's mobile but it was answered only by the 'automatic operator', she would need to try again later. She was beginning to realise that he wasn't the 'illiterate peasant' she had originally taken him for.

"I had a terrible night's sleep..." Gabriella's voice disturbed her train of thought as she entered the lounge slumping down into the opposite couch. Her hair was a mess and her eyes puffed up. "Is Sui Lin up yet? I need a coffee... Sui..." she called, without waiting for an answer.

"I sent her out, make your own..." Kristianna snapped at her.

"Oh... what for?" Not receiving an answer, she staggered from the couch, returning some minutes later with her coffee.

"How was last night?" Kristianna sipped her coffee and pulled the silk dressing gown tighter around her legs and settled back, not really bothered whether she was answered or not, just conversational curiosity.

"Well, it was so strange." Gabriella brightened, the smile beaming across her face. "At first he seemed absolutely terrified of me."

Kristianna scoffed, finding that impossible to imagine.

"...we were in my cabin." She pretended not to hear her sister's derogatory grunt. "Initially, I had to do 'everything'. I almost raped him... it was so strange. Then it was over and done with, like that." She snapped her finger and thumb together. "I wondered if he was a virgin, or even 'gay'... but I think he was just out of practice." She sniggered, took a sip of her coffee and continued, feeling excited as she relived it. "But he revived so quickly... and the second time... oh dear... the second time was just..." She jiggled on the couch. "... fantastic... just drove me out of my mind."

"Don't get attached to him..." Kristianna said firmly and without smiling. "Just play him along until we are out of this mess, give him whatever he wants. He has a girlfriend by the way..." she said, spitefully letting it 'hang' there for a second. "Rather plain, country bumpkin type. Quite ordinary really, I thought." She smiled, glancing quickly over at her sister, her mind turning back to the situation in hand.

Gabriella was silent, hating her sister. It had always been the same, all of their lives. Kristianna just had to destroy everything she touched. Even as children, she would take away anything I had. She wondered if she realised just how destructive she really was. "How do you know that?" she tried to make her voice sound... 'Casual'.

"He has a woman..." Was all she would say? Spite and anger and bitterness creased her brow. Anger at how long she'd had to spend with 'The Caretaker' and spite for the 'prey' she had lost after following 'that damned Webbley' for hours. Never mind, she would pick up the 'trail' later.

Chapter 13

Webb wondered if there was anything else to be done before they arrived, but he was certain that he'd covered everything. He touched the briefcase by his side, feeling nervous. This was a meeting of his 'piers,' or they would have been, ten years ago. Now he was well 'out of practice'... one thing he was very certain of was that he would need to be absolutely straight with them... or as straight as he could be... anything that sound like 'bullshit', they would pick up on immediately and walk away from it. They were the consummate 'professionals'... as he had once been.

The main difference now was that if he got this wrong... he would be dead... there was no way on God's earth he could do this alone.

"Can I get you something else, sir." The pretty waitress who had served him earlier startled him.

"Yeah... sure. I'll just have another Coke until my guests arrive." He smiled at her. "They're late, not like them at all. Oh, and could you bring over some menus. Please."

He had managed to book a table, well off to one side and next to the window so that he could watch the car park. At this time of day and because it was a Monday the pub was almost empty, just a couple of 'rep. types' at the bar and two women seated three or four tables along from where he sat and over to the right, a young couple that seemed to be full of each other.

The rain had started again, slightly obscuring his vision so he wiped the window to clear the condensation. It was that misty, fine rain, typical 'English weekend weather', really.

He watched as the big B.M.W. seven series pulled into the car park, followed by another smaller B.M.W. close behind. A huge black man got out of the 'seven series' and walked back to the following car and spoke to the driver. Webb knew instantly who it was; there could be no mistaking Peter Copping... At six feet seven and weighing around the two hundred and fifty pounds mark... there was just no way he could look, 'Inconspicuous'.

Webb raised his hand as they entered, signalling to the big man...

"...You old bastard." Peter Copping threw his arms around Webb and lifted him off his feet as if he was a 'light-weight toy', his character as big as his smile. "Damn good to see you again... damn good. What you been up to now? This sod could never keep his nose clean."

"... and good to see you too, mate... but can you put me down now... it's getting a bit uncomfortable and you're creasing my suit." Webb beamed it really was good to see him again. There was always a feeling of 'safety' and security around him. If anyone could get him out of this mess he was in, it would be Peter Copping... without a doubt.

"So..." Peter was still smiling. "This is what I've got for you." He introduced the two people with him. "This is Beth Westwood and David Coulter. Beth was the first female to pass the S.A.S. full 'Selection', and David was ten years with the Marines. The last three attached to the Special Boat Section. They know their stuff."

Webb would have put David Coulter down as a Marine, for sure. He was almost as tall as Peter Copping, muscled and toned like a rugby player with a huge wide neck and square jaw. His suit would have been specially tailored for him, no 'off-the-peg' suit would have fitted and he looked immaculate and thoroughly professional. Beth Westwood was wiry, her face almost gaunt and she looked like an athlete, a runner or a gymnast. She was five feet eight, he thought, almost flat chested and her bright green eyes were alive and seemed aware of everything around her. She held his gaze, unflinching as if searching his soul as she shook his hand. The pinstriped suit and a simple white blouse, buttoned almost to the neck suited her. He shook their hands, glad to be back in 'his' kind of company.

They both looked thoroughly professional. "Have a seat, folks." He hoped his voice hadn't wavered. "We'll order some drinks and eat later, if that's okay with you?"

They ordered their drinks, as he thought, no one had ordered alcohol. He would have been disappointed if they had.

"Christ man, are you still rolling that crap... you never packed it up then?" Peter pointed at the cigarette Webb was rolling. He was smiling but Webb knew that Peter had been serious about the smoking 'bit', he'd always been a bit of a 'fitness buff'. "That crap will 'really' kill you."

Webb laughed. "Nag, nag, nag... like me bloody mother." To his surprise, Beth produced a silver cigarette case and took out a pink Sobranni and lit up. He would never have put her down as a smoker. "Right, I'll just run you through the basics. I don't want to go into the minutiae of every little detail, but stop me if there is something you don't understand or you need more info on." He was back in his 'briefing room', deep in the jungle... gaining more and more confidence as he spoke.

He ran through the exact situation, exactly as it happened, but told them only of the briefcase and just two suitcases one filled with money the other with Daniel's clothes, and of the two ledgers, adding that there had been two large bags of diamonds in there also. He briefed out Alejandro de los Santos's proposal, not sure afterwards why he had mentioned the diamonds, but it just seemed to add a little more 'drama' to the story and just maybe a little more 'credence'. He also told them about the two women Kristianna and Gabriella.

"Were they the ones who did the original robbery?" Beth asked, her eyes were still fixed on his.

Webb nodded. "I think so..."

"Wouldn't it just be better to 'shop' them?" Peter added. "It would give you a lot more credibility with this Alejandro chap."

"You hardnosed sod," Webb was annoyed. "... I don't want to be responsible for 'their' deaths... I actually quite like the younger one, but that aside, I'm not turning them in, not unless I absolutely have to."

"Why don't you try going down the negotiation route first, worth a try, surely?" Peter shrugged his shoulders. He hadn't taken his eyes from Webb since he'd started talking. His work made him automatically suspicious of everyone. "Ha... it's that bloody 'kitten' again, isn't it..."

Webb ignored the 'kitten' gibe from Peter. "I thought of that, trying to negotiate, but they'll know I've read the journals, how do we get over that?" Webb sipped his coke. "... and these buggers don't take prisoners by the looks of things. I couldn't believe how hard they came at us, no pissing about with talk... just straight in."

"We've got negotiators, Peter, why don't we send them in first. It'll give us a better lay-of-the-land," Beth added.

"Mmm, don't know. Not sure if I like that approach." Peter scratched his balding head. "I've heard of Met Corps, got their bloody fingers in all sorts of pies, any time they are pulled by the cops, their lawyers have them out before you can say 'Jack-in-the-box.' Slippery sods."

"What's in the journals?" It was the first time David Coulter had spoken. "Have you read through them?"

"Names, dates and payouts to the cops, lawyers, judges, even some bloody high ranking politicians. Makes pretty grim reading I can tell ya. I never imagined we had that many bent coppers and judges." Webb finished his coke and signalled the waitress over. "I need something stronger..." He ordered his usual large gin and tonic.

"Sounds like shit to me." Peter's prickly-heat was playing up again, as it always did when he couldn't solve a 'riddle'. "Look... okay. We'll try the 'negotiations bit' first, see where that takes us, but we'll do it from a distance. No names, no tie-ups to me or you... I'll do it as if you have organised it yourself. They don't need to know we are involved at all. Gimme the number..."

"Are you blackmailing them, Quill?" Beth's gaze almost made him wilt. She said it without smiling. His old army 'nickname' seemed sort of strange coming from her. The question came right out of the blue and almost caught him out of 'kilter'.

"No... I think too much of my life to go up against people like this. I told you, I'm just a 'chippy'." He held her gaze, hopefully convincing her that he wasn't lying. "I'm quite happy to walk away from the whole bloody thing... maybe a bit of compensation for the damage they did to my van, but that's about it, really. I certainly don't need all this hassle."

"So you just need 'looking after' for what... a week... fortnight?" Beth questioned him again.

"Pretty well... that's about it really... just someone to watch my back until this is settled or I'm out of the country."

Peter watched Webb's face trying to identify the lie that he knew was in there... 'somewhere'. "I just get this really bad feeling about all of this... you've told us everything that we need to know, Quill?"

He nodded, holding Peter's stare. "Everything you need to know... sure," he said noncommittal.

Peter leaned across the table and slowly eased Webb's lapel a fraction. "What's with the cannon?" His pink, white eyes trying to penetrate Webb's inner mind. "You obviously think it's pretty serious to be carrying that."

Webb nodded... "Yeah I do, they had one 'pop' at me already. They'll get a bloody big shock the next time they try."

"Well I don't know, I'm still concerned about my people." He looked at his two companions, his raised eyebrows questioning them, silently.

"Were you concerned two weeks ago when they were in Bosnia? I shouldn't think you had enough control from here to 'be' concerned." He was worrying a little now, needing them to cover him whilst he made his arrangements and didn't have an alternative other than to get on a big yacht with two 'strange, volatile women' that had 'supposedly' murdered three people already.

"True..." Peter conceded. "What do you think?" He put the question to Beth and David.

"It's fine with me... we just need to sort out the odds and sods, really". She was the first to answer, but there were still questions in her own mind that she wasn't too happy about... still not sure of the opposition. David nodded consent, casually sipping his Fanta.

"How do you feel about being 'tooled up'?" He referred to them carrying guns, knowing full well that they would all have them tucked away in some secret little corner out of the way of prying eyes and hidden from the law, as he used to have until the British government brought out that ridiculous firearms law as a 'knee-jerk' reaction after the Dunblain shootings.

"Only on 'special occasions'..." She was the first to answer again. "I don't want to be caught walking around with one, particularly." All knew that possession of a firearm was an automatic ten-year custodial sentence.

"Yeah, I'm okay. With that..." David followed. "We can always leave them handy in the car."

There was something 'needling' Webb about David. The 'strong silent type' always had that effect on him, he would far sooner have everything open and transparent from the outset and discussed, with all potential problems thrashed through. "If there's anything that you're not happy with or unsure about..." He was careful how he put his words; these were professional, temperamental and sensitive people. "...any doubts in your mind... I would sooner know about them now. If you're not happy with the arrangements, I'd be happy to sort out your expenses for today and part as friends." He looked at all three.

"Sure... count me in." Beth seemed much more assertive. She reached forward and shook Webb's hand, smiling.

David followed suit, but Webb could see by his eyes that there was something he wasn't quite happy with.

"Well, I think we're on then..." Webb nodded at the briefcase next to him and then to Peter. "I'll sort this out in your car when were finished. There's fifty grand in there... I'll need a couple more people by the middle of the week... Wednesday? I'll put in an additional thirty grand bonus for everyone at the end of the fortnight... Yeah?"

They shook hands on the deal, everyone seemed perfectly happy with the financial arrangements. Beth wondered if it would be enough for her to start her little riding school and farm, then she could get out of this business altogether. She was thirty-one years old and her mind and body weren't as sharp now as they should be... it was time to 'call-it-a-day'... With the money she had already saved and this contract it was now a real possibility that she might just be able to put down a decent deposit.

"If you want another couple of chaps, I've got one straight away that would be perfect for you already, and he needs the money... badly. He's a 'Rupert', but brilliant." The name 'Rupert' was given to all officers of the Special Air Service... in a way it was a 'compliment'. "He's a lord... a real one with a bloody great big castle in Wales. He's trying to pay off his death duties... fat chance really, it runs into millions..."

"Who's that?" Beth's eyes sparkled over the rim of her Coca Cola. "Simon... Simon Le Croix?"

"Yeah..." Peter nodded.

"Mmm... You're right, good bloke to have with you in any circumstances, especially in a scrap. I was with him in the Radfan... real handy." She smiled to herself as she thought of Simon, one of the most genuine people she had ever met.

"Right... are we done, business concluded?" Webb put the question to them and when nothing more was forth coming. "... let's eat then, I'm starving," and signalled the waitress over.

Peter smiled; these were 'his kind' of people, these were the young, modern 'Spartans'... the warriors that in their own small way 'stabilised' some of the madness in the world. "I'll agree with that... I'm starving..."

Through lunch, the conversation was easy and casual, never touching on past exploits or past contracts until...

"This feller..." Peter pointed his fork at Webb, smiling. "...is a nutter... he got himself a bloody D.D. out of the regiment, over a cat..." A D.D. in army parlance was a 'Dishonourable Discharge,' and in most civilian establishments it would be looked on as a 'disgrace' and the recipient, unemployable... by any respectable company. "Over a bloody scabby cat..."

Beth was intrigued, raising her eyebrows, questioning, but when nothing was forth coming from Webb she asked Peter.

Peter chewed the last vestiges of 'usable meat' from the huge T-bone steak he had ordered. "This scabby old, flee ridden kitten took to living in his spare boot, one of the other blokes, when he was pissed took it out and chopped its head off... Quill was on patrol at the time... When he came back they told him what had happened... so this dopey bugger gets his Gollock out... walks into Burnett's 'bivvy'... Burnett was the twat that cut the kittens head off... grabs Burnett by the scuff off the neck and chops off all his fingers on one hand..." He laughed again... after all of these years still finding it highly hilarious... many a night he had 'dined out' on the story.

"Oh... I love cats." Beth wasn't laughing. "Is that right, Quill?"

He shrugged his shoulders, remembering. "Yeah... something like that. I didn't even like the scabby little thing really... it just seemed to adopt me, must have thought that I was his mummy or 'daddy', or something."

"They kicked you out for it...?" David asked, intrigued.

"Well... it had been coming for a while... not just the cat... Burnett's fingers were just the last straw really." Webb shrugged again, not really caring much to elaborating the story. The outcome of the Dishonourable Discharge had caused him multiple problems when he had tried to get a job... hence the reason he had pretty well always worked for himself in the last ten years.

"Oh..." Beth touched his arm, understanding, feeling his sadness herself. "I think I'd have done the same to the sod."

"Well when he cut the poor little buggers head off, I was going to do the same to him... but I took his fingers instead."

Beth watched Webb's face, it was full of emotion and could see that he was covering his true emotions with 'bravado' but she knew that he had really cared for the cat... What a strange contradiction of anomalies this man is, she thought, he seems to be a 'hard man', calculating... maybe a little ruthless, and yet underneath all of that... he could show care for a kitten that would cost him almost everything... at the time. She decided she liked him and wondered what had 'truly' brought him into this situation... not fully believing his story... But there... sometimes it didn't do to dwell on motives too much, some of the 'jobs' she'd had over the past few years had been desperately 'motiveless' and pointless and yet she had risked her life for it, in foreign countries even, knowing that if she'd been caught they would have taken a very 'dim view' of her involvement... especially as a female... and for what, money... excitement... adventure, 'love of country', what? She knew she wasn't a 'danger junky' or a just a thrill seeker. Originally she had sat her exams to be an accountant... the thought chilled her bones now... hardly able to imagine the destructive, mental anguish she would have suffered staring at balance sheets all day... every day... praying for retirement, what else was there for her, her social life was almost nonexistent, was she to wait for 'Mr. Right' to come along and sweep her off her feet? But that wouldn't have worked either, he would have wanted children... two, maybe even three. The thought appalled her, or she could have gone into Tesco's, stacking shelves all day... No! This is what suited her, her biggest regret was that her father hadn't lived to see her pass the S.A.S. selection. He had been 'first generation S.A.S.', in the last war. She was sure he would have approved and been very proud of her, but she wondered sometimes how he would view a 'female' in 'his' role...

"Go on, mate... show 'em your scars." Peter teased. "He got shot three times... in the bloody groin for Christ sakes." He felt his own groin... already feeling the pain.

"Bugger off, you prick..."

"Come on... we're all in the same 'mob' here. Drop your 'caks'." Peter was enjoying himself.

"Piss off... you're such a prick sometimes and don't embarrass me..." Webb was getting irritated. This was one of the main reasons he never went to any of the reunions, they were all 'piss takers' and 'piss heads' living off their memories as 'hard men' who loved talking about past 'glories', some of their 'exploits' had only ever existed in their own silly minds...

"We got ambushed on a patrol in Borneo..." Peter was on a roll now. "I was alright being right at the rear. We lost two blokes, Porky Reader got shot right through the bloody eye, and Quill got shot, but he was lucky really, the three rounds that hit him had already gone right through Porky... we had to airlift all of them out... almost unheard of in those days. They wanted to send him back to the U.K. but he wouldn't have it, after two months in a hospital in Malaya he just wanted to get back to his Eban's... silly brave bugger..." Peter leaned across the table, wrapped his big hand around Webb's neck and kissed him on the top of his head.

Beth felt Webb's discomfort, in a way she envied him, for his shyness and courage. She also had been in Borneo, many years after him and at a time when everything out there was stable and the political climate safer. She too had fallen in love with the Eban people who were always so friendly and compassionate and had accepted her without question, even though they had never seen a woman as tall 'and' who was a soldier to boot, and carried a very big gun... she could have quite happily settled down there for the rest of her life

Somehow this 'Webb' or 'Quill', or whatever he wanted to be called... 'was' different. She could see that he was uncomfortable with the normal 'male' macho banter that was already developing and expanding between Peter and David. It was the same 'macho exclusion' she had suffered through her entire 'Selection' into The Regiment, but she had proven that she was more than up to the task, asking no one for favours or special treatment because of her gender and she had achieved a distinction by coming second in a Selection of eighty men... What was it about these damn men? They could absolutely hate each other... fighting... arguing amongst themselves when they were in barracks... but when the 'crunch' came and they were under fire... they would die for each other a dozen times. Over the years she had seen extraordinary acts of bravery from them, unnoticed sometimes by others, and just loved them to bits.

"Shut up, Peter, or I'm going to get really pissed with you..." Webb's hand unconsciously touched his inner thigh, the horrors of that day still vivid in his mind and would be forever... "Talk about something nice or pleasant, not crap that happened donkey's years ago..." He realised Beth had seen him rubbing his leg, so he stopped and placed his hand on the table. "Don't forget I need another two people."

"I don't get the connection with the name 'Quill'." Beth skilfully diverted the conversation.

"It's my 'sir name'." Webb nodded at her, silently thanking her. "... Pendleton... Pen... Quill... You know what the bloody army's like... nobody ever gets called by their real names... do they. Ya know… 'Chalky' White…'Dusty' Miller. We even had one feller called 'House' so they nicknamed him, 'Bungalow', for Christ's sake."

"Mmm... Mine was 'Betty Booth'," Beth said with distain. "I didn't like that very much, though."

Webb smiled... he liked her, a lot.

"Get another car down to me, Peter. It needs to be clean and legal. Something big... I can't drive this one much longer before they pick me up in it." The 'meeting' had exhausted him, emotionally. After the last few days he hadn't really rested. "Do me a little favour, Peter." He took a tissue from his pocket and unwrapped it on the table, inside was, what looked like a piece of 'glass', very rough and coarse and about the size of a thumbnail. "Just get a valuation on that for me. Let's see what we're dealing with here, because I have two bloody great big bags of those."

"Is that a..." Beth leaned towards the table and inspected it. "...Diamond, a real one?"

"I think it must be... it's probably what all the fuss is about." Webb didn't look at her eyes.

He took the mobile from the briefcase and dialled the Motel. "... Hiya, Jonti... its Webb." He told her that he needed another two rooms immediately, for a couple of days. She said there was only one double left, but that it did have two single beds. Webb repeated it to David and Beth.

"Fine with me..." David shrugged his shoulders. "Just hope you don't snore... or get too randy."

'It was there again that damned 'male... macho thing'. They just couldn't help it' but Beth smiled anyway...

"... Right then." Peter Copping stood up and offered his hand to Webb. "I'll go along with this for now, but let me tell you, 'brother' I can smell a rat. There' something you're not telling me here... but be sure that I'll 'weeddle' it out of you soon."

No one spotted the grey Mercedes as they left the pub... why would they? They had been to a simple 'business meeting'... and to meet with an old friend, why would anyone consider danger in that?

Kristianna eased the car into the midday traffic following the B.M.W. seven series. She was curious; the huge black man looked like a professional wrestler and his two 'companions' who had followed Webbley, had the distinct look of the 'military' about them... She knew they weren't ordinary 'business' people, just in the way they carried themselves. It was easy enough to identify a fellow professional... She knew exactly where Webbley was going so it was pointless following him. It had taken Mister Tanner some time to locate the 'stolen car', through the electrical signature tracker installed by Mercedes Benz on all of their top of the range cars. Somehow he had achieved it without having to notify Mercedes that the car had actually been 'stolen'. She loved his efficiency. Kristianna eased the car back a little staying four cars behind the black man whom she knew could well provide some critical answers to this intriguing little problem... and anyway, it excited her...

Chapter 14

"Well don't you look like the cat that got the cream..." Jonti smiled at her friend Claire and gave her a hug as she came into the reception.

"Mmm..." Claire seemed a little 'dreamy'. She had just come on duty to relieve her friend.

"Go on then... tell me," Jonti said excitedly. "Was it... good... brilliant... disaster... what?"

Claire smiled, but seemed uncertain. "Oh... I don't know... yes wonderful... I suppose, but..."

"But what... you ungrateful bitch..." She hugged her friend. "That's just half a story. What happened?"

"It's just that... well; it's too good to be true... isn't it, really?" She touched her face with her hands fretting again. "I don't know anything about him... who is he... what does he do... where does he come from, really?" She shrugged her shoulders.

"Well, dear, I can see that something gelled between you two... that's for sure. I've never seen you like this before... Anyway, oie think it's me he fancies... oive jost bin talking to yer mon." An older couple came into the reception and Jonti took their keys, and smiling thanked them, telling them to have a nice day, whilst Claire had to wait impatiently for an explanation until they had left the reception.

"You've what..?" She jumped straight in as soon as the guests closed the reception door behind them.

"Oh yes..." She teased her, flicking her long hair away from her face. "In fact oie think he's got the 'hots' for me... really."

Claire rose from her chair and quickly grabbed Jonti, playfully by the hair, holding it firmly. "Tell me... you Irish 'She Devil', or I'll pull this lot out by the roots... what... what do you mean, he called you?"

"Ooow... He asked me for a date, but oie turned him down flat... I said oie couldn't do it because you were my friend." But she could see the hurt on her friend's face and capitulated. "... you silly soap... oim jost joshin'." She freed herself and rubbed her scalp, ducking under Claire's arm and dashed to the other end of the counter holding a chair in front of her. "...he wanted another two rooms... oie bet it's for his 'floozies'."

"Don't tease, Jonti; please... I'm not in the mood." Claire returned to her seat and leaned heavily on the desk. "Is that what he really wanted?"

Jonti wrapped her arms around Claire. "Silly... it's probably just two of his customers... his business has over run on time and they are going to stay the night... That's all, isn't it?"

Claire dabbed her eyes with a tissue and leaned her head on Jonti's arm. "You see, that's another thing... he came back with an almost brand new Mercedes sports car that was registered in London... and... he said his mother is in a nursing home in Fareham, that's only twenty miles from here... but he said he lives in Cornwall... I don't get it."

"Oh... there's no such thing as a 'local' car number plate these days, dealers bring cars in from all over the place... and... Well, I don't know, perhaps his mother wanted to be up here... perhaps he has a relative up here, people do move away you know."

Claire nodded, wanting to believe her friend. "But he's so good-looking and rich, why hasn't someone snapped him up by now?"

"Perhaps he hasn't found the right woman... until now." Jonti returned to her own chair. "... anyway, forget the gloom... was the 'sex' good?"

Claire threw her head back dreamily, smiling. "Mmm... Wonderful."

Jonti watched the 'far away', dreamy look on her friend's face, knowing she wasn't exaggerating, feeling envious. "Well then... let things run their course... just save 'something' for yourself. Don't go falling head over heels for him straight away... keep a little part of you for yourself, a part that can't be hurt...?"

The glow left Claire's face and she felt a little flat. It was already far too late for that, she thought.

It seemed an odd location to base a security companies' offices... in the middle of an industrial estate. Kristianna counted fifteen cars in the car park and the impressive, hand painted sign over the windows read simply. 'Global Securities International.'

She waited for the B.M.W. to park and slowly drove past, her eyes following the external overhead telephone wires. She stopped two hundred yards along the road and removed the binoculars from her glove compartment and scrutinised the junction box and the terminals at the top of the telegraph pole and then dialled a number on her mobile...

"I have an urgent job for you," she said simply. "Meet me at four o'clock..." And then replaced the mobile and drove out of the industrial estate.

Chapter 15

It was five-thirty before he drove back into the Motel car park and stopped at the reception to collect his keys and get David and Beth settled. Claire was on duty and he leaned over the counter to 'peck' her on the cheek... but she seemed tense and a little irritated.

She smiled at David and Beth and asked them to sign in and summoned the porter.

"Are you going to be alright while we dump this stuff?" Beth asked, pointing at their small overnight bags and a single case.

Webb nodded. "Mmm. I'll catch up with you in the bar in ten minutes." When they had left he turned to Claire. "You want to do something tonight, mate, I can get free for a few hours?"

"Are you sure you have time..." Her response was curt and sharp. "Who are they?"

It irritated him a little. "Just business colleges..." he said simply. "Anyway, I need a shower and a change of clothes... and a large drink. What about tonight?" He tried to smile but her 'frostiness' stopped him.

"Mmm. I get off at six... Twenty minutes." She didn't look at him. "Oh... there's a message for you from a Sue

Mcgillacuddy, she'd like you to phone back as soon as you return. She sounded 'nice'," she added... flatly.

Webb simply nodded and left, parking the car outside his chalet.

"Sue, how are you... my lovely?" He always liked talking to her, deeply regretting that he hadn't been down to see them for such a long time. "Did you manage to get that sorted for me?"

"I did, boy..." He loved it when she called him that, even though they were almost the same age. She always wanted to mother him. "But... and it's a big 'but', they want twenty thousand on deposit. I knew there would be a deposit but I didn't think it would be that big. But then so is the motor yacht. As soon as I said where you were going, they put the 'normal' deposit up by ten percent. Is that going to be alright? Or you just want me to cancel it?"

He said it was okay for her to go ahead with it, and that he would get a bonded courier down to her tomorrow. "I'll pop down briefly on Wednesday, if that's alright, Sue."

"Of course it is, you don't even have to ask that, do 'ee. You wait 'til I tells are Steve, he'll be pleased as punch." She was excited; he could tell by her voice how excited she was. "It's been almost a year... did you know that, you bad bugger, since weem last seen you... you devil?"

If only the rest of the world could be like Steve and Sue McGillicuddy, he thought, what a pleasant world that would be to live in. He apologised again and said that he was looking forwards to it, but that it would only be a 'flying visit' for the day. "We can catch up 'proper' when I bring the clients down, Sue. Christ, I've missed you two."

Afterwards he removed his jacket, shoes and socks and flopped out on the bed with a cigarette. He needed ten minutes relaxation before his shower and the next 'onslaught' to his senses still worrying whether he was going about this the right way, but at the moment, couldn't think of a suitable alternative. Maybe something would come to him later. He started to worry about hiring the boat from Steve and Sue's charter company... now he was involving other people again... too many 'other' people in fact and people that he cared about... deeply. Yes, there was plenty of money to go around, if he could just pull it off, but it was still fraught with dangers. The plan was only different from Kristianna's original plan by the simple fact that 'he' was in control of it now and that they would know nothing of it until he was ready to take them on board... with his 'own' people to cover him... but he still worried.

The telephone rang as he came back into the lounge of his chalet from his shower. "Yeah..?" He asked simply, wrapping the towel around his waist...then a knock on his door made him jump; he tucked the automatic back into the bedside locker quickly. "Gimme a minute Peter..." and opened the door to Claire, pecked her on the cheek and signaled for her to come in and that he was on the 'phone. "Be just a minute..." He whispered with his hand over the mouthpiece. "Sorry...go on Peter."

"... The meeting with our two negotiators is on for tomorrow morning at nine, so we should know something by midday." He clicked his teeth. "Let's just hope that we can get something sensible out of it, aye?"

"You didn't give any names away, did you?" He was cautious about what he said with Claire present.

"I run a security company and I'm not a twat..." Peter grumbled. "What's the best way to reach you tomorrow?"

Webb thought for a moment. He'd planned on taking the 'package' for Sue over to the Securicor office first thing, but he could get Claire to do that and he really needed to get hold of Kristianna and Gabriella as soon as possible... but that could wait. "Try this number first, failing that, ring me on my mobile."

"Oh and that little 'package' you gave me... as it is, uncut... about sixty grand... cut and mounted, it could be double that... and you say you have a bag full of them? No wonder they want your bollocks in a sling, mate. I think I would too."

"Jesus! Mmm... that's a lot aye, a hell of a lot." He couldn't begin to calculate the value of the whole damned bag.

"Was that 'another'... lady?" Claire asked as he replaced the receiver. She looked radiant in a simple knee-length frock and leather jacket over.

Webb clicked his teeth, patiently holding his temper, yesterday he'd found out from her that her birthday was November the sixteenth...'A Scorpio'... the most 'insecure' star sign of all. "Hey..." he pulled her to him but felt her tension and resistance to his touch so he smiled and turned away from her. "I have to get dressed, d'you want to wait in the bar for me or...?"

"Who's Sue...Webbley?" She pouted, not wanting to look at him.

"My mistress..." He was joking, but looking at her face... wished he hadn't.

"Really?"

"Christ, Claire, what is this?" He turned on her sharply. "We've known each other what, two days and you suddenly own me?"

"I just..." her eyes welled up. "... don't know anything about you, that's all, and I would like to."

"What could you possibly know about someone in two days? I don't know anything about you... who your last boyfriend was... who your parents are... nothing." He walked over to his wardrobe and ripped the towel off from around his waist and started dressing and didn't hear her leave, only the door closing behind her. 'Damn...' Tonight he would have liked to be with her, not really fancying a night on his own...

Chapter 16

Tuesday 9:30 am. "That certainly went a lot easier than I expected." Brian Stourbridge straightened his tie as they walked back to the car and checked his briefcase again.

"They seemed a little... I don't know... reticent to deal with us at first, as if they thought we were holding something back. Didn't you think?" The other negotiator was Jacob Isla, one of Peter Copping's senior lawyers.

"I'll telephone Peter as soon as we're in the car. But yes, I know what you mean, there was certainly an undercurrent. I don't fully trust them though. In fact, I think they were quite intimidating."

Stourbridge fastened his seatbelt and dialled Peter's number on the bulky mobile as Islet drove. On the dashboard was a family photograph of Jacob Islset's wife and his two daughters'. "Yes, Peter... hello it's Brian. Look, I have a few misgivings about some of this..."

"How do you mean?" Peter flicked nonchalantly at the stack of paperwork on his desk with his pencil.

"It went well enough, but I'm not sure of their motives..."

"How do you mean?"

"Just something one of them said. I don't really like it at all, but we'll see. They seemed to be interested in the exchange... but."

"What, for fuck's sake?"

"I think they want your chap dead... regardless, because..."

The line went dead... Peter flipped through the buttons, cursing modern technology. "Jenny, is your phone okay, this one's just gone off?"

His secretary lifted her own telephone and put it to her ear. "Yes, boss... mine's fine..."

The fireball at the end of the hotel car park could be seen for two miles. People rushed out into the foyer, women screamed hysterically... the hotel receptionist quickly phoned 999, not wanting to look at what she imagined was another atrocity by the I.R.A. Knowing that nothing at all could have lived through that blaze...

10:30

The constant ringing woke him from a deep, dreamless sleep and when he forced his eyes open to check the bedside clock saw that it was just after ten. "Christ..." He couldn't remember the last time he had laid in bed for that long, but then last night 'had' been pretty 'heavy' and could barely remember David and Beth getting him back into bed... "What for fuck sake..." He rubbed the sleep from his eyes and sat up, rested the handset between his cheek and his shoulder.

"They fuckin' blew up my negotiators, both of them are dead. What the fuck is this?" Peter screamed into the handset.

He was fully awake now. "Both... what, what do you mean... they're both dead, how could that have happened?"

"I don't fuckin' know... but I sure as hell will find out. Get David and Beth to phone me straight away."

Peter slammed the receiver down, and Webb felt the cold sweat of fear as he leaned back into the headboard, wishing now that they had taken his warnings more serious. 'Why would they kill the two negotiators, it didn't make any sense?' He ran the scenario through his head. 'I thought they wanted their fucking stuff back'.

Chapter 17

Tuesday 12:30

"We've located the white van of the builder, Alejandro." Paul Kyso didn't sit, waiting to be invited. "Young Daniel was there... dead, but none of our property, unfortunately."

Alejandro nodded, deriving some small pleasure from Paul's discomfort. "Do we know who he is... 'what' he is?"

"Yes sir... from the receipts we found in the van we have a name and address and a fare idea now." He shifted his weight from one foot to the other, nervously. "Webbley Pendleton, it seems he is what he says he is... a carpenter, small time builder. We also know that he bought a grey Mercedes estate less than two hours after the... um... 'Incident'. But we have already found that car; abandoned at Southampton railway station... his fingerprints were all over it..." He was at a loss to add any more to it.

"And this man is a 'carpenter'? Do we actually believe that?" Alejandro's stare was withering. "He seems to be running circles around us at the moment. Why is that?"

"I know, sir... I agree. He is a carpenter 'now', but there must be something more to him than that. I have our people in Special Branch looking into it. The police road blocks were set up within an hour of the incident and he still evaded them. I think that there is a lot more to learn about our 'Mr. Pendleton.' I've got a lot of our people onto it now..." He fidgeted again, uncomfortably wanting to sit down, but dared not.

"For God's sake... sit down," Alejandro shouted.

"There's... something else." Sitting seemed less comfortable than standing, now; it put him closer to Alejandro. "The Negotiators... their car was blown up... fifteen minutes ago... just after the meeting with our people."

Alejandro sat upright, shocked. "By whom?"

Paul Kyso shook his head. "I don't know, sir..."

"Tell me something that you do know..." Alejandro screamed. "You are the head of my security… what is it that you 'do' know. Mr. Kyso…?"

"I know... that we are not being... put up against a 'carpenter'... sir." He fidgeted again. "I will know more about this man in an hour or so."

Chapter 18

Webb threw the two suitcases into the back of his car. "Stupid bloody car..." He cursed the tiny sports car as he slammed the boot down again, this time securing it and then rushed over to the restaurant to find Beth and David, almost knocking Claire off her feet as he bumped into her in the foyer... worrying that she'd heard part of the conversation between Peter and himself.

"Webbley..." she said sharply, in her hands was a small notepad. Cautiously, she handed it to him and then stood away.

"In a minute..." He took the pad and rushed past her into the breakfast room. "We need to move..." he whispered hoarsely to David and Beth. "They've killed the two negotiators..."

Within seconds they were on their feet... nothing they had brought with them was of major importance, if necessary it could be collected later...

"I'll go with Webb..." Beth took the lead. "You bring up the rear in my car." David nodded but said nothing as they quickly moved to the cars.

As they passed through reception Claire grabbed at Webb's coat and held it fast. "Webbley... I am trying to..." She gasped as the zip on his bomber jacket top, revealing the automatic in its holster. Horrified, she touched her face with her hands and backed away from him, holding the pad out for him to take it... "It's... your mother... she's been... brutally murdered... you have to..." Slowly she moved behind the reception desk and held on to Jonti's arm. "I... saw it on the television... and I telephoned the home... are you... a... gangster?"

"Webb, we need to go..." Beth gripped his arm firmly and dragged him from the reception. "Get in the passenger seat." She shouted as she wrenched the keys from his hand. "Webb!"

He stared at the neat handwriting on the pad, blankly... as she drove quickly from the motel, stopping briefly at the road junction making sure the road was clear and to check that David was following... a single gunshot rang out from the wooded area in front of them and David's car swung off the car park road, crashing into the tree almost alongside them...

From twenty feet Beth could see David's head... almost torn apart by the impact of the high velocity bullet. Hair and body parts were strewn over the headrest of his seat mixed with patches of leather upholstery and the remnants of the shattered windscreen...

Beth hit the accelerator... hard... and gunned the car into life, skilfully negotiating the bends in the road ahead. Webb was fascinated with her calmness... as she speedily selected each appropriate gear. He tried to look back, but the tiny windows of the Porsche restricted his vision.

"David?" Webb asked, but he thought he already knew the answer, knowing now that this was getting really serious and everything had suddenly gone in a different direction.

Beth shook her head... "What are we onto here, Webbley?" She dropped the car into a lower gear and eased the speed back.

"I'm not sure..." He looked at the notepad again. "It doesn't make any sense... none of it. Why would they kill the negotiators, and my mother for God's sake? I don't get it."

"We need to get rid of this car..." she said simply, calmly. Someone will have taken the number plate and they already know who's driving it. I need to get to a phone.

They had driven for about ten miles before Beth pulled off the main road onto a 'B' road, driving much slower now until she spotted a telephone box and deftly stopped alongside it. "Wait here..."

Webb removed the small 'filofax' from his shoulder bag and dialled the number as he watched Beth in the red telephone box... A feeling of absolute desolation came over him as he dialled the number, the blood draining from his face. He listened to the curt, polite voice...

"Good morning, Alderbrook care home... nurse Hampton speaking... how can I help you..?"

"This is Webbley Pendelton..." His voice shook uncontrollably. "My mother is with you... in the care home. Is she... alright?"

For a moment the line was silent until... "Could you just hold for a moment, sir...?"

And then a different voice, a male voice... "Mr. Pendelton... this inspector Dowling of Southampton police..."

"Police... where's my mother... I heard on the news that..." He felt his heart sink. Claire must have been right... but why?

"Yes... yes, I'm afraid she is... deceased, but I think you probably already know that, sir... don't you? Where are you?"

"What happened was she...?" But he couldn't finish the sentence, his throat had seized up, and a severe pain in his chest was making it hard to breath.

"My understanding is that you booked in to see her at 9:30, this morning, is that correct?" The cold voice continued.

"No!" He screamed into the mobile.

"You were seen, sir... here... you signed the visitors book."

"No..." He tried to clear his head, for a moment he had forgotten Beth. "I was..." He wondered what he could say... nothing really.

"Can someone corroborate where you were, sir?"

He knew there was no 'sensible' answer he could give to him. "I... I wasn't there."

"Were you also 'not there' on Saturday morning at The Whiterings when two men were murdered, one a member of the public that was brutally shot to death," Inspector Dowling asked.

He felt the cold finger of death touch his heart. It was happening already, Kristianna had said 'they... these people' were all powerful. How then did he think he could 'take them on'? This wasn't a game... not some sad... awful game... a game that he was now... totally unsuited for. "Yes... I was there, but he was not a 'member of the public'. Check his credentials, his number plate... do your fucking job, you wanker. You think I killed my own mother, what sort of cunt are you?" He felt the tears welling up and coughed to clear his airways.

"I think you had better tell me where you are, sir; we'll find you eventually you know. We just need to eliminate you from our enquiries." The voice seemed a little more sympathetic.

"How... how did she die?" He felt himself choke up again.

"We cannot discuss this on the telephone, you must understand that. Tell me where you are... please; I can get some people to you straight away. If necessary we can give you protection... if what you say is true, but let me tell you, Mister Pendelton, if this 'is' you that has committed this awful crime, I will hunt you down like a dog. Is that clear?"

"Check on the dead man from the Mercedes, he must work for The Met Corps," Webb said wearily. "They are the key to all of this..." Slowly, methodically he turned off the mobile and replaced it in the briefcase, as Beth came back to the car. "Poor old bugger..." He mumbled out loud, wiping the tears from his face before Beth could see them.

"What?"

"She got killed for me... because I got myself mixed up in this crap..." He couldn't look at her.

"We'll talk about this later; the main priority is to get shot of this motor. Peter's sending down some people. Are you listening?" she shouted at him, shaking his arm, violently. "One of them is Simon ... and they'll bring down a spare car... They'll meet us halfway at Woodsbrooke Park, twenty minutes from here... I've got a 'safe house', but I'm not even too sure about that now." She shrugged.

"No, don't worry about that, I know where we'll go." His head was clearing now. He dialled Gabriella's number and when she answered. "Gabby... I need you to move the yacht... now." He reasoned that the Southampton area was getting far to 'congested', but where? "Get it to Poole; you can get in there at any state of the tide, now that they have dredged it. There's a new marina for 'Super yachts' just inside the entrance, the captain will know it." The trouble with Poole was that it also was an island with one way in and one way out, but the benefit would be the amount of tourists that would still be there at this time of the year would help to cover his tracks and could easily mix with them, unnoticed. There was no other alternative, nothing east until Brighton... nothing west until Dartmouth, and that could be a five or six-hour drive, if the traffic was heavy.

"I don't know, Webbley, Kristianna's not here; I don't want to make that decision on my own..." She sounded frightened.

"Gabby, we're in trouble, please just do it you can phone Kristianna... just tell her where you are." He softened his voice worrying that her fear might cause complete apathy and inaction on her part. "Will you do that for me, Gabby... please?"

She said she would try, hoping that she was doing the right thing. "Has... someone else been hurt, Webbley?"

"I'll tell you when I get there. Oh and, Gabby... I have two other people with me make sure the security at the marina know we are coming... three people right and log it as..." He ran through some names in his head. "Log it as Edward Smith..." It wasn't very original but the best he could come up with under the circumstances.

Inspector Alan Dowling replaced the receiver and scratched his chin, thoughtfully. He was angry, angry at the man he had just spoken to... but most of all, angry at himself for losing his temper and that was unforgiveable.

"Boss... 'Scenes of Crime' are done in there, but forensics says they need about another hour." Sergeant Tracy Gould spoke loudly, as she always did. "Are we done... you alright, boss?" She had inadvertently developed the 'loudness' as a defensive mechanism to hide her innate shyness. It seemed to work as most of her colleges and the people she knew, tended to avoid her... which suited her fine...

Over the last eight years she had been with him, he had grown accustomed to her brusque, direct manner. "Yes... I think so..." He turned towards her, liking the chubby, round face of his assistant. He actually liked her briskness, her efficiency and her frankness... and he could see right through her defences. She was tidy and rarely forgot or missed anything and was exceptionally efficient. He knew that if she smartened herself up and spent a little more time being 'tolerant' towards other people, she would make 'Officer Grade' within a year or two... she already had the necessary qualifications for the job anyway. 'And where does she get those clothes from'? The trousers and blouse and chunky pullover, looked like she had retrieved them from the wash basket... 'Before' they had been washed...

"You sure you're alright, boss?"

He nodded, still a little pensive. "Mmm. That was the old lady's son... say's he wasn't here today and that he knew nothing about this until he was told about it. I have a strange tendency to believe him... Good lord, what son could do 'that' to his mother?"

"Did he deny being at the Wittering's as well?"

"No... That's the odd part, he didn't."

Sergeant Gould said nothing, knowing that he wasn't finished yet...

"Although nothing ever surprises me in this job... nothing. Or with people for that matter, God there are some evil people out there, it makes you fearful of opening your door in the mornings, doesn't it?" He spoke as they walked back to the cordoned off area, Tracy lifted the tape for him and he ducked under, re-entering the scene of the crime room. The body had been taken to the morgue and most of the 'carnage' they had seen earlier had been cleared away. Some of the 'weaponry' used in the attack had been bagged and labelled for forensics to deal with later and were stored neatly in plastic containers.

A man and woman were dressed in white, disposable paper overalls were on their hands and knees combing through the fibres of the carpet...

"Find anything?"

"Plenty really... lots of bits and pieces to sieve through later. Certainly enough to get us started."

He recognised the female voice immediately. She always seemed to 'turn up' at his 'Scenes of crime'. "Any idea's yet?"

"Oh hi, Alan." She stood and removed her gloves and mask. "I wish I could say it was nice to see you again, but we only ever seem to meet under these circumstances, don't we. I have a few ideas." She looked back into the room. "'Incidents' like this, I wonder why I do it sometimes... should be used to it by now I suppose, but how does one ever really get used to that? Even now, it still sickens me."

He agreed. "What savagery goes through someone's mind to commit an atrocity of this magnitude, it's beyond my comprehension?" His mind remembered the scene vividly, as if the old lady was still lying there. Her hands and feet bound with duct tape, her mouth gagged brutally. The tape had been wound around her mouth and part of her nose so tightly that it had almost torn the flesh down to the bone. The doctor had said she was probably dead before the main assault took place, dying of either asphyxiation or a massive heart attack caused by the shock of it all.

She had been found, kneeling in front of an old wooden, bedside locker as if she was praying. Two six-inch spikes had been driven through her hands into the top of the locker, and then her assailant had smashed her head repeatedly with a baseball bat until it was almost 'pulp'. The baseball bat had been tossed casually on the bed and left there as if the assailant didn't care about leaving a clue behind.

A shiver ran through the whole of his body at the thought of it, and hoped the doctor was right... that the old lady had died before the assault.

"The old girl put up a fight though," The white overalled, forensic lady said. "The 'chap'... sorry, 'the person' you are looking for will be pretty badly scratched about. She had enough blood and skin under her finger nails to keep a plastic surgeon happy for a month. God, I really hate the job sometimes... at times like this."

"Yes... I know what you're saying, Carole, but without you and your people, we would all be back in the dark ages... and nothing would ever get solved." Alan watched the kindly face of the middle-aged, not unattractive lady. He knew she was a widow. Several times she had invited him out to dinner, years ago now, but he had politely declined her. Since the death of his own wife through breast cancer five years ago, he had lost interest in all 'social affairs'. Certainly any that would involve his emotions... He cleared his mind of clutter. "Tracy, let's get back to the office. Be kind enough to send that over when you are finished, Carole. Please..."

Chapter 19

"They're here now..." Beth's voice sounded like a warning. For the last thirty minutes they had waited quietly, at the back of The Old Dog and Duck car park. Hardly a word had passed between them, each sorting out their own 'special demons'.

The big 'seven series' pulled up fast behind them, followed by three other cars that boxed them in.

Webb stood by his own car with Beth as Peter charged over, like an enraged bull charging a fence. The other cars emptied of people. Two of the men from the last car stood quietly by the side doors, each held a small Uzi type machine pistol across their waists.

"What the fuck is this man?" Peter grabbed Webb by the collar and pulled him into his body, lifting him easily off his feet with one hand, the vice like grip almost choking him. "Three fucking men dead... what the fuck?" Peter slammed him back against the car.

Web put his arms out to his side hands facing up. "I don't fuckin' know... I know as much as you do."

Peter lifted him again and slammed him back onto the car. "Fuck... I haven't lost this many people since... agh... fuck knows. What's the answer here then, man... tell me?"

"There's got to be another 'organisation' involved in this, Peter. It's all I can think of. Why would they kill the negotiators... why?" Webb rubbed his throat. "Or it's someone in their own set-up that's doing it. Christ, think it out... they have no reason to kill them... or David."

"Well I'm pulling everyone off... that's for fuckin' sure. Sort out your own shit." He turned away, mainly to stop him smashing Webb's face to pulp. "Take that car..." He pointed at the Range Rover. "It's clean, although with you... it probably won't stay that way for long..."

"Peter..."

"What?"

Webb shrugged. "Is that going to solve anything, you pulling out of it?" He was really worried now, knowing full well that he couldn't do this alone... but the cost had already exceeded his wildest nightmares...

"Get in the car..." Peter pointed at Beth.

"No... I think I'll stay, boss, with him," she said, almost casually, folding her arms across her chest, her jaw set. "I took this on and I've never pulled off a job... ever."

Webb nodded at her. "Thanks... you sure?"

She said nothing; her eyes were on the tall handsome man with the immaculate suit and blonde hair standing by one of Peter's men. He nodded at her when he caught her eyes.

"Why?" Peter was still angry as he watched Beth. "This bugger's going to get you killed..."

"Well, boss, if you'd done what he said... you may well have had two negotiators that were still alive." She faced up to him. "And perhaps we would have been pre-warned about David. I'm staying..." And then she walked over to Simon de la Croix.

"Was he... married, Peter... David, I mean?" Webb pushed the mop of hair from his eyes'. "No... Don't tell me, I don't want to know..."

Peter looked at him... a look close to hatred, or disgust. "Yeah... he was married... got a young baby, four months old. Do you want to tell her?" He turned away, signalling for the others to get into their cars. "Or you gonna leave that to me?"

"I'll stay also, Peter..." Simon's voice was articulate, perfect 'Queens English'. He shrugged his shoulders and walked over to Peter. "You know how it is with me... I need this money more than any of you and from what I understand, this job is likely to pay far more than normal."

Peter tapped him on the shoulder and nodded. "Keep your head down and don't take any chances, especially with 'him'. That bastard never could stay clear of trouble." He nodded in Webb's direction. "I'll keep in touch; I need to find out more about all this shit..."

When the all the cars had left Beth introduced Simon to Webb. "You sure you want to do this?" Webb asked.

Simon nodded and smiled. "Oh, I think so... Webb," he said confidently. "What the hell."

Webb felt at home. A strange, long forgotten feeling of camaraderie flooded over him... a feeling he hadn't felt since leaving the army. "I'll bump up the money, three hundred grand each when I leave the country."

They both smiled, a little ruefully...

Chapter 20

Tuesday 2:30. Anastasia de Los Santos sat quietly in the outer reception of her grandfather's office. She had spent the last thirty minutes flipping through the endless pages of the Vogue fashion magazine... bored... she glanced at her watch, 11:30, she had already waited almost an hour, but her grandfather's secretary had said that her grandfather was in a very critical meeting and had left strict instructions that under no circumstances was he to be interrupted, not by anyone... absolutely 'no one' was to interrupt the meeting...

"Is there something I can get you, miss, whilst you are waiting?" The elegantly dressed secretary smiled.

Anastasia pouted and shook her head. She was eighteen years old, five feet six inches tall. Bright and intelligent and exceptionally beautiful and her life circulated around her schooling and her social life, although on a percentage basis, schooling was a very low priority. Most of all... she loved to spend time with her grandfather.

When she was short of money or in trouble, as she was now... she always came to her grandfather, for help. She wore a very short Gucci miniskirt and button fronted, cream blouse that exposed a little too much of her breasts, but then she knew her grandfather liked her to dress like that. He said she reminded him so much of his own wife...

long deceased... when they had been teenagers. In contrast to her six-inch, designer shoes, skirt and button fronted blouse her coat was and old army 'great-coat' with a moth-eaten fur collar and assorted stains down the front. It was heavy and had belonged to a male friend and she had instantly fallen in love with it the moment she spotted it in the charity box, ready to be taken to the shop... Somehow on her, it looked like a very expensive, designer Versace...

Anastasia was in trouble 'again' and she had known, instinctively where to come. Her only savour was her grandfather... as always. He was, 'as always', the only one who could save her from the anger of her father... after she had just 'flunked', for the third time, her latest attempt at passing her 'silly', 'A' Level exams.

She smiled as she watched the boring, suited men leave her grandfather's office, their heads bowed fearfully as if they were naughty little boys. One day, 'she' would wield the same power over the same suited men... and she would enjoy it, so much, she thought.

The secretary signalled to her that she could now go in. "He's not in a good mood I'm afraid, miss..." she whispered.

It felt so good to be able to control 'men', and Anastasia was exceptionally good at it. Except for her own father... somehow he could see through her and she rarely managed to get her own way with him... unless she went through her grandfather... first.

Earlier, before coming here she had booked a table at the Dortmund Suits, the most expensive restaurant outside of London and would take her grandfather to lunch... he would pay, of course... her allowance for the month had already been spent in the first week. But never mind, that didn't matter... one day she wouldn't have to worry about the friviolities of 'money'.

"Grampa…" She 'swished' into his office, pushing the wide-rimmed sunglasses over her forehead and before he could rise sat on his lap kissing his cheeks several times and then pressed her mouth against his. "I've been waiting an age, Grampa… an absolute age for you. I was beginning to think you didn't want to see me."

For the first time today, Alejandro smiled. "I know, child…business first I'm afraid." He wrapped an arm around her waist and rested his right hand gently on her knees. "I would sooner have been with you."

"I've book us a table… and we're almost late already." She pouted, snuggling her mouth into his neck.

"I really don't know if I can get away, child… at the moment all sorts of silly things are happening." He shrugged, wishing that everything else… except her, would just go away.

"No… you can't say that. It's our day." She opened her legs a little allowing his shaking hand to fall between her thighs. "Gramps?"

He snuggled his head into the cleavage of her breasts. "Child…" he said solemnly. "You could make a wicked old man out of me… do you know that?"

"Yes… Grampa…" She whispered.

Chapter 21

With the congested traffic and the bottleneck to get into Poole, the sixty-mile distance had taken almost two hours, in a way it had been beneficial in getting to know Simon Butterworth better. He had spent six years as a Special Operations Officer with the Special Air Service and had served with distinction earning the first of his Military Crosses in the Yemen after a successful outcome in a battle with one of the local tribal chiefs and had added a 'Bar' to the Military Cross three years later in the South America conflict. However, with crippling death duties he needed to earn far more money than the army could ever offer him and so had entered the 'private market' of the burgeoning 'security industry'... that was taking over many of the roles of the military.

"What I don't understand Webbley, is that if these two are the people who perpetrated the crime, why are you still dealing with them?" Simon had asked cautiously, not wanting to offend.

"It's a death sentence for both of them if I don't help." He leaned back to look at Simon. "I know, I should have just thrown them to the wolves... but." He shrugged his shoulders. "We'll just have to watch ourselves around them, especially Kristianna... she's a cold hard bitch, she's the 'brains' behind all of it..." He needed to change the subject. There had been quite a few times over the last day or so that he wished he had... 'flung them both to the wolves', but he quite liked Gabriella, she was different... kind and seemingly sincere.

For the last thirty minutes Simon had commanded the conversation about his beautiful home in Wales and the costs of the upkeep and death duties and... "Is there no other way around these death duties?" Webb asked him, knowing nothing of the subject. "What happens if you don't pay?

"I'd lose Holmeness House." Simon had accepted his position and his duty to the family many years ago. "I just couldn't allow that to happen, it's been in the family for over five hundred years."

"Big place?"

Beth laughed...

"Mmm. Quite big..." Simon stretched over the front seat and touched her shoulder. "Beth's been there several times."

Beth was driving, but she could see Simon's face in the rearview mirror and smiled to herself. "Go on then, you devil... tell him how big." She had been to Simon's home on three or four occasions and was always staggered at the size and beauty of it.

"It has three hundred and fifty rooms. Four of the reception rooms are capable of holding two hundred people." He seemed a little embarrassed. "In fact, in the Great Hall we once held a dinner for twelve hundred people..."

"Why's it called 'a house'?" Webb asked, innocently.

Simon smiled. "Typical English 'understatement' really. We took it from them, three hundred years ago and wouldn't give it back. It's like an anchor around my neck, sometimes though, not just the death duties, it's the upkeep as well, impossible to keep up with the repairs and we have had to close down the east wing completely."

Webb parked as close as he could to the yacht, fortunately it wasn't the only 'Super yacht' in the marina and certainly not the largest so at least it wouldn't stick out like a sore thumb... "Are you 'tooled up', Simon?"

"Yes... I always am. Even in Britain these days, with what we do, it's always wise to carry..." He touched the holster under his left arm. "Are we likely to need it... here?"

"No... I hope not, these are supposed to be 'friends', but I wouldn't trust that dictum too far. Not after the last couple of days. Beth?"

"No..." She didn't seem overly worried about it.

"There's one in my suitcase in the boot." He raised his eyebrows and she nodded. "I'll sort it out for you."

"What is it?"

"A 9mm Glock..."

"Good lord... if there's a Glock in the boot, why do you carry that damn great big Colt .45." She tapped his holster with her hand.

"Just what I got used to out there I suppose." He meant Borneo. "It's almost the same as my Browning really, about the same weight and feel, just a lot more reliable."

She smiled and looked back at Simon. "God I used to hate those damn Browning's, heavy useless things. Never used one seriously, but on the range they kept jamming. Not very good when you really need it..."

Webb nodded at the yacht. "Look when we get in there, they'll ask all sorts of questions." He shrugged his shoulders, knowing that he didn't really have to tell 'these' people not to say anything, so he didn't continue. "I want to be here no more than one night and then we need to find somewhere else until I can get my end sorted out."

"Why don't you come down to Hartness until you are ready to leave, Webbley?" Simon asked as they walked up the passeral to the yacht. "They would never get to you down there you know. The 'House' is guarded by the village and no one could ever enter the village without being identified as a stranger... Think about it."

"I don't really want to get anyone else involved in this, especially your family..." Webb tapped at the glass patio door, he could see Gabriella and Kristianna in the lounge. "Christ!" He swore under his breath. "They've got every bloody light on again, they've probably invited all the 'neighbours' over for the evening party, or something."

He watched Gabriella as she rushed over to open the sliding doors and flung her arms around him almost knocking him off his feet. "Webbley, I am so sorry... so very, very sorry. I heard it on the news this morning... your poor mother. It was such a shock."

Kristianna touched his shoulder and 'air-kissed' his cheeks. "Likewise, Webbley... I'm so sorry." Her eyes were cold and hard and her face emotionless. Unlike Gabriella who seemed to be genuinely moved, deeply by his loss. Gabriella hugged him around the waist as they all entered the lounge. "What can we do?"

"Not a lot at the moment." Webb introduced them to Beth and Simon, he offered no other information, just that they were friends. Even when they sat, Gabriella wouldn't let Webb go sitting close to him on the big couch, her hand linked through his arm. "I'm sorry..." She seemed to be blaming herself. "They are such animals... life means absolutely nothing to them."

"For that to have happened they must have put out a 'Termination Order' on you, Webbley." Kristianna sat opposite, a small glass of red wine in her hand. "That means they will kill off every member of your family and every friend that you ever associated with..." She smiled behind her eyes, but no emotion showed on her face as she spoke, to her it was just... business... nothing else.

"Seriously?" Simon asked. He looked worried now. "I've never heard of that before."

"It's the only way The Met Corps can get total obedience and loyalty from its staff... and it works very well." Kristianna couldn't see what the problem was... every dictator in history had successfully employed the same tactic... to very great effect.

Webb shrugged, it wasn't that he was not concerned, on the contrary he felt quite frightened and his mind a little 'disjointed' and didn't really believe that 'they' would go through all the trouble and complications of 'eliminating' all of his family. What benefit could they possibly gain from that? "We'll be out of here by the end of the week... just ride out the storm for now and wait. That's all."

He saw Kristianna watching him, her beautiful 'dead' eyes, never leaving his. "You have something planned, Webbley?" She touched his arm with her fingers seductively as she walked past him.

"Yeah, we'll be gone by Friday evening." He couldn't seem to hold her intense gaze and looked away from her to Gabriella and then back to Simon. "I might take you up on your offer..."

After a light dinner of Chinese fried vegetables, rice and expertly cooked noodles with charcoaled ribs and sautéed prawns and pork loin scallops cooked in a delicious red wine sauce, they retired to the saloon, a large uncomplicated sitting area beyond the lounge, Gabriella Leaned on Webbley's arm struggling to keep her eyes open.

"I have to go to bed, Webbley, I'm sorry... just too much emotion for one day." She leaned over and kissed him on the cheek. "Wake me if you want to, when you go to bed... I would like that." She whispered close to his ear.

"And me, boss... if you don't mind." Beth raised her eyebrows. "As long as you don't need me anymore."

Webb nodded. "Simon? I need to talk to Kristianna."

Kristianna asked Sui Lin to show them to their cabins and as soon as everyone had left sat opposite Webb. She wished now that she had changed into something more 'appealing' something a little more 'sexual and revealing', but there had been little or no time to prepare. She had felt the callousness of his hands when they greeted, he was an oaf... an uneducated 'clod-hopper' and for her he held no sexual appeal at all... and yet there 'was' something about him that 'did' appeal to her... she couldn't put her finger on it, maybe it was his roughness, his 'coarseness.' 'Did he, in some small way remind her of her own father... could that be it... possible?' The roughness of his hands and manner were similar... but there any similarity abruptly ended.

"Again, I'm sorry, Webbley." She sat straight backed, her eyes unflinching, her knees discreetly together and at a slight angle to her body, her hands on her lap as if she was about to pose for a Vogue magazine photoshot. "We can count on further killings from these people, that's why it is so important for us to leave immediately." She allowed her knees to part... just a fraction. Knowing exactly what she needed to do, even if it was just to gain his trust... his 'obedience' would come later... by tomorrow morning he would be eating out of her very soft, delicate hands. "We need to leave the yacht as soon as possible. You have seen how efficient they can be and it won't end, not until all of us are dead, or in their hands." She smiled her 'softest', most appealing smile.

"I know, I'm making the arrangements at the moment, by tomorrow we'll know for definite." He sipped his third large gin and tonic, normally he would have restricted it to two. "Christ, you people stirred up a bloody hornet's nest... didn't you? Couldn't you have gone for something a little easier?"

"I considered it to be 'my' money. They took the company from my father." She edged the bitterness with a shallow smile. "They deserved to lose everything... everything."

"But why so much, couldn't you leave them with something? Surely you didn't need to take everything, did you?"

"Believe me it was necessary. They have a shipment due in some time very soon, only a handful of people know the location or time, or how it is to be delivered, but it is the biggest shipment of cocaine that has ever been delivered in Europe, almost a billion dollars' worth, the street value would be twenty times that amount. The money and bonds I took is the payment for it, if they can't meet the payment date then they will all meet the same fate as your poor mother."

She thought she would add the last statement as a simple 'sympathetic gesture' of solidarity with him. She stood and walked over to his couch and sat with him, her hand on his thigh, cursing him inwardly. Damn him... damn him. She knew she would have to go along with his madness, what else could she do? More delays, delays that may well spell death to all of them... delays that were totally unnecessary. "We have the yacht here, Webbley, what more do we need, why can't we just go... now, and you have your own people with you?"

"They'll know the yacht by now." He nudged her arm away from his thigh. "Put another one in there for me." He handed her his empty glass. "Your captain has to submit a 'last port of call record', before departure. They may not have the name of the yacht... yet, but if they're as good as you say they are, they'll have it pretty soon. Christ, they're not dummies... they know you can't get that amount of money out of the country by air, it would be far too risky and sure as 'eggs is eggs', they'll have every airport and private runway monitored, an hour after they discovered the robbery."

"What is your plan?" She handed him back the refilled glass and resumed her seat next to him.

"I'll tell you when it's complete, and there won't be any 'cock-ups' in it like yours..." He eased himself away from her, feeling uncomfortable at her closeness and her heady perfume. In reality he 'wanted' to touch her... what man wouldn't, she was stunningly beautiful. He had felt the softness of her skin when they shook hands and her perfume was 'heady', almost... 'orgasmic'. It would be so easy to reach over and touch her to start it all off... she would be a 'willing participant', of that he was absolutely positive... but then what? He had seen her 'strength of character' and didn't doubt her courage for one minute. "I spoke to Alejandro..."

For a second she was visibly shocked, so much so that her hand tilted the glass, spilling some of her Champagne into her lap, but she hardly noticed. "You spoke with... Alejandro, when?"

"Yesterday, before the team of negotiators went in." He turned slightly to watch her face, but it gave little away. "He said you killed three of his people in the robbery, one of them a young lady who has three children. Is that true?" Webb watched her eyes.

"He would say that." She retorted instantly, her eyes not leaving his. "It's a lie just to gain your sympathy... of course he would say that, wouldn't he." She shrugged.

"I hope it's not true, Kristianna. If it was..." He grasped her short cropped hair and pulled her head towards his. "If it was true... I'd kill you myself," and then pushed her head away from him.

Kristianna allowed the glass to slip from her hand to the carpet and forced the blood into her cheeks and the tears to well up in her eyes. Slowly she lowered her head to his shoulder and wept... uncontrollably. It would need to be her very best... 'Oscar winning performance'... she knew that... and it was. The emotion rose from the very pit of her tummy and her body shook, quite violently, her tears spilling over onto his cheeks and down onto his shirt. She hugged his neck and kissed her tears from his face.

"That is... such an awful thing to say... Webbley." She sobbed. "Terrible... I hate that man so much for his vicious lies and deceits. How could he say such a thing?"

Webb laid his glass carefully on the side table and placed his hand gently on her cheek...

"Alright... alright." He kissed her cheek, his hand soothing her, wiping the tears from her face, hating to see a woman cry. "He seemed a bit of an arsehole when I spoke to him... vicious bastard. Hey come on... pull yourself together, please. We have lots to do tomorrow we need to keep our heads about us... Mmm?" He stood, making her stand with him and kissed her face. "Bed, we're all knackered..."

It was almost twelve-thirty before he had showered, long after his 'normal' bedtime... but then these were not 'normal times'. He towelled himself down and looked at the mobile telephone on the bedside locker, pleased that he hadn't switched it on for most of the day, fearing that it might be traced... or bring in another disastrous message.

Was it too late to phone Claire? He wanted to, needing someone 'sane' to talk to, someone who wasn't involved with any of this 'madness', but he doubted she would want to talk to him anyway, so he decided against it.

He switched out the light and lay back on the bunk, desperately tired, knowing that sleep would probably elude him again, desperate just to close his eyes and drift off in to oblivion, wondering if he should have knocked at Gabriella's door.

A movement of the door handle jolted him back to reality and he quickly grabbed for the automatic and pointed it at the door as it opened. Kristianna was framed in the doorway, her naked, tall frame easily distinguishable as she closed the door behind her, quietly and approached, stopping only as the barrel of the automatic touched her tummy...

"I... I couldn't sleep and I was frightened." She spoke softly, like a child... her hands touching her cheeks. "Could I... stay with you... just for tonight?" Slowly her hand reached down for him.

Chapter 22

Wednesday 9 am. "That's a beautiful lady, Webb." Beth held her coffee to her lips with both hands, her eyes mocking him over the rim of the cup.

"Who?"

Beth looked at Simon and winked. It was almost nine o'clock and they were in the main saloon of the yacht waiting for Sui Lin to call them in for breakfast. Webb was surprised how well he had slept after the 'tonic' Kristianna had administered...

Beth tapped his hand lightly and smiled again. "The tall, pretty lady... do you remember her?" she teased.

"Oh, Kristianna... yeah, not bad I suppose." He didn't look at her.

"Not bad!" She slapped him on the shoulder. "I watched you go 'all rigid' the minute she touched you."

Simon laughed with her. She spoke as if they were 'two chaps' talking about a 'good lay'.

"Webbley!" Gabriella charged into the saloon as if she was being chased by the devil, startling them. "Ooooh... switch on the television..." She charged across the saloon and switched it on herself, not waiting for them.

"...the police have confirmed a definite similarity between these four murders and the brutal murder of an old age pensioner, resident in a care home in Fareham. At the moment the police have no leads but would especially like to interview the pensioner's son, who at present can't be traced."

The newscaster selected the next topic. "The war in Iraq continues with the deaths of two more American advisers in the Anmmar region..."

"Oh, Webbley... they have killed your sister and husband and... oh God... the children..." Gabriella was beside herself, distraught as she hugged him.

"Wow!" Beth touched his arm, but could find nothing else to say.

Simon put his hand on Webb's shoulder. "That's real bad, my friend. I'm so sorry."

Webb felt a 'coldness' touch him, it seemed to pervade his whole body every muscle seemed to freeze. He felt fear and anger and bitterness... but he also felt a strange calmness... the same calmness when the doctors in Malaya had told him that he would live... and that all of his... 'working parts'... 'down there'... were fine. He nodded and walked away from them, easing Gabriella's arm away from him, not in an unkindly way but gently, wanting to be alone for just a moment... He slid the big patio type doors aside and dragged himself into the cockpit area and rolled a cigarette, feeling the tears welling inside him... another four people had died because of his greed and selfishness...

Kristianna came into the saloon, still wrapped in her bathrobe, the noise had disturbed her. Gabriella quickly explained. Kristianna cursed silently. 'Now he would crack... he would offer them all of the money and bonds... and everything back... just for a bit of peace... and everything would be wasted.' But she knew there would be very little peace for anyone until this was completely resolved, somehow she had to convince him to fight back... and that the Met Corps would not allow him just to 'capitulate'.

She brushed the wet hair from her eyes as she walked through to the cockpit her fingers easing the neckline of her bathrobe opening it to her waist. "Webbley..." She threw he arms out to him, hugging his neck, not caring that the belt on her robe had untied and the front of the robe had parted. His hands encircled her waist she was pleased to feel the coarseness of his hands on her naked flesh... again. "What are we going to do?" she asked, pretending hopelessness.

"We're going on the offensive..." He looked at the others over her shoulder. His calmness surprised her. "What we should have done in the first place... after mum... Let's go back in..."

Sui Lin brought in coffee and then discreetly retreated to her galley...

"I'll pay you off..." He nodded at Beth and Simon. "I don't want you getting involved in any more of this crap."

"No, I'm in... We need to put a stop to this." Beth answered almost straight away. Simon nodded agreement.

"You're sure?" He felt calm now, plans were already formulating in his mind. "Thanks. There must be some way we can get to this Alejandro chap." He looked at the two faces who knew Alejandro better than anyone. . "What's he like, what are his habits?

"No... you can't get to him, he's too well guarded. He's an old man, his passion is The Met Corps nothing else matters to him." Kristianna smiled inside, he had surprised her. "He has no lovers or mistresses. He's escorted by armed guards whenever he leaves the office or his house, the house it's self is like 'Fort Knox', so that is out. As I said, his two permanent guards are the best in the business, as are the reliefs. They do three-hour shifts, and these are not the sort of people that could be 'diverted'. What ever happened they would stay with Alexander... and they don't fall asleep on their shifts and they take their job very, very serious. Paul Kyso maybe, he would be an easier target but Alejandro would 'sacrifice' him without a second thought... No, Alejandro is out, there is just no way you can get to him."

"If the President of America can be got to, so can this feller..." Webb added, his mind flipping into overdrive.

"Believe me, Webbley, it would be far easier to get to the President than Alejandro," Kristianna said, glumly.

"We need to know more about him." Simon sat back into the couch and took a cup of coffee from the tray. "It's no different than any other 'campaign', we just need more information."

"There might be a way..." All eyes turned to Gabriella. She was holding onto her sister's arm tightly, for comfort and confidence, unused as she was with public speaking or initiating ideas. Kristianna was almost ready to 'poo-poo it', when... "Anastasia..." she blurted out the name, fully expecting Kristianna to dismiss her idea, instantly.

Webb was mystified. "Who's, Anastasia?"

"Anastasia is..." Kristianna took up on it straight away.

"Anastasia is Alejandro's granddaughter...his absolute favourite. It's my idea Kristianna, shut up... please." Gabriella snapped back, interrupting her sister. The idea was still formulating in her mind. "If we... kidnapped her, he would capitulate immediately. He would never allow any harm to come to her..." Gabriella blurted it out feeling a little faint and light-headed... but pleased with herself. 'What if I make a fool of myself again... I usually do'. The thought raced through her mind.

"Good lord, it might work... yes it would... it would work." Kristianna was overjoyed, her face lit up like a Christmas tree. "Yes, it would. She has one guard with her at all times, but he's just a baby. Normally, no one would ever dare touch Anastasia. I should have thought of it myself. Well done, Gabriella." She hugged her sister and then rushed back to Webb. "It 'would' work..."

"Who's this Paul Kyso?" Simon asked.

Kristianna explained that he was the head of security. "He would have organised all of this." She looked at Webb, amazed at how he was holding up and how well he was handling the situation. But she knew that at all costs she needed to keep control of it, fearing that he might charge off at any minute and attack them outright, as if he was back in the army charging into the 'trenches', getting himself killed in the process... That wouldn't suit my plans, she thought, well, not until I have 'my money' back. "Yes, brilliant, forget Paul Kyso... if we took the girl and just held her for a few days... just until we are out of the country." She loved the idea.

Gabriella smiled. It was all of her idea... for once she wasn't following behind her sister. "We could take her at the disco... she always goes there, three nights a week, Saturday, Sunday and Wednesday... tonight.

"I'll go along with it if we guarantee no harm comes to the girl, agreed?" Simon was worried, that if something went wrong they would need to make sure the girl stayed safe, regardless. He had young children of his own. "How old is she?"

"Eighteen." Gabriella still couldn't comprehend her good fortune that all these people were discussing 'her' idea.

For the first time since the whole of this 'mess' had started Webb felt a little surge of relief and the return of his confidence. "Look, I have a couple of calls to make and I have to be in Cornwall today..." In the tearing hurry to get out of the motel he hadn't sent the money down to Steve and Sue McGillicuddy, and they wouldn't make the arrangements without the deposit. He would need to do that today if there was any chance of being out of here by Friday night. "You come with me, Beth, and I'd appreciate it if you could stay with Gabriella, Simon. Kristianna, you need to find out for sure whether this girl is going to the disco tonight. We need a complete layout of the area... what time she leaves... who's going to be with her... everything!" He felt good, now there was something he could concentrate on... now he would truly make them pay for all of this pain... "Could you ask Sui Lin to put us up a packed lunch, then we won't need to stop anywhere."

Peter Copping slammed the office door shut and flopped down into his swivel chair resting his elbows on the desk, settling his head into his hands. He had just returned from seeing David's widow and it had torn him apart so much that he hadn't been able to face the widows of the two negotiators and had sent someone else to do that job, a job he really should have done himself... He felt like a gutless coward, justifying it only by the fact that he had known David well, but had never really got to know the other two men, even though one of them was his accountant. Accountants were just 'accountant's', faceless people... and anyway, the job had been arranged through another agency. It was a poor justification...

Chapter 23

"I would like to meet up with you, inspector." It was Webb's first call. He'd 'call' Sue McGillicuddy straight after this call, on his mobile as they drove. He had asked Beth to stop at the first telephone box she saw on the outskirts of Bournemouth, before they hit the motorway proper. "But I need your assurance that I won't be arrested and that I will be free to leave afterwards."

"Where were you last night, Mr. Pendelton, at around midnight?" Inspector Dowling ignored his request.

"Don't worry, inspector, I have an absolute, concrete alibi. I can't tell you where I was, that would give away my location, but be assured I was not at my sister's house..." He flicked the cuff of his sleeve up to check the time. It was going to be tight. "Do we have a deal?"

"No, of course we don't have a deal. Good lord, I'm a policeman, how can I make a deal with you?" His telephone was on speaker so that Sergeant Gould could hear and the outer office was already placing the trace. "For goodness sakes, man, come in, let's sort this business out. You will be perfectly safe here I can assure you of that."

"I don't think so." Webb's patience was wearing a little thin with the inspector's stupidity. "Look, let's take another tack here then you might just understand why I can't come in. I'm going to give you a list of names. Along with the names, I'll give you listed offshore account numbers, some in Switzerland others in the Cayman Islands and I'll give you the dates of payments. Most of these are senior policemen, some judges and some are lawyers. Don't interrupt me, I'll phone back at eight or nine this evening to see what you think, if you are anything of a policeman after you have checked these out, you will understand my reluctance to come in..." He read out the names and numbers of the people he wanted checking, just five... that would do for now... and then, before he rang off. "Oh, inspector. I need you to put an armed guard on my wife and kids." He gave him the address. "It's real important... do you understand?"

"Right, let's go..." he said to Beth as she started the car. "We've got a long drive ahead of us."

"What d'ya think, boss?" Sergeant Tracy Gould asked.

"This can't be right, I know some of these people." He pointed at the open door, waiting until she had closed it. "There are three, no four Chief Inspectors here, mainly with the Met."

She leaned over his shoulder scanning down the list. "That one, Chief Inspector Watson of the Met, don't you remember two years ago he was accused of complicity in a robbery that resulted in two deaths. Nothing was ever proven and he was cleared, but it left a dirty taste in everyone's mouth for months."

"Well we all get 'mud' thrown at us from time to time, don't we, but this chap." He pointed to the name. "Edward Stouridge, I've known him for... twenty, no twenty-five years. I went to one of his children's christenings. Good lord." He glanced around him making sure that she had shut the door properly.

"Let me show you something, sir." She rushed over to her filing cabinet and took out a bulging lever arch file and opened it to 'W' "C.I. Watson has the highest conviction rate for Class 1 drugs of any police force... and yet if you look here." She flipped the page. "All of the convictions are only of one drug organisation... do see that?"

Alan Dowling turned the lever arch to the cover. "What is this?" He flipped back to the 'W' section, mystified.

"It's just something that I do, in my spare time." She fidgeted. It was the first time she had shown it to anyone. "I keep records of any serious accusations or incidents that occur relating to police corruption. I... well, I wanted to know if there was any connections... I, well sort of get all the information from the classified files... that's probably not 'strictly' legal, is it?"

He quickly scanned through the beautifully handwritten accounts all neatly categorised and dated. After each section she had written comments and findings of her research. "Good God, you did all of this? How did you ever find the time?" It looked like a 'work of art'.

"I sort of... made a hobby of it really and it sort of became an obsession. I'm a bit of a sad 'bugger' really boss, s'pose it makes up for my lack of a social life." She leaned over him and pointed again at the name Watson. "Do you see what I mean, sir... it's only ever one 'cartel'."

He did see it, straight away. "Why didn't anyone else pick up on it before?" He scratched his head, fascinated with her work. "I... just can't believe you did all this."

"That's only one file... I have another five..." She nodded towards her filing cabinet.

Chapter 24

It was almost one-thirty before they crossed into Cornwall from Devon. He was driving fast, too fast for Beth's mind and the road was still crowded with three lanes of traffic. She wished now that she hadn't agreed to the changeover, content with her own, safe driving. "I don't feel very comfortable when you do that, you know." She watched nervously as he held the wheel with one knee whilst he rolled his cigarette. "If you want to smoke why don't you let me drive... I'm perfectly happy driving all the way."

"Sorry..." He smiled at her with his best, 'little boy smile'. Now he wished he'd left last night as had been originally planned. But then last night wasn't exactly his 'usual' night. Now he wasn't clear whether he had made love to Kristianna or whether she had just 'raped' him... there wasn't too much that he'd needed to do really... she was in charge of the whole 'procedure' from start to finish... "Agh, yer alright, mate... the next lay-by we come to, we'll change back." He felt nervous and apprehensive about seeing Steve and Sue again, especially under these circumstances. It had been over a year and now this visit would be less than an hour long... Sue wouldn't like that very much at all.

Eventually they drove into the old boatyard at Penryn. It seemed not to have changed a jot since his last visit. The same decrepit, half-finished boats along the side of the yard, propped haphazardly or 'rough moored' to the equally tired old dock. It made a stark contrast to the new, well managed marina further along. The new marina sported the modern facilities of a very 'posh', super clean toilet and shower block, housed in a brand new complex which contained a small shopping area for basic supplies and chandlery, a sail maker and a small engineering workshop selling out board motors and advertising engine and boat repairs. But as with most waterside facilities, it all felt so 'alive', even though people went about their business in the typical 'unhurried', no hassle sort of 'West country' manor... where nothing ever seemed important enough to break into a run for. Things 'got done', but only in their own good time, he loved the place, wishing now that he had taken Steve up on his original offer to come in as a full partner. That was almost eight years ago now. Thinking of it with hindsight, they would have made a good team.

There was one exception to the, seemingly 'organised chaos' of the yard, a gleaming, navy blue hulled, twin mast yacht in the inner dry dock basin. "Pull over..." He pointed to a spot twenty feet from the yacht's stern. "That is 'orgasmic'..." Webb opened his door and walked along the quay admiring the yacht's lines and the beautiful teak laid decks. On the side of the superstructure was a small, handwritten sign that simply read 'For sale', and a couple of telephone numbers for interested clients to call.

'She' was pristine and took his breath away. "My lord, why would anyone ever want to sell something as beautiful as that?" He hadn't realised he'd spoken out loud.

"You like that a little bit then?" Beth had followed him. "Not really my 'bag', I absolutely hate the water."

"God, 'she's' so bloody beautiful, wonder what they're asking for her?" Webb was 'bog-eyed'.

"You can't bloody afford that, boy." The heavy Cornish accent interrupted his thoughts and was easily recognisable, instantly.

"You old bastard, how are you, mate?" Webb shook the hand of his friend and gave him a bear hug. "Bloody good to see you again... real good."

"Better 'an yo, by the looks of 'e, lad." He grasped Webb's hand and with his free hand slapped him on the back.

Steve McGillicuddy was a huge, larger than life, jovial character. At six feet three inches he seemed to tower over Webb, but it was mainly the great 'bulk' of his chest and tummy that made him look even larger. He was Webb's senior by eight years, and they had met when Webb was doing his S.A.S. selection and Steve had been Webb's instructor. There seemed to be no 'apparent' age difference in them now though, but when Webb was nineteen and Steve was twenty-six he appeared much older and a lot smarter and mature. Steve had become, almost a 'father' figure to him. They had been friends ever since.

"How much are they asking, there's no price on the sign?" Webb pointed at the yacht.

Steve squinted his eyes at him. "What you up to, boy, you won the pools, er somptin'?"

"Sort off... how much?" Webb felt a tang of 'caution, knowing that Steve could easily read him 'like an open book'.

"Quarter of a mill." He became silent, searching Webb's face for an answer that at the moment... wasn't there.

"Oh this is Beth, a friend..." For a second, because of his concentration on the big yacht... he'd forgotten her.

"Let's git op the 'ouse," Steve said after shaking hands with Beth. "'Ar Sue... she bin bakin', 'alf the blinking night, expectin' you, she is." He tucked his arm around Beth's waist as they walked. "I 'ope you ain't fallen in love with this bogger... luv. 'E's a sod for a pretty woman... an' don't believe a word 'e tells ee' unless it's written down."

Beth smiled and said she was a little concerned about leaving the car there, but Steve assured her that no one would touch it. She would have been much more concerned if she'd known the true value of the contents of the red suitcase in the boot.

"Webbley!" A plump, red-faced lady ran down the path of the pretty little cottage at the end of the quay, and threw her arms around him. "I missed you, lad, that's for sure." They were almost the same age and yet she had always called him 'lad' or 'boy', not in a disparaging way but in a more homely, affectionate and kindly way. "You didn't tell me you wos bringing yor young lady, you devil... I only got one spare bed prepared..." She gave Beth a hug. "And you lad, need to stop all yor silly wonderin's and settle down 'ere... with us. You know's yor always welcome."

"No Sue, she's not my..." But it was too late, Sue had taken charge and introduced herself to Beth and then, slipping her hand through Beth's arm... whisked her away up the path to the house.

"Er's a bit skinny lad." Steve commented as they watched the two ladies disappear into the house. "You normally goes for the bigger, rounder version of that..." He shook his head, pointing at Beth's tiny, almost nonexistent backside with the stem of his old pipe and clicked his teeth.

"She's just a friend... look, I can't stay, Steve... I did tell Sue but I'm not sure if she understood." He rested his hand on Steve's big shoulder. "I've just come down to give you the deposit. You reckon the motor yacht will be alright for Friday morning?"

"More like Monday... I reckon. The skippers not back 'while Sunday', anyway, and there's a minor problem with one of the engines. You don't want to be out in 'The Bay' at this time of the year with a 'dicky' engine." He referred to The Bay of Biscay. Steve was completely unphased by the delay... what was another two days, how could that matter? After all... they were in Cornwall.

Unconsciously Webb's fingers clenched and he felt the tension deep in his bowels knowing the sooner he was out of the country, the sooner people would stop 'dying around him.' "Sure that's the earliest?" He tried to show no outward concern. Steve nodded. "Ah well, can't be helped then, I s'pose. Tell me about 'this' yacht, Steve. She must be a Van Dam Nordia, I should think." He looked back over his shoulder at the beautiful gleaming yacht.

Steve said it was and had been built at the Van Dam yard in Amsterdam. "She's sixty-five feet. Young couple had it built, sold their house and everything they owned. He's a boat joiner and a very good one so he did all the fitting out himself. Van Dam did the hull, deck and superstructure, all the ballast, floors and bulkheads and fitted the engine and rudder. Christ! You talk about 'silly dreamers'. They even had a Gardener engine put in, with what they paid for that, they could have fitted the whole boat out. Visions of grandeur I suppose." Steve looked enviously at the beautiful yacht as he had looked at it for the past three months, every morning since its arrival on the dock. "But usual story, overambitious and then of course, they ran out of money... now they're facing virtual bankruptcy... unless they can sell it and make some of their money back. Poor buggers."

"Bloody beautiful." Webb wanted to jump on board to look over the yacht but knew there was not enough time.

Steve nodded and mumbled something indiscernible. Before they went inside, he took Webb's arm and eased him back into the porch. "Go on then... what's this all about?" He changed the subject deliberately and looked into his friend's eyes, watching for the 'lie', knowing that nothing to do with Webb was ever straight forwards and simple... it never had been.

"I... I can't tell you all of it, it wouldn't be safe..." He had thought his plan through carefully in the car on the way down, but after seeing the Van Dam Nordia, he'd 'slightly' modified those plans, and was now finding it difficult to commit himself to another 'series' of 'lies' to his friend. "The charter is for a client..." It wasn't 'entirely' a lie, he could easily pass Kristianna and Gabriella off as the 'client' and in one respect, 'they were'... the second part of the lie he had only thought of when he'd seen the big yacht for sale. "That..." He pointed at the yacht. "I want for me..."

"Oh?" Steve's stare hadn't altered. "I sort of get the feeling that there's trouble coming from somewhere, aye? Don't you put my Sue in any danger... d'ya hear me, lad. Seems to me there's too much money involved in this already... and money does bad things to good people... You hear me?" He tapped Webb's left breast pocket, feeling the gun, "...specially when them things start to come into the equation..."

"I know..." Webb shrugged, already worried that he had gotten these 'people' involved. "I got a little... problem at the moment... but I'm trying to resolve it, but I've got an idea..."

Steve watched his face, especially his eyes. "You just remember what I said, boy, about my Sue."

The lunch, as was normal with Sue... was enormous. It started with a huge homemade pasty that the locals called a 'Teddy-Oggy', basically a Cornish pasty... but consisting of fresh meats, pork and beef, hot spicy pepper and vegetables, especially Swede. It was surrounded by a thick, rich gravy that would have been considered a 'food group' on its own. The 'pudding' was late season, fresh strawberries from Sue's own garden, topped with fresh Cornish, double cream.

"Oh my God..." Beth held her stomach. "I can't move, I think I'm about to burst... that must be the biggest meal I have ever eaten and it was absolutely delicious."

"You stay here for long, my dear, and you'll be as big as me..." Steve laughed. "When I first met Sue, I was a 'twig'... just like you." He patted his oversized tummy.

Webb found it difficult to leave but knew it was critical that he did so. A glance at his watch told him that he was already late, it was five o'clock and they had a four-hour drive in front of them... and that was with good road and traffic conditions.

"Steve, with the money I've left you there should be about twenty grand over... it's yours." He had roughly counted out an additional three hundred thousand from the suitcase and stuffed it into an old holdall. "And this is for that Van Dam, get on and buy it for me... I'll tell you all about it the next time I'm down here which will be over the weekend if everything goes right."

"I don't want bad money, lad... you jus' mark what I said about my Sue..." He edged him off to one side out of earshot of the two women as they walked back to Webb's car. "But I'll put the offer to the young couple and let you know. They'll probably jump at a cash deal." He thought for a long moment. "There wus some chaps snooping around here yesterday, looking for you, that's how I noo you were in trouble. Said they wus Special Branch but I didn't get a look at their warrant cards."

"Here?" He was startled, his mind racing ahead, hoping that they 'were' special Branch, and not just another part of The Met Corps men. But then the thought occurred to him that even 'bent coppers' carried fully legitimate warrant cards. Why wouldn't they?

"Mmm. We said we hadn't seen you in an age... and you turn a social visit into what... trouble?" Steve puffed at the stem of his old weathered pipe and spat a 'gob of 'jibber' on the floor. "Jus' keep us out of it..." He pocked Webb sharply in the chest. "...an' you too, boy...you keep yor 'ead down... keep safe." He wrapped his big arms around Webb's shoulders and hugged him. "Now piss off..." He laughed.

Webb chest tightened and he couldn't look at him...

"They seem like nice people." Beth spoke quietly as she drove to the car at the top of the speed limit.

"Yeah, bloody salt of the earth really. They're about the most genuine people I have ever come across." He rolled his cigarette and tried to relax. "I'm wondering what the hell I've gotten them into here. Christ, if anything happened to them..." He cast the thought from his mind, dreading the consequences of such a thing...

She didn't ease the speed off until they were in sight of Poole Marina. For Webb it had been a difficult journey... a journey of deep thought... now he had involved his best friends in this awful 'folly' of his, a 'folly' which would undoubtedly involve putting them in grave danger. 'But then...' He reasoned, trying to justify himself, what other answer was there? Kristianna had said The Met Corps would target his family 'and' his friends also, better that he was able to 'take care of them'... wasn't it'?

He dialled the number that he'd memorised and when the deep African voice answered... "You still going to help me?" He wasn't sure of the answer he'd get from Peter Copping.

"Why, why the fuck should I?"

"You've lost three people, Peter, I've lost five... and I've got a good chance of losing more, without your help." He bit his lip... Beth kept her eyes on the road ahead, not making any comment. "Come on, man... we need to get back at these bastards, I've never seen you back off from a scrap, never... let's hit the bastards really hard." He waited for a second. "I've had to get Steve and Sue McGillicuddy involved now... wish I hadn't. We... you can't let anything happen to those two, Peter, can we..."

After a long silence, Webb was about to turn the mobile off... "You goin' after them, then?" Peter's voice was less angry. "How?"

"Not over this mobile... I'll call you in the morning... but, Peter, I need a favour." He spoke quickly before Peter could reply. "Steve and Sue McGillicuddy? The Met Corps are going to target them next... I'm sure of it, I've got this really bad feeling, I'm almost certain of it. I need a couple of good people down there, discretely, straight away and tooled up to look after them... it's no bloody good asking for help of the cops, is it. Would you do that for me, mate?"

Grudgingly he said he would. In the past they had all been good friends and the McGillicudy's usually turned up at his reunions.

"And, Peter, don't forget you need to make sure they 'are' tooled-up, I'd prefer not to see any more dead bodies... especially from my own blokes." He pushed the hair from his face and shrugged. "If it means anything... mate... I'm sorry about your fellers."

Chapter 25

Sue waved them away until she couldn't see the car anymore as it disappeared around the end of the dock. "That lad's in trouble again, Steve, isn't he? I can always tell with him."

Steve nodded. "Yep... and this time it's not his usual petty... marriage... bail me out of jail, kind of trouble, is it. It's something much bigger, 'grown-up' sort of trouble I reckons." He tapped the bowl of his pipe out on the upright of the porch and wrapped his arm around the one person in the world he had ever truly 'loved'. "Did you see what he left us in the bag?"

Sue shook her head, her brow frowning. "No, lad, I didn't."

He nodded at the bag laying on the floor of the hallway and then walked in and unzipped it. "There..." He nodded at the piles of money, neatly sealed in polythene wrappers. "Bit too much for him to have earned... honestly. Don't you think?"

"My, oh my. What's that silly devil into now? He told me it was the deposit from his clients... but there seems to be an awful lot there, Steve." She didn't want to touch it. In the whole of her life she had never seen so much money... not all in one place, that is.

"Well... for sure it ain't honest, is it." He watched Sue's face, worried now. "I already tol' 'im. If 'e gets us into trouble I'll bloody brain him."

Sue slipped her hand into his. "Do we go ahead with the charter, Steve? I suppose so."

"Yeah, that can't hurt I suppose. If it comes to the law, we're just fulfilling an obligation to a client." He frowned. "The thing that worries me more than anything else is that he wants me to buy the big Van Dam Nordia... cash. I wonder how much problem that will cause, and what does he want us to do with it? Mind you... we'll be doing that young boat couple a real big favour, I reckon."

"Where is he then?" Kristianna said angrily to her sister. It was nine-thirty and she had already waited an hour. They needed to rehearse the events for tonight... or people would get killed... unnecessarily.

"I've told you, Krisy, I don't know, his mobile is not switched on." She loved calling her 'Krisy', knowing how much she hated it. "He said he would be here and that is good enough for me."

"He's a stupid man..." She kicked at the sofa. "We need to be off of this damn yacht by tomorrow at the latest. You know that and so does he and yet he's playing around like this... damn." She slammed her shoulder bag down onto the coffee table tearing a deep scratch into the varnish with the buckle and cursed again.

"I'm sure he is just as aware of our situation as you are." Gabriella spoke in his defence, but knew she wouldn't dare challenge Kristianna too much. "He said he had some business in the West Country and that he would be back, early evening... that is all I know."

Kristianna stormed out of the saloon, still cursing out loud. She needed a shower and a change of clothes... the prospect of tonight excited her, but she didn't want anything to go wrong with her plans…

Chapter 26

9:30 pm. Paul Kyso, the head of security for The Met Corps, paced the floor impatiently railing at his four 'lieutenants' seated in front of him. He was holding a large buff folder.

"We just can't find a trace of this damned man, Paul." Dick Cordon was the first to speak. He was tall and stocky, well-built and balding, prematurely. At thirty years old he was second in charge of security, next to Paul Kyso. He was also a 'Third Dan' martial arts expert and had spent almost four years in a Buddhist temple in the mountains of Japan, studying the subject, before joining The Met Corps eight years ago. This was the first 'major crises that he'd had to face… and was bitterly disappointed that he couldn't come up with a satisfactory answer to solve it. "It's like he's just disappeared from the face of the earth. Why did we need to take out a termination order on him, wasn't that a bit 'previous'? I don't understand that. It's made him go deeper undercover, and Christ, to send that goddamned lunatic Preston to carry it out. Jeees! Anyone but that fucking lunatic." His American accent was still strong even after all these years. "Like I said before, I thought we'd stopped using him because of his brutality."

Paul nodded in agreement. "That was taken out of my hands, unfortunately, I told you that already." He spoke quietly as if he could be overheard. "Somehow we need to do more. I have to report 'something' back to Alejandro … by tonight or I'll be having my bollocks chewed off again… anything!"

"What about the Yanks, can't they help us out with their sat. tracking gear… an' all?" A younger man William spoke nervously, he had been with the company just six months and liked his job, but the last thing he wanted to do was to upset the 'status quo'.

"Or our other contacts with Special Branch, can't they help?" another added, a little sheepishly.

"Mmm. They're looking into it for us." Paul still had his contacts with his last organisation. "Let's get everything that we know about this 'carpenter… builder', or whatever the hell he is." He looked at the 'tack board' on the wall. Everyone had contributed 'something' to it but it still didn't make any sense or give them any clues to Pendleton's whereabouts. "We know that he was in the army, but what we don't know at this moment is what branch he was in. My MI 6 contact says he thinks it was the Special Air Service… but he's working on it at the moment. So that sort of blows the 'carpenter' theory out of the window." He was met by a stony wall of silence. He paced around again. "Look, Dick, get everyone from all the other field sections, everyone that can be spared. I want every hotel, guesthouse and whorehouse within a fifty-mile radius visited, and check on every friend he ever had… every relative, no one can just disappear off the face of the God damned earth… not even me."

The telephone rang and Paul lifted the receiver. "Right thanks, David. I owe you one… big time." He scribbled frantically on his pad as he took the message, when he replacing the receiver he grinned. "Now at least, we're getting 'something'… it's coming through on the fax, now…" He walked over to the machine as it printed, reading quickly through the text. "Fuck it… fuck it, that's great... he 'was' S.A.S. Gimme a Goddamned break here... will ya." He touched his forehead, sweeping a wisp of hair from his eyes. "No wonder we can't find the bastard. He served in Aden and The Radfan, but mainly in Borneo..." He tore the sheet from the machine as it finished printing and handed it over to Dick Cordon.

"Where's Borneo?" someone asked, but it went unanswered.

Paul carried on speaking, leaning over Dick Cordon's shoulder. "Christ! At the height of the Borneo campaign in '63 he was doing thirty-day patrols... alone... and working on 'covert stuff' for MI 6 at the same time. Jeees and we thought we were dealing with a damned 'amateur'. We'll have our work cut out here, looks like we stuffed our fingers into a dam hornet's nest... Christ he's a renegade and a 'boy scout' all rolled into one. He was awarded the military medal and then had it taken away a year later for assaulting another soldier... nearly killing him, and was then given a dishonourable discharge. The soldier killed his... cat! What sort of fuckin' guy is this?"

"So, how do we get to him?" Dick Cordon asked.

"At the moment, I don't know." He scratched his balding head, trying to put together a thought.

Paul Kyso stood away from them, worry clearly written on his face. "Well, 'we' started this damn 'bloodbath', so we'll have to carry on in the same vein, I suppose, now we certainly can't negotiate our way out of it. We need to take someone close to him, flush the bastard out. If he is this 'bloody boy scout' he'll play ball with us. I just need to convince Alejandro to back off a little... I need to persuade him to drop the damned 'Termination order', for a start or this whole thing will escalate out of hand. I don't need to tell any of you the importance of this. The shipment is due in soon and this guy has our money that was to pay for it... we're all dead if we don't get it back... you understand that? If we fuck up the yanks… we're all dead. Get onto every one of your leads, your contacts; chase down every scrap of information you can, regardless of how small it seems, chase it up. Promise them anything. There's a half-mill in it for the person who comes up with something definite… But for God's sake, let's get something moving here, fellers, remember, this man must not be 'touched' he is to remain unharmed… at least until we have the money returned… then you can do what you damn well please with him. Now get your arses out of here and find the son-of-a-bitch!"

Anastasia de Los Santos sat on the edge of her very large bed and pouted, sulkily. She was alone and surrounded by most of the contents of her huge wardrobes. She wore only the briefest, white panties and a simple, halter-necked top that barely covered her ample breasts

She picked up the Gucci frock, string backed and thigh length, its delicate pink and white fabric glistened as she ran it through her fingers but then cast it to one side and rested her chin in her hands. It was already eight-thirty and she was late… again.

In 'desperation' she settled for the 'Paul Roddan'. The frock was an original from his spring collection which had taken Paris by storm… and to date… she had never worn it. In fact most of the dresses, shirts and frocks strewn around her had only ever been worn once or twice, at most. Anastasia bounced from the bed and flung her bedroom door open, clasping the tiny frock to her chest. "Xavi… what do you think?" She pirouetted around her startled young bodyguard. He had stood up so quickly that he'd spilt the plate of sandwiches he'd been holding on his lap onto the floor or halfway down the trousers of his suit…

"Senorita…" He wiped his mouth quickly and brushed the remains of the sandwich from his waist band and looked away from her almost naked body. "Senorita, you startle me... and, senorita please, you should not be... dressed like that... not in front of me... please." He looked at her briefly and then turned away from her embarrassed to see her like that and so close to him.

"Oh don't be silly, Xavi. What do you think...?" She held the tiny frock in front of her again, smiling, pretending impatience, loving to see his red face when she teased him.

"I think it... looks so beautiful, senorita... beautiful." Xavier Maria Carlos Aguilera would have thought the same if she had appeared in a potato sack with holes cut out for the arms and neck... But then, for the first time in his short twenty-one years of life... he was 'truly in love'... or what he 'perceived' as love. If that was ever reciprocated even in some small obscure way... by her, he would be the happiest man on this earth and his life would be forever complete... but he knew it never would be...

Xavier Maria Carlos Aguilera came from a small, remote village in the Sierra Madras mountains of South west Spain... in a tiny village called Montenegral Alto. The village in common with many others of this region was struggling to enter into the twentieth century. Poverty, hardship and the lack of sustainable work was part of the ritual of 'normal' daily life for the peoples of these regions, already living below what would normally be considered, 'the poverty line'. Three severe drought years had contributed to the vast poverty of most of southern Spain and to the huge numbers of the unemployed, which the central government seemed unwilling, or just incapable of assisting. Most local authorities were usually controlled by corrupt or inept councillors, or mayors. The fact that the people 'did' survive and in general, were relatively happy was a credit to their own strength and courage and fortitude against adversary. It had been barely five years since his village had been connected to the main, government facility for the supply of electricity. The more 'affluent' could now watch television and see how other people in the world lived. Xavier was the youngest of eight brothers and four sisters, but had never been 'pampered'… that was not the way the family system worked in Andalucía, everyone from birth was taught to survive… everyone had to fight for their own 'rough-hewn' spot in life. But he had grown to be the strongest of them all and the smartest too… At an early age he found he had a superior skill at wrestling and could fight and beat boys much older and stronger than himself. Eventually he became the regional champion and to the absolute delight of his parents and family, had become a local hero.

It was sheer good fortune and luck, two years ago that his third cousin on his mother's side paid a visit to one of his bouts and was so impressed that after talking extensively with him arranged a meeting in England with his boss… Paul Kyso.

Xavier had never travelled further than a hundred miles from his own village… and yet now… he was in England with the job of his dreams. On the firing range he found that he also had a natural talent for shooting and with training from his cousin Manolo, within a few weeks he could hit the bullseye with a pistol shot easily from thirty yards. Occasionally he had been asked to step in as security for Mr. Kyso's 'himself'… and then, six months ago he had been detailed to guard senorita Anastasia… and he knew then that his life was complete…

"Oh!" Anastasia pouted again and stamped her foot, angrily. "You say that about everything I wear, you are so silly. I can't wear some 'old rag' that I've worn before… can I?"

"No, senorita… Miss…"

She turned and ran back into her room, giggling and slammed the door behind her. Men… She often wondered what made their minds work... they always seemed so preoccupied with 'breasts'... especially hers... and yet they were just 'muscles', almost like any other 'muscle' on the body. She loved what she could make these men do for her. In the 'true' sense of the word, she had never had a 'sexual relationship', as yet. Yes, there had been some 'heavy petting' and groping of sweaty, inexperienced, clammy hands on her body... but she had never actually... had sex, and had never found anyone she felt she wanted to 'give' her body to.

She just loved it so much when the boys and even older men admired her and told her how beautiful she was. Grandpa though 'was' special, she thought... she never minded 'him' 'touching her...'

Out of frustration she decided that she would wear the silk frock, a 'micro-mini', halter-neck, and virtually 'see-through', but she would discard her brassier, she felt much 'freer' like that. To accompany it she chose a thick, heavy woven pair of multi-coloured socks that should have been worn knee-length but she pushed them down to her ankles and laced up her huge brown 'Doc. Martin' boots. Her coat would be her favourite 'tramp-coat'. She looked at herself in the mirror and flicked a loose strand of hair back, and then, almost satisfied... just one small thing to change... she lifted the hem of her mini-shirt and removed her tiny white panties throwing them towards the bed... now she was ready.

Chapter 26

"If you do that again I'm going to kick your 'gonads' up to your throat." Beth said flatly, emphasising the point by lifting her knee to the inside of his groin. In reality, she was actually enjoying his closeness, and having his arms around her, inside her coat. She could hardly remember the last time someone had held her as close.

"Sorry... it was an accident," Webb sniggered. His elbow had 'nudged' Beth's breast 'again', for the second time. He lifting his head from her shoulder, to give him a better view of the disco entrance and then tickled the inside of her ear again with his tongue, breathing his hot breath into her ear and down the side of her neck, smiling when she wriggled against it. "It's... just a 'natural reaction', isn't it? Christ, I think I'm getting a bloody 'hard-on'."

"Oh for God's sake, man." She brought her knee up sharply just to remind him of the 'danger' he was in. "God you're so gross... sometimes." But she smiled anyway and pulled him in a little closer, comparing his warmth to the coldness of the Glock automatic in her right hand tucked under his coat. "And now that I come to think of it... I'm not too sure whether I put my safety catch on..." She tapped the small of his back with the barrel, knowing full well that she was far too professional, 'not' to have applied the safety... but it would give him something else to think about, rather than his... erection.

The rain had started again, a fine constant drizzle now. It seemed to slowly soak through their coats and dribble down their necks, penetrating right through to the skin, and it was cold, too. It blew a misty haze along the road, partly obscuring the view of the disco entrance. They had arrived later than they had hoped to, mainly due to his 'faffing' around' on the yacht, sorting through his last bits and pieces, holding everyone else up, but then even under 'normal' circumstances he always seemed to 'faff-around'. His wife used to remark sometimes that he was like a 'big girl' getting ready to go to her first prom, with all the unnecessary 'departure checks' he did before leaving the house.

But no matter, everything was in place with the exception of his Range Rover. They had parked further down the street than he had hoped too, due to the unexpected heavy traffic. He worried a little about that, it would mean an extra thirty or forty meters for Kristianna to drive after they took the girl. Simon was parked on the opposite side of the road from the disc, ready to pick up Gabriella as soon as she exited... they had all equipped themselves with the 'walky-talkies' from the yacht and had, hopefully selected a channel that no one else would be listening on... well... not at this moment in time.

"I thought this bloody girl had to be home for midnight?" A glance at his watch told him it was almost that time now and that she was obviously going to be late.

"Were you always on time at her age?" Beth pinched the skin at the small of his back to make him 'desist'. He had passed his free hand across her breasts again to look at his watch, and she was finding it difficult to concentrate.

Suddenly, the 'walky-talky' around Beth's neck, crackled and burst into life. "They are just coming out now, but so is half of the town, by the looks of things." Gabriella's voice was calm and precise, but the reception wasn't good. "She's with a young man in a bright green coat and blue jeans, but I still can't see Xavier…"

They knew no one could make a move against the girl until Xavier 'was' spotted. "Anything yet?" Webb whispered into his own radio. He could see the boy in the green coat and recognised Anastasia from the photograph Kristianna had supplied. They were almost fifty yards away and the car they knew Xavier to be driving was ten yards in front of them. "Walk up a bit, we need to get closer." He eased the big .45 from under Beth's coat and held it against the small of her back and then leaned into her and kissed her neck, slowly walking towards Anastasia… as if they were lovers.

"Where's the fucking bodyguard?" Webb whispered hoarsely into the walky-talky.

"I can see him he's behind them, by about five metres." Gabriella's voice shook a little. "Against the wall… can you see him? He's wearing a grey suit and a grey scarf around his neck. He looks very… big, Webb."

Webb cursed her silently. The last thing he had stressed to all of them was not to use names… at all. Never mind, it was done. "No, damn it I can't… you?" he asked Beth as they slowly jostled past the crowds of people, but she shook her head.

Beth freed her gun hand from around his waist squinting her eyes against the drizzle. "I don't like this at all… too many damned people about, this could end up badly."

A young girl and two teenage boys pushed past them, huddled under their coats, bumping his shoulder roughly, giggling. The girl looked back at them and apologised. Couples were gathering outside of the entrance, hailing taxis… or being picked up by friends or relatives, or… God knows who. "There..." he nodded towards the well-built, very smartly dressed young man... in the grey suit. He was walking close to the wall. "Watch him... he looks like he knows his stuff..." It was just the way that Xavier walked and the way he held his hands, his head upright and aware, oblivious of the rain. He was forty yards away, but Anastasia and her boyfriend were almost up to them. "Go for it now... I've got the boyfriend." He freed Beth and slowly headed closer to the body guard.

Webb heard the screeching tires of the Range Rover to his left and knew that Kristianna was in position. She exited the car and fired three shots into the air... just to clear the street, but Webb didn't look over at her, his eyes solely on the bodyguard. He knew Kristianna was more than capable of handling her end of the job. The noise of the shots had, had the desired effect of causing havoc. Women screamed and rushed hysterically with their partners to clear the area, in seconds the whole area had been turned into bedlam. Within a few more seconds no one was standing... with the exception of Xavier, who already had his automatic in his hand and his body braced as he ran firing two random shots at Beth and Kristianna, but the range was too great to be effective... Webb was much closer to him.

Had Xavier been older and a little more experienced, he would have just dropped to his knee and taken careful aim at Beth as he watched her neatly clip Anastasia's boyfriend with the butt of her hand, dropping him instantly to the floor and then pushed Anastasia towards Kristianna.

But experience can only be leaned with years of intensive training and dedication and most of all... practice... lots and lots of 'real' practice. Instead he chose to run at them, firing quickly, his arm at full stretch as he ran to save Anastasia. One of his shots ricocheted along the pavement hitting a fleeing bystander in the leg, sending him sprawling to the floor screaming. Xavier only saw Webb, after Webb had fired his first two shots... and by then it was too late... far too late. The impact of a .45 caliber round could sever a man's leg or arm instantly, so Webb had aimed high, aiming at the high point on the shoulder where hopefully it would miss the main body mass... It could have proved fatal for him, as a complete miss would draw the other shooters attention and enable him to return more accurate fire. But both shots found their marks. Xavier seemed to stop in mid 'flight', the bullet heaving him over to one side, throwing him to the floor. But he pulled himself to his knees and shakily fired two aimed, but impossible shots at Webb.

Webb felt the tug of Xavier's first bullet as it passed through his coat and shirt, high on his collar and he slowly took aim as the second shot passed harmlessly to his right, he had heard the 'zeeet... zeeet' of the rounds and felt the air pressure build-up as he unhurriedly fired a third and then a fourth, carefully aimed shot...

In the back of his mind he could still hear the screams of the women and the crying but had blanked everything from his mind, except Xavier. Now that part had been dealt with he slowly stood up, his eyes still on the body of Xavier, his automatic still pointing at the prone figure. Cautiously he knelt beside Xavier and removed the pistol from his hands and flicked the safety to 'off' before tucking it into his own pocket. His first bullet had hit Xavier in the shoulder, high and to the right and appeared to have passed right through. However, the second bullet had hit him in the side of the throat, shattering the collar bone, cutting through part of the jugular artery. Xavier twitched and opened his eyes, his bloody lips quivering.

Webb unwound Xavier's scarf carefully and padded it into the wound. He knew by the colour of the blood and the strong, pulsed spurts that it must have hit his jugular or some other main artery. "Try to hold that on there, son..." he said to Xavier, but the boy couldn't move his arm. "I'm sorry... mate, it looks like I killed you." He touched the boy's handsome face. "You did your best..."

Xavier slowly shook his head, blood gurgling from his mouth as he tried to speak. "Don't... hurt her..." His eyes begged. "Please don't hurt her."

"Webbley... Webbley!" He heard Kristianna screaming at him and Beth tugging at his arm.

"Leave him, boss... leave him," Beth pleaded. In the far distance they could hear police sirens already approaching.

"You..." Webb signalled to a teenage boy laying on the pavement six feet from him. "Come here... come on, you won't be hurt." The frightened, distraught boy crawled over to him hardly raising his head. "Hold that on there, 'til the cops get here." He forced the boys hand onto the rolled up scarf on Xavier's neck. "Put pressure on it."

"Boss... we got to go... now..."

Beth rushed over and dragged him into the Range Rover...

Kristianna slammed the big car into gear and sped off, tires screaming, already the sirens were much too close, it would be barely more than a couple of minutes now before the police and emergency services arrived and surrounded the area completely...

"Christ!" he cursed, wiping a smear of blood from his hands, another patch of blood stained the sleeve of his coat. He tried to wipe it off but just made it worse so he let it be. "You alright?" He directed his words to the young girl huddled in the corner of the rear passenger seat, besides him. She cradled her knees to her chest with her arms, almost curled into a ball. Even in the intermittent flashes of light he could see the terror on her face. "Please don't scream... you won't be hurt."

She shook her head frantically but said nothing... the eyeliner had smeared around her face and run onto her cheeks, making her look a little 'freakish' and weird.

He made a move to touch her knee, just to reassure her, but she was shaking so violently that he withdrew his hand and moved to the far end of the seat. "Listen... you are going to be alright, no one will harm you... you are going to spend the night with us and then maybe tomorrow when we have spoken to your granddaddy, you will be going home tomorrow night, yeah?" His words seemed to make little or no difference.

He wasn't sure if she had understood, but she seemed a little calmer.

"You alright, boss, is that your blood?" Bethe was worried.

"No... well, I don't think so..."

"Too many bloody people there. I didn't like it like that at all. People could really have gotten hurt, innocent people." Beth checked her automatic before holstering it.

They had only travelled about ten miles or so when Kristianna pulled into a lay-by. "I need to stop". She leaned over the steering column and fidgeted in her seat. "You'll have to drive, Beth. I've been shot..."

"Shot!" Webb was out of the car and alongside her helping her out. "Where? Christ, I thought I saw you go down, but I thought you'd slipped, or something. Shot where?"

Kristianna mumbled something that they couldn't really understand...

"Where?" Beth asked, trying to see any bloodstains in the half darkness. "I can't see anything, see if there's a torch in the glove compartment."

But before Webb could look. "In my... backside..." Kristianna mumbled again, her hand on the cheek of her backside.

Webb sniggered, starting Beth off laughing...

"In your what?" He tried in vain to stop himself from laughing.

"It doesn't matter... just drive." Kristianna sounded irritated as she staggered into the passenger seat alongside Beth.

An hour later they were back in the yacht. Gabriella had arrived with Simon thirty minutes earlier, beaming at the success of the 'mission'... at 'her' success. As soon as Webb entered she gave him a hug and put a large strong gin and tonic in his hand. "We all deserve that tonight, I reckon." She stretched herself to her tiptoes and kissed him on the mouth, but then seeing Kristianna, her smile changed to worry as she saw the patch of blood staining the outside of her slacks. "Kristianna, what's happened, did you get hurt? Webb, look." She pointed at the seat of her sister's slacks.

"I need to take a look at that." Webb touched her arm, to escort her to the sofa. "Gabby, take the girl through and get her cleaned up, please... and you had better find her something a little more... less revealing... more comforting to wear. She looks cold."

"No... leave me," Kristianna protested loudly, pushing Webb's hand away, her dignity and pride a little bruised. For the first time in as long as she could remember... she felt embarrassed. She would deal with it herself in the privacy of her own cabin... the last thing she wanted was for someone to be 'picking about' at her.

"Shush, you big baby... don't be such a squinny... come on." Webb took her arm and led her to the sofa. "Lie down." He released the belt on her slacks and made her lie on her belly. "Lift up a bit..." He eased her slacks down to her knees and then her panties. A sudden macabre thought touched him... that he had 'made love' to her and yet had never actually 'seen' any part of her body. She had the most beautiful bottom and legs he had ever seen on any woman. "Bugger, that looks really bad." He winked at Beth. "What d'ya reckon... cut it out, or should I just probe for it?"

"I think we're going to have to amputate..." Beth smiled as she looked at the wound. The bullet had broken the skin for about six inches along one cheek and some blood and bruising was evident.

"Will you stop...?" Kristianna struggled to be free, but Webb held her down so that she couldn't really move.

"Well, perhaps not all of it..." He smiled with Simon and Beth. "We could just cut this bit out, maybe." He smiled as he 'scribed' an imaginary line around the bruised area with his finger. "Have we got a suture kit on board, Gabby and a decent scalpel?" He gently pinched her bottom, and she winced a little. "Keep still. There... half a dozen stitches should do it... I'm looking forwards to this. I haven't sewn anyone up for years..."

"No... damn it. If it needs anything at all, just put a few 'Steri-stitches' over it, you're not going anywhere near me with a Goddamned needle." Kristianna struggled to raise herself, but he held her down. Eventually he let her sit up, taking her weight on the undamaged 'cheek'.

"I think that leg will have to come off you know..." Beth smiled again, enjoying the situation.

"Oh dear..." Gabriella was taking it all very serious. "Really... it doesn't look very deep."

"That's alright..." Kristianna huffed. "Have fun at my expense, I don't mind. Just stick something on it. We'll see how funny it is when one of you gets shot... then I'll have the laugh."

"You were dead lucky there though. The bullet just creased the skin, another inch to the right and you'd have definitely lost your 'virginity' for sure." He bent and kissed her buttock, her scent making him a little heady, if the others hadn't been present, he would have ripped the rest of her clothes off and ravaged her... there and then. Instead he wiped the wound clean with the hot wet towels Sui Lin had brought up and then dried it, gently applying the antiseptic wipes and deftly attached the three 'Steri-strips' to hold the wound together. When he was satisfied that the wound was clean he covered it with antiseptic Elastoplast. "There, that'll do for now... next surgery ten o'clock tomorrow morning and don't be late... surgery closes at ten-fifteen."

A whimper from the armchair brought them back to the reality of their evening's endeavours. Gabriella had given Anastasia a clean white dressing gown to dress in and she was crying. She held a glass of hot milk shakily in her hands that Sui Lin had heated up for her. "Grampa will be so cross with you Kristianna and you too, Gabriella..." She sniffled. "He will be so very cross... do you realise what you have done?" Her words seemed a little immature, even childish, given the situation she was in.

Kristianna sat up and removed her slacks completely and threw them at Sui Lin and then looked at the 'child' in front of her, hating her. Anastasia, above all the others had made her life purgatory at one time, a thorn in her side any time she had dealings with Alejandro.

Anastasia was 'the favoured one', there were lots of other grandchildren but for reasons known only to himself Alejandro de los Santos had selected her as his favourite...

"Don't worry about your grandfather, Anastasia, you have much bigger problems than that," Kristianna said cuttingly. "Just hope and pray that 'grampa', is in the mood for negotiating..." She ran her finger across her own throat threatening her.

"Whoa, miss..." Simon touched Kristianna's arm. "Nothing is going to happen to this girl... right." He increased the pressure on her arm. "Webb... is that right, yes?"

Webb nodded...

Kristianna turned and smiled at him, enjoying the pain in her arm. It amused her that this 'Superman'... this 'Special Forces man'... who held her arm so tightly, would be totally defenceless against her if she chose to react now. "Ah... that's hurting me." She placed her hand over his and made a face of distress and pain until he released her. "Sorry, I'm just irritable... I need a shower." She smiled as she walked away from him. She would sooner have just turned on him... on them all and killed them... but it was far too early for that.

But the look of pure hatred Kristianna had given Anastasia had not gone unnoticed by Webb. The smiled drained from his face as he realised he would need to protect the girl closely from now on, at least until such times as she could be safely returned to her family. He was beginning to doubt whether this plan of theirs would work and that he might well have to think of something else... pronto!

"I think we all need to turn in..." he said not really feeling tired now... nor it seemed were the others, the adrenaline was still running too high, so they sat and talked into the late hours of the night...

"Shall I keep the girl with me for the night, boss?" Beth yawned. "I think I'm about ready for the 'pit'."

Gabriella cuddled into Webb, her hand entwined through his arm. "And us, Webbley, we need to get some sleep, there is so much we have to do tomorrow."

Simon stood and yawned again. "Do you want to come to Wales tomorrow, Webbley? You would be much safer there."

Webb had been considering the offer from the outset but still worried about further involving other people. "Mmm, maybe, as long as you are sure about it. I have some other business here tomorrow. There's something I need you to do for me but I'll go through it in the morning. Gabby was saying she has a cottage, that's registered in her aunt's name so I'll take Beth with me and we'll stay there for tomorrow night and then come on down to you for Friday... if that's okay?

Chapter 28

Thursday 1 am.

"What! Are you sure?" Paul Kyso leapt from his bed and shoved his feet into his slippers and then switched on the light. His young female companion groaned as the light burnt her eyes. "When… who was with her?"

"Just the boy, we don't have anyone else… They're all out tracking down Pendleton." Panic was clearly evident in Dick Cordon's voice. "We never even thought that anyone would dare take Anastasia, Paul. Who would take her for God's sake… everyone knows that anyone who touched her would be 'automatically' dead."

"Goddamn it! How the hell do I tell Alejandro that his granddaughter has been taken? What the hell do I say?" The situation had escalated out of control now and he knew it… the situation was bad enough before this, but now. "Hell… the world's going to explode now…"

Thursday:

It was almost ten before Webb woke. His mouth was dry and his throat sore and raspy. The oversized gin and tonics of last night had not had the desired effect of wiping his memory clean from the fact that he had killed a young man...

Slowly he unwrapped himself from Gabriella's arm and slid out of bed, gently pulling the quilt back over so that he wouldn't wake her... Brushing his teeth twice didn't remove the taste of his excessive drinking either... he needed several coffees and half-a-dozen 'fags' to put his head and mouth to rights.

His dulled mind mulled over the events of the past few days, tragedy, fear and excitement and now... death... again. He looked at his reflection in the mirror, not entirely happy with the new sets of wrinkles under his eyes. "Late night's..." he mumbled out loud, his 'normal' bedtime was ten to ten-thirty... not two o'clock in the morning...

But at the back of his mind there was something that excited him about all of it... he hadn't felt this 'alive' since he had left The Regiment, and realised how much he'd missed it all... Even when he had first started courting his ex-wife, J.C. he'd told her that he was a 'lifer'... in the army for life and that there was nothing else he wanted to do other than be a soldier. Funny... her name was Jane-Claire and yet from the outset he had shortened it to J.C. in those early days he had believed that marriage also was 'for life'... but then, what the hell... "Nothing lasts forever" does it?"

Now, however he could understand things about his temperament that he couldn't at the time... the irrational tempers that used to completely take control of him and the 'manic, self-destruct button' that used to live in secret ... inside his head... waiting for the appropriate 'trigger' to explode. It was the main reason he'd been kicked out of the army in disgrace. Not just the irrational incident over the cat, resulting in him cutting Tom Burnett's fingers off... that had just been the final straw for his commanders, some of whom had always thought he was too much of an independent, undisciplined and unstable individual anyway and were very eager to get rid of him... 'Not a team player...' one senior officer had said. These days' things were a lot more stable, in his head... at least he hoped they were.

Beth and Simon were in the main saloon as he entered. Both had stuck with coffee last night... as his head told him he should have. On the opposite sofa Anastasia sat quietly sipping her tea, wrapped in a huge towelling dressing gown, her hair still wet from her shower. She was humming a silent tune, seemingly unperturbed by the danger she was in.

"Oh dear..." Beth smiled over her cup and winked at Simon. "We look a little worse for wear this morning, boss..."

He had put on Daniel's silk dressing gown and had 'sort of' smoothed his hair down. "Now I wished I'd stuck to the coffee," he mumbled, nodding at Simon, who looked like he was dressed for the 'court'. His jeans were pressed and the casual sports coat, blue shirt and cravat suited him to a 'tee'. "Quick coffee and then I'll have a shower."

He ran through what he wanted Simon to do. "I'll phone Steve in a minute tell him you're on your way down. Just check on the situation with Peter's chaps for me, make sure they're tooled up and know how serious this all is. If they get sloppy they'll get themselves killed... you know the drill, mate."

"We're a bit short on clothes for the girl, Webb." Beth nodded at Anastasia. "Hopefully Gabriella might have something more 'appropriate'."

"What... will happen to me?" Anastasia asked, she seemed brighter, less frightened now.

He hadn't realised what a beautiful girl she was until now. Her short cropped, brunette hair, was scissor cut just below the jaw and tucked neatly under her chin, emphasising her perfect almond face and tiny 'button' nose. She wasn't dissimilar, in looks to Kristianna, although far prettier and more 'kittenish'. He could easily understand why she would be her grandfather's favourite. She looked the sort of young lady that any man, young or old would have difficulty refusing anything…

"As soon as your grandfather gives us safe passage, I'll get you back to your parents… hopefully today, yeah." He touched her head affectionately and she didn't pull back from him. He wished he could just sit here for a couple of hours with nothing else to do… just idle chat… like 'normal' people would be doing. "Don't worry, you won't come to any harm, I give you my word."

"But what if he doesn't agree…" She tried to hide her nervousness with a smile but found it impossible.

"From what I understand, there's not much chance of that." He worried a little bit about that himself. 'Would anyone really sacrifice the whole company for the life of an eighteen-year-old child? Of course they wouldn't. He answered his own question. "But if he doesn't agree… you can leave anyway, we'll just have to think of something else."

"Really, really?" she said excitedly, bouncing on the sofa. "Honestly?" She pulled her dressing gown around her knees. "Do you think I could… telephone my mother? Please, she will be so worried."

Webb nodded. "Sure, but not until I phone Alejandro…"

She smiled at him. "Thank you… so much." She liked this tall man he was rough and ready and yet very charming at the same time.

"I need a shower." He looked at Beth. "You'll be alright here for a moment?" He indicated with a nod towards the girl. "Where's Kristianna by the way?" He couldn't imagine her still being in bed, somehow."

Beth told him it wasn't a problem… with the girl, and then… "Not sure, she went out earlier said she had some things that needed to be done."

"Bloody woman's never still is she…"

"I just as well get off then, Webbley." Simon held his hand out and Webb shook it enthusiastically. "Watch your back. Beth knows the way to the 'house'. Telephone when you are ten minutes away."

Chapter 29

Thursday 8:45 am.

Peter Copping turned slowly into the last junction that would take him into the Docklands and his offices. He loved the area, in fact he loved all of London... as far as he was concerned it was the greatest city in the world.

He was still smarting over the loss of David Coulter and the two negotiators, trying to put it out of his mind was difficult, if not impossible. He'd tried to look at it from a different angle... it was no different than any other 'Opp'... casualties of 'war', etc. etc. But that hadn't worked either... This was England for God's sake, not some jumped up 'rag-head' country, where people were murdered and slaughtered every day of the week... so much so, that it became the 'norm...' This contract with Pendleton, he had assessed the risk as 'minimal to medium'... How wrong can you be?

Initially he had been delighted to take on the extra work from Webbley 'bloody' Pendleton... it was far more lucrative than most of his other clients... but at what cost? Now... it was almost impossible for him to pull out of it.

The car park outside of his office was clearly marked on the tarmac for positioning cars neatly in line and yet there were three huge, black cars parked haphazardly, one outside of the main office door and the other two, angled across the entrance... and his entire office staff were standing around in a huddle.

"What the fuck?"

His brow furrowed further as he pulled into the forecourt and Amanda, his P.A. rushed over to his door. She was distraught and besides herself, the nervous twitch had returned to her face, something that only happened to her when she was under extreme pressure.

"There are policemen all over the office, Mr. Copping." She rubbed her jaw furiously. "They are going through all of our filing cabinets. I don't understand it."

"Calm down, Amanda... please." He took her arm and nodded at the rest of his staff as he walked her to the front door of the office, where two burly men blocked their entrance. "What is it they want... did they say?"

She shook her head, her hands fretting with her face... "They didn't say, but it seems they have a search warrant..."

"I checked it, Mr. Copping, it seemed genuine," Jason, the trainee office boy added.

"I'm afraid you can't go in there, sir." One of the men held his hand out in front of Peter.

Peter grasped the man's hand and pulled him forward violently, tripping him with his foot, sending him sprawling across the tarmac. The second man took a pace forward, but Peter knocked him out of the way and went through to his offices...

He was met inside by another man, tall and wiry. "You need to stay outside, sir, until we are finished... please," And pointed at the door.

Peter ignored him and walked through to his own office. Through the glass divider screen he could see another man sat in his swivel chair. "Get out of that chair..." He spat the words viciously at the bespectacled, thin man, "...you in charge?"

The thin man nodded and leapt out of the swivel chair and backed off to the far wall. "Yes, I am... Chief Inspector Richard Brian Richardson." He spoke confidently and a little arrogant, although cautious of the big black man. "I have a legal search warrant to search these premises." He took an envelope from his pocket and made to hand it to Peter.

"Where's your warrant card?" Peter demanded. One of the burly men from outside stood behind Peter. "Warrant card..." Peter shouted, holding his hand out...

The policeman shuffled through his inside pocket and produced the document and handed it to Peter, who verified it and then threw it down onto the table...

"Show me the warrant..."

He read through the warrant, slowly and then reread it. "Right, 'Chief Inspector of Police... Richard Brian Richardson'. Your mother didn't have too much imagination either... did she. I am as familiar with the law as you are. What's this about?"

"We were reliably informed that there were weapons in this establishment..."

"Bollocks!" Peter voice boomed around the office, but no one moved to challenge him. "If that had been the case you would not have just walked in here without half the 'armed response team' behind you." He held the warrant up. "I deal with these all the time, 'Chief Inspector', and this one is illegal... It has an illegible signature and the stamp has not been countersigned by a county court judge..." He threw the warrant back at the Chief Inspector, but he wasn't quick enough to catch it and it spiralled slowly down onto the carpet, amongst the other documents that had already been removed by the police. "So... what's this really about?" He pushed past him and dialled a number. "You…" He took the Chief Inspector by the lapel and propelled him towards his colleague by the doorway. "Wait there… I need to make a call."

The Chief Inspector started to protest but Peter held up his hand, stopping him mid-sentence…

"Julian… Peter." He watched the policeman's moustache twitch. Peter explained the situation to the man at the other end of the telephone, and then handed the handset to Richardson…

Richard Brian Richardson knew exactly to whom he was talking. Everyone in the law enforcement agencies of Greater London knew Julian St. Claire… the foremost criminal barrister in the city. What Richard Brian Richard didn't know was that Julian St. Claire had been the Colonel of the S.A.S. and that Peter Copping had been his sergeant major… Julian St. Claire was a regular attendee of Peter's 'Old Comrades Reunions'.

"Yes, sir… yes… I do understand that… yes." Richardson blustered.

Peter enjoyed the fragmented debate the two were having on the telephone… He had known instinctively that there was some not quite right with the warrant, but had not been able to study it in detail.

"Yes, sir, I will… straight away…"

"Now get out…"

The police left with the sounds of gears wringing in their ears. Richardson cursed… another ten minutes and he would have obtained from Copping's office what he had been told to get… namely the location of his 'agents' attached to Webbley Pendleton… Now he would have to answer to his own 'masters', who had specifically said… 'Handle it with a 'light touch'.

"Get that bastard Pendleton on the phone," Peter shouted at Amanda.

Thursday 11:30

"We need to make a deal, Mr. Alesander." Webb had showered and dressed and eaten his breakfast of two fried eggs and bacon on toast and felt much better, the 'grease' had settled his tummy perfectly, now the effects of last night had almost gone and felt confident that this call would bring about the result he wanted. "I want safe passage out of the country for myself, and my companions. Is that clear?" He heard the old man sigh.

"My name is 'Alejandro… sir." Alejandro corrected him… grumbling wearily and coughed. "Can I speak with her, Mr. Pendleton, please?" His voice sounded old and very tired.

Webb cupped the mouth piece of the mobile. "Say nothing of where you are, Anastasia. If there is anything I don't like, then you won't get to talk to your parents… yeah?" He rested his hand on the receiver arms, ready to flick the telephone off if Anastasia said anything untoward.

She smiled excitedly and took the handset from him. "Grampa…" Tears poured from her eyes and Gabriella handed her a tissue, then sat next to her, her hand on Anastasia's shoulder.

Webb allowed her to talk for several minutes before he gently eased the handset from her fingers. His hand touched her wet face. "It's alright." He whispered… Gabriella took charge of the girl… and then to Alejandro. "What do you think, do we have a deal, sir?"

"Mr. Pendleton… I love that child as if she were my own, more than I have ever loved anyone in this world, I think. She means that much to me…" He sniffled. "But I cannot give you what you ask of me… it is just not possible for me to grant it… and I think you know that."

"Don't be a fool, Alejandro." Webb felt clammy and hot…he never had been a good poker player. "You would sacrifice the life of a child for…for…what…money, prestige, what?"

"You have seen the child, Mr. Pendleton… spoken to her." The old man wasn't pleading with him. "Could you really harm her? Could you?"

"If necessary…" He knew the bluff wasn't working. "You thought nothing of hurting my people, did you?"

"Mr. Pendleton, I read your army report, sir. How could a man that sacrifices his whole army career and reputation for a small kitten… how could that man then harm 'my', little 'kitten'? Mr. Pendleton, how?" Alejandro's voice wasn't smug or belligerent, just pitiable.

Slowly Webb touched the off button of the telephone, knowing he was beaten… and sat on the sofa.

"No go, boss?" Beth asked.

He shook his head. Somewhere in the distance he heard a telephone ringing, it seemed miles away, but he was conscience of Gabriella answering it and then screaming at him…

"Did Gramps say it was alright?" Anastasia interrupted his thoughts as he bounded over to Gabriella.

"It's Kristianna… she says it is desperately urgent…"

"What… what is it?" He snatched the handset from her… "What?"

"Webbley, you have to get to your wife and children… now! Preston is going after them…" Kristianna's voice was controlled but urgent.

"Preston…?" At first the name didn't register, but then he remembered Kristianna telling him about Adrian Preston, the assassin that would have been responsible for his mother's death. "They have an armed police protection unit with them, they should be safe. How do you know this?"

"That doesn't matter... you need to get there now, forget the police, there is only one unarmed policeman with them. Go, Webbley, please." She urged him. "I might be there before you. If I am I'll do what I can..."

He threw the phone in the general direction of the cradle, but it missed and landed on the carpet. "Jesus! What do these bastards want, from me?" He pushed the hair from his face, frantically...

"I heard most of that, boss... I'm coming with you." Beth grabbed her coat and checked the load on her Glock and tucked it into her shoulder holster.

"Christ!" He was frantic. "The girl... my bloody gun..." He realised he'd left it in his cabin. "Get the car started, Beth, I'll be there in a minute." He took the frightened girl by the arm and quickly led her to his cabin. "Gabriella!" He shook her into life, signalling for her to get moving and threw on his shoulder holster and cocked the .45, making sure the round entered the chamber cleanly. "Keep her locked in here 'till I get back... do you understand?"

"Please..." Anastasia pleaded with him. "Please don't hurt me... I'm so frightened now." She tugged at the heavy pullover Gabriella had given her.

He looked around the room and grabbed another three ammunition clips for the .45. The only suitcase that mattered was still in the Range Rover, anything else he could collect later...

Anastasia grabbed his arm, her panicked face contorted with fear. "Don't leave me here... please don't, I'm so frightened."

"Listen, you'll be safe with Gabriella." He shook her shoulders. "Be quiet and nothing will happen to you, I promise. Your grandfather has sent people to kill my family... do you understand?"

"Just call out the direction, boss, in plenty of time." Beth drove fast and skilfully, weaving in and out of the traffic. Her driving assessment in the S.A.S. had been 100 1/A, the highest rating of any previous class, it was a natural skill enhanced by her father's tuition. She had seen the manic, almost demented look in Webb's eyes and feared for his powers of reasoning, but she needed him to concentrate.

On the surface he appeared calm, but she knew from past experience of people under extreme pressure, the difficulty in forming rational thought. "Calm down, keep it together, concentrate on the 'immediate problem'... forget the 'vengeance bit', you can do that later." She touched his arm, encouraging him.

"We'll be alright when we clear that damned causeway and get onto the A27, its straight though from there to Christ Church." He felt calmer, there was no chance of getting lost... he had lived there for almost twelve years. "We should get there in..." he checked his watch. "About fifteen... twenty minutes..."

The traffic was heavier at this time of the day and even with Beth's skilful driving, it took almost thirty-five minutes before they were turning into the 'cul-de-sac' where J.C. lived...

"Slow down... there." He pointed to the big Toyota Land Cruiser parked in what used to be his driveway.

Beth eased her speed, but she was still travelling at nearly twenty miles an hour when he jumped out, rolled across the pavement and lawn and charged at the front door...

"Webb, wait... damn you..." She screamed after him as she braked behind the Toyota. She knew he hadn't heard her.

As he ran at the big mahogany door that he'd built, all those years ago, a thought momentarily passed through his mind that if it was locked with both top and bottom 'deadlocks', his efforts would be in vain... fortunately only the day lock was on and it splintered the keep plate into a dozen pieces as his shoulder hit the centre mass of the lock. The doormat slipped from under his feet and a huge splinter of wood from the rebate drove into his leg... but he didn't feel it. He smashed the barrel of his automatic across the neck of the tall thin man, as he stood astride J.C; the hammer raised, ready to shatter her brains across the maple flooring...

Webb dived at the man, crashing into his body, knocking him to the floor, but he was fit and wiry, the first blow had just glanced across his head and he fought back as Webb sunk his finger and thumb into Preston's throat, squeezing harder, like a pit bull terrier with a rag, refusing to release it... digging his thumb deeper into the man's oesophagus... and then smashing the automatic at his face, again and again, feeling the bones and teeth shatter as the metal impacted with his flesh.

But Adrian Preston wasn't done yet. Somehow he freed his hand and drove the hammer at Webb's face giving him a glancing blow across the upper cheekbone and eyebrow. Sensing blood he tried to stand, but Webb drove him back to the floor with several blows from his automatic across the face until he was virtually unconscious... his face a bloody mess.

Webb pushed himself up from the inert body and rested on his knees as Beth came through the back door... It was only now that he became aware of the terrified, muffled screams of his wife and daughter...

"You alright, boss?" Beth held the Glock in both hands, pointed at the floor, cocked and ready. She touched Webb's shoulder and kicked the hammer along the hallway, out of harm's way. "Leave him, boss... don't think he's got too much fight left in him..." She helped Webb to his feet. "Did he get you?" She looked at the blood streaks on his face.

"I'm alright... cut them free..." He pointed at his ex-wife and daughter by the staircase and calmly returned the .45 to its holster and secured it. Suddenly feeling very tired now that the adrenaline had left his body. "Jesus Christ." For the first time his eyes were taking in the scene of 'carnage'. He looked at his wife and daughter and then over to the semi-conscious body of J.C's. 'boyfriend', laying at the bottom of the staircase, his arms outstretched to the fourth tread... his hands had been nailed through the palms to the wood... "Did you fuckin' do the same to my mother, you bastard?" He took a short run at Adrian Preston and kicked him in the ribs and then again in the face, the blow smashing the remainder of his teeth into his shattered mouth.

Webb watched as Beth untied the two terrified women on the floor next to him, unable to help, his mind appalled with the brutality of it all. "Who... who could do this, what sort of fucking animal could..." He kicked at the inert man's face again, feeling the squelch of blood around his toes.

J.C. ignored him and rushed over to her 'man', holding his head against her chest she gently removed the grey masking tape from his mouth. "He's alive!" she screamed. "He's still alive... get an ambulance... someone call for an ambulance..."

"Daddy..." Katrina, his daughter hugged him around the waist, tightly. "Daddy..." Her eyes pleading with him.

He lifted her and kissed her face, it had been so long since he had carried out such a simple, loving thing to her. "It's alright now, 'Twinkle'"... his pet name for her. "It's alright..." He smothered her face with kisses, pulling her closer into his body. "It's alright..." He repeated it again and again to her...

"Webb, there's a dead cop in the backyard... and he wasn't armed..." Beth nodded at the back door.

But he didn't really hear her. He lowered the fourteen-year-old to the floor, gently. "Phone for an ambulance, darlin'... please."

Webb kicked at the plumber's bag and walked over to where Preston lay, the contents sounded 'metallic'. When he opened it he found a selection of steel, spike nails, some ten inches long... rope and cord and several rolls of duct tape. In one of the pockets were different lengths of cable ties the same as his family had been bound with.

Adrian Preston stirred, his hands seeking out the injuries to his face. He tried to sit up but Webb placed his foot on his chest and forced him back down to the floor.

"Let's see if some of these fit you..." Webb rolled him over onto his belly and wired his thumbs together with the shorter cable ties and then joined three of the longer ones together and wound them around Preston's neck and back onto the cable ties around his thumbs. "I think that'll probably hold you for a while, then I'll see if I can't return some of the 'favours'."

"Webb, the cops are going to be all over this place in a minute. What do you want to do?" Beth had her arms around J.C., cuddling her. "I can't do anything at the moment for him." She nodded at J.C's boyfriend, nailed to the staircase. "We'll need the fire brigade to get him free."

"I..." The door handle moved and he quickly pulled the big .45 from its holster, waiting.

"Webbley... Webbley..." The hoarse, heavily whispered voice of Kristianna against the door. "I'm coming in..." Slowly she pushed the door open, in her hand was a huge, silver 'Peace Maker' revolver... She was wearing an immaculate grey suit with a pleated, simple A-line skirt as if she had just attended a meeting with her 'bank manager'... "You have him..." She smiled, impressed. "Clever boy..." She touched his face lightly with the tips of her fingers and kissed his mouth. "You are a very resourceful man..."

"Jesus! I'm glad to see you..." He holstered his automatic and tapped her on the arm. "I need to get this bastard somewhere quiet where I can 'talk' to him..." He whispered close to her ear. "Where?"

"Right, I know where he lives," she whispered back, excited. "Get him in the car... and his little bag of tools..." She smiled and gently touched his cheek with her lips.

"You!" J.C. screamed at Webb, frightened to approach him as if he was the 'Devil' himself. "You bastard... I knew... I just knew this had to be something to do with you... you fucking lunatic..." She screamed again, hysterically, her words manic, her face completely distorted, with anger and grief and fear. Tears poured down her face and she whimpered as she slowly slid back to the floor. "Every time you come near us you ruin our lives, you ruin it... everything... everything you touch always gets destroyed."

"Daddy... what's going on... who are all these people?" Katrina staggered over to him and hugged him again.

"You stay with this nice lady, aye?" He nodded at Beth. "She'll take care of you. Gimme your stuff, Beth... you don't want the cops finding you with 'a piece' on you..."

She knew exactly what he meant and handed the holster and the Glock over to him.

He took her by the arm and walked her to the front door. "When the cops come ask to speak to Inspector Dowling, no one else... you hear? Be 'selective' about what you tell him, most of all tell him that I need to meet him... that's real important." He kissed her on the cheek and squeezed her arm. "Phone me as soon as you're released..."

"Webb, I know what you are going to do and I can't be part of that. Hand him over to the police, let them deal with it. Please." Beth touched his arm, pleading with him.

"I need some information... and you know I can't let him live... can I." He shrugged, understanding what she was saying.

Kristianna and Webb dragged the semi-conscious Preston to the Range Rover and threw him into the rear passenger well with the 'plumber's' bag of tools on top of him.

Several people had gathered in the street, some huddled around in tight little groups discussing what they thought was going on. Two men, one with a long garden hoe in his hands approached the back of Webb's car. He was a big man with a shaved head, bare chested and tattoo's covering most of his exposed body, spoke first. "You want to tell me what's going on here, matey?" He pointed the sharp end of the hoe at Webb, prodding his arm with the blade.

"Fuck off..." Webb said as he walked around to the driver's door, ready to get in.

"I'm talking to you, mate." The big man persisted and poked Webb in the back again.

Webb turned slowly pulling the .45 and fired two shots into the lawn, either side of the man's feet. "I said... fuck off..."

Preston's house was a picture of a bygone age of splendour and luxury and absolute elegance. It had been built originally for a wealthy landowner and his growing family in the early eighteenth century. Set in thirty acres of arable land, of which a goodly portion had been fully landscaped, colonnades of rose beds and arches of laburnum and rhododendron, all at the moment in full bloom, designed to follow the along each side of the long curved driveway to the house entrance.

No expense had been spared in the original construction, skilled labour in those days was cheap. But over the years the mansion and grounds had fallen into disrepair, until Adrian Preston had purchased it and spent a small fortune on the complete renovation… restoring it back to its former glory.

"We came here several years ago, Gabriella, and I for some sort of medieval banquet he was hosting… he loved having lots of people around him. If only they had known what he was really like, maybe they would not have been so eager to come here." Kristianna spoke quietly as if frightened of disturbing the 'ghosts of the house'. "Wait until you see inside, it's magnificent."

"How in God's name can a man like that afford such a place?" Webb pushed and shoved Adrian Preston towards the front door. "Bring that bag of tools, I need to give him a feel of his own medicine."

"I don't think you can imagine how much people like this make from their murder and torture… millions." Kristianna lifted the heavy bag and swung it easily on her shoulder, oblivious of her immaculate coat. "I thought they had stopped using this animal though, he's the most brutal of all of them... Those um, spike things, he uses them on all of his victims... it's his trademark. He 'crucifies' them."

Webb shuddered. "Does he? So he would have... done the same to my... mother?"

She nodded...

He kicked and pushed Preston towards the door and then opened it with Preston's own keys. "Take the ground floor, make sure there's no one else in the house, I'll take this cretin upstairs."

"There won't be anyone else here, he lives alone."

Webb told her to check anyway. "Just humour me then. I'm not going to get caught with my pants around my ankles again."

He pushed Preston into the huge, beamed entrance hallway and up the magnificent, Gothic staircase. Webb cranked his head to one side as they reached the landing, the .45 pointed at Preston's head... He listened, hearing the sound again... it sounded like the cries of a baby or a very young child. Slowly he opened the door where the sound was coming from and shoved Preston in. It appeared to be the main bedroom suit, dominated by a huge, double, four-poster bed. The posts were carved and sculptured into intricate gargoyles and dwarves and elves cavorting in exaggerated sexual acts.

He poked his head around the door cautiously, 'fanning' the huge room with his automatic. The floor was the original, wide boarded, stained oak, covering the whole area. The only floor covering was a huge Persian carpet around the dressing area and at the far end of the bedroom was a full-sized billiards table.

"Some pad aye?" He clipped Preston 'lightly' across the back of the head and forced him to kneel at the bottom of the bed. "Now you just sit there like a good boy..." The sound was coming from the bed, under the heaped quilt. Slowly with one hand still on the pistol, he threw back the quilt. The sight of the young naked girl, her lower body covered in blood horrified him. "Jesus Christ! It don't get any better with you, does it..."

He quickly untied her, freeing her hands and feet that had been tied 'spread eagled' across the bed. She was so terrified that she didn't move, not even to cover her nakedness from his stare, her face a picture of absolute fear...

"Kristianna!" he shouted, hearing her bounding up the staircase. She rushed in, still carrying the heavy 'plumber's bag' and holding the big silver 'Peace Maker'. The noise was ear splitting when she dropped the bag to the floor. "Look at this for Christ's sake... what a fuckin' animal..." He didn't want to touch the girl, fearing she would go into hysterics...

"Damn it, man... I thought you had been shot, or something." She lowered the big gun and looked over into the bed. "She's probably one of his floozies..." ...and turned away, unconcerned.

"You hardnosed bitch... what's up with you?" He tucked the automatic back into its holster, looking at her, disgusted. "Help her up... get her into the bathroom and clean her up... her clothes must be here somewhere."

"Me? Clean her up?" She was appalled. "Why me?"

"Because you're a fuckin'... woman." He threw his hands in the air as the girl on the bed stirred herself and moaned loudly, covering her body with her hands. "I can't take her in there ... can I? Look at her, I should think she is going to be terrified of men for the rest of her life."

Reluctantly Kristianna helped the girl from the bed, but not before she had removed a pillowcase to cover the girl's arm where she would have to touch her. "You don't have long, Webb," she said as she eased the girl into the bathroom. "The police won't take long to identify his car..."

He cursed her under his breath and turned on the hapless, semi-conscious Preston. "Now, my friend..." He dragged the bag over from the doorway. And removed the big hammer and a handful of the heavy metal spikes and threw them at Preston's feet.

Webb pushed him over onto his back and stood on his chest and then bent to him, removing his shoes and socks. "Is this what you did to my mother, you bastard?"

"I... I have money." Preston forced the words through his broken teeth and the bloody pulp around his mouth. He tried to sit, but Webb forced him back to the floor with a quick blow of the hammer and then picked up one of the longer steel spikes. Touching it to the top centre of Preston's foot he drove it through skin and bone to the floor beneath with one blow. "How's that feel, did she scream like that?" He spread Preston's legs as wide as he was able and repeated the process.

The horrified screams were ear-shattering, bloodcurdling and didn't stop until he passed out... into a fitful, erratic contortion of pained movement.

Webb left him and walked over to the billiard table and taking a cue, smashed the end against the side until it shattered into a jagged sharp point, four feet long. He lifted Preston and threw him onto the bed, his feet still spiked to the floor. The additional pain roused him as Webb ripped his trousers and underwear from him.

"Good..." Webb's voice was manic, his eyes bulging, almost insane, realising that Preston was conscious again. "I wouldn't want you to sleep through this." And then drove the billiard cue up Preston's rectum... "How's that feel?" He saw the hammer on the floor and picked it up, wanting to smash his head into pulp... but stopped himself. Instead he drove a further two spikes into the floor behind Preston and at angle, as if he was arranging the supports for a tent and shuffled through the bag selecting enough of the cord to throw over the bedhead and made it fast, in the other end he tied a spike and then eased the screaming Preston from the bed until the billiard cue in his rectum just touched the floor. It almost looked like he was in the 'perfect position' for 'horse riding' with his back straight and his knees bent.

"Money… I have money…" He pleaded, his eyes begging Webbley, his hands frantically trying to remove the cue. "In the tall-boy, cupboard… lots of money… Oh God help me, please help me." He gazed into Webb's unsympathetic eyes. "The… the shipment… I can… tell you about the shipment. It's in… on Friday. It is the…" He screamed as his body lowered slightly onto the cue. With a Herculean effort he forced his muscles to lift his body from the pain. "It is the biggest European shipment ever." He spat the blood from his mouth trying to clear his throat… "You… have their money for it… the money you stole from them…Pier sixty 'A', Friday, on the American tanker 'Mariana'." He gasped deeply for breath, praying that by some slim chance he would be spared. "The inner holding tanks… it's all in there…" He pleaded.

"I have lots of money…" Webb jammed the spike, tied to the cord into Preston's mouth and readjusted the length until the whole of his weight was leaning back on the billiard cue and then refastened his hands with the cable ties behind his back. "Now… you look like a pretty strong chap, let's see how long you can hold that in your mouth, before that cue impales you." He smiled a slightly crooked, demented smile. "Oh… Just so that you won't cheat…" He tied a long cord around Preston's neck and then the loose ends back to the offset spikes, as if he was rigging the 'guy ropes' for a tent. "Hang onto that one in your mouth… now there's only one way for you to go… and that's down…"

A movement to his left made him jump. Kristianna was standing in the bathroom doorway, a look of demonic pleasure on her face her eyes alight with excitement watching him. For a long time he had forgotten she was here. Her hands were pressed tightly to her groin... massaging herself, slowly.

"Get the girl and let's get out of here." As he turned, she smiled at him, a strange unusual smile as if she were in a dream. Webb grabbed a pillowcase and stuffed Preston's money into it. "Come on, let's go..." He didn't even give Preston a glance as he left...

***

"Webbley, its better you don't go back to the yacht. I want to close it all down now and get rid of it." She touched his arm and pulled him out of earshot of the girl, in the passenger seat. "It's better that you follow me to the cottage now and I'll send Gabriella over to you with a new car, park this in the garage of the cottage. The police will have a warrant out for you and the car by now. So better you don't drive it too far." She leaned forward and kissed him on the mouth. "You were superb in there... I enjoyed that so much..."

***

As he followed her with his eyes he wondered why he had agreed to the arrangement, there was nothing about Kristianna that he could trust. She had assured him that the girl, Anastasia, was of no use to them anymore and that she would pack her up and send her back to her parents.

"Why do you associate with 'shyte' like that?" he asked the young girl next to him. Outwardly, she looked calmer now. "You look quite bright and you're very pretty."

She sniffled. Earlier she had told him her name was Kyle. "My mum named me after the Australian singer." She found talking difficult after the shock of being tied to the bed and brutalised by Adrian Preston. "I... It was raining and he offered me a lift home..." She sniffled again and took a handful of tissues from the holder on the dashboard and blew her nose. "I thought he was a nice man... I've seen him around Mr. Kyso's office. I work for Mr. Kyso you see... as a junior accountant. Nothing like this has ever happened to me before. I'm not a bad girl or anything like that... my mum will be so worried..."

He looked at her bleached, blonde hair and her too short... too tight miniskirt, and her long painted, scarlet finger nails and clicked his teeth. "Look, in the back there's a sack of money... take it when you leave, do something useful with it, change your life, but don't spend it all at once, or someone will want to know where you got it."

He dropped her at the Tesco's supermarket, next to the taxi rank and watched her 'waddle off' carrying her 'sack' of money as she staggered across to the nearest taxi, in shoes that were either too small or the heels to high, wondering if she actually would change her life.

Chapter 29

Thursday 4:30 pm.

The cottage was homely and set in a small woodland at the top of a windy track, unseen from the road up a short winding track. Webb thought it must have been built just after the war as the brickwork was a mixture of Staffordshire blues and red clay's. The chimney was so ornate and large that he knew to build it at today's prices, would cost a fortune.

"It'll be safe here, at least for a couple of days." Kristianna opened the door to the cottage. "Hopefully no one knows anything about this." She handed him the bunch of keys. "Or should I stay here with you…" She kissed him on the mouth, but all he could smell was the stench of blood and death on her breath… or was it his.

Most of the furniture was covered in white dust cloths, but it still felt homely, albeit a little… musty and 'unloved'. He drew the curtains and pulled off some of the dust sheets and bundled them into a corner out of the way. Kristianna showed no interest in helping, but he had grown to expect that from her. He wondered how these people could amass such wealth that a beautiful cottage such as this could be purchased and then just left… used only on very rare occasion. The cottage, he thought would probably fetch a quarter of a million, even in this condition. 'Ah well.' He thought. "Perhaps 'I' can share in some of that 'wealth' from now on.'

After she left he parked the car in the garage and brought in the suitcase, hiding it under the stairs and then after locking the doors, flopped out on long, soft sofa, rolled a cigarette and laid out full length.

A sudden wave of emotion overtook him and he felt his stomach well up, but he held it. In the past he'd been a little 'bullheaded' and 'impulsive', prone to do idiotic things... but never... never had he killed someone in such a violent, premeditated and evil way... All of this had turned 'him' into an 'animal' as well. He sat up and rested his head in his hands... even the cigarette tasted of blood, so he threw it into the fireplace... and rushed up to the bathroom...

Paul Kyso knew that the situation was starting to unravel. He also knew that he had to take back control of the situation, but at the moment nothing came to mind of 'how'.

Anastasia was his biggest problem... he hadn't seen that coming and knew now that he should have doubled her guard and forbade her from leaving the house until all of this had blown over. Of that he was sure, but in the meantime... 'What?'

Two hours ago Alejandro had called a meeting of all senior heads of the company. He had fumed, ranted and raved about the inefficiencies, the incompetence of his security and the downright stupidity of most of the members and railed in despair at the kidnapping of his granddaughter.

"A company as significant, as powerful as The Met Corps has been bested by an 'amateur' and two stupid women." He had torn into them, coming close to threatening all of them with their very existence and standing in the company. "I want that child back here... safely. Or everyone here will suffer the consequences..."

Paul didn't give a damn about the girl personally. His main concern was for the shipment... which fortunately for everyone concerned, had been delayed in the Atlantic due to bad weather and would not now dock until Monday morning. He silently thanked the unknown 'God' that had looked after him all these years. A two-day delay might, at best save his job and at worst... his life.

He had decided to call off the termination order on Webbley Pendelton, without informing Alejandro. It was a huge gamble and one that may well cost him 'everything' if it went wrong, but it was a chance worth taking. He also knew that he had to bring back some 'sanity' to all of this... chaos.

To that end, and as a safeguard for himself, if things turned 'sour' on him, he had instructed his deputy Dick Cordon to handle Adrian Preston, and that no word of it was to be leaked to Alejandro... or they would all find themselves 'swimming' along the bottom of the Thames in a very large pair of concrete boots or concreted into the footings of one of the many Met Corps construction sites around the town.

In the meantime he felt it only prudent to put 'his own house in order'. Just in case nothing else worked. He had instructed his bankers and stock holders to consolidate all of his assets into one portfolio, for easy access and had hired a private jet to be on standby, twenty-four hours a day, at least for the next ten days...

Desperate measures... he thought. But necessary...at this time. He flicked at a smudge of ash that had fallen onto his trousers. If everything goes to plan, then all well and good, he would resume his rightful role as head of security, if not, then he could immediately put the other plan into action, whichever way it went he would be safeguarded.

He wondered about the boy in hospital, who Pendleton had shot, Xavier, possibly dyeing, with a bullet hole in his chest and a badly lacerated throat. The boy's condition was of little concern to him, only the implication perceived by others... that The Met Corps... were suddenly 'vulnerable'.

It was almost five o'clock before Gabriella arrived. He noticed that she made a point of turning the car around so that it faced back down the drive, the way she had entered... He was pleased to see that it was another Range Rover... this time a Vogue. The car suited his temperament.

"Hiya, it's good to see you." He 'pecked' her on the mouth, but she held onto the kiss, wrapping her arms around him.

"And me, I couldn't wait to get away from that awful boat." She kissed him again. "Webbley, this all frightens me so much, so very, very much, everything is going wrong... all our work and planning to take Anastasia and that boy being shot... all for what, nothing."

"Ah, don't worry, nothing's ever for nothing. I should have realised that Alejandro would see right through me... he knew I wouldn't hurt the girl. I hadn't backed on that. Their intelligence service must be pretty good, they knew about my army record. Pretty impressive, I thought." He returned her kiss, the warmth of her body relaxing him. The last four or five hours had pretty well been the only time he had spent alone in the last four days, and he hadn't liked it very much. "Did you get the girl back to her parents?"

She shook her head, a little uncertain of herself... and what his response might be. "No... Kristianna said she would do it." She followed the worry signs on his forehead and touched his cheek. "It's alright, Webb... she wouldn't hurt her... what would be the point now? She gave me her word that within a couple of hours she would have her packed off, back to her parents. She needs to clear all the evidence of our being on the boat. I believed her, Webbley... she's not that stupid. If anything happened to Anastasia, the whole 'Empire' of The Met Corps would come down on us... far worse than it is now, she knows that." But at the back of her mind she wasn't so sure, not at all convinced in her own mind of what she had just said would happen as Kristianna had promised...

There was nothing he could do about it, he knew that. "I wish you had done it though." It wasn't a 'scold', just a thought set into words. "Bugger it anyway, like you said Kristianna isn't stupid enough to harm the girl. Did you manage to bring my clothes, I don't have anything to change into."

She beamed. "Of course, but better than that..." She opened the passenger door and produced a carrier bag... the contents still steaming hot. "I remembered you said your favourite food was Chinese. I've even got sweetcorn and crabmeat soup. If it's gone a little cool we can pop it into the microwave oven for a minute, 'and'..." She popped her hand into the second bag and produced a bottle of Beefeater gin, then opened the bag wider to show him half-a-dozen bottles of Schweppes tonic. "I have a bag of ice in the freezer bag, also..."

"Wow... The perfect woman, now I really do love you..."

It came out suddenly... just as a 'thank you'... not as...

"Do you really, Webbley, really?" Her face lit up with a sparkle as her hand touched his cheek gently. "I felt the same..."

Webb held her head between his hands and kissed her on the mouth and then hugged her long and hard. How could there be 'love', anywhere in the world at this moment. For a second, despair almost overtook him.

"Mmm... let's eat, I'm starving." But he could see by the disappointment on her face that she had wanted her question answered.

Chapter 30

8:30 pm.

For Marcos and Petra de Los Santos it had been the longest day and night of their entire life. In the past their daughter Anastasia 'had' stayed out all night, but only under the strictest supervision in a 'sleepover' at a friend's house or at the house of a close relative. There had been several times she had disobeyed her 'curfew' time of twelve o'clock, but 'this'! They had been given the news at twelve-thirty this morning by Paul Kyso that Anastasia had been taken, and that her bodyguard had been shot. They hadn't slept or rested since the news.

It was now eight thirty in the evening and still no news of her. Kristianna, that 'traitorous woman'… the child they had accepted into their own household after the sudden death of her worthless father… had turned on them like a snake. Paul Kyso had told them she had contacted Alejandro on her own account with a new proposal, but that Alejandsro had turned her down, as he had with the first enquiry… and had demanded more information and proof that Anastasia was still alive, but that Kristianna had refused.

That was many hours ago and nothing had been heard since…

Marcos wrapped his arm tightly around his wife's shoulders as she sobbed. There were no tears left in her... just dry, heartrending sobs, and worry for their daughter... their only child...

They had tried for a child for years but nothing had ever happened. Then late into middle age, when they had completely given up hope of ever having children, it happened... Petra had become pregnant with Anastasia. They were overjoyed, as was all of the family.

There had been times through the pregnancy when Petra and her doctors thought she might lose the child because of her age... fifty-two years old was not the best age to be carrying a baby... so for the last four months of her pregnancy, rather than risk a miscarriage, Petra had to be confined to her bed. With the best medical care and total rest and love from her husband... their beautiful baby was born... four weeks early and with the lung capacity of five grown babies.

Marcos kissed her face and pulled her in closer. "Why doesn't someone call?"

She sobbed, warily looking into his eyes. She ached to be in her bed with her child asleep in the next room. "And that poor boy. Do they know if he will live, yet?"

A knock on the lounge door brought them out of their reverie. "Sir, madam..." The tall butler entered the room, his sadness for them grafted into every wrinkle on his old face. He had known Anastasia from birth from the very second she had been born and looked on her as if she was his own... "There are five packages in the hallway they were delivered by two Chinese people to the front gate." He dusted an imaginary crease on his immaculate sleeve. "Our security people have scanned them and given them the all clear for you to open them. They are all numbered... from one to five... I... I just don't understand. There is a handwritten note with it... in Miss Anastasia's writing..."

"Bring them in, Charles. Please, quickly." Marcos was first to react. "Put them on the table." He took the note and tore it open, instantly recognising the scrawly handwriting of his daughter.

A line of servants brought the parcels in and laid them on the table in front of the fireplace and Charles the butler sorted them in order of number listed on the box, making sure the number one was to the left. Then he ushered the staff from the room and leaned on the closed door.

'Dear Mamma and Papa, just a little surprise for your anniversary. All my love 'A'' The note read.

"Oh dear, that is one date she always remembers… bless her." Petra leaned into her husband as she read the note.

She turned the neatly wrapped box so that the 'number one' was facing her and tore at the wrapping.

"I don't like this at all, dear, perhaps I ought to do it…" He touched his wife's arm, lovingly…

Outside of the lounge door the butler stood 'guard' against the melee of staff crowded into the hallway.

"What is it, Mr. Summersville, something to do with the young Miss Anastasia?" the housekeeper asked, she whispered so that only the butler heard.

"I don't know, Mrs. Wakefield." He whispered back. "But I will be so pleased when all this awful business is over and done with. I'm so worried for the mistress and master…"

The deathly… earsplitting scream from inside the lounge cut his words short as he tore at the door handle…

Though he hadn't seen his mistress cut through the last tape and wrapping paper of the box marked 'Number one', or Anastasia's bloody, severed head roll from the box onto the carpet… He knew the whole of his world as he had known it for five decades had come to a sudden… awful end.

Chapter 30

10:30 pm.

"You watching the T.V., boss?" Sergeant Tracy Gould spoke quickly into the handset, and a lot louder than normal.

Detective Inspector Alan Dowling had been feeding his budgerigars', watching television in the evening was not something he would normally do, not unless there was a David Attenborough wildlife program on or something similar. Television to him was far too close to his own work to be 'entertainment'. He told her he wasn't...

"Anastasia, the girl they kidnapped has been returned to her parents... dead." The crime had been committed out of their jurisdiction, but it 'was' still part of their own investigations into the Webbley Pendleton inquiry. "They've mutilated her... I think we ought to get over there."

"Damn it. What the hell is going on here, it's starting to look like the nineteen-fifties 'turf wars'. Get over there, sergeant, you're closer, I'll be there as soon as I can."

Earlier in the afternoon he had been the first detective on the scene at Adrian Preston's house. Even after all his years on the force... the sight of Adrian Preston bound and gagged and impaled on a billiard cue revolted him. The cue had exited from just below his collarbone, and yet through some miracle, he was still alive... barely but the doctors had said that his injuries were so severe there was little hope of him surviving. 'What manner of human being could carry out such barbarity'?

Kristianna had showered and changed her clothes. The light grey slacks and cream blouse made her look taller. Her bags were already in the car and Sui Lin and her husband had left earlier, she would meet with them again later before going to the West Country. She stepped tentatively around the pools of blood, most of which Sui Lin had mopped into the bilges. It didn't worry her that her sharp, high heels dug into the pristine teak decking as she locked the saloon door behind her and glanced at her watch. There was still fifteen minutes left before the timer ignited the detonator attached to the four large gas bottles... and the ten pounds of plastic explosive she had taped to the sides of the gas bottles. She would have liked it better if she could have sat off at a safe distance to see the effects... but time was already running short.

She waved at the woman on the adjacent yacht as she played with her three children in the cockpit, chasing them around amidst happy shouts and enthusiastic yells...

"Would you like a coffee?" The woman cupped her mouth and called over, smiling, her beautiful softly spoken English accent sounding strangely out of place somehow.

Kristianna pointed at her watch and smiled. "Later, thank you maybe later, but I have to dash."

She smiled to herself as she started her car and drove off, she had done everything she had promised... cleared the yacht of evidence... tidied everything away... there would be no loose ends left, and most of all... packed Anastasia off to her parents...

Chapter 31

10:35 pm.

"Now I feel a little more 'human'." Webb had showered again and put on a fresh clean dressing gown. The smell of blood in his nostrils was almost indiscernible, only when he wasn't concentrating, did it return. "Are you sure we're safe here... who knows about this place?"

"No one, darling... I promise you."

Earlier they had eaten and for a brief moment, managed to relax. It had been one of the most traumatic days of his life and he had seen a side of himself that he didn't know existed and didn't like it very much either. It was a side that put him into the same 'animal' category as Adrian Preston.

"My turn then..." Gabriella touched his hand as he came back into the lounge and hugged him around the waist, feeling excited. "Can I take that awful thing away from you, please?" She touched the holster of the automatic he carried loosely in his hand. "We don't need that now. No one knows we are here..." She eased it away from his reluctant fingers and walked over to the sofa and stuffed it into the corner, covering it with a cushion. "There... now it's out of the way. I absolutely hate those things." She slipped her fingers into the gap of his dressing gown and ran her fingers along his thighs. "Let's do something nice tonight... something special. Mmm. Something... sexual. I loved it last time when you…" She coddled next to him a little embarrassed. "You know… you were very… energetic."

"Out of practice, more like…" He smiled, wrapping his arms around her and kissed her mouth, worried about the growing feelings he was starting to have for her…

"I kind of, didn't get that impression… not at all." She folded herself into his body, returning his affections, hungry for the touch of his lips on hers… wanting to feel him inside her again.

"Go and have your shower… I love it when you're all wet and moist… there." He touched her tummy, his hand slowly moving towards the mass of pubic hairs. "Jesus!"

Gabriella turned her back on him and giggled, her fingers separating his dressing gown… so that she could feel his nakedness, her hands reaching behind her cupping the cheeks of his bottom, pulling him in closer, edging him towards the big sofa. "There is always time for this, darling." She could feel his hardness touching her skin… radiating its heat into her.

Webb lifted her dressing gown above her waist and leaned her slowly over the arm, his hands feeling for her breasts and tummy and then lower… gently seeking her out… knowing that they couldn't stop this now… even if Beth popped her head around the corner and said 'Hiya…'

Chapter 32

Friday morning 10 am:

Webb sipped his coffee as he walked through to the lounge. Last night had relieved him of a lot of stress. Even so, the nightmares of the 'barbarous' act he had committed played heavily on his mind and had woken him several times throughout the night. Waking in a strange place and with a companion by his side that he hardly knew... hadn't helped the situation. To make things worse, Kristianna hadn't turned up at all, even though he hated being around her, but he hated it even more when he couldn't see her... or know where she was... that really worried him, he mistrusted her so much.

The ringing of his mobile disturbed his thoughts... He wondered if this was her now.

"They've let me out, boss, just kept me overnight, they couldn't really hold me on anything." Beth's voice was welcoming.

"Oh, mate... bloody good to hear from you. Are you alright?" He almost spilled his coffee as he tried to put it onto the coffee table. "What happened? God, that's so bloody great."

She briefly explained that the police had taken his family into hospital and placed an armed guard on the door and that the 'boyfriend' was still in intensive care but out of danger. "They knew they couldn't hold me... found traces of gun cordite on my hands but that was just circumstantial, I'd handled that animal's gun... so they had to let me go eventually. Oh, I met that Detective Inspector, Dowling... he seems a decent chap, you know. He's interested in meeting you, I think."

"He's an idiot..." Webb was angry. "I told him to put an armed guard on them, but he obviously didn't take it very serious."

"Christ, Webb, you can hardly blame the poor sod for that. Who puts 'armed guards' around 'ordinary people's houses? This is England..."

"Yeah, I suppose. Anyway where are you?"

"Well, I've had to hire a car. Initially I went back to the boat but it was just a chard, burnt out hull, virtually nothing left of it or most of the boats around it. What a sight... Eight people were killed in the explosion, including three kids, damned awful sight."

"Kristianna?" It was his first thought, hoping that she had been one of the victims.

"Don't know. I didn't stay there too long. There were still cops and firefighters all over the place. They're saying that it was a gas leak." Her voice seemed a little flatter now.

"Christ, it just gets worse, doesn't it?" He scolded his mouth on the coffee. "What do you want to do, Beth, come here or go straight down to Simon's place?"

"No, I need to be with you, man. That's what you pay me for." She felt a touch of excitement at the thought of being with him again, looking after him. Something she hadn't felt for years on any of her 'jobs', and she really liked him, even though there were times when he was totally irrational.

"You sure?"

"Sure I'm sure, boss. Otherwise I have to go back to that big black bugger, don't I."

He gave her the directions and she said she would be there within the hour, or sooner as long as she didn't get lost. "And, boss, don't worry... no one's good enough to follow me there." He shut the mobile down and rolled a cigarette, flicking the top of his Zippo lighter, cowboy style to light it, at least 'something' was going right, at last.

Webb smiled, knowing she was probably right about anyone being able to follow her she was far too good at her job to let that happen. "We'll leave as soon as you get here... and, Beth... thanks again..." He shut the mobile down and rolled a cigarette... flicking the top of the lighter as if it were a toy.

"Who was that?" Gabriella called down from the top of the stairs. She did a little 'pose' for him, slowly opening the top of her dressing gown, flicking her head back... smiling. "Was it Kristianna?"

"No, Beth. She's on her way over." He could see her framed against the light, dressed only in the thin, fine dressing gown she had worn last night. He loved the 'pose', there was something so absolutely sexual in how she held herself. She was one of the most sensual women he had ever met. There was just something about the more 'rounded figure', larger busted woman that appealed so much to him... these women had so much more to offer. "Have I got time for a bath, I could do with it, I'm still full of sperm." She giggled and crooked her knee towards him opening the dressing gown further to her waist. "You could come up and scrub my back and maybe 'fill me up' again." She turned herself in profile, opening the dressing gown... holding it around her back so that he could see 'all' of her. "Mmm. You're not tempted? Or we could just fool around for a bit." She brushed her hands along her tummy and up onto her breasts, lifting each one in turn, seductively. "There's plenty of time before Beth gets here... at least an hour. What do you think... big boy?" She was trying to imitate something she had obviously seen on the television or films.

"Get on with you..." He smiled, feeling himself being aroused already, just with her words, really wanting her now, more than he had wanted her last night. "Get on with you... you little 'devil woman'... you 'temptress'". He teased. "Later... I'm going to pack the cases, if we start anything 'now', Beth's just likely to barge in on us. When we get to Simon's I'll rip your drawers off with my teeth..."

Gabriella giggled...

***

Sue McGillicuddy came back into the dining room and looked over at Steve, worry clearly written all over her face. "I... um, just counted that money, 'lad'." It was her favourite name for him. As big and tough as he was, she knew she had to 'look after him', as she always had. She had hated it when he was in the army, away from her... then she worried... in 'there', she 'couldn't' look after him and there were always nasty people, trying to hurt him. He never talked about any of his missions only that he would be away for one... or two weeks... or longer. Every time she read through a newspaper and saw that a soldier had been killed... she would sit in the kitchen and wait for the knock on the door expecting an officer from The Regiment to tell her he had been killed in action... in some awful far away land. But now... he was 'safe', because he was with her all of the time. She just loved having him around her. "There is over four hundred and fifty thousand in there. I can understand the money for the charter, but that is only thirty-two-thousand for the two weeks and he said about the twenty for us... but, there is just so much more, Steve."

"I know, darlin', he wants me to buy the big Van Dam, but I can't imagine where he got the money from." He touched her hand as she approached and squeezed it. "And that chap yesterday... what was his name?"

"Simon de le Croix. He was in The Regiment as well, with Peter. But Peter said it was okay, didn't he... he's was just here for our protection... against who, lad?" Sue sat down on the arm of the old worn armchair and rested her hand on his shoulder. "From what, Stevie?"

"I don't know old girl." He patted her handed affectionately. Earlier he had dug out his old army automatic and the shotgun, cleaned and greased them, leaving them both charged and tucked away. The automatic in his jacket pocket and the shotgun leaned against the door jamb behind the curtain of the front entrance. "But the next time I see that bogger, he'd better have a bloody good explanation."

***

Friday 12:05 pm.

Webb watched the yellow Ford Fiesta as it turned into the driveway of the cottage, he held the Glock loosely in his right hand until he could clearly make out that it was Beth driving and then tucked it in his belt at the small of his back, beneath the 'bomber jacket'. It had only been about thirty-five minutes since her call.

"Good to see you, mate... I was worried." He hugged her and 'pecked' her on the cheek. "We'll stick your gear in the Range Rover straight off and get away as soon as Gabriella has stopped 'faffing' around... be damned glad to be clear of this whole, soddin' area."

Beth followed him into the cottage, after loading her cases into the Range Rover. "Wow, this is really my dream home." She looked around the room, impressed with the layout and the homely, cottagey style of it. "This would be absolutely perfect for my little riding stables... wow." She closed the door behind her, unconscious that she was still holding onto his arm.

"Hi, Beth…" Gabriella shouted from the landing, still in her dressing gown, still with a towel wrapped around her head. She waved at her, smiling. "I'm just finishing off, be down in a mo…"

"Aren't you ready yet, you little sod?" Webb scolded her lightly, as he dumped his heavy suitcase by the door ready to be loaded into the car. "Come on, gal, let's get out of here."

Beth smiled and made a face, waving, and then turning back to Webb. "We seem to be up against a pretty vicious bunch of buggers here, Webb." She showed her concern. "We'll have to work out how we're going to play this," And almost tripped over his cases.

"I know what you mean, but somehow we just need to stay ahead of them, out think them." He pulled her into him, his hand gently on her neck and kissed her forehead. "Our biggest advantage is that they don't know where we are. Over the next few days we'll see if we can't 'expand' on that". He was as concerned as she was. Simon's place seemed to be a safer option at the moment. "Is that what you've always wanted then, a riding stables?" He needed to change the subject to something more… 'normal'.

Beth nodded. "Yes, one day… maybe." She shrugged her shoulders. "But I'll probably need to go onto another job after this one."

"No, mate. See this through, gal, and I'll sort your riding stables out for you." He touched her shoulder, affectionately.

Beth shrugged her shoulders, non-plussed. "Whatever… We'll see."

A car hooted in the lane and Webb watched the bright red post office van pull into the driveway. "Okay, it's just the postman…"

Beth opened the door as the postman knocked...

"Webbley!!!" Too late, he heard Gabriella scream at him. "We don't have a postman..."

Two shots rang out as the door burst open and huge man dressed in an ill-fitting postman's uniform charged in... Webb heard Beth scream and blood exploded from her back as she fell to the floor in front of him...

Frantically he reached for the Glock but the barrel foresite caught in his belt and stuck fast and felt the big man's gun strike the side of his head as he staggered backwards, dropping to his knee.

"Stay! Stay where you are, boy... stay there." The man screamed at him, the barrel of his gun touching Webb's head. "I'll make another mouth for you if you dus anyfin' stupid." He smiled, showing gritty yellow teeth against his pock marked face. "Just be still now, boy... you don't want me to put a couple in your legs now, do you. I will, and my Christ I'd enjoy it... sure as little apples, mate, I'd really enjoy doin' that. So be still now..."

A shorter, thickset man came in behind the first man and stepped on Beth as she lay moaning on the floor. "Over there..." He motioned towards the sofa. "Sit yer fuckin' arse on that and don't move. Alby... get that 'tart' down here." He nodded at Gabriella, still on the staircase, petrified to move and touched his friend's shoulder, nodding at the terrified Gabriella on the stairs, not taking his eyes from Webb for a second, his gun pointing at Webb's head. He patted Webb down and found the Glock and tucked it into his own belt. "There now... things is a bit safer... ain't they just."

Slowly Webb stood and cautiously moved backwards, his hand cradling the bloody wound on his head, until the backs of his knees touched the sofa. "Can I?" He feigned more pain than he was really in. "Can I check on my friend?" He nodded towards Beth on the floor.

"Sit down!!!" The man smiled and flicked the gun across the side of Webb's head and nodded in the direction of the sofa.

'Alby' strolled over and dragged Gabriella from the stairs, his arm around her waist, his hand inside her open dressing gown, savouring the touch of her breasts and then pushed her in Webb's general direction. Webb held her as they sat his arm around her shoulder. Gabriella hastily pulled the dressing gown closer around her body, covering herself against their stares...

"Jesus! Davey... I can't believe ar' fuckin' luck... can't believe it... Jesus!" He 'jiggled' around in front of Gabriella and Webb, his feet doing a little dance, his fingers lightly holding the pistol, swinging it cockily in front of their faces. "We's gonna be fuckin' rich, mate... richer than yor wildest fuckin' dreams. Man oh man oh man!"

Casually Davey joined his friend to stand in front of his captives, mindful of getting too close to them. "Go and check the house, make sure there's no one else here... and watch yourself."

Alby grinned "No... they're all here. They said two women and 'im... that's all, mate."

"Check anyway..." Davey was clearly in charge. "Christ... you seen the tits on this one here." He extended his gun hand and with the tip of the barrel opened the neck line of Gabriella's dressing gown, but she slapped his hand away. "Feisty little bitch... ain't she, you won't be that bloody feisty when yor swivelin', 'round the end of my dick... that I can tell you." He grabbed a handful of his groin, thrusting it towards her, so excited he just couldn't stand still. "Jeees! I jus' can't believe ar luck, mate, we're bloody 'quids in' for taking this lot'. Bloody 'quids in.' I'm going to ask the boss for that one as part of my bonus." He nodded at Gabriella. "Yeah... you kiddo... I'm going to shag the arse off you... every bloody orifice."

"Don't worry about tits boy." Alby kicked Beth in the ribs as he moved towards the staircase, and she screamed again. "You'll have more 'tits' than you can shake a stick at after this. We'll be fuckin' heroes."

Webb rose quickly, pushing Davey away from Gabriella, but Davey tapped him across the head again with the barrel. "Sit down, you cunt... do that again and yor fuckin' dead."

"You can't kill me, you fucking idiot." Webb shouted at him. "Or you'll never see any of your stuff again." He felt a trickle of blood run into his eye and rubbed at it.

Davey pointed the gun and touched it to Gabriella's head. "This one first then." He smiled. "And then yor fuckin' knees, one at a time, that'll take some of the spunk out of you."

"Alright... alright..." Webb held his hands in front of him. "No problem... just leave her alone, man."

Beth moaned as she lay on the floor, the pain in her shoulder was excruciating. She could feel the fire of shock burning her as the blood drained from her. She lay as still as she could, fending off the panic, delaying the inevitable as long as she could fearing the onset of shock more than the immediate pain, knowing full well that it was the trauma of shock that would kill her faster than the pain. . Slowly she monitored her breathing, biting her lips against the pain. Her brain trying to reason why she had opened the door without first checking... Stupid cow, she thought cursing herself.

Davey backed up to the fireplace and lifted the telephone from the alcove and placed it on the coffee table. His eyes and gun fixed on Webb. Laying the handset to one side he dialled a series of numbers...

"Look... we can make a deal, man," Webb pleaded. "I've got more money in that suitcase than you ever dreamed of... take it... it's yours. There's even more, if you want it."

"Ha... you silly bugger." Davey scoffed. "Have you any idea who you're dealing wiv? We wouldn't get ten miles up the road wiv a deal like that, man. You'll tell them where the money is, don't worry about that. They got ways... they'd skin you alive. Christ, man... I'd give you ten minutes before you was talking like a trained parrot. You'll wish you was dead a thousand times over, before they's dun wiv ya."

Webb looked into Gabriella's eyes, and then down at her partly exposed breasts, his eyes pleading with hers... and gritting his teeth, gave her an almost indiscernible nod of his head... hoping, begging her to understand what he was trying to say. He groaned, leaning into her, nodding his head at the partly exposed butt of the gun behind the cushion, until he felt she understood...

At his left elbow he could feel the hard metal of his .45 behind the cushion. He knew it was still in its holster. He knew also that there was a round in the chamber, he had gotten used to carrying it like that... unsafe, but ready. But the biggest problem was the safety catch... it was 'off' and the gun was on his left and he was right-handed. Somehow, he needed to get to the gun before they had the sense to tie him up, as soon as that happened... they were all as good as dead anyway. The biggest problem of all was that the safety catch was operated by the right thumb... damn. He leaned forward more and moaned deeply, touching the deep cut on his head... pretending extreme pain and gave Gabriella a sideways glance... indicating with his eyes what he wanted from her and she seemed to understand... he needed a 'diversion'... He glanced up at Davey and back to Gabriella, knowing that he needed to do something 'now'... any delay would make it more and more difficult.

He knew it would be an impossible chance... but it would be the 'only' chance he would get... to snatch the gun from under the cushion with his left hand, flick off the safety... somehow, aim and fire... 'and' hit the target in the split second he would have before this man 'Davey' blew his head off...Webb knew he would have a virtually impossible shot. But then what else was there, whichever way he went, he was almost certain to die anyway. The outcome really didn't matter...

"Yes, sir... we got the buggers... yes, sir... they're right in front of me, all three of the buggers." Davey stood, excited, tentatively holding the handset between his shoulder and jaw, hardly able to contain himself, a smile as wide as the moon across his face. He jiggled from one foot to the other, excitedly. "It's a little cottage... one of the one's on the 'closed list'." He gave the address and telephone number.

Webb gave a tiny nod to Gabriella again, praying she understood. A second later Gabriella screamed and tried to stand, her hands in front of her as if she was about to faint and rolled forward, her shoulder bouncing along the edge of the sofa as she fell onto the carpet on her back, her legs open exposing the whole of her frontal, naked body.

"Jeees..." Davey grinned and for a second his eyes left Webb...

It was all the time Webb needed, the metal of the hammer gauged a deep cut into the palm of his hand as he snatched at the automatic, but he didn't feel anything... for an instant he caught a fractional view of Alby at the top of the stairs, but cast it from his mind... 'he' wasn't the 'immediate' threat... Davey was. He felt the solid butt in his hand as he dragged the gun out... cocked the hammer with his right hand and, overreaching the barrel, flicked off the safety catch... and fired once.

Davey seemed to fire at the same time, his bullet struck the cushion on Webb's right. But Webb's bullet had struck his target six inches above the knee and the bullet had gone in at such an acute angle that it had travel halfway up Davey's leg before exiting from the cheek of his right buttock... He screamed in agony as he fell back to the floor, the automatic falling from his hand as he grasped at his leg, blood pouring from the entry and exit wound... but even more from the exit. His mind seemed not to comprehend, his fingers frantically feeling for the now, nonexistent cheek of his right buttock. He picked up a huge piece of flesh and shattered bone, trying to put it back where it had come from and screamed again when it wouldn't fit exactly...

Quickly Webb swapped the automatic to his right hand and knelt on the carpet, taking careful aim over the top of Gabriella. His mind watched Alby struggling to get his automatic from the waistband of his trousers... he smiled, momentarily amused at the sudden role reversal. It was difficult to concentrate with the screaming Davey eight feet to the left of him. But he fired once at Alby. The first round hit the handrail in front of him and ricocheted into Alby's hand and he screamed as a huge, jagged splinter of wood drove itself through his hand and tore into his side. Webb quickly returned to his aim, taking one long, deep breath and then held it while he aimed a second deliberate shot at 'the mass' and fired twice.

He didn't check to see the hit... the screams told him enough as Albi toppled over the balcony and crashed to the floor... and lay still. Webb walked over to Davey and picked up his automatic...

"What were you going to do to me, you cunt?" He spat the words at him, smashing the barrel across his face, enjoying seeing Davey's smashed teeth and the bottom lip torn down to his jaw. "Skin me alive?" He smashed the barrel across his face again and then picked up the handset.

"Are you listening to this... Mr. 'Fuckin' Kyso?" He screamed into the mouth piece. "You're next...You murdering little worm... you despicable bastard, you're next. I'm coming for you next... you fucking lunatic... hide wherever you want, but I'll fucking find you." He raised his own gun to Davey's head and fired twice and then threw the handset at the hearth.

Davey's head seemed to explode as the back of his scalp splattered into the fireplace. It almost looked as if he had decided to 'remove his wig'. Bloody chunks of splintered bones splattered against the white stonework of the fireplace. One of the bullets ricocheted around the hearth and tore into Webb's leg, but he didn't feel anything...

Slowly he walked over to Alby, he had fallen on his shoulder and dislocated his neck and collarbone his right arm was at an odd angle, with the tibia bone of his lower arm protruding through his jaw. Yet... surprisingly, he was still alive. Bubbles of blood gurgled from his broken mouth as he tried to speak... but it just seemed to make the bubbles grow bigger.

"More practice, son..." Webb kicked the bone further through Alby's jaw and scoffed as he leaned over the terrified man. "With more practice you should have had me from up there... perfect position. But you panicked. You're just a punk... a scab with a big gun." He saw Alby's eyes widen, pleading as Webb touched the gun to his head with the barrel and fired once...

Beth looked up from the floor, propping herself on her arm and winked at him. "You're a dangerous bugger to be around, boss." She tried to smile before collapsing to the floor again.

"Gabriella quick, get me some clean linen... sheets or something... quick." He cradled Beth's head on his lap and tore open her shirt. The bullet had entered just above her right breast and had passed right through. He felt around the exit wound. The hole was big and jagged, but he couldn't feel any pieces of bone... just torn, ragged flesh. That was good. But he'd seen wounds like this before and knew how essential it was to get her immediately into proper medical care.

"Boss?" She smiled weakly. "You got to get your life sorted out... it's a bloody mess." And then she passed out.

He felt himself well up and cradled her head, kissing her cheek. "I know, mate... I know, I'm sorry."

Gabriella handed him a polythene package with newly washed sheets inside and he tore it open, ripping the sheets into strips, packing the wound back and front before binding it tightly. "Get the cases into the Range Rover, Gabby... you drive that and follow me, we need to get her to hospital... Now!"

Gabriella leaned into his shoulder and sobbed, her left hand touching the inert Beth, soothing her face. "Oh. Webb... this is just... awful... what can we do... will she be alright?"

He put his arm around her and pecked her on the side of her cheek. "I just need you to hold it together, just for a little while longer. Mmm?" He pulled her into him. "Listen..." He lifted her head. "Listen to me, darling'... we need to get Beth to hospital... now... yeah? One thing at a time, get the cases into my car... I'll take Beth in the hire car and you need to follow me... yeah?"

Beth raised her head a fraction and protested, wincing in pain. "Silly bugger... you can't go near a hospital... can you... they'll... pick you up..." and then flopped her head back into his lap.

"Shush... let me worry about that." He smothered her face. "Look... I'm going to have to hurt you, I'll be as gentle as I can, but I just need to get you into the car."

The journey seemed to take forever and regardless of how carefully he drove, the movement of the car over the bumps tortured every fibre of his body every time Beth groaned. He had laid her across the back seat, but it was a small car and her legs were slightly bent which he knew wasn't the best situation, but the only feasible one.

He turned sharply into the hospital grounds and followed the signs that read A & E. Emergency... and pulled up outside the entrance, as an ambulance, still with flashing blue lights, disgorged the last of its patients. Nurses and other white coated medical staff were ushering patients to and fro, some walking, some in wheelchairs with drip bottles attached.

Webb rushed over to the first male Paramedic crew member of the ambulance and grabbed his arm. "Bring that gurney over here, mate, I've got a woman that's been shot."

At first he seemed not to understand, his female partner in the ambulance popped her head out. "Shot?" She seemed more concerned with the, now, drying blood on Webb's hands and face. "Where?"

Webb almost dragged the Paramedic over to his car, followed by his female companion. "It's bad... real bad." He opened the car door for them.

"Christ, Jacky... get the gurney." The Paramedic spoke rapidly, urging his partner, and then crawled cautiously alongside Beth. "How are we, miss?" He touched her face and lifted the bandage slightly. "Can you tell me what your name is? Look at me... yeah, that's good, we're just going to get you out... just a little pain and then we'll sort you out, dear." He shone the little pen torch in each of her eyes. "Right, let's get you in now." He called over another two assistants and together they managed to get Beth onto the gurney.

Webb bent over Beth and kissed her on the mouth. "You're in good hands now, gal…" He felt his face redden and the tears swell in his eyes. "I'll check on you later."

Beth smiled. "You keep away, boy, or they'll have you in irons."

The Paramedic eased Webb away from the gurney. "You stay there…" He signalled to the security guard at the entrance. "Someone will need to talk to you…" before rushing the gurney through the doors.

Webb slammed the doors to the car shut, leaving the keys in the ignition. The security guard rushed over, his 'walky-talky' pressed to his ear, already out of breath after his short run, and touched Webb on the shoulder. "You'll need to come with me, sir." He struggled around the bulk of his stomach to remove the night stick from its holder on his belt, wheezing heavily…

Webb slowly, without rancour brushed the man's hand from his shoulder and stepped back away from him. "You don't want to arrest me, my friend…" He opened the left breast of his jacket, clearly displaying the big .45 automatic. "Not unless you've got one bigger than that."

He mingled with the melee of nurses and patients and visitors until he was through the main entrance and out of the hospital grounds where he had asked Gabriella to wait. "Let's get the fuck out of here…" he said simply.

He was on his third cigarette before he asked Gabriella to pull over, indicating a small lay-by. It was only then that he realised she was still only wearing her dressing gown. "Did you manage to get any of your clothes in?" It seemed strangely odd, watching her control the big car in bare feet.

"Some…" She sniffled. She had driven for about ten miles. Gabriella lifted the armrest and burst out crying, snuggling into him. "Will she be alright, Webbley, do you think? I'm so ashamed of myself... all of this is our fault, mine and Kristianna's and Daniel."

He nodded, hugging her to him, his arm around her shoulders. "Agh don't take on some much, mate... it's as much my fault as yours, damn it. But yeah, she's strong. I think she'll be alright..." He wasn't sure. "Look, I need to make a couple of calls..."

"You need to get some stitches in that, Webbley." She touched the wound on his head, concerned for him. "Oh, it looks awful." She rummaged through the glove compartment until she found a small medical kit. "Let me see to it."

He rolled another cigarette and lay back whilst she wiped some of the blood away and applied a thin layer of antiseptic and then a plaster. "That'll do, darlin'... I need to make these calls." He kissed her on the cheek, still worried about Beth.

A ladies voice answered, rather curt and precise introducing herself as Mrs. Maud, housekeeper for the de le Croix residence. Webb asked to speak to Simon and after a short delay, he came to the telephone.

Before Webb could speak... "I hope you weren't anything to do with that, Webbly... the girl, I mean..." Simon's voice was flat and angry.

"What girl?"

"Anastasia... she's been murdered..."

"What!!!" He was horrified. In his mind's eye he could still see the face of the beautiful girl... clearly. "How? God damn it! It must have been that bitch Kristianna... I'll kill the fucking cow... Damn!"

"Hum..." Simon stammered for a second. "It couldn't have been her she arrived here late last night. She was as shocked as we were... she..."

"There, how did she get down to you?" He interrupted. "I don't get it... she didn't know where you lived. Did she?"

Gabriella grabbed his arm. "What is it, Webb?" Her voice a little frantic... terrified even.

"She... well... telephone and I gave her the directions." He seemed to falter. "She was very upset. When I queried her she said she had put the girl in a car and telephoned those people to pick up the girl..."

"What is it?" Gabriella's face was full of fear.

"Anastasia's dead..." Webb explained it... briefly.

"No..." She cupped her head in her hands and cried. "Kristianna wouldn't do that..." She sobbed heavily. "She wouldn't... I know she wouldn't, not that... she couldn't."

"If I find she has had anything to do with this, I swear to God, I'll kill her myself," Webb said angrily. He took the directions from Simon and told him they were setting off now. It wasn't until he rang off that he realised he hadn't said anything about Beth being shot. "Damn it. Now I don't want to make the other call..." It was to Detective Inspector Dowling.

Gabriella wiped her eyes. "What a terrible thing we've started off." She rubbed the tissue around her face and sniffled again. "Terrible..." She lowered her seat and sorted through her suitcase, selecting clothes at random, not worrying what she put on really as long as it covered her.

"Sod it, I'd best call Dowling... get it over and done with." He rang the number and Sergeant Gould answered.

"I'll put you through," she said, without a trace of emotion in her voice as she put the handset on 'voice'. "It's Pendleton..."

"Cheeky bugger." Inspector Dowling switched the telephone over to voice, and picked it up. "Dowling."

"I've... just heard... about the girl."

"Really?" His critical voice said of his disbelief.

"Yes... really... for fuck sake." Webb pushed the hair out of his eyes, for a moment forgetting the cut on his head as he knocked the drying scab. "Bugger! It was nothing to do with me... I give you my word, inspector."

"Your word, Mr. Pendleton? Is that worth anything... do you think?" His voice was heavily sarcastic.

"No, probably not." He felt the emotion well up inside again and had a job controlling his voice. "There was a time... when it 'was' worth something."

"What about the chap up the Meon Valley, was that anything to do with you?" Dowling voice was scathing.

"Yes... yes, it was. I... yes... that was me." His voice broke a little, but he controlled it. "I'm not proud of it, not at all, all I could see was my mother... He was the bastard that killed her... and I felt... aggrieved, damn it."

"You are absolutely sure of that? Why didn't you telephone me, instead of handling it yourself? We could have dealt with him..."

"What like you handled looking after my ex and my daughter? Fuck sakes, you must have shit for brains. I told you what we were up against, you stupid bastard, didn't I." He felt spiteful. "You got that copper killed... you, you stupid bastard. I told you to arm him, didn't I?"

For a long time there was silence. "Yes... I underestimated that."

"And very nearly got the rest of my family killed. Fuck sake. Anyway that aside for the minute, we'll deal with that later, how did your findings on the names come out?" He changed the subject... slightly, wanting to get away from 'death' for a second.

"It looks like you were right... at least on the names we have checked," Dowling conceded. "You need to come in, Mr. Pendleton, we need to talk..."

Webb laughed. Not a happy, satisfied laugh but a 'critical, cynical' laugh. "I wouldn't be alive ten minutes after I walked in to the bloody station, talk sense, man. According to these journals, there are people far higher up the chain than you... inspector." He thought for a moment. "I'll tell you what I will do though, I'll meet you... at a place of my choosing and under the strict condition that you come alone and inform no one else... and... I'll bring a copy of the journals with me. What do you think?"

Sergeant Tracy Gould nodded her head, furiously at her boss, to accept...

"I don't like it..." was all he said.

Sergeant Gould switched off the telephone, frantically signalling to him. "Accept it, boss, at least we get to talk to the bastard... find out what makes him 'tick'." She pressed the 'on' switch.

Reluctantly he agreed, on the condition that he could bring his sergeant. "If you kill me, every copper in England will hunt you down," he added.

"You seem to be an honest copper, Dowling, and I haven't seen your name in any of the journals... not that, that seems to mean much, but I'll take you at your word. I'll phone you this evening, around eight..." He drummed his fingers on the dashboard. "By the way, have you got someone in customs that you can trust?"

"Of course, why?"

Webb gave him all the details he knew of the shipment, the name of the boat, location and docking details. "Oh, and, inspector, you might want to send someone around to a little cottage here, there's another two bodies... and they 'are' my work..." Webb told Dowling that he would call as soon as he had made the arrangements on where they could meet.

***

"We'd better go armed, boss." Tracy Gould opened her draw and produced a Smith and Weston, 9mm automatic and a shoulder holster. She removed her jacket and slipped her arms through the straps of the shoulder holster and then checked that her three ammunition clips were fully charged. "In fact, from now on, I'm not going anywhere without it."

"I can't carry a gun for goodness sakes, I haven't been rated in years. It would be illegal." He puffed.

"I don't think anyone would complain about your 'legality' if you killed a bastard like this, boss." Over the years, she had made sure that her firearms rating was always at A1 Plus, visiting the firing range at least twice a week, sometimes more. If she ever became bored at home she would go to the ranges in the evenings on a very regular basis.

"I'm confused…" He removed his spectacles and laid them carefully on the desk and then massaged his face in his hands. The huge 'china-graph' board on the wall was covered in names, dates and places, times of incident and locations. At the top of the board, written in large capitals were the words 'Met Corps'. "He couldn't possibly have been in all of those locations at the same time." Dowling scribbled a few notes. "He admits to the murder of this chap Preston… an admission that could get him, what, thirty years… minimum? And yet seemed genuinely disgusted at the murder of the girl… now he 'says' he has another two, that 'he's' killed… there's too much of an anomaly here… something doesn't quite fit. Unless of course he's telling the truth…"

"The location he gave us is only about twenty-five miles from here. I'll get some back-up organised." She seemed not to have heard him, liking the excitement. Even though they hadn't been given the exact meeting place, she could easily have back-up waiting within a stone's throw of it. Unlike her 'boss', she was glad she had kept her firearms rating up.

"Jesus, how much longer?" Webb complained. They had been driving for almost three and a half hours and had gotten lost in the foothills of the Brecon Beacons. At Senybridges they had, had to 'concede defeat' and phone Simon, who told them to stay where they were and he would come out to them. For the last thirty minutes they had been following his tail lights, driving through bleak, high mountain ranges with streams cascading down the sides. In the fading light the peaks looked stunning. Startled sheep with long, wrangy, uncut tails rushed across the road, in front of the headlights, and then dashed off to the relative safety of the hills. Occasionally a ray of moonlight broke through the cloud cover, almost making it seem like daylight, as if an unforeseen giant held a huge torch aloft for them.

Conversation had been limited each with their own, very individual thoughts and recriminations. For part of the way Gabriella had slept and he was glad about that, she looked exhausted and he needed the time to think things through, anyway.

He watched as Simon indicated a right turn and pulled off of the road onto a hard shoulder of the tiny mountain road they had been on for so long, and got out of the car.

"I just wanted to show you this," he said as Webb joined him for an explanation. "That's Hartness House... my home."

Webb looked at the massive, grey stone 'ugly' castle in the valley, illuminated by the moonlight, for a moment, struck dumb by the size of it. It's huge, medieval, pointed turrets seemed to disappear into the clouds. Most of it was hidden by the shadows of the valleys beyond, but even the valleys couldn't hide the enormity of it.

"Good God, why do they call it a 'house'?"

Simon laughed, proudly. "It's a very typical British 'understatement' really." He slapped Webb lightly on the back. "Your 'forebears' built this about five hundred years ago to keep us out of England, but it all backfired when we took it from you at the battle of Senny in 1640 , albeit by treachery, but we wouldn't let you have it back."

"No wonder you smiled when I asked you if you had enough room for all of us." But his mind was too preoccupied on other things to be able to concentrate on 'fripperys' like this

The smile left Simon's face, replaced by a strange, deep, melancholy gaze. "I love this place like most men would love their most ardent woman. That is probably difficult for you to understand and for me, sometimes, it will remain a ball and chain around my neck until the day I die, and then the debt will be passed on to my children. But it is a passion that I cannot rid from my blood, no matter how hard I try, or how far I am away from it, it pulls me back... and will do so until my last breath.

"Where's Kristianna?" Webb asked, the second they stepped into the entrance hallway. He hadn't even noticed the grandeur. Or the beautifully, hand carved staircase or even the complicated construction of the massive, oak ceiling beams, if the situation had been different he would have 'drooled' over the fine timberwork.

"I'm not sure, probably in her room." He pointed casually towards the long balcony above the staircase.

Webb was already taking them three at a time as he charged up the staircase...

"It's the large stateroom... the one with the head of a lion carved over the headstone." Simon shouted after him, and then to Gabriella... "I think we had better go up and follow him, I'm afraid he may well hurt her."

Webb charged into the room like a raging, angry bull, Kristianna was seated at the small dressing table brushing her hair, a towel around her head and dressed only in a thin, fine white dressing gown.

She smiled as he rushed into the room towards her so she stood to greet him. His anger was quite evident. Stupid man, she thought. So many years ago her father had taught her the basics of 'close combat', but she had expanded the 'basics' to such a degree that she was listed as a Second Dan with the federation of combat sports of South Africa. 'Never, never be angry when you fight. Calculate your opponent's weaknesses, but most of all his strengths,' he had told her. 'Breath slowly and deeply to pump the oxygen to the brain... and be relaxed, but most of all... choose your ground.'

A smile touched her eyes as she stood away from the stool, her right leg trailing behind her to give her balance for her own attack. She checked her breathing and lowered her arms, her fists relaxed, waiting to spring into action. "Darling, your head..." She held her most disarming, worried expression, not reacting to his attack, allowing his hand to throttle her throat. He almost lifted her from her feet, dragging her across the room and threw her onto the bed.

He knelt by her side, his hand returning to her throat, fingers and thumb digging into her larynx. "Did you have anything to do with that girl's death... you fuckin' bitch?" He tightened his grip.

Kristianna coughed, unable to speak. Her dressing gown had been torn open and she lay naked under him. Painfully she shook her head, her hands resting lightly on his hand around her throat. Behind her eyes she smiled again, even now she could kill him... easily. The whole of his side... his delicate kidney area was open to a powerful, destructive strike from her knee, or her hand. It would break most of his ribs and before he could 'recover', she would deal a 'death blow' to his throat. She forced the blood pressure into her face and the tear glands in her eyes to explode... and relaxed herself. This time she would let him live... she still needed him... for now.

"Webbley... Webbley." Simon forced Webb's hands open and held him back from Kristianna as she rolled onto the floor, gasping for breath, coughing, rubbing her throat. "You'll kill her. Leave her... for God's sake man, what's the matter with you?" He held him away from her whilst Gabriella helped her sister back onto the bed, still coughing violently, her hands massaging the bruising around her neck and throat.

"I..." Kristianna coughed again to clear her airways. "I told Simon... I left her tied in my car for... Paul Kyso to collect." She made no attempt to cover her nakedness, loving the sympathetic look from Simon and his eyes wandering across her body, 'ravaging her'. Gabriella handed her a glass of water and she drank a little. "He has... his own agendas." She forced the tears into her eyes again and leaned on her sister, weeping. "She was... my cousin... I thought she was a bitch, but I couldn't hurt her... I couldn't... I couldn't."

Simon took Webb's arm. "Come on, man, down stairs... you're overwrought. Leave her, please."

***

It was three, or maybe four large gin and tonics later, he couldn't remember before he had calmed down. "Maybe I 'was' wrong about her," he conceded. "It's just that she's such a... calculating bitch. I wouldn't want to trust her as far as I could throw her."

Simon nodded. "I know what you mean, old chap." He sipped at his whiskey. They were in what he called 'the den', a 'small' room about thirty feet square that he used as his office and 'retreat'. The only entrance was a small doorway, hidden beneath the staircase, and two large windows that looked out onto the rear vegetable gardens, sent shafts of natural light around the room. Heating in the winter was provided by an oversized Inglenook fireplace. "But I consider myself to be a jolly good judge of character and to me she seemed to be telling the truth. Anyway, women don't generally do stuff like that... not decapitation... one has to be pretty twisted to do that. Mmm?"

"I didn't know about that... the decapitation thing..." Webb shuddered at the thought of that pretty body being... "Christ, what a bloody mess." He looked at his two suitcases and his briefcase piled by the door and wondered over to them, opening the briefcase. "Do you know anything about these?" He handed a bearer bond to Simon.

"Good God! It has the user certificate with it. You can't just carry this around in your pocket like that, Webbley. With these two pieces of paper together, any 'Tom, Dick or Harriet' could exchange them for cash, anywhere in the world." He was stunned at the stupidity, but didn't say so. "They must be kept separate, it's like carrying a..." He looked at the value of the bond, boldly printed across the front. "My Lord, this one is for almost two million pounds, sterling." He flopped back into his armchair, flabbergasted. "It's like walking around with a two million pound bank note, Webb... guaranteed by the bank of England."

"If she dropped the girl off and left her in her own car, how did she get down here?" His mind was back on Kristianna still working on the assumption that Kristianna had, had something to do with the girl's death.

"Mmm. Don't know..." Simon handed the bearer bond back, his mind elsewhere. 'For that amount of money I could almost finish the renovation of the roof.' He thought.

Webb looked at his watch, twenty past eight. "Fuck... I should have phoned that copper." He rushed over to his briefcase and removed the mobile.

"Ah, sorry, old chap, there's no mobile coverage here, were sort of out in the sticks. If you go to the top of the rise, where I showed you the house, sometimes it's okay there." Simon seemed concerned.

"Bugger..." It threw him a little. "Could I use your main line phone? If I keep it short, they won't be able to trace it... hopefully."

"Inspector Dowling, I'm going to make this really quick. I'll meet with you tomorrow at one o'clock, in the Belmont..." He gave him the location and directions. The Belmont was the pub he had taken Kristianna and Gabriella on their first meeting. It was the only place he could think of that he knew well enough and knew the layout. "I'll bring the journals with me. I still have your word, inspector, that you won't set a trap for me?"

Inspector Dowling affirmed his word. "This is the only time, Mr. Pendleton... the only time, after this, as far I'm concerned you will be a fugitive."

***

In the loft above her bedroom, Kristianna removed the wire taps from the telephone cable wire and tucked them neatly back into the custom-made box and then closed the top. Earlier she had 'begged off' from Gabriella's company with the excuse that her throat was paining her and she needed to sleep... no one would check on her.

Before opening the door to the loft, she slipped out of the neat paper overalls and removed her latex gloves and tucked them into the tiny alcove at the side of the eaves and made sure that she was alone as she slipped downstairs, back to her own room. 'Tomorrow would be interesting', whatever happens she couldn't allow the journals to fall into the hands of the police. In a way they were much more valuable than the money, they held the absolute power of

The Met Corps and had been compiled over a great number of years.

"Let's get pissed…" For the first time in a week Webb felt safe. "This time last week I was just an ordinary 'chippy', without any of this crap going on." He explained the circumstances, deleting what he felt wasn't necessary.

"It's sort of like winner the pools but in reverse, isn't it?" Simon refilled his glass and then did the same for Webb.

"How much is all this going to cost you then?" Webb waved his arm. "The 'house' I mean."

"In total?" Simon's brow wrinkled. "The quotation for the roof alone comes to around four million, mainly because of the dry rot and the death watch beetle and of course the work has to be done by absolute professionals such as Renta-Kill, or the Richard Starling Corporation. It most certainly can't be done by amateurs or we would be doing it all again in a few years. For the whole house, probably in the region of fifteen to sixteen million…" The figures frightened him just the thought of finding all that money scared the living daylights of him. "Hum, as I said, it will never paid off in my lifetime…"

"That's some commitment, man." He admired Simon for the effort and the commitment and dedication to something as large as this project. "You ever thought of just walking away from it all?"

Simon laughed. "All the time, but I know I never could. We do everything possible to raise money for the restoration of course, it helps but it's never enough. Tomorrow we have a banquet for about three hundred, medieval dress etc; all the 'trash' from all over will be in here… gorging themselves. That will raise about sixty thousand, but it only ever goes into 'maintenance', rarely on renovation. If we don't fix the roof completely, then everything we do below it gets ruined again."

"Christ what a task… maybe I could help out a bit. Start a trust or something." It wasn't 'his' money, did it really matter what he did with it. Kristianna had said there was the equivalent of six hundred million pounds, what would it matter if ten or twelve million got siphoned off… at least it was for a good cause. He handed the bearer bond and the 'user certificate' over to Simon. "Stick that in the kitty…"

Simon's mouth fell open. "Really… do you mean that?" His hands shook as he took the document. His eyes watching Webb's, frightened that he was only joking and that he would snatch it back.

Webb shrugged his shoulders. "At least it's going to a good cause… I'll sort you out some more when I can get the rest of my stuff down here…"

Chapter 32

Friday:

"I don't like this governor, not at all." Sergeant Gould spoke quickly, as she always did when she was nervous. "We need backup if we're seeing this bugger. I don't care what you told him…"

"I do, I gave him my word." Alan Dowling looked over the rim of his spectacles at her. "I get this really bad itching at the back of my neck when I feel someone is lying to me you know… and for some reason, I'm tending to believe Pendleton."

"I still think it's too risky." She interrupted him again.

"I know, but even if half of what he is saying is true, then there are a lot of rotten 'coppers' about and we somehow or other, need to route them out." Dowling scratched his chin, anxiously. "Damn it, I know some of these people. I've socialised with them as friends, met their kids and spent pleasant evenings in their company. I just hope it's all just an awful mistake, or something."

"What about our appointment with the commissioner, do we tell him?" She worried constantly about her boss and hated the thought of him 'sticking his hand out', maybe just to get it chopped off.

"Not until I'm absolutely sure of my facts, I'm too close to retirement to make a cock-up of my career now."

Earlier they had made an urgent appointment with Roger Harrington, the Chief Constable for Hampshire. The appointment was for two-thirty, it would be tight after his meeting with Pendleton, but 'doable', as long as nothing went wrong... and as long as Roger Harrington's name didn't appear in any of the journals... that's what he had to verify more than anything else. If it did... where would he turn to then? He wondered how any of this could have happened, and to so many. Pendleton had said there were at least several hundred names on the list. "Damn..." He mumbled under his breath. The 'average British copper' was admired throughout the world for its integrity, reliability and above all... its honesty. How would all this look?

"Bad business if the Daily's get hold of this before we sort it out, even a 'snip-it'. There'll be all hell to pay." Inspector Dowling always worried too much... or not enough. "What are your thoughts on it?"

"It's beyond me, sir." She leaned further back in her chair, her hands behind her head. "I just find it as incredible as you. I suppose there has always been 'bent coppers', but like you I would never have imagined it on such a large scale... and 'high rankers', too."

A tiny finger of panic touched Kristianna as she drove steadily down the main street of Winchester. The big white Mercedes she was following for the last hour had turned right into Main Street, across the traffic and had stopped outside a block of modern styled office buildings. She made the turn and pulled up a hundred yards in front of them. Through her rearview mirror she watched Paul Kyso and his two bodyguards leave the car. The bodyguards stayed with the car chatting to the driver still at the wheel with the engine running, as Paul entered the building.

She had left Hartness House at three-thirty this morning but was already running late, whatever happened she needed to be in position for Webbley Pendleton's meeting with the police inspector, in good time.

She looked again through the rearview mirror, nothing had changed. Somehow she needed to get to the front of the office block to find out what Kyso was doing here. Checking her watch she knew time would be tight before Pendleton's meeting with the inspector, the drive would take her almost an hour.

Kyso, she had decided would have to be eliminated, he was far too influential in The Corps to be left alive, as soon as she convinced Webbley Pendleton that her 'new' plan would work. She touched her sore throat and eased the bandage Gabriella had given her. Without looking around her, she left the car and pulled the head scarf closer to her face, tucking it into the collar of her jacket, it would hide her distinctive blonde hair also, men had a habit of looking at blondes more than any other colour of hair and all of Kyso's guards were men, some even knew her. The risk she was taking was great and could result in her capture, or even worse, but she knew it was a risk worth taking.

Kristianna edged her way through the shoppers and traders as she walked back up the street, until she was opposite the office block… the brass name plate read, 'J.P. Darling-Stockbrokers'. She made a mental note to get Mr. Tanner to check it out. It made no sense to her that Kyso would be visiting his stockbrokers in the middle of this massive crisis… unless of course, he was about to 'run'. 'But why would he do that?'

In the offices of J.P. Darling Paul Kyso was tense. "This is very radical, Paul, and certainly not the best time to sell... are you sure you want to?" David Manner's voice was precise, and softly spoken, as always he was never taken up with wasteful 'emotion' or 'sentiment', just purely business. He had been the senior partner of J.P. Darling Stock's Division for almost fifteen years, his specialty was in handling commercial investment and short sell bonds. When Paul had first telephoned, late yesterday instructing him to consolidate all his investments and holdings, and that the consolidation was to be immediate... he was not a little confused and very perturbed, fearing the accusation of 'insider trading'. 'Why would a client as influential as Paul Kyso want to sell everything he owned, especially now as the market was on the rise?' Paul had been one of his most ardent, prudent and productive investors in his portfolio to date.

"I know..." Paul fidgeted in his seat, wanting their meeting to be over and done with as quickly as possible. He was seated in front of David Manner's huge, 'U' shaped desk. "Of course this must stay absolutely confidential, you understand that David, don't you?"

"That goes without question, of course and I won't ask the reasons, why you want to convert all of your holdings to cash. Although, I must say it intrigues me but I can only advise you, as I always have. I know it must be pretty serious. This kind of 'quick sell' is bad for the markets as well as for the individual. Brokers don't like uncertainty. Such a shame, you'll be down by..." He fanned through the paperwork. "Probably as much as twenty-five percent..." He walked across to the wide, vertical blind and 'twiddled' the cord holder allowing more light to enter the room.

Paul winced. "Can't be helped..." If everything went to plan and he was able to stay on with The Met Corps, he could make up for the loss.

Now that David had tilted the blinds he could clearly see into the street below, it had always been his 'window into the world outside'. "Good Lord, isn't that Kristianna Van Ouden... there?"

Paul was out of his seat in a rush, roughly thrusting the blinds to one side. "Kristianna... where?" He pushed David to one side. "I can't see her..."

"There... in the black coat and white, flowered head scarf. I would know her anywhere." He smiled, pointing his finger towards the alleyway, opposite. There had been a time when he had been 'close' to her and a brief 'affair' had taken place. He remembered the perfection of her body and that he had never touched skin as soft. "Who wouldn't?" He felt the emotions arousing his body just thinking about their short time together. "You see her?"

Paul followed his pointing finger. "Yes, damn it... He glanced at his car, both of his men were standing by the driver's door, smoking... chatting to the driver, oblivious of anything else around them. Guiamo was even facing in Kristianna's direction. "Damn them... get the blasted paperwork sorted out now, I'll be back in a moment!" He cursed as he charged from the office and down the stairs, flinging the front doors open.

At the entrance to the office complex, he took the stairs two at a time, startling his men. "You Goddamned idiots." He gasped in mouthfuls of air, his body badly out of condition for any kind of exertion. He grabbed Guiamo by the collar and spun him around. Guiamo was the closest to him. "Kristianna..." He puffed again, his lungs unable to cope. "There..." He pointed at the empty alleyway. Shielding his eyes from the glare of the sun, he scanned down the road and spotted the head scarf and a tiny wisp of blonde hair. "There..." He threw Guiamo in the direction of the head scarf.

Both men saw her, almost at the same time and took off after her...

"One of you, damn it… one of you." Paul screamed after them. "Idiots, Goddamned idiots."

Tomo, the big Mexican stopped in his tracks and returned to the car, whist Guiamo charged off down the street in pursuit of Kristianna.

"I pay you idiot's top buck…" Paul leaned on the car wheezing, out of breadth, his American accent always stronger when he was angry. "Because you're supposed to be the best…" He pushed Tomo in towards the car. "Damn well act as if you 'are' the best."

A short time later, Guiamo returned, he was breathing steadily. "Sorry, Mr Kyso… I lost her." He looked embarrassed and felt distinctly awkward.

"Probably for the best." Paul had regained some of his composure. "She would have probably killed you with her bare hands." He spat the words at him, venomously and then without looking at either man, walked up the steps. "Try not to fall asleep, I'll be ten minutes."

Chapter 33

They were already two and a half hours into the return trip to the public house for the meeting with Inspector Dowling. Webb still had some trepidations about the outcome, or whether he was just walking into a trap. He knew he had so much he could offer the inspector, but doubted whether the inspector would have the authority to authorise what he wanted. To be allowed to leave the country, unfettered… Bugger it, it's worth a try, he thought.

"And with the money you kindly donated, Webb, we could get the contracts started for the roof straight away." Simon was excited.

For the past two and something hours Webb had 'endured' Simons ranting's about that 'damned', Hartness House. "Simon… mate!" He wanted to put it 'diplomatically, holding back his anger but found it 'difficult.' "I need to concentrate on the job in hand, and so do you…"

"Good Lord…I'm sorry…I'm so very sorry." He looked mortified, briefly taking his eyes' from the road. "I'm so sorry…sometimes I don't know I'm doing it, like then…sorry old chap."

Webb smiled. "It must be wonderful to have something in your life that you are so passionate about, but at this moment we need to be thinking of the job in hand."

Simon apologised again...

"It's good about Beth though, aye?" He quickly changed the subject. Early this morning he had telephoned the hospital, telling them that he was her brother. They had informed him that Beth, although still in intensive care was out of danger and should make a full recovery in time and that the operation had gone well. "She's one of the most genuine people... and the nicest, I've ever met... I'd really hate anything to have happened to her." There was compassion in Simon's voice... and something else too.

"She said the same about you... mate." Webb smiled, wondering if at one time in the past the two of them had more to their relationship than just a 'professional' association.

Simon flushed a little. "Oh...?" He fidgeted in his seat, needing to change the subject. "Did you want to come to the banquet tonight, Webbley, although I'm not sure if it's your 'thing'?"

Webb thanked him, but declined his offer. He just wished for a little peace at the moment, rather than the constant, banter.

"I've um... invited a couple of people over that you really ought to meet, they're not part of the banquet, you understand." He glanced across at Webbley for a second. "Bankers... commercial, mainly, but if you have any um... 'cash' that you um, need to 'filter away'." He hedged around it gently. "They can set you up legitimate bank accounts in any currency you wish and in almost any country... might be of interest to you... hum?"

It irritated him but sounded intriguing. Bastard gentry, he thought. They can get away with things the 'ordinary man in the street' would get hung for. "Mmm, set it up let's see what they can come up with."

"They 'normally' charge about twenty pence in the pound. But they 'guarantee', legitimacy."

They arrived at the pub thirty minutes early and he felt good about that. The rain had started again and it definitely felt a little cooler, typical early autumn, unpredictable and changeable, feeling almost like the middle of January. He directed Simon to a spot close to the pub and asked him to turn the car around, just in case they needed to leave in a hurry. The car park was quite full and the pub bustling. "Worst damn day of the week to go anywhere." He complained. "Every man and his damn dog will be in there today…" He shrugged his shoulders, wishing he was somewhere else, there was nothing he could do about it now…

"We have a separate suit for you, sir, as you asked." The pretty waitress who had served him on the two previous occasions, took his arm and led him through the crowds of people. "I'll take your order if you like and bring it back through. You don't need to get back into that crush." She smiled sweetly.

Webb thanked her and followed her through. The room was quite large and was dominated by a huge, long central table dressed with an embroidered table cloth and a huge boquet of flowers in the centre and a dozen or so chairs as if it was to be used as a boardroom or conference room. . To one side was a sealed jug of water and several glasses, other than that, the room was quite sparse.

"I know it's a little early but I need a very large gin and tonic with plenty of ice." He saw Simon frown but didn't really care. He needed something to take away the shaking in his hands and relieve the 'jitters' in his belly. He paid her the two hundred for the room and pressed another three fifties into her hand. "That's for you, just look after me 'til we leave. Please. I've told my guests to ask at the bar, if you would be kind enough to bring them in when they come I would appreciate that very much."

It seemed to be the longest thirty minutes he had ever waited. Sipping his drink it tasted a little 'rank' and put it down to the earliness of the day to be drinking, not really wanting it now. Standing by the window he could still see all the way up the road and most of the car park, almost full now, he hoped the cars wouldn't block him in, that really would give him a problem... and the rain was steadily getting heavier. "Miserable blood weather, it's blowing 'ten bastards' out there," he moaned.

Simon answered the knock on the door, pulling his headscarf closer to his face so that only his eyes were now visible. Webb thought that he looked like an Arab terrorist.

"Your guests are her, sir." The pretty waitress smiled as she ushered them in and seemed seriously perturbed by Simon's 'headdress'.

Webb felt his stomach turn over as the inspector and his sergeant entered so he stayed at the far end of the table, not wanting to get too close to them, 'or' shake their hands, fearing they might identify him as the 'fraud' he really was...

"I'll need to search you, inspector. Are you 'carrying'?" He leaned forwards onto the table trying to still the shaking in his hands.

"No need to..." The inspector slowly opened his coat and nodded. Simon removed the old, army service revolver from the inspector's shoulder holster and laid it on the table and then searched him thoroughly...

"You, miss?"

Sergeant Tracy Gould removed her own 9mm automatic, slowly with her left hand, pushing Simon to one side as she did so and placed the gun next to the inspector's, saying nothing.

Webb nodded at Simon to search her, but she backed away. "This doesn't go any further if you don't allow him to search you, miss. Clear?"

"Sergeant..." Alan Dowling scolded her.

Reluctantly she allowed Simon to approach her. He traced her shoulders and under her arms and then between her very large breasts... and then ripped the front of her shirt open to reveal another 9mm automatic in its harness strapped between the cleavage.

"Naughty girl..." Webb teased her.

A further search between her legs and buttocks revealed nothing else. "That's all, boss." Simon walked over to the door and stood with his back to it, his arms loosely at his sides.

"A revolver, inspector?" Webb frowned at the inspector's revolver. It looked like a relic from the Second World War. "Unusual..."

"Before this, when would I ever need a gun?" He shrugged and then removing his old, battered trilby, placed it on the table and then sat in the last chair, at the very end of the table. "I think this is probably only the second time in thirty years I have carried one, and anyway, revolvers are far more efficient, they are far more reliable, and they don't jam. Do I get the same courtesy?"

Webb nodded and laid his .45 on the table and then approached Inspector Dowling sitting two seats away from him. "I've taken photocopies of some of the more relevant items in both journals, inspector." He placed the briefcase on the table and took out a sheath of papers. "I'll hang on to the originals for now but most of the 'relevant' names are there, there are plenty of others but I haven't printed them out yet. Those are what I consider to be the most prominent, most important ones."

Dowling scanned through the photocopies, occasionally going back to a page he had already read, and then, tapping them all into a neat, tidy pile, folded them once in half and tucked them into the inside pocket of his raincoat. "For the sake of my own profession, I hope these 'are' fabrications."

"How did the others check out?"

"Not good, for us... that is." Dowling frowned, feeling distinctly uncomfortable. "Can we get down to the reasons we are here, Mr. Pendleton? I would like to conclude as soon as possible." He leaned back in the chair and took out his pipe. "Do you mind?"

"Not at all, I'll join you..." He had already rolled half-a-dozen or so cigarettes on the way up and lit one. "I'm going to tell you how all of this mess began right from the start... whether you believe me or not doesn't matter, I don't really care, that's up to you."

Webb ran through the events of the past few days from the beginning, telling the inspector everything as it happened... everything, including the six suitcases, but not divulging the contents, considering that with Simon present it wouldn't be wise. "Initially I was quite happy to return everything and go on my way. I had agreed with them that I would keep the contents of the briefcase, as a sort of 'finders fee', there was probably about a hundred grand in it, well I'd guess there was about a hundred grand in there, more than enough for my needs... but then of course it all went to 'rat-shit', as soon as they started killing my family... that bit I couldn't really understand at all. So... as far as I'm concerned... they get nothing back, and if they want a war... then I'll oblige them with a war."

"It sounds like a work of pure fiction to me, Mr. Pendleton." Inspector Dowling puffed a cloud of dark blue smoke into the air.

Webb felt angry. "Well, like I said, I really don't give a fuck whether you believe it or not, inspector." He shrugged his shoulders. "And anyway, look at it all from this perspective... who in their right mind would make up a stupid story as bizarre as that? I could have thought of something far less complicated if I had wanted to bullshit you."

"So... what is it you want from me?"

"I want immunity from prosecution... and an unhindered safe passage out of the country, for myself and anyone that has been involved with me on this. I'm leaving the country soon anyway, so it won't really matter to you, one way or the other." Webb softened his tone.

Inspector Dowling smiled thinly, shaking his head. "No..." he said, simply. "Not a chance in hell. You are a self-confessed murderer, of at least four people that we know of... possibly more, who knows but you, it's ridiculous... you want me to just let you walk away from all of this?" He shrugged and drew again on the old pipe. "What I will do for you, however, is take you into 'protective custody' and promise you that you will be given an absolutely fair trial in front of a jury, of your peers. That is the best I can offer."

"Fuck sake!" Webb stood and walked back to the end of the table where he had left his automatic, picked it up and re-holstered it. "You still don't get it, do you, inspector. Look in the fucking journals, who in that lot could you trust... or even in your own teams. What bloody 'protective custody', from whom?" He nodded to Simon. "You made a complete fuck-up of looking after my family, how in God's name are you going to look after me and my people?"

"I promised you nothing when we arranged this meeting, Mr. Pendleton... it's the best I can do."

"Be reasonable... for God's sake, man. What's up with you, how can I let you take me in? I wouldn't last a day in custody, you must know that. I was thrust into this situation, anyone I killed was in self-defence... and anyway... they were bloody 'vermin', all of them."

"And the courts will decide whether that is the case… or not." he said, stubbornly.

"Bullshit. It's a great pity your fellow officers don't hold the same views and values on honesty and integrity that you seem to hold, inspector." He raised his voice, in frustration, more than he'd wanted to. "Then perhaps none of this would have happened in the first place, don't you think?"

Dowling stood, pushing the chair away from him with the backs of his knees. "I'm a policeman." He was angry at the accusation. "I can't agree with this, you know I can't. I would be as bad as these people." He tapped his breast pocket where he had put the lists.

"Then who can?" Webb knew he wasn't getting anywhere. "What about someone higher than you, someone you know you can trust? Can't we at least take that route?"

Dowling shook his head. "No one in legal authority would agree to this arrangement. They couldn't."

"We could…" Sergeant Gould started to speak, but Inspector Dowling raised his hand, stopping her.

"What were you going to say, sergeant?" Webb watched her eyes.

"Nothing…nothing." She answered him, curtly and turned away from his withering stare, feeling that she had 'betrayed' her boss.

"Well…" Webb zipped his bomber jacket halfway. "I think that's about all we can progress too then…" He pointed to the weapons on the table. "Take them, I still have your word, inspector… you go first, please. You can keep the journals, think of it as a 'freebie' on me. Oh, what about the drug ship, or did that get cocked up as well?"

"No… I passed on the information, apparently the ship is delayed through bad weather. It's due in on Monday now."

"Are you sure, or has one of your 'honest contacts', given them the jolly old 'tip-off' again?" he said, acidly.

At the front entrance to the pub, Simon opened the door for the inspector and his sergeant, allowing them to lead the way. Simon's 'headdress' had turned a few heads as they left the pub to escorted Inspector Dowling to his car.

The rain had stopped now, leaving huge puddles of water around the car park so that they had to negotiate their way around them.

"I'm sorry I couldn't do more, Mr. Pendleton." Dowling nodded. He looked genuinely sorry. Taking the copies of the documents from his pocket he tapped them in his hand. "One thing I will promise you is that these will be thoroughly investigated."

Webb shrugged his shoulders, hardly caring any more... but his eyes were focused on the white Mercedes parked across the entrance to the pub car park, forty yards away. He felt a tingle along his spine as three men exited the car, two staying with the car as the third approached them. Webb signalled to Simon with his eyes, who moved to the back of the inspector's car.

The man came to within twenty feet, his attention only on Webb, seemingly unaware of the others, but his eyes were conscious of them. He was slightly built, but as tall as Webb, and dressed in an immaculate grey suit. He walked and held himself in such a way that Webb knew immediately what he represented. His steps and body language controlled and precise and calculated...

"Mr. Pendleton..." He spoke slowly with a slight 'North Country' accent and his words were directed only at Webb, never taking his eyes from him. He held his hands relaxed, balled loosely in front of him... balanced. "Mr. Kyso would like a word with you... sir."

Webb eased the zip of his jacket and rested his thumb inside the opening, watching the man in front of him and the bulge under the right armpit. "You see what I mean, inspector, what's your answer to that?"

The inspector seemed completely oblivious and initially unaware of the imminent danger the man in the suit posed or what the two men by the car represented. Then suddenly the realisation dawned on him. "Stop..." He raised his hand in front of him and then, slowly with his right hand reached into his pocket and produced his warrant card... flipping it open with his finger and thumb to show them his photograph and insignia of rank. "I'm a police officer... Inspector Dowling..."

"Mr. Kyso needs to see you, sir," the man said politely, ignoring the inspector as if he hadn't even spoken. "And I need to take you with me... now." He turned slightly and nodded at the two men by the car as they reached inside and produced small Uzi type machine guns, each holding them loosely against their legs.

Sergeant Gould moved slowly to one side of the group... slipping her hand inside her raincoat to touch the butt of her automatic.

"Stay where you are, miss... please, we don't need anyone to get hurt here..." The man in the grey suit waved Sergeant Gould back into the group. "What do you think, Mr. Pendleton? We wouldn't want anyone to get hurt, now would we? It's best that you come along with me, now."

"What do you think now, inspector... is this the England you know." Webb stroked his lower belly with his fingers, slowly easing them inside his jacket until they rested on the butt of the automatic. Things were starting to look bad. From the corner of his eye he could see Simon, off to his left and slightly forwards. He was in a good position, but Webb wondered if he was 'carrying', cursing himself for not checking before they entered the pub. He knew that a shot with a pistol from thirty or forty yards, against two men with Ouzzis would be a difficult shot, almost impossible. Now he wished he'd brought the rifle... Kristianna had offered him, but they were always so difficult to conceal. "Can you protect me against this... do you think?"

The inspector looked a little bemused. He was a brilliant detective but thirty years in the force had left him unprepared for a situation such as this. In all of those years he had never had to draw or use his weapon... ever, this situation to him was totally unheard of and would be reserved for the 'armed response' teams not a simple 'rural detective.' And now, at the most critical juncture in his life... his weapon was empty...

Webb flicked his hand onto the butt of his automatic and withdrew it, almost at the same time as the 'grey suit' both held their aim for a second... not firing. A woman behind them screamed and rushed with her group back inside of the pub, others stood away, away from the scene, cowering behind the cars transfixed with fear and excitement. Webb was at a slight advantage, standing obliquely behind the inspector there was a small chance that the bullet would hit the inspector first.

Another woman behind them screamed, and rushed back into the pub, others just glared through the safety of the windows just the tops of their heads showing, watching in awe as the situation unfolded in front of them.

A cloudburst overhead swept past quickly bringing with it a light, fine drizzle, partly obscuring the two men with the Uzis, for a second. Webb felt the rain on his face... a tiny droplet of water dripped from his eyebrow onto the side of his face and he tried not to blink.

"Alright... alright." The 'grey suit' spoke quickly, his 'free' hand raised in front of him and then lowered his weapon to his waist, holding it loosely by the trigger guard with his index finger. "No need for this... or someone's going to end up dead. I'll make you a deal... yeah?" He shrugged his shoulders and lowered the gun further. "Look. They tell me you're supposed to be a bit of a 'hard man', a 'scrapper'. So am I..." He smiled, throwing down the gauntlet, offering Webb the challenge as he tucked the automatic back into his shoulder holster. "Fight me for it... if you beat me, you walk away... but if it's the other way around." He shrugged his shoulders again, smiling. "You come with me. Right, Mr. Pendleton?"

Webb smiled. "Jesus, you fucking people, what's up with you... you think this is some sort of fucking game... aye... do you?" He raised the automatic and without pausing fired once... The bullet hit the 'grey suit' just above the nose and he was dead before he hit the ground. Webb knelt and quickly fired off two shots at the men by the car, he could hear shots from Simon and also to his right from Sergeant Gould but accuracy was almost impossible from that distance, fortunately the same applied to the two Uzis, their small 9mm rounds were almost as ineffective... but the biggest advantage for them was the volume of rounds they could lay onto a target... at any given time and with a much better chance of a hit.

The inspector was the only one who hadn't knelt, or taken any sort of cover. He stood, waving his hands frantically screaming for them to stop firing... oblivious of any danger he might be in.

Webb watched as the man to the left of the car threw his hands forwards, the Uzi falling from his hands as his head exploded into a mess of bone and flesh... and then what seemed like a 'micro second' later the sound of a much larger, far bigger calibre gunshot sounded... and then a second. He stood and looked across to Simon as the second man at the car fell. "Fuck... that's a..." He didn't get the words from his mouth before the inspector's body seemed to leap into the air before crashing to the tarmac, most of his throat and neck had been torn to pieces by a third shot.

"Sniper..." He heard Simon scream out, un-panicked as he ducked down behind the bumper of the car. "Webb, get in... it's coming from the top of that hill... there, at the end of the road."

As Webb dived behind the car he could just make out the puff of white and blue smoke, three quarters the way up the wooded hill... He heard Sergeant Gould screaming, she was out in the open, firing randomly in the direction she imagined the shots were coming from and then as her clip emptied, knelt and cradled Inspector Dowling's head in her lap. Webb rushed over to her, pushing her to one side and dragged the inspector to the cover of the car, as another long range round struck the tarmac, in front of Sergeant Gould.

"Get in for God's sake, get in..." Webb screamed at her, and then crawling quickly across the tarmac grabbed her by the collar and dragged her behind the car. Two more rounds thumped harmlessly into the body of the car. He recognised the heavy 'crack' of a high-powered, long range rifle. He edged himself to the corner of the bumper until he could see all the way up the long road to the wooded hillock, as two more distinctive puffs of whispery smoke drifted across the face of the hillock.

A group of people had started to leave the pub until his first shot had sent them screaming back in. Occasionally a curious, more adventurous individual poked a head up to the window... but ducked back down as the shots started to come. One shot ricochet through the pub window causing mayhem and eliciting more screams.

He looked at the bodies of the two men by the car... they had been taken with one shot each... as had the inspector... the remaining shots, he knew were 'warning shots' for him... nothing more, he knew also that if the sniper had wanted to kill 'him', he could have done so...easily.

He touched Sergeant Gould's shoulder as she cradled the dead inspector, but she screamed at him and threw his hand away from her, her eyes full of hate. "Stay low..." He pleaded with her not knowing what she was likely to do. "Listen to me." Desperately trying to calm her down. "Don't move from here... that bugger can't stay up there for long. Do you understand?" But he knew she couldn't hear him. Tears poured from her eyes and her face and clothes were covered in the inspector's blood, making it appear that she also had been shot. "Tracy..." He shouted at her again. "Do you hear what I'm saying..?"

She raised herself to her knees and swung her hand at his face, her fist smashing into his jaw, the inspector's head still in her lap. "You bastard... you useless fucking bastard." She dragged the automatic out from its holster and would have shot him if he hadn't tackled it away from her before she collapsed back onto the head of her inspector and wept. "He was a good man... a good man... a decent man... and you scum bags have murdered him." Her body wracked with sobs. "I was here to look after him... he didn't expect any of this, you bastard, and now this..."

"I didn't do this..." he screamed at her. "I told you people what you were dealing with. You thought you could handle it, damn you... you can't control these bastards with ordinary police methods... you have to exterminate them... as if they were just vermin."

***

On the little hillock above them, Kristianna meticulously removed the telescopic sight and unscrewed the barrel of the big Mannliker rifle, carefully wiping the water from them and replaced them into their respective positions in the case. She unclipped the butt and bipod, her fingers touching the metallic parts affectionately as if they were 'living organisms', before placing them in position alongside the barrel. Satisfied, she closed the lid and returned it and the case to the boot of the car, later, as soon as time allowed, she would clean and oil it thoroughly.

The rifle was unique and had belonged to her father it had been his favourite hunting rifle. At 7.95mm it was one of the most powerful rifles ever made and was capable of stopping a two ton elephant at full charge. In the 'trade' it was known as a 'one-in-twenty-thousand', the term used only by gunsmith's around the world and was only given to the 'first of the line', the 'model' that all other rifles would be made from. From this perfect sample, would come all of the standard 'production models' that would then be bought by the 'masses'. It was loosely based around the 7.95mm. Mauser which had been so successfully used by the German's in the Second World War with such devastating effect by their snipers, especially at long range.

As she drove, she pondered her shots. The first one she was very proud of. It had found the exact mark she had aimed for… three inches above the lower neck, but the second… she gritted her teeth… the second was bad, it had struck the very top of the second man's head, another inch higher and it would have been a 'miss'. "That's not good…" She spoke out loud to herself and shook her head at her own inecifiency. But anyway, she consoled herself, her father would have been proud of her, she knew that. She had correctly estimated the range at about eight hundred yards with a cross wind of ten to fifteen knots and the rain had doubled the difficulty. "Dear me…" She smiled a happy contented smile. With the wind and the rain combined she had, had to aim almost two feet high and eighteen inches wide to obtain the shot… But she chastised herself for the last shot that had been aimed at the upper chest of the older man she knew to be the inspector. She knew she had slightly snatched at the trigger… "Never mind…" Satisfied that she had achieved her goal and that the results were 'acceptable'. She smiled again. "What would have happened if I had taken the shot at Simon de Le Croux. "I was so tempted, but maybe it was for the best ..." She mused, considering that it might well ruin her 'new plan...'

So far her plan was working well... 'so far', she was determined that the journals would never reach the authorities, at least she had achieved that. For her 'new plan' she would need all of the judges, politicians and police... when she took over The Met Corps... Without them it would be so much harder, everything would have to started all over again... in a way, they were worth more than the money...

Kristianna touched a dab of moisturiser to her lips, the rain and wind had chapped them a little and then put her foot down hard on the accelerator as she headed back for Cornwall, knowing she would need to be there before her 'new partner' arrived from his appointment with the inspector... In her new Porsche it wouldn't be too difficult... She made a mental note to add an 'extra bonus' to Herbert Tanners account... He had earned it.

Chapter 34

Friday 4:30 pm.

Roger Harrington had been Chief constable for Hampshire for the past six years; and had been a policeman since the age of sixteen, thirty-five years ago. He enjoyed his work and could think of nothing else that he would rather have done, above all... he was exceptionally good at what he did. The rank of Chief Constable had been 'earned', for him there had been no 'fast track'... no accelerated, young graduate system available in those days he had worked himself through the ranks, all the way to the top.

In all of those thirty-five years he had never come across a situation such as he now faced. Yes, there had always been 'bent coppers' or members of parliament that had been corrupted, or a high ranking officer who had 'stepped out of line', but they could almost be counted on the fingers of one hand, but never, never to the magnitude suggested by D.I. Dowling in his latest report.

He paced the room, fretting again. A glance at the wall clock in his lounge told him it was eight o'clock, almost two hours since he had sent a car to bring Sergeant Tracy Gould over to his New Forrest home, not something that he would normally do, but under these tragic circumstances... it just seemed the right thing 'to do'.

Methodically he flipped through the report on her police career... for the third time... failing to understand why she had not already been promoted to Detective Inspector, her record was impeccable. Alan Dowling had written glowing reports of her...

He thought she would have been here, long before this time, but knew that the traffic on the A 27 would probably be backed up again all the way to the Ringwood junction. "I'll be damned glad when they finish that damned bypass." He hadn't realised he had spoken out loud.

"Talking to yourself again darling, not a good sign." Naomi, his wife of twenty-eight years came into the lounge and quietly closed the door behind her. "Coffee, or would you like something a little stronger?" She came over and kissed him on the cheek and squeezed his arm. She was a 'homely' woman, tall and very elegant. Her hair was starting to 'grey' a little at the crown and some of the 'crow's feet' around her eyes hadn't been there just a few years ago, but she would have been considered a 'handsome woman' in any circle. As usual she was dressed in an artist's smock and breaches. Blotches of plaster hung from a strand of hair and there was another small patch on her cheek where she had touched it with her fingers.

"Thank you, no... coffee's fine." He returned her hug. "Tragedy! Damned awful tragedy, that's what this is." His mind was still on the killing of his D.I. "I didn't like the chap, not very much, humourless sort of character, no personality... well, none that I ever saw, but a superb detective, one of the best on the 'force', without a doubt, such a stupid, terrible waste. I would say he had few equals in conviction rates, better than my own in fact, when I was in the same position as him."

She hugged him again. A smudge of white plaster rubbed off from her potter's overall and fell to the carpet. "Oh dear, I shouldn't be wearing this in here. Yes it's such a bad business, that poor man." She had a soft, kindly manner and in the twenty-eight years she had been married to her husband there hadn't been a day that she hadn't loved him, reminding him every day of that fact before he left for the office. "Did he have a family?"

"No... I don't think so. Yes, yes it is... bad business, very bad." He stared blankly out of the window to the illuminated lawn. He loved that view and would always leave the lights on until they retired to bed so that they could get the full effect of it. Beyond the lawn, hidden by the darkness was The New Forest, acres of nibbled grass and further out, forests of pines, oaks and cedar, and tall, fir topped pine. In the daytime the wild forest ponies would come to graze the lawn, even the flowerbeds were not 'sacrosanct' to them, given the opportunity they would devour every flower and every shrub in the garden. "Unfortunately we need to be different policemen now. The whole country is full of drugs and guns and all sorts of awful things. Most of the time we appear to be powerless to do anything about it, perhaps Dowling's report holds some of the answers." He pulled her in closer seeking comfort from her warmth. "Sometimes I feel we are just losing control of everything. This past week has been like a war zone out there." He sighed. "Everything is changing so fast, I wonder if it's time for silly old sods like me just to get out of it altogether, leave it to the youngsters, maybe."

Naomi rested her head on his chest. 'If only' She thought, her mind wondering. How many nights had she lain awake unable to sleep worrying about him until he came back in... safely tucked up with her. How many times had she secretly hoped he would take his 'early retirement option' before it was too late, but in her heart she knew he wouldn't.

"Excuse me, sir... ma'am. She's here, sir..." His sergeant called to them from the doorway. He was a big man, with a huge barrel chest. Thorough with his work and highly efficient but carried a grossly oversized tummy and had been with Roger Harrington for over ten years.

"Thanks, George, show her in for me will you, please." He kissed his wife and patted her 'fulsome bottom'. "Back to work, I suppose. Best you leave now, darling."

Naomi touched Sergeant Gould's arm affectionately as they passed in the doorway and tentatively 'pecked' her cheek. "I'm so very, very sorry, Tracy." She had never met her before this evening but felt her pain.

Roger shook her hand and holding her forearm escorted her into the lounge. "Sit down, sergeant. Please. I'm sorry that you are here under these circumstances." He eased her into a comfortable armchair and then sat opposite her, as close to her as possible. "Can I get you something?"

"I… I could do with a very large Scotch, sir…" she said, still a little tearful, her eyes red and sore. She stared at him defiantly, angry as if he was her 'accuser'.

He poured the drink and handed it to her. "When you are ready, in your own time run through the details for me… everything you can remember." He could see by her eyes that she was suffering, she had obviously cried away some of her pain. "You were very close to Alan, I know that, this must be absolutely terrible for you and I'm sorry to have to put you through this again, but as you know, it's necessary that 'I' fully understand the situation, first hand."

It took almost thirty minutes for her to run through what she could remember of the shooting and the lead up to it. Occasionally she broke down in floods of tears and he had to console her. On several points he interrupted her rendition of the events, asking her to go back to a certain part, until it was clear in his own mind and he was able to form the whole picture. Most of the facts were still indelibly printed on her mind. Her analytic, 'police trained mind', able to separate emotion from actual fact. But she was unclear about events immediately after the shooting. At first she thought there were three shots fired but then after further deliberation thought there might have been as many as five… or six.

"Do you think the shot was aimed specifically at Alan?" He eased her steadily along.

Sergeant Gould nodded. "Yes… without a doubt, he was the target." She stammered with her words. "He just fell… there was no sound at all… he just fell to the ground." She held the glass to her lips with both hands, her fingers shaking violently. "And his head, oh God, his head." She wiped her face with the cuff of her sleeve. "There was almost nothing left of his head… I tried to gather it all…" For a moment she broke down again. Roger handed her a box of tissues and she took a handful to wipe her face. "I need a fag, sir… can I smoke?" She blew her nose, loudly and continued relating what she could remember.

Roger nodded. Neither he, nor his wife had ever smoked and under 'normal' circumstances would never have allowed it in his home. He found a small dish for her to use as an ashtray and placed it for her on the arm of her chair. "It was a high-powered rifle shot, from a long distance." He tried to keep his own emotions in balance, but was finding it difficult. This was 'one of his own', not some unknown person, not just some total stranger that he could deal with, dispassionately.

He continued, slowly. "The report that I've just received says that the shots were taken from a small knoll at the end of the motorway. They found the exact spot, but nothing in the way of evidence, no shell casing, just a few very muddy car tire tracks. It must have been a professional hit… but why Alan… I don't understand that?"

She lit a long tipped cigarette and drew deeply on it. "It has to be something to do with this case… Pendleton. Did you know that he lost his wife to breast cancer, two years ago?"

"Pendleton?"

"No... Alan." She sniffled again and dabbed at her eyes. "He was a good man, like a dad to me... sometimes. That's why I stayed with him for so long... like a dad."

Roger Harrington felt his throat tighten and felt supremely guilty. Up until the faxes he had received less than two hours ago, he knew almost nothing of Alan Dowling's personal life. He felt guilty because he 'hadn't' known... and should have made a point of knowing 'all' his staff.

He coughed, clearing his throat. "Just go back a bit Tracy, run through the last bit again for me, when you first went into the car park after leaving the pub and just before the shooting took place."

She repeated the details, bringing in more and more 'snippets' as she remembered them...

"Did the man Pendleton shot, have a gun?" He hadn't made any notes, everything she said was being recorded by George in the next room. Later they would go through everything in the transcript in more detail.

"Yes... but he had holstered it, he wasn't a threat, not at that moment, initially he was holding it down by his side at first and then he holstered it. He wanted Pendleton to fight him... hand fight him, I mean."

"That's odd... why?"

She shrugged her shoulders. "It's just this bloody stupid 'macho' thing, I suppose."

"And he just shot him, out of hand?"

She nodded again...

"What's he like... this Webbley Pendleton fellow?" He refilled her glass and it seemed to be relaxing her. "I know this must be so difficult for you, but it's vitally important that we get everything down while it's still fresh in your mind. I know you understand that, Tracy." It wasn't the first time he had referred to her by her Christian name.

She told him everything she knew about him from the initial incident, and to date, adding a few of her own 'suppositions'. "I think I'm tending to believe his story, sir... like 'he' said, 'it's too stupid to make up', who would believe it anyway."

"Do you think he was involved in Alan's murder?"

"No, sir... not a chance. I saw his face when Alan... Inspector Dowling was hit. He was as surprised as all of us were."

"Who then had the motive... a rival gang?" He stood and paced the carpet. "Was there another rival gang, do you think?" He was talking out loud, mainly to himself as he did when considering a major problem. "The money motive was certainly strong enough. But not to deliberately target a senior police officer... damn." He smashed his fit into the palm of his left hand angrily. "This other man with Pendleton, what about him, bodyguard?"

"Not the usual type, I'd say ex-special forces, something like that, just the way he carried himself. He wore an Arab style headscarf to hide his face..." She was thinking much clearer now. "But when the shooting started, his veil slipped and I caught a glimpse of his face, very 'gentrified'... looks and speech. I'd say definitely 'top draw' and the suit he was wearing... really expensive. Probably cost a thousand pounds." She clicked her teeth. The tears had dried now and she was a 'detective' again. "Really cool character though. Most men would be too embarrassed to 'properly' search a woman... but not him... he was an absolute 'professional' alright."

"How do you mean?"

"He went inside my bra, to find my other gun. Most men wouldn't do that. He was too thorough to be an amateur and he felt right up into my crotch just to make sure I wasn't wired or carrying anything else. That's real unusual for a man to do."

"I see. What about these journals?"

She produced three sheets of still soggy A4 sized paper from her briefcase and handed them to him. "They're not a lot of good I'm afraid. Our forensic people went over them but they got too wet, everything blew out of Alan's coat pocket when he fell. I tried to gather up as much as I could but it was really windy and pouring down…"

"Pity…" Roger looked at the sodden paper, some names were still visible but blurred and the 'figures and dates' alongside the names were illegible. There was nothing that could safely be used as evidence. "I'd love to get my hands on the originals…."

"I saw the sheets before this happened, some of the names I recognised, but that would be useless without written evidence or proper proof." She shrugged. "The main thing I'm worried about, is that they'll all 'go to ground' now, until this blows over, unless we act quickly."

"Mmm, I was thinking along the same lines." He nodded agreement, his mind still trying to comprehend the brutal assassination of one of his men.

"What are we going to do about Pendleton, sir?" She sipped the last of her whiskey, feeling it burning her tummy. "If it had been down to me, sir…" She hesitated, sensing a betrayal of her late 'boss'.

"No… no… go on." He was intrigued.

"Well…" She continued hesitantly. "I would have made the deal with Pendleton for the journals. Let's face it, sir, he'd already given us details of the biggest ever drug deal that Europe has ever seen… and all he wants is to get safely out of the country. It must be worth a deal, don't you think, sir? Let the bugger get out of here. We don't want 'his type' here, anyway."

311

Harrington nodded agreement. "It's not 'exactly' legal, but yes, I agree I would take the chance with it." An idea was beginning to form in his mind. "Let's forget the drugs for a minute that all looks like it's in hand. More than anything, we need the journals. To me they're worth far more than the money. Without the journals, 'the moles' in the force will just carry on as if nothing has happened. Even if they go to ground now, they'll resurface at a later date. No, we need those blessed journals. How do we get hold of this Pendleton chap?"

"I have his mobile number but I've tried it several times, it's either switched off or he's just not answering."

"Look, sergeant..." He felt enthused, a glint of an idea forming. "I know this has been pretty tough on you, but I want you to take over the case, take it over... completely."

"Me?" She was startled and a little frightened at the prospect of total responsibility. "I'm... just a sergeant."

"Not any longer. As of now, you are an acting inspector, with full, overall responsibility for the enquiry. Pull this off and you can keep the promotion, with back pay...." He turned to face her, watching her face, encouraging her. "You're admirably suited for the job, don't you see. No one knows more about it than you do. Who could I bring in from fresh... no... Tracy, the job's yours if you want it. Do it for yourself, but most of all for Alan..."

She smiled weakly at him, feeling her hands shaking again as she sat on the edge of her seat. "Alright... I'll give it my best crack. I'd like to get back at the bastards who shot Alan, anyway."

"Good! I'll give you full authority over anyone that doesn't outrank me. If you hit any problems with 'anyone', refer them straight back to me. We might still be able to pull something positive out of this tragedy."

"That was just an unbelievable shot... shots." Simon corrected himself. They were just rounding the last bend before Hartness House. It had been the first time either had spoken in the two and a half hour journey since they had driven away from the carnage at the pub. "I consider myself an excellent shot, but I could not have made 'that' shot..."

"Mmm. I was thinking the same. How many people could actually make such a shot, not many, I'd say." Webb simply mumbled. He was deep into his own thoughts of the day's events. What he had decided was that for sure there was another 'element' involved here, another 'player', someone, somehow was obtaining details of their movements... and for some reason his mind always came back to Kristianna and yet he still didn't understand how she would know...

"The shot was down wind, that would make the bullet 'weave', and it was raining pretty hard. He was certainly a professional." Simon continued, enthralled by the shooter. "...but why did they target the inspector, I thought they wanted you?"

"No... they can't pop me, not until they have their stuff back." Webb said it casually, but inside his guts were in a tangled mess. The same question still remained in his own mind... 'why the inspector'? That didn't make any sense, what he did know was that from now on, the 'shit' would really fly, the cops wouldn't let one of their own go easily, not without a massive manhunt for him and any of his associates. Now, they would pull coppers in from all over the place to find him... it was still two days before the motor yacht was ready to leave... and wondered if he could stay alive until then...

As they pulled into the courtyard of Hartness House, Simon edged in between a black Porsche that had parked at an angle, almost blocking the entrance. "Good lord. What silly arse parks like that?" Simon pointed at the black Porsche Carrere parked diagonally across the front of the driveway. "Probably one of those damned guests." He shrugged, as soon as he could he would get Thomas to ask the owner to move it. "Unfortunately we have twenty guests staying for the weekend and for the ball tomorrow... such is life, I suppose."

"Whose is the Porsche, Maud, do you know?" Simon touched the housekeeper's shoulder, affectionately as they entered the Great Hall. She was 'rotund', with a happy, cheerful and very red face, and had been Simon's nanny until he was sent off to boarding school at ten years old.

"I believe it is Miss Van Ouden's car, sir..." She smiled, accepting a 'peck' on her cheek from him.

Webb watched Simon's face, knowing he was thinking the same. "I hadn't realised she'd gone out today... and a 'new car?"

"Yes, sir, very early apparently, one of the herdsman, Peter saw her car at about half three this morning," Maud added, cheerfully.

Webb opened Kristianna's bedroom door, entering without knocking. She was dressed in silk, flowing pantaloons and a cream top to match. The cloth seemed to flow around her as if it had a life of its own, there seemed an over 'abundance' of material, that 'flowed' around her legs as she moved making soft 'whooshing' sounds against her skin.

"Darling, how very pleasant..."

"Where were you all day?" He walked towards her, cautiously watching her eyes. Above the 'makeshift' bandage around her neck he could clearly see the green, blue bruises on her throat.

She smiled sweetly. "I had some business to attend to and to visit my doctor." She unconsciously touched her throat and gave a subdued cough. Her voice was raspy and she seemed to be finding it difficult to talk.

"Business..." His voice was critical. "What business could you possibly have, you would have been gone by now, if not for...?"

She coughed again, a little more dramatically this time and held her throat. "Your... not going to hurt me again are you?" She stepped backwards, away from him, outwardly showing signs of 'fear'.

"No... I'm not." He felt embarrassed. That had been the very first time he'd ever struck a woman in his life. "But I need to know where you were... today... what business?" He glanced around the room, wondering whether there would be anything here to tie her into the shootings. But there was just a long narrow suitcase and another smaller case and several handbags... He raised his eyebrows, wanting an answer.

"We have an additional passenger... you... you were not included on the original 'manifest'. So I have had to make 'adjustments'." She walked over to her handbag on the dressing table and removed two official looking documents. "Such as your new passports..." She handed them to him.

Webb flicked them open, staggered at the authenticity. "James Whales and... Thomas Sanderson.?" He smiled a little at the names, liking them.

"I thought you much more a 'James' or a 'Thomas', far more 'dignified' than Webbley... don't you think?" She touched his arm affectionately. "I think we got off on the wrong foot from the outset, we really ought to put that right, you know."

"Where... where did you get the photograph?" He was still suspicious of her.

"From your passport..."

"My pass…" He opened his shoulder bag and removed his own, slightly crumpled, dogeared passport. "Good lord…" The space where the passport photograph 'lived' was bare. "That was very clever, you never said anything about this. They look real."

A hurt, pained expression surrounded her face. "That is because they 'are real', darling."

"But I…"

She touched his lips with the tips of her fingers. "No need to thank me, 'James Whales', maybe we can be friends now. You certainly can't travel on your own passport… can you? That would be rather silly, don't you think?" She briefly turned her head away from him lest he see the lie in her eyes, and then turned back to face him, touching her lips to his and held it. "Your arms are so strong… I like a strong man…"

Gradually she 'eased' him over to the bed and sat with him, feeling him respond to her probing fingers. He smelt musty, rough, just like her own father used to, when they had been out hunting in the Veldt and she loved the feel of his calloused hands on the softness of her skin as he struggled with her overly complicated blouse…

Webb felt decidedly uncomfortable. In the midst of all this carnage and death, there seemed to be a glimmer of hope and compassion in her, even if that was just fleeting… he felt the arousal in his loins. Slowly he eased himself away from her… a little regretful… a little fearful of the consequences being this close to her and stood away.

"I don't think this is exactly the right time, for this… regrettably." He shrugged, trying to read her.

"Kristy…" Gabriella burst through the door. "Oh…" She wrongly interpreted the 'scene', instantly. "I'm sorry…"

Webb saw Kristianna's jaw harden. "Go away, Gabriella... we're talking," she shouted at her sister annoyed at the intrusion.

Kristianna's 'miracle recovery' had not gone unnoticed and Webb smiled inwardly at the deceit and then went over to Gabriella. "Hiya, Gabby..." He touched her neck, fondly and kissed her on the mouth. "I think we're about done here anyway." He waved the passports at Kristianna. "Thank you for those..." And then left with Gabriella...

In the hallway she snuggled into his side. "What do you want to do now?" Gabriella teased him, with her arm around his waist, her fingers tickling his ribs, as they walked along the hallway back to his room.

"At the moment..." he said wearily. "I just want to have a steaming hot shower, a bite to eat and then a very, very large gin and tonic. Hopefully get pissed out of my brains for a change..."

"Can I have a shower with you? Perhaps we can add one more thing to that long list..." She giggled excitedly.

Chapter 35

The New Forest: 8:38 pm.

"Your call's through to the home office, sir." Sergeant George Dobkin spoke softly as he always did when addressing his boss, Roger Harrington. He was a quiet, placid man, normally 'unflappable' and a good man to have around in a crisis and extremely efficient...

Harrington thanked him and waited until he had left before lifting the receiver. "Good afternoon, sir. I wish I was calling under better conditions than this." He controlled his breathing, feeling a slight 'panic attack' coming on. Although the indication from the journals placed the corruption as nationwide, most of the 'heavy action' seemed to be centred in or around his 'patch' and he felt decidedly uncomfortable about it. "The situation seems to be far more serious than I first thought..." Slowly and methodically he related the events of the past four or five hours, in detail and then without interruption, tied it into the past six days... "When I spoke to you yesterday part of this was just supposition, now... unfortunately... it's fact. We've lost a damned good D.I. Almost irreplaceable. As a 'stopgap' I have promoted Sergeant Gould to Detective Inspector."

"Is that wise, Roger?" The Home Secretary seemed concerned. "What do we know about her and what about someone more senior?"

"Until we get to the bottom of these journals, I'm not sure who I can trust." He felt impatient and hated dealing with politicians and their 'sideways' talking and 'non-committal' attitudes'.

"Good God! It's as bad as that?"

"It's worse. Some of the names I saw on that slip of paper, alarmed me greatly. With regards to Gould, if she worked with Alan Dowling for any length of time, she must be good, he would not have had it any other way. When she was a young training constable she handed in a bag of cash, almost a hundred thousand in old used notes, money that the swat teams had missed, so I don't think her integrity or honesty could ever be questioned. No, I need her on this… and… she has more reason than any of us to bring these people to justice… she was really fond of old Dowling…"

"Well, we need to do something pretty fast, Roger, if the press boys even get the tiniest 'sniff' of this, all of our heads will be on the block." The Home Secretary had cleared his own office of people, on Roger's advice and they were speaking on the 'secure line'. His voice was agitated and sharp.

"I know, sir… believe me, I know…"

"Why can't we just arrest the damned man?"

"Mainly because we don't know where he is. We know what he looks like, but if I broadcast his photograph, we'll be swamped with the press and it will drive the 'real rats' underground." He felt even more irritated now, desperately wanting to get on with it all, but his 'radical ideas' had to be approved first. "Look… sir… I want to do a deal with him…"

"Who…"

"This Webbley Pendleton character, he has most of the answers to this anyway... I'm sure of it." Harrington bit his lip, hoping that he wasn't going to get too much opposition.

"Seriously, what sort of a deal?"

"He wants clear passage out of the country, unobstructed and indemnity for his people, for that he will hand over the journals, complete." Roger drummed his fingers on the desk and gritted his teeth.

"I don't know... if something goes wrong on this... where does that leave us? In the 'pooh' by the sounds of it."

"We need those damn journals Sir, otherwise everything we are doing here is just a waste of time." He hated politicians even more now. "And... if what he has told us about the drugs shipment, turns out to be true, think of the 'feather in your cap', all of our caps for that matter."

"Mmm, I'm not sure I like this at all. What about the murderer of Dowling, how's this stand with his involvement?" The Home Secretary hedged his bets, thinking more of the consequences of failure... and his own job. He had held the job for barely a year and had gained the position only after his 'indiscreet' predecessor had been secretly photographed in a compromising situation with an under aged girl... 'Now this!'

"What would you suggest then, sir?" He kept his voice level and under control. 'Apathetical sod.' He thought. "I'm open to anything at the moment."

"I'm not sure... What's the chance of your plan failing?" He sidled around making a decision, preferring the other man to do so...

"I don't work on failures, sir... only successes..." Roger knew he had sealed his own fate now, but he was desperate for some form of 'positive answer'. One slip up on this case, one tiny 'whiff' of a scandal and he would be out of a job, throwing away thirty years of impeccable policing...

"There are a couple of... um... things that you need to know about Pendleton, Roger, before you make your decision." The Home Secretary seemed nervous and somewhat reluctant to share his information.

Roger sensed that 'politician thing' again. "Things, what sort of 'things'?" He felt anger at the thought that Pendleton was already known to the Home Office and that 'he', as the senior investigating officer on the case had so far been kept out of the 'loop'.

"He... um... he was 'special forces', served six years with the Special Air Service, Aden Borneo, Somalia, the usual places for those days. But the main 'thing'..." There was a long pause. "He executed a Malay army officer and one of his Sergeant Majors and... an MI6 officer..."

"Oh what! Good lord... He's a bit of a lad then," he said, sarcastically. "When were you going to tell me that?" Roger Harrington was hopping mad now, almost foaming at the mouth at the revelation. "Damn it... sir, that information would have been useful a week ago. Don't you think?"

"I'm sorry but I had to get clearance on it myself before I could to tell you," he admitted, grudgingly.

"This is getting better... by the minute, 'sir'. Clearance, from whom?" Rodger paced around the room.

"Things were different then..." He tried to avoid the criticism. "What I am about to tell you is not to go further than your office, Roger." There was a long delay again. "In '62 we were taking a lot of casualties in Borneo and we couldn't figure out why so many of the Indonesian fighters were getting through, so they dropped two S.A.S. men over the border, one of which was 'your man' Pendleton... to cut a long story short... they identified the problem as the Malay army who were guarding that section of the border. The Indonesians were coming over the border in company strength, having breakfast with the Malays, who of course were supposed to be on our side, and the Indonesians were going down to kill our chaps. Anyway… it was decided by 'the powers' at the time that the Malays needed to be taught a lesson and sent a patrol of S.A.S. in to deal with it… plus… an MI6 officer. Dear me, I just can't imagine it now, some of the things my predecessors' got up to, makes my blood run cold, but they all still had the 'Colonial mentality' then, you understand." His voice broke a little. "Apparently a certain number of Malays were selected to be shot… just low ranking soldiers, 'for cowardice' in the face of the enemy. I can hardly bear to think about it… It all ended in a complete mess after three 'privates' from the Malay army were shot dead by their Malay officers. That's when 'your chap' intervened and shot the officer and sergeant major. The MI6 officer tried to stop Pendleton and Pendleton shot him dead…"

For a long time neither spoke. "Good God! Why… wasn't he sentenced for murder, I don't understand?"

"Think about it for a second, Roger… how could they charge him with anything, 'we' were… the murderers… we 'instigated' this, not just him." The Home Secretary's voice trembled. "As I said, 'things' were different in those days… much different. They kept Pendleton 'under wraps' for a time but it completely backfired six months later when he assaulted another soldier, some sort of incident over a cat… that doesn't matter, what does matter is that Pendleton was kicked out of the army with a dishonourable discharge… on the condition that he signed a 'non-disclosure' contract. If he broke it, it would mean a life sentence for him. So I guess he is probably quite a dysfunctional, aggressive sort of character, certainly not a team player."

After the call, Roger replaced the handset and leaned back in his chair, resting his elbows on the desk he lowered his head into his hands… breathing steadily. His hands felt clammy and shook a little. The information the H.S. had supplied, changed everything. Initially they were just chasing 'a fugitive' from justice, but now... what? This man Pendleton wasn't just 'any' fugitive... he was a highly trained, efficient 'killing machine' that had been forced by circumstances into 'extreme' retaliation.

'So be it...' Somehow they would have to deal with it but first he needed to be found. He dialled 'Inspector' Gould's number. "Any luck with the mobile?" It was just a slight chance.

"No, I think they're out of coverage, but..." She sounded hopeful. "I've had an idea. There was a gunshot case admitted to Southampton General, two days ago. Some of the 'local's' who were dealing with it, couldn't get anything out of the victim... a woman... but... I bet a 'pound-to-a-pinch-of-shit,' that it was something to do with him... Pendleton."

Roger winced at her crudity but applauded her intuitive mind. "What makes you think she's involved?"

"Because she was ex. Special Air Service and I don't believe in coincidence, sir. That's all."

Roger's mood lifted. "Right I'll meet you there, at the hospital. It'll take me about thirty minutes. George!" he shouted as he replaced the receiver. "Get the car out..."

***

It was eight o'clock before the housekeeper called them down for dinner and as Hartness House was near to capacity with weekend guests, they ate in the private lounge, normally reserved entirely for family use.

"We don't allow the public in here, of course... otherwise, we would be completely overrun by guests and their awful children," Pipa said, curtly.

It was the most Webb had heard her say since they'd met. She wasn't beautiful, not in the true sense of the word, not like Kristianna or Gabriella. 'Pretty' would be a better word for her, and very elegant. She was 'countryfied' and could have been taken easily for a 'country squires daughter', which in fact she was. Her rosy, healthy cheeks gave her face that 'country glow' of the 'hunting, shooting brigade', the 'fox and hounds' look. But he noticed also she had that 'gentrified face' and seemed to walk around all day as if there was an awful smell under her nose, worst of all he knew she didn't like him much... either. "Your kids don't normally eat with you?"

"Normally yes, but they're with their nanny and grandma tonight. It's... nicer like that sometimes, when business is to be discussed." Simon spoke as if he was defending his actions.

Tensions were still running high from the events of the day and it showed in the faces of everyone at the table. With the exception of Gabriella, who had seated herself next to Webb and constantly beamed a huge smile in his direction, occasionally slipping her hand under the table to touch his knee. Kristianna had arrived late, much to the chagrin of the cook, who had put her dinner in the oven, grumbling that it would all be 'spoiled' now. Throughout the whole of the dinner, Kristianna had hardly spoken and picked around at her food, eating almost nothing, which added to the tension.

"What's the next move, boss?" Simon finished of the last of the roast beef on the tray and added a huge dollop of English mustard before popping it into his mouth.

"I'm not sure, get the bloody yacht sorted out, I suppose, so that we can get the hell out of here." He dabbed his lips with the serviette. "That was the best roast beef I've eaten since my gran's, thank you." And it was. Coupled with the fresh vegetables from the garden and the deep rich, beef gravy, it had been superb. He pushed the empty plate away from him, patting his tummy. "At the moment I feel like I'm being 'arse fucked' from every angle."

"Mr. Pendleton!!!" Pippa slammed her knife and fork onto her plate, making Gabriella jump and glared at Webb, her eyes inflamed and venomous. "This is 'my' house and you are sat at 'my' table, please have the courtesy to respect that and refrain from using language more suited to the barrack room... or some other den of iniquity that you are probably more familiar with."

He stood, throwing the serviette onto the table. "I'm sorry, you're right. I'll leave you all to it... I need a walk anyway."

"I'll come with you..." Simon rose and walked over to the gun cabinet on the far wall.

"No! Please..." Pippa added sharply, turning to face her husband, but stopped herself going any further. She had never seen Simon like this. Never, never had he brought a 'client' into the house, before. She had spoken to him on his return and he had outlined briefly, the details of the day. She could see that he was clearly shaken by it, even though he pretended it hadn't affected him. She knew him far too well for him to hide that, sick with worry for him, and not 'just' him... for the safety of the whole family and had forbidden anyone to go down into the village until this 'business' was over and done with. Why had he brought this awful man here, there was just something terribly 'sinister' and truly 'noxious' about him. She fretted. 'He was the 'carrier of death'. She could feel the aura of death surrounding him.

"It's okay, Simon, really." Webb held his hand out. "You stay here, I'm alright. I just need a walk and some fresh air." He had been a little startled by Pippa's reaction to his swearing, understandable he thought, but it wasn't just that... he had seen the look of hate and contempt she held for him in her eyes.

"I'll come with you, Webbley... we need to talk anyway." Kristianna was on her feet and 'marching' out of the door before he could say anything, or even protest.

As they left the house Webb checked the load on his automatic, making sure there was a round in the chamber and then set the safety catch before returning it to its holster. Tonight it felt 'heavy' and 'cumbersome' under his armpit, at one time the 'feel of it' had been a comfort, but not anymore... now it was just becoming a burden.

They walked to the top of the tree-lined lane, and then, to spite her, and her immaculate cream and grey suit, he stepped over the fence stile and onto the single mud track that led all the way up to the top of the hill, starting off at a fast pace, testing her fitness and his.

Kristianna removed her black, high heels as they reached the stile and tying the straps together, threw them over her shoulder, unphased as a chunk of wet mud smeared across the front of the delicate blue jacket she was wearing. By the time they reached the top of the rise, the legs of her slacks were covered in mud to above her knees, but she paid little attention to it. Strangely she felt happy, even though he hadn't spoken to her all the way up to the top.

To her, 'She was hunting again, with her father in the Rhodesian bush, hunting the lioness that had nearly killed her, two days earlier. Her father had only managed to wound it... now they knew that the lioness would be even more dangerous. Kristianna always thought of her father when she was in trouble. He'd been first and foremost... her father, her tutor, her mentor and at the age of thirteen... her very first lover. But... then even 'he' had betrayed her, as all men will, eventually... how well she knew that now. He had been weak and allowed that 'body-eating cancer' to kill him when she was just nineteen and yet he had promised her he would always be with her...' She felt his presence now though.

Wiping a splash of mud from her face she looked at Webb, walking in front, the pace not worrying her in the least. 'This man has the potential to be something great'. The thoughts raced through her mind. He had obviously grown soft over the years, but she could see in his eyes that the will to survive was still strong in him and if necessary he had the strength to kill, as he had already demonstrated. 'If only he would let me 'teach him.' She had watched, fascinated through the rifle 'scope as she fired the calculated headshot into the old man, outside of the public house, cold and callous and calculated, the only 'downside' was that she had wished she could have heard the conversation preceding the shot. 'Yes…' she decided. 'He was worth training. He would be her deputy, as soon as she took over The Met Corps.'

The track wound through great old oaks, interspersed occasionally by a few elm and ash. Most of the area beneath the trees was covered in bracken, in places overgrowing the little used track. For Webb it felt, in parts like the jungles of Borneo that he had grown accustomed to and had come to love so much. The trees and the foliage were different of course but the bracken, though smaller, looked like the tall 'Baluka' that grew so high in Borneo, sometimes growing as high as twenty feet tall in secondary jungle. It was just the feeling of being 'held', lovingly by the immensity of it all, like being back in the womb… protected.

Even though he had set a good pace, he was impressed and surprised that she had kept up with him. By the time they reached the top he was a little 'winded' but hoped it didn't show… Kristianna was breathing steadily, her face a little flushed, she smiled as he flopped down against the roots of a big oak and rolled a cigarette, shielding it under his coat against the fine drizzle.

"I'm a little out of condition." She kneeled in front of him, her hands on his knees. "I haven't done anything like that in years, I've missed it. City life makes people soft. They all shelter in their cosy, centrally heated houses, secure from the world, or so they think but it is never as secure as they believe it to be... is it Webbley? Can I have one of those... I've earned it."

"I didn't realise you smoked..." He handed her the one he had intended for himself and rolled another.

"Sometimes... when I feel happy, content and in good company." She accepted his lighter and drew heavily... coughing. "I like to sit by myself and smoke a Sobrani, or an American cheroot."

He pulled the coat around him. The night had become much colder. Through the break in the canopy of the trees above, he caught fleeting glances of the full moon, when it broke through the clouds it almost became 'daylight'. "I can't figure you out..." He tried to see the expression on her face, but the moon had ducked back behind a cloud.

"Nor I you..." she countered. "Tell me something about 'you'... I like you... very much." Her hand gently caressed his knee.

For the first time since he had known her, he detected a slight South African accent... almost imperceptible, hidden at the back of her impeccable English. "Where were you born?" He puffed on the Cigarette.

"Rhodesia..." She took the leather pouch from him and rolled herself another one. "It used to be the best country in the world and the most beautiful. That was until the 'Kaifer's' took over... Ian Smith just completely failed us, if he had given The Selos Scouts their head we could have hung onto our independence. Now... nothing. Nothing is grown there, they don't take care of the game... and tourists wouldn't dream of going there now, it's just not safe anymore since that bastard Mugabe took over..."

"I thought they were there first," he countered.

"Ha... they won the country from the original inhabitants and we won it from them. It's called 'survival' and down to the tenacity and perseverance of the strongest." She sounded bitter. "If South Africa had stayed with us and allowed Ian Smith full reign, we would still have been there now." Looking at him, she wondered again if he was 'really' worth it... worth the trouble of 'teaching'... or was he still too soft? "My grandparents were first generation, they hacked it out of the wilderness, dying by the hundreds as they did so. That was when the blacks were just worthless, wandering tribesmen, which is the way they will return to, eventually."

He noted how strong her accent had suddenly become as she spoke so passionately about her birthplace. "Why did you leave?" He was sat on his haunches, as he had, hundreds of times when talking to the tribal leaders of the Eban, but now it felt uncomfortable, so he shuffled back onto his backside and rested his elbows on his knees.

She looked wistful. "Now's not the time..." she said simply. "One day, if we ever have time, I'll tell you."

She stubbed the butt of the cigarette out and buried it in the mud and then turned back to face him speaking softly, more feminine, the bitterness gone from her voice now as if 'on cue'.

"Webbley, there is another way around all of this, you know..." She raised her hand and touched his lips with her fingertips as he was about to speak. "Let me finish... please." Her hand moved from his knee to the inside of his thigh. "So far we have achieved almost nothing, we are basically no further forwards than we were a week ago... and a lot of people have been killed along the way. But... we 'are' still here, thanks, in no small part to your tenacity and your skills..." She edged in closer to him, opening his legs, her hands playing gently around his groin.

Her voice had returned to the 'perfect English' again, with little or no trace of an accent and he felt annoyed at her 'ham-fisted' attempt to get him onto her side. "Go on…"

"At first we only had it in mind to take the money and run with it, as far as we could and that was right… then. But now… I see the weaknesses with 'The Corps', we have broken through their once impregnable 'armour'. Now, we have the greatest opportunity… you and I… to take over the whole of The Corps. Don't you see that?"

"Are you fuckin' mad?" He wriggled out of her touch, and stood, leaning more against the tree. "Jesus! What's up with you, you think I can put up with more of this bloody carnage… Jesus!"

"Listen to me…" She stood with him, her hand on his shoulder, touching his arm. "Alejandro is old and weak and has become careless, but no one, up until now dared to challenge him, until you, Webbley, don't you see what that means. His time is nearly over anyway, the only obstacle is Paul Kyso and I can deal with him…Webbley… we could have it all. We could make our own arrangements with the Americans."

"It's madness… madness." He stormed. She was too close to him now, close enough to smell her perfume. "Why would I want to?"

"For a multitude of reasons. Think of the power… the money… together we could rule most of the underworld of Great Britain, don't you see that? To be safe forever…" she said simply, forcefully, raising her hand she touched his face. "Just think, Webbley, you could be the head of one of the largest companies in the world… a multimillion dollar company and all you would have to do is turn up occasionally for a board meeting. I would do all the running of the company for you… doesn't that sound appealing?"

He held her at arm's length. "You mad bloody bitch. No, not at all, Christ, I couldn't think of anything worse..." He hated her with a vengeance now after seeing into her soul. "You would be the last person on this earth I would want to make any sort of 'partnership' with... even if it was 'making dolls' clothes' or something."

Kristianna held her emotions, giving nothing away on her face. She could just make out the outline of his face in the half darkness, full of hatred, for her. Maybe she had been wrong, all the time... he didn't have the hunger... he couldn't see the opportunities here... opportunities that would never, ever come along again. "Webbley, he's the man who ordered the killing of your mother... doesn't that mean anything?" She could see that she'd hit a 'cord' and progressed with it... "Well at least kill 'him'."

But he turned away from her and walked away...

"I've done all the killing I'm going to do..." He didn't look back as he walked on down the hill...

"No, you haven't," Kristianna mumbled to herself as he walked away from her. "Not by a long ways... there is much more that I need you to do for me... before I kill you..."

It was past eleven before he returned to the house and joined Simon in his little 'den' under the stairs.

"Hi, Webb, can I get you something?" Simon didn't look at him and seemed distracted.

"Mmm. Gin and tonic mate, please. Ice if you've got it." He shrugged his shoulders and flopped down into the old, threadbare armchair, feeling emotionally drained.

"Sorry about Pippa tonight, old chap." He handed Webb his drink and returned to his own chair. "She's a bit 'strung out' with everything: the kids, the house and this blessed banquet."

"No, it was my fault, it's me that should be apologising, not her. I think we're all a little strung out to be perfectly honest. I wouldn't normally have used language like that around someone like your wife. You'll have to apologise to her for me." He took a big 'swallow' and settled down. Webb noticed how very different Simon was around his wife, tense and a little 'subservient', maybe, far different from the confident, self-assertive character when he was 'working' away from the house.

"Oh Beth phoned..." He said it as if he wasn't surprised or excited.

"Beth! Here... she phoned here, from where?" Webb almost spilt his drink. "Christ... when?"

"From the hospital, about an hour ago. She left a number for you to call. I wrote the number down..." He pointed to the telephone table. "Piece of paper next to the phone. She said it was urgent, that you need to call as soon as you return." He realised he had blundered a little but his mind was still on Pippa and the discussion they'd had as soon as they were alone. He had never seen her like this before, she seemed obsessed with Webb. 'You must ask him to leave, please, he is a 'carrier of death', I can feel it on him...' She had insisted. "She's okay now, Webb, out of intensive care and onto an ordinary ward." He tried to make amends, but he could see by Webb's face that it hadn't worked.

Webb fumed inwardly but said nothing as he dialled the number. 'How could Beth have rated 'this character' so highly, he's an incompetent idiot...' He almost spoke the words out loud.

The telephone rang just twice. "Webb, good to hear from you again, how are you?"

"More to the point, mate, what about you?" He choked up. Her cheerful voice was the best present he'd had all week. "Fuckin' good to hear from you, mate... you worried the shit out of me... but you're okay... you sound it? Christ, mate... this must be pretty important."

"It is, Webb... I um... I'm sat with a gentleman that needs to talk to you..." Her voice sounded soft and reassuring.

For a second he panicked... instantly. 'God no! They must have gotten to her... in the bloody hospital'. "Who..?"

"He's the Chief Constable for Hampshire, Webb... Roger Harrington... he wants to make a deal with you. I have his absolute word that this call will not be traced and he looks honest."

Webb felt the hairs on the back of his neck bristle. The past week had put him badly on edge and his thought process had become a little irrational at times. He looked around the room, positioning himself against the big bureau, half expecting a swat squad to charge into the room. "Roger Harrington? I know him..."

"You do, how? Forget that. Look I'll put him on in a minute, but he has convinced me that he has your best interests at heart and has the authority of The Home Secretary, no less... to offer you a deal... I think you need to talk to him Webb, he sounds genuine."

He heard her talking to Harrington as she handed the telephone over, her voice a heavy whisper. "He said he knows you..."

"Mr. Pendleton, Roger Harrington."

"Yeah, we've met, Roger... I fitted your conservatory." There was silence on the other end of the line. "Your wife is a potter, does those beautiful, hand painted plates. I had her make me a complete set. You live in the New Forrest as I recall... yeah?"

"Good God! I knew that name was familiar, it's not exactly a 'Smith' or 'Jones' is it. I just never made the connection. Good lord." His voice stammered a little with nervous tension. "How the devil did you get mixed up in this mess? No, forget that… maybe sometime in the future… we can sit down and have a laugh about it. Let's get to the business in hand. Tell me about the journals…" He quickly laid out the terms, namely, that the journals would have to be in his hands and looked over before any concrete deal could be made 'and' that there would be no more killings…

Webb agreed. "And for that I get what?"

"You get an immediate amnesty from prosecution, and at your own expense, you will be required to leave the country within a week… and with no return. What you do with the other 'goods' is of no concern to me at all. All I want is the journals… would you agree to that?" He rushed through it as if eager to have the words out of his mouth.

"The journals are no problem, you can have them any time, but the 'no more killings', that's completely out of my control, there are still a lot of people out there that want me dead… and I can't just stand around and take it… now can I? I need to defend myself." For the first time in a week he was swept with an overwhelming sense of relief. "I won't do the delivery myself, but I'll send someone reliable up with them tomorrow." He looked over at Simon. 'Make the bugger work for his money…' He thought.

They spoke at length, working through the details of the meeting place, the car Simon would be driving and what clothes he would wear. "Now this conversation is only known to you and me and Simon, who is with me now." Webb ran through what he wanted to happen in his mind and then repeated them to Harrington. "Could I suggest that you pick only the people you 'personally trust' and no one else and that you tell them the meeting location ten minutes before you send them out. The world is a 'sieve' as far as information is concerned at the moment, or seems to be." He took a big swallow of his gin and tonic, the tonic now flat, but it didn't matter, at least there seemed to be an end in sight to all of this damned mess. "If we're done, Roger, I'll get my chap to phone you as soon as we have discussed everything. Ten minutes, yeah? Could you um... put me back over to Beth, please."

"I'm going to book myself out of here tomorrow, Webb," she said cheerfully. "So I'll see you sometime tomorrow, hopefully."

"No, I don't like that too much, mate. I'd sooner you stayed away from here, the shit's not stopped flowing yet." He was concerned. "You promise? Just get on and buy that riding stable you wanted, I'll leave the money with Simon, at least you can get out of this shitty bloody business once and for all." He would make sure that she had enough money to last her for the next two lifetimes... "You promise?"

"Yeah, maybe... but I won't promise, and anyway... I'd like to see you again before you bugger off..." She laughed down the line and hung up.

Two floors above them, in the loft void she had used before, Kristianna removed the ear pieces and disconnected the tap wires from the telephone wires and leaned back against the wall. She was freezing cold and soaked to the skin, but it didn't matter. She would wait for another ten minutes or so, as soon as she had the exact location she could telephone Mr. Herbert Tanner with the details. Pulling a blanket from the tiny bed she wrapped it around her shoulders, shivering with the cold now, and then reattached the ear pieces...

Kristianna chuckled to herself... people were such fools, especially in their own homes... if only they realised, 'that' was where they are at their most vulnerable... just when they felt relaxed and started feeling secure... and of course... why shouldn't they. Their home was their 'secure cave' with the cave entrance barred from the wild creatures outside. But! Be very careful whom you allow into your 'cave', especially after dark...

Tomorrow she knew that everything 'had' to go right... In the cottage where she had directed the two 'Kyso' men, she had underestimated the capabilities of 'Mr. Webbley Pendleton'... that would not happen again... ever. But then... she convinced herself... it was because she hadn't been there 'in person' and that her instructions to Mr. Herbert Tanner had been 'slightly' altered. She had instructed him to make the call to Paul Kyso's two closest men and then just wait for them to enter the cottage. They should have waited no more than a few minutes before entering the cottage by the back door and then her instruction to them was to 'exterminate' Kyso's men and rescue Webbley and the others. They would then have been able to tell Webbley Pendleton that they had been sent to look after him by Kristianna. His trust in her would have been 'absolute'... but something had been 'lost in the interpretation'. If it had worked out as she had planned it, he would have been 'eating from her hands by now.'

'Never mind... there was nothing lost', but tomorrow, she knew must be perfect... absolutely 'no slip-ups' and it would have to be 'dramatic!' She would take the 'long shots' herself, but whatever happened, she was determined the journals would not fall into the hands of the police...

Chapter 36

Dick Cordon stood nervously in the library of his boss's house. Paul Kyso was the only boss he had ever worked for who he actually liked… truly liked. Paul had always been very fair to him and had treated him well, promoting him to deputy head of security over others that were, in his mind more… capable than he. He put it down to the fact that they were both Americans and that they both thought along a similar vein… He fidgeted his feet, nervously, his hands behind his back. He had been summoned an hour ago, just as he was settling down for the evening with his girlfriend, she had been difficult to convince that it was purely business and not something or 'someone' else.

His eyes abstractly followed the rows of books… thousands of them, displayed in immaculate, impeccable order, shelf after shelf from floor to ceiling. He assumed it was the collection of a lifetime. There were no windows in here and the room was temperature controlled, mainly to preserve the more priceless items from the devastating, destructive effects that sunlight would have on them. He remembered Paul saying he just loved the solitude. For his part, he had never been much of a 'reader'… maybe the odd newspaper or adventure story, but reading as such, had never interested him.

"You like books, Dick?" Paul Kyso spoke softly as he always did, nevertheless Paul's quiet entrance still startled him.

"Yep..." He lied, when he regained some of his composure, he wasn't able to remember the last time he'd actually read a book. He had a faint idea why he'd been asked by Mr. Alejandro de Los Santos to fetch Paul and that it didn't look good... not at all, for Paul. He shrugged his shoulders. "One day... maybe... I would like to have a collection like this."

"Why are Henry and Joseph in the hallway, Dick?" Paul held a steady gaze on his deputy's eyes.

Henry and Joseph were the personal bodyguards of Alejandro and under 'normal' circumstances would never leave his side.

"Um... ain't no easy way to say this, boss... or do this..." He fidgeted from his right to his left foot. "Mr. de Los Santos, phoned me at home and told me to come over for you... take you into his office. He needs to see you... now. Seems important."

"That's very unusual, Dick, especially this time of night, any idea why he wants to see me?" Paul walked across to his desk and sat behind it, seemingly unruffled, but he could feel his fingers shaking and there was a distinct 'hollowness' inside his gut. He opened the draw and removed a long Cuban cigar and lit it. Through the luxurious cloud of blue smoke he could just see the butt of the loaded automatic at the back of the draw, hoping that this wasn't going to be the day he would need to use it... "Any idea what this is about, Dick?" He watched his deputy over the huge leather bound desktop.

"No idea, boss. It was as much a surprise to me." Dick shrugged and made a face. He was just following instructions, not wanting to get into the 'why's and where-for's of it.

"Mmm." Paul closed the lid of the box and tucked it back into the draw. Momentarily his finger touched the butt of the automatic. I wonder what he 'thinks' he knows? Paul thought. It went through his mind to kill all three of them now... and have done with it. He could do that without even leaving his desk... but it was too soon. He would listen to what that 'old fool', Alejandro had to say... and then make his move if necessary. What had he done wrong that warranted being dragged in at this time of night like some fool 'common soldier'? He was sure that it was a mystery that would unravel within the next hour or so...of that he was very sure.

"Best go see him then," he said, with a confidence he didn't feel and headed for the door.

"Paul..." Dick blurted out, his hand on the door knob, blocking Paul's exit. "He knows about your money, cashing everything in and all..."

Paul felt his gut knot up and for a tiny fraction of a second his 'inner strength' almost failed him. He bit down on the butt of his cigar, controlling his emotions. "Oh that..." His voice was flat and unemotional, hiding the nauseating turmoil. If his courage failed him now... by midnight he would be at the bottom of the Test River...

As he entered the outer office he spread his arms and legs for Joseph to search him. No one... not even the Queen of England could go in front of Alejandro de Los Santos without being thoroughly searched...

***

It was well after midnight before Roger Harrington returned home. He had gone with Tracy Gould to see for himself where the 'incident' had taken place, just to have it all clear in his mind.

His wife, Naomi greeted him at the door and hugged him, glad that he was home safely. She could never have gone to bed alone whilst he was out. "How did it go, darling?" She knew he wouldn't tell her about the assignment or the danger, but knew him well enough to read between his words.

"At the moment it all looks very good. Just hope it will last until I can get my hands on those damned journals." He held her, feeling her warmth. "You shouldn't have waited up. "What a mess, aye?"

"Come in by the fire, I lit it earlier... you feel cold." She held his hand as if they were still young lovers, as they walked through to the lounge. "I'll make us some hot Cocoa. Does that sound nice?" She leaned forwards and kissed his cheek, her hand briefly touching his chest, affectionately. Feeling the hard metal under his armpit, her heart almost froze. Slowly she opened his lapel, her eyes fixated on the shoulder holster and the automatic under his arm. "Oh, darling, is that absolutely necessary, do you think?" She had never known him leave the house... armed before.

He 'pecked' her on the cheek. "It's just a precaution... really." He shrugged, trying to console her, trying to make light of it. "This is a sort of... unusual case, really." He kissed her on the cheek and held her for a 'long' second to console her fears.

Chapter 37

Friday 11:30pm.

"Take a seat, Paul," Alejandro said coldly, through the haze of cigar smoke, indicating the armchair opposite. He had wrapped a blanket around his shoulders against the night air, even though the room was unbearably hot and the log fire was blazing in the hearth. After the death of his granddaughter, Anastasia, he had changed inexorably, there was little compassion left in him now and the whole of his world had seemed to have collapsed around him. The funeral two days ago had drained the last vestige of energy from his tired old body. In fact the only thing that was keeping him alive now was 'vengeance!' He was determined with the last breath left in his body that he would seek out and destroy everyone connected with the death of Anastasia... regardless of cost.

Since her death the whole weight of The Met Corps had fallen on the shoulders of his son Marcos, a role he was completely unsuitable for and was totally out of his depth. Since the brutal murder of their daughter, Anastasia, Marcos's life circulated around his wife's mental illness and he seemed to be spending more time in the private sanatorium they had found for her than on the affairs of the company...

"You look tired, Alejandro." Paul forced a wan smile, hiding his fear. He watched Joseph from the corner of his eye, standing with his back against the door, his hands folded ominously across his huge chest. It was the first time he had been able to speak to Alejandro since the girl's death. "I can't begin to tell you how sorry I am, Alejandro…"

"You as good as murdered her…" The old man wheezed and spat a gob of brown phlegm towards the hearth. "You were there to protect her…"

"That's not true, Alejandro… not true at all." He protested his voice passionate but pleading, sitting on the edge of his seat. "We… were all there to protect her… we all failed her. It was…"

"What?" he spat out the question, almost screaming. "We, you say 'we'? It was your job, damn your eyes…"

"I can't take all of the responsibility Alejandro. You know the circumstances…the situation we were all in…looking for that damn man and Kristianna. I was as devastated as everyone about the 'child's' murder." He tried to defend himself, knowing full well that almost nothing he could say would ease the old man's pain. "Yes… sir, I will accept responsibility, because the 'buck' stops with me. But now… we have to think further along…" He knew he was treading on very thin ice, but felt that Alejandro had already decided his fate and if he 'cowered now', it really would be his ending. "We have to find them… or the Met Corps will exist no longer, sir…"

In reality, Paul didn't give a damn about the death of the 'stupid little tart', he had hated her from the very second he'd met her, with her stupid, overly privileged, unreasonable, demanding life style. But like everyone else he had responded to her demands and fickle temperament, her stupid requests for escorts and anything else she wanted on a silly whim, purely because of her relationships with

342

Alejandro. He knew, that in a way, she had singlehandedly demolished the power of the most powerful man in The Met Corps, namely her grandfather, simply by showing everyone one that he had his weakness… 'Yes'. He thought. 'I should have put more men with her…but you wanted all of them to chase around the country… damn it'. Instead he said. "She had the best security available at the time, Alejandro, you know what the situation was like, we needed to find Kristianna… The boy died by the way… Anastasia's bodyguard, he never recovered from his injuries, poor chap." Paul could see that the old man hadn't heard him.

"She was just a child." He wiped his face with his handkerchief, sounding a little demented. Not even hearing Paul's words. "A child… why would anyone want to kill something as beautiful and harmless as that?"

"No one could have imagined that she would be a target. She was a… civilian, not a…" But then so were Pendleton's family, Paul thought. In a way he knew he was right. If Alejandro had not issued the 'Termination' order without first trying to negotiate a deal with Pendleton, things may well have been different, the child may well be still alive… Stupid old fool, he thought.

"Tell me about the money, Paul…"

"Money?" The instant 'change of subject' threw him for a second.

"Your money…"

In a moment of madness he was tempted to tell Alejandro to mind his own 'Goddamned business', but his 'self-preservation' instincts kicked in, warning him to 'tread lightly' here. "I am a banker, Alejandro, I work the markets. There is nothing unusual about what I am doing… nothing at all." In the past they had argued, but their 'discussions', had never been the subject of a direct 'threat', as there was now. He made a mental note to track down Alejandro's source of information at the bank or at his brokers and crush them into total oblivion. In future, that 'source' would never work again, either in a bank or as a 'road sweeper'.

"You have consolidated all of it?" Alejandro's eyes never left Paul's.

"As I see fit, Alejandro." He said it as 'kindly' as he could. Not wanting to 'tilt' the balance of his fate more than he dared to. "I'm not sure I understand the implications of what are you suggesting?"

"Simply, that you won't mind easing my concerns a little by loaning 'all of it' to The Corps, on a temporary basis of course." Alejandro indicated the leather desk in the centre of the lounge with his finger. "You will find all the necessary documentation for you to sign, there."

"That's not fair, Alejandro. We have known each other for what, almost twenty years, and now you are saying that you don't trust me anymore, now it has come down to this? How can that be possible?" He knew he had been 'out played' by the old fool, and that there was nothing he could do about it... not if he wanted to walk out of here alive, tonight.

"And what of the shipment?"

Paul didn't really care anymore he knew one way or the other his time with Met Corps was at an end under the present 'regime'. "I've instructed them to divert it, with the agreement of the board, of course. At the moment it's standing out to sea, sixty miles off the Cornish coast awaiting the codes to bring it into either Brest or Calais. Calais I hope." He felt deflated.

"How far have we got with this Pendleton chap?" Alejandro didn't take his eyes from Paul's.

"He caught us... he caught 'me'... off guard..." He corrected himself. Everything else had been blamed on him, why not this... "With my Goddamned pants down. I assumed he was just some 'ordinary Joe'. Now I find that he is ex British Special Forces and has surrounded himself with mercenaries..."

"And paying for it with our money, by all account." Alejandro turned the screw, harder.

"I didn't expect..."

"I pay you to 'expect' the 'unexpected', Paul." He spat the words out contemptuously.

"I know..." There was almost nothing else he could say. What else was there? Even now he couldn't think of a satisfactory solution to the problem. "Will I be allowed to carry on... I would like to catch this man as much as you."

The old man nodded. "I am disappointed in you, Paul, bitterly disappointed. I expected more." He coughed through the smoke, wheezing heavily and turned away, his fingers touched the 'secret' button under the arm of his chair, pressing it once. The corresponding bracelet on Joseph's arm would vibrate... once only. Alejandro had been tempted to press it twice, which was the prearranged signal for Joseph to 'terminate' Paul's 'contract' with The Corps... but he held back. "Sign the papers before you leave," he said coldly.

***

Saturday morning: 8:30

"Kristianna!" Webb shouted across the courtyard as he ran towards her car. "Where are you going?" He opened her driver's door and leaning on the roof, reached in and took her keys from the ignition.

She smiled, placing her hand on his arm. "I have some business in town. I'll be gone most of the day... is that alright?"

"I want you to stay here today, please." He was a little winded and still dressed only in a thin T-shirt and jeans and an old pair of slippers he'd borrowed from Simon. "I have something on today… involving Simon." He guarded himself about expanding on it. "Therefore I would like everyone to stay here… for the day, well… at least until about one… until he gets back that is." He opened the door wider waiting for her to swing her legs out. The cold autumn air and the drizzle cut through his thin shirt, chilling him.

But she stayed seated, waiting, enjoying his discomfort as his eyes flicked back and forth from her 'too short' mini-frock and her plunging neck line and then back to her face… "Do I need to know about it, darling, we are supposed to be 'partners', you know?" She slipped her hand between his legs, gently massaging along the insides of his thighs and then pulling him closer to her… "You don't feel that you can tell me?"

"Not at the moment…" He stepped back, freeing himself from her. "When Simon returns, we'll all have a meeting and I'll run through everything with all of you, put you in the picture… yeah? As I said, at the moment, I don't want anyone leaving. Hopefully we can be out of here tomorrow, completely. You'd like that… wouldn't you?"

She swivelled in her seat and faced him, her mini-frock riding along her thighs revealing the tiny white panties… teasing him and held out her hand for him to help her out. "It's not important, darling…" She spoke softly, provocatively and slipped her hands around his buttocks. "But what could I possibly find to do here all day? I don't knit or sew, and this place just feels like I have been thrown back into the Stone Age. We could…" She kissed the side of his cheek and ran her tongue across his lips. "Go up and have a shower together and… well… think of something more 'constructive' to do…"

Webb held her forearms and gently pushed her away from him. Last night, at the top of the track, had been enough for him in his dealings with her, the sooner he was shot of her, the better.

She seemed to read his mind. "Or... we could go back up there..." She nodded at the fence stile. "And finish off what we 'almost' started last night." Her fingers fiddle with the zip of his fly... disappointed when he pulled away from her, but she smiled inwardly...knowing that she would need to 'rearrange' her plans for today... but that it wouldn't be a problem, one way or the other, Mr. Tanner was a very capable man, and very resourceful.

"You're incorrigible, dear..." He tried to speak dispassionately, but felt her closeness already arousing him. At the top of the house in the room he knew to be his he could see Gabriella, framed by the light, looking anxiously down at them. 'If only her elder sister was as little trouble.' He had grown fond of Gabriella this past week and liked her easy going manner... 'and' her vast sexual appetite. She seemed honest and genuine but he was still a little unclear whether he could totally trust her, or whether she was still heavily influenced by her sister... Kristianna.

"I think I'll change and go for a walk..." She walked away from him smiling, inside she was fuming. Again the day's plans would need to be changed... She hoped her mobile worked from the top of the hill, Herbert Tanner wouldn't go ahead with the plan if she didn't turn up, or at least be given the okay for it to go ahead.

"Let's just go through everything again, Simon." Webb felt tense and nervous. They were alone in Simon's office and he had checked the door several times to ascertain no one could possibly over hear them. He knew it was imperative that no one else needed to know anything about any of their arrangements... not until it was over, at least. What ever happened in the next few hours he needed this to go well for his own sanity and the security of his own 'people' and for them to be safely out of the country by tomorrow. "Your appointment isn't until three... its ten o'clock now. Maximum, four hours' drive, even with bad traffic. Give yourself plenty of time and for Christ sake, drive under the speed limit. You can't afford to get picked up, not for anything."

"I don't see why we don't just fax the documents through, boss. Wouldn't that be just as easy?"

"I'd thought of that, but Harrington says they wouldn't be admissible in a court of law, they wouldn't accept what they consider as 'copies'. They need the 'real thing' for a conviction." He tapped Simon's breast pocket, both sides. "You're not carrying…"

"I will be but it makes Pippa a little nervous in the house." He shrugged his shoulders, pushing the mop of blond hair from his eyes. "Pippa hates it when I'm tooled up in the house. Mind you, if the last time was anything to go by, it won't make too much difference. If somehow they know about this, then the 'long-range shot' will bugger all of us up."

"That's true…" He was already starting to worry.

Simon shrugged, he had done all he could to safeguard the delivery and himself there was nothing more he could think of to add to it. "And don't forget, boss, I'm meeting a whole 'bundle' of policemen… it 'should' be pretty safe… with that many cops around, don't you think?"

"Anyway, just watch yourself, mate." He slapped his arm, leaving his hand on Simon's shoulder for a second, knowing that he should be doing this himself, really. "If anything looks out of place, anything at all… just back off out of it, right?" He handed Simon the heavy briefcase containing the original five journals. As a safeguard he had spent most of the night photostatting them, intendin to keep the copies for his own safety. "Now you're absolutely clear, Simon, on everything? I can't overstate the importance of what you are carrying." He was starting to worry again.

"Webbley…" Simon interrupted him and nodded, smiling confidently. "It's okay. We've been through it a dozen times. I have everything I need," he said eloquently. "This is my job; I do stuff like this all the time. I know the dangers and the risks... I'm a pro..."

"Sure... sure." He felt chastised but understood. "It's just that this bloody business is screwing up my head. Fuck it... just be careful. Or should I come with you?" he added as an afterthought.

Simon smiled. "You need to get down to Cornwall, make the arrangements with the McGillicuddy's or nothing will ever get resolved. Yeah? That's more important." He tapped Webb's arm. "I just need to see Pippa before I leave, just to put her mind at rest."

***

Paul Kyso rose late, it was unusual for him to be still in bed at nine-thirty in the morning. Initially there seemed little point waking up and doing anything anyway, after last night. With the exception of a few thousand pounds and some change, he was completely broke now. With one simple stroke of his pen he had signed every penny over to Alejandro and The Met Corps almost fifteen million dollars... Damn. It represented every penny he had put aside for an event such as this...

For the first time in his life, he had entered the world of 'penury'. He was loath to sell anything in the house, especially his book collection, which had taken almost a quarter of a century to collect. It might come to that, but not yet. He caught a glimpse of himself in the hallway mirror as he passed and then retraced his steps and stared at the 'unsatisfactory' image reflected back at him. How had he ever allowed 'this' to happen? How had his once superbly, muscular body developed into a grossly overweight... grossly unfit image he could now see... for a moment he despised himself. 'Too many years of luxury...of the 'easy life'...he decided, dejectedly.

He wasn't a tall man by any means, standing barely five feet six inches in his stockings. The hairline had receded dramatically, now only forming a thin semicircle around the crown of his head, unlike his belly which had developed a huge paunch, giving the impression that he was actually shorter. He attempted to pull his tummy in and 'puff' out his chest, but it seemed to make little or no difference. Over the years his tummy and chest and buttocks had conspired against him, assisted by the overwhelming force of 'gravity', giving him the shape of an enormous 'barrel'.

At university there had been a time when he had run marathons and been captain of the football team. 'Where had all those years gone', up until this morning he had been admired, respected and by most, even feared, albeit grudgingly. It wouldn't be long before everyone in Met Corps would know of his demise, from the office junior up, before that happened he had to act… and act now. The 'way back' to favour was there in front of him, but the solution just hadn't materialised yet. A feeling of despair and fear swept over him, there was a way… there just had to be.

He looked again at the image in the mirror… 'it lied to him'… The overall 'shape' might be that of an overweight sixty-three years old man, but the 'mind' was as sharp and as 'athletic' as it had been as the twenty-year-old student that had captained the college football team… A dim spark 'twinkled' at the back of his mind. Tzu Cheng, in his book, 'The Art of War', had written… 'Treat adversity as a friend and command that friend to do your bidding…'

He needed to 'attack' and now, but how? 'There was weakness in every strategy' Tzu Cheng had said. He walked into the lounge and drew the curtains and poured himself a Scotch, then placed a single ice cube in the glass. Thinking was much easier on your feet… 'How would that twenty years old captain of the football team handle this?'

All their endeavours to find Pendleton had been fruitless, with the exception of a brief encounter at the bungalow. He wondered where that information had come from… but there, there 'was' the 'weakness', someone in Pendleton's 'camp' was helping to betray him. Pendleton was crafty, surrounding himself with highly competent mercenaries and he was elusive, never staying long enough at one location to be caught. "Clever… very clever." He spoke the words out loud, it seemed to make more sense like that. The Scotch stung his throat, drinking before midday was not a normal habit with him, but it helped to clear his head of the constant fear. "So, if the mountain won't come to Mohammed, then Mohammed will have to go to the mountain…"

Pendleton would need to be flushed out of his 'hole'. Paul paced the floor in front of his grand, marble fireplace, he'd had it shipped over from an Egyptian monastery, in the days when things were much 'simpler'. His mind whirled with fresh ideas, fresh new thoughts bombarded his brain… most he discarded immediately, Pendleton's friends in Cornwall were surrounded by mercenaries and legitimate police, his own men were there but they had already told him that the target was too well covered… so what then? He needed something easier… something more definite… "No… there's a much easier target…" He was so elated that he shouted it out loud. "Much easier… and much more commanding,"… and… he already had his men on site.

He rushed over to the telephone and dialled the number. 'Why hadn't he thought of it before… it would be so easy… and above all… it would flush Pendleton out.' "Dick…" He felt a surge of his old confidence returning. "I need you to do a job for me… now."

Chapter 38

Saturday:

It was almost four o'clock before Gabriella and Webb returned from Cornwall. She had begged to go with him rather than stay in what she referred to as 'this awful old house', for another second longer. And he was glad she was there, her light, idle banter and constant sexual overtones lightened his mood and took some of the worry from his mind.

The visit to the McGillicuddy's had been barely thirty minutes long, much to the chagrin of Sue who had wanted them to stay longer, but that was all he dared to spare, needing to get back to Hartness House as soon as possible, just in case anything went wrong with Simon's delivery.

He had, after a long time, managed to convince Steve and Sue however, to follow his instructions to the letter and get out of the country tonight at the latest. The next high tide was at 2 am. Sunday morning and they were to take the new Van Dam Nordia, 'quietly' over to Cork, in Ireland and wait there. Once there they were to make a call to Roger Harrington's home, and using Webb's old army 'nickname' of 'Quillian', say simple, 'Get a message to Quillian that S. and S. are well'. "Nothing else," Webb insisted. "I'll send two of Peter's men with you. They're all ex S.A.S. and they'll be tooled up, you can trust them, don't let them call anyone, whatever happens and take their damned mobiles off of them, just to be sure." After the brief conversation he had hugged Sue and given her a big kiss. "I'm sorry about this, darlin', most of it wasn't of my making. If anything ever happened to either of you two, because of me... well, it doesn't bear thinking about." He had 'bear hugged' Steve. "You take care of her for me, mate... remember, one night in Cork only, unless the weather is shit, then back up to Dartmouth... I'll meet you there in a day or so, when I can..." Before he left he handed Steve a large holdall. "There's about two mill in there. It's yours. When this is over, do what you want with it. I just hope this all goes right..." He had choked up and left quickly, silently praying that no harm would come to them...

Steve's words still rang in his ears as they drove. "You hope..." he had said. "Tell me what you hope for, Webbley, that the usual shit that surrounds you doesn't get 'splattered' across the faces of 'all' your friends at the same time or that 'you' come out of it alright. It's one thing to help out a 'friend', mate, when he's down on his luck or just needs a little 'handout' once in a while... but this?" The disgust had been evident in his voice. "We don't need your money, boy... we had a good, simple life before this and that is all we ever wanted... what was it that 'you' wanted, Webbley?"

He had countered, unconvincingly, telling Steve that even if he hadn't come down to see them, they would have been implicated... "Simply because we're mates. These bastards are ruthless... and I just couldn't let them get to you or Sue without doing 'something'. I'm sorry." Webb knew that he had lost one of the most important things in life... a mate!

The return journey had seemed interminable. "Jesus! I can't let anything happen to those people. I have to do 'everything' I can to look after them... if anything ever happened to them..." It didn't bear thinking about, so he changed his thoughts to the 'in hand problems'. "Wonder how they got on?" He parked the car outside of the front entrance of Hartness, talking to himself, not really caring if the car blocked anyone in.

"Who?" Gabriella asked sleepily as they entered the house and walked through to the main lounge. Half-a-dozen maids were still busy cleaning up from last night's party in the main Great Hall and the music was so loud that she didn't hear his reply. "Who?" she shouted.

"Any calls...?" he asked Kristianna, not answering Gabriella, his eyes watching Kristianna closely, wondering what she had been up too for most of the day, not really caring.

"Calls, no... what were you expecting. I'm sure 'that' awful 'Pippa woman' would have told me if there had been anything of importance." Kristianna sulked. She was seated in the old armchair with her feet resting on the pouffe. "I doubt whether that wouldn't be too complicated, even for her... would it?" She walked over to the wine cabinet, and freshened her Martini, ignoring the needs of the others as if they weren't there.

Webb mumbled something incomprehensible and she asked him to repeat it... but he just mumbled again. "Nothing, just chuntering... what are you so damned grumpy about?" he grumbled as he made Gabriella and himself a large gin and tonic.

"Such a delightful colloquialism... what does 'chuntering' actually mean?" She tried to control the tenseness in her voice, just as eager as he was to get some kind of information.

"Will you just shut up fuckin' 'babbling' for a minute, for Christ's sakes? Sometimes I wonder about the crap that comes out of your mouth." He felt irritable and bad-tempered and knew that his comment was uncalled for and totally unnecessary.

Kristianna just shrugged and made a face. As usual she was dressed impeccably in a grey miniskirt suit, the skirt far too short for her endlessly long legs and the white blouse was exposing far too much of her. He couldn't remember seeing her in the same dress or suit, twice. She never seems to just 'flop' like 'normal people' did, just to 'lounge about', but always had to sit with her back straight and her legs neatly tucked to one side or crossed, as if someone had stuffed a steel ramrod up her backside, he thought. "What do 'you' do for relaxation, Kristianna? You're always wound up like a coiled spring." he asked her, a little cuttingly… just to annoy her really. "Learn to fuckin' relax. Jesus!"

"I am relaxed now, darling, completely relaxed." She smiled her 'favourite' disarming smile at him. "But you must remember, while you two have been gallivanting around the country enjoying yourselves. I have been cooped up in 'the land that time forgot'." She cuttingly referred to Simon's house.

"But really 'relax'. Go on tell me, what do you do for 'entertainment', honestly?" He continued to probe, knowing that it was annoying her, regardless of the happy content face she was portraying.

"Darling, I have always had a very full life, you know that, Webbley." She smiled again, her body or face betraying nothing of her true feelings and the hatred she felt for him at this moment. 'If only you knew… you stupid man. If only you knew.' She thought.

The telephone rang in the hallway, cutting short their conversation. Webb's gut tightened up. They could hear the telephone being answered but it was too far away to make out the conversation.

Pippa appeared in the doorway, the lines of stress across her forehead seemed to dominate her countenance, completely. "It's the Chief Constable for Hampshire, Roger Harrington, for you…" She looked at him disparagingly he could feel the hate in her eyes. Pippa pointed to the telephone on the table next to Kristianna. "I've put it through to there…"

His fingers shook as he lifted the receiver from its cradle, knowing that this had to be trouble. Why would Harrington phone here before Simon had… that wasn't the arrangement at all. The arrangement with Simon had been that he alone would telephone the house and then only after successfully completing the assignment and that only 'he' would phone the house to confirm it… no one else. "Roger, what's up?"

"Problems, old chap… I'm afraid, big, big problems. Was that Simon's wife who answered?" The voice shook with trepidation.

"Yes, it was…" Webb turned to face Pippa, still leaning anxiously on the door jamb, listening… waiting, nibbling dejectedly at her fingernails. Her mother-in-law, Rowan stood behind her, her arm around her daughter-in-law's waist.

"Damn…" Harrington cursed. "Bad business… look, good lord I don't even know how to say this. They were all ambushed at the meeting place… slaughtered, all of them. Three of my men and two of yours… No one survived…"

"Jesus fuck… how...?" He heard a sharp intake of breath from the 'shadow' in the doorway.

"Is… it… Simon?" Pippa stuttered, taking a pace towards him… panic already in her words, now barely able to speak, her hands clasped around her mouth, a terrible fear shrouding her eyes.

Webb looked away, wanting to walk over and hold her, comfort her, but his feet wouldn't move. He looked away, unable to face her. "All of them, 'two' of my men, I only sent one...?" he whispered into the mouth piece.

"There were two in the car one was dressed in a sort of Arab headdress... with a sort of Arab scarf over his head."

"Jesus...! There must have been a leak... from your end... only Simon and I knew about it from here." He held his forehead in his hands, leaning his head on the wall in despair, his fingers crushing the receiver, his chest tightening with grief and fear. Slowly he looked over to Pippa and she knew by his eyes that her husband was dead.

Pippa rested her head on the door jamb, stumbling tears pouring from her eyes as Rowan hugged her. A terrible, deep wailing sound came from her mouth and rose to a deafening crescendo, like a small calf with its foot trapped in a snare. Slowly Rowan eased her into the hallway and closed the door behind them... ...

In the distance they could still hear the screams echoing around the walls. Webb made a move to follow her but Kristianna stood and held him, her arms around his neck, hugging him. "Don't, Webbley, please... she needs to be alone with her pain... leave her." She kissed his neck affectionately, her heart jumping with relief and joy... So Mr. Herbert Tanner has performed his 'miracle', again... after all... she thought.

Gabriella huddled into his side, weeping, her tears wetting his shirt... unable to control her emotions.

"It couldn't have been my end, Webbley, I told no one, not until they were a few minutes from the rendezvous. No one could have set up such a thing in that time. The long-range shooter was there again... how could he have known... I don't understand?" Roger's voice broke, still finding difficulty understanding it all... "I... I don't know what we are into here, but I have never seen anything like it... so many deaths... It is violence of the first magnitude..."

"Tell me... what happened... as far as you know it... Roger." He struggled to regain some of his composure.

Roger stammered with his words, still finding it difficult to talk. "As I said, my men were just told to head along the M27 motorway, and then when they were just minutes from the rendezvous I gave them the exact location, their final instructions... literally five minutes from it... there is just no way anyone else could have known, even if they could have intercepted my transmissions, they couldn't possibly have gotten there in time. The sniper knew exactly where to set up, he was waiting for them." Roger blew his nose and continued. "And you say, you and your courier were the only people who knew? Who was the second man, then?"

Webb said he didn't know. "It must have been someone that Simon brought in to help him. It's the only thing I can think of." He was desperately trying to keep his head balanced.

"They took the journals... of course." Roger's voice was flat. Now he had three dead policemen and he would need an explanation to give to the Home Office of why he had failed. "These were not just ordinary policemen, Webbley, they were a highly trained, highly efficient S.W.A.T. team. Dear me..."

"Roger, I need time to think... let me get back to you later, an hour or so... right." Slowly he replaced the receiver and flopped down into the old, worn sofa, his head in his hands, despair surrounding him. Slowly, methodically he explained the situation to Kristianna and Gabriella and leaned back into the sofa. "What the hell do I say to Pippa... and the kids?"

Gabriella wept and knelt at his feet, her head in his lap. Kristianna snuggled her head into his neck, her arm around his shoulders as she sat on the arm.

"These men... The Corps, they are totally ruthless, I told you that. Life means absolutely nothing to them, they don't care who they hurt. Good lord, that poor woman." Kristianna had to snuggle deeper into his neck to hide her face and not allow him to feel her heartbeat that was pounding so hard against her breast, lest he see through her deceit. She was a consummate actress, but even 'she' wasn't sure whether she could hide the look of pure pleasure in her eyes from him. If she had been alone she would have 'brought the house down' with her screams of pure joy, she would have telephoned Herbert Tanner and congratulated him on a job 'well done'... but that would have to wait... time for that later when she had the journals safely in her hands. With those she could 'build her own' Met Corps. Even without the money the journals would be worth an absolute fortune, now.

The telephone rang again, disturbing the mood. Gabriella reached over, sniffled and lifted the receiver. "It's the policeman again..."

"What?" was all he could manage as he put the handset to his ear. "What now for fucks sake?"

"Webbley..." Roger Harrington seemed to be having difficulty speaking at all. "I really don't know what we are into here, but..." There was a long pause. "I... have... just been informed... that... your wife and daughter have just been killed... Oh God..."

"What, how do you mean... what is this? They were in protective custody..." Webb stood, knocking Gabriella to the floor and screamed into the handset. "Your fuckin' 'protective custody.' How the fuck did that happen? They were in your 'safe house'... how could that possibly happen? My God, and you still don't think you have a leak?"

"It's so crazy... I'm so sorry... it appears... on the face of it, that the attackers were the two... relief policemen..."

The grief was evident in his voice. "They... they have left a note with instructions... and... your son, they have taken your son... kidnapped him."

Webb looked at the handset and threw it hard against the wall. He rushed over to the door and flung it open almost standing on Gabriella ... but he didn't notice. "I need to get out of here..." he said simply.

"This has Paul Kyso written all over it, Webbley." Kristianna touched his arm but he pushed it away. "I know how he works..."

As soon as Webb had left the room, Kristianna collected the pieces of the handset and screwed the mouthpiece back on. "Are you still there?" She spoke calmly, coldly.

"Yes... yes, I am..."

"Mr. Pendleton is a little upset at the moment. I will get him to telephone you later... thank you," she said curtly and replaced the handset in its cradle. "This has all the hallmarks of Paul Kyso, I know it does." She said again not realising she was speaking out loud...

Gabriella crawled up to the sofa and placed her hands on her sister's knee hoping to gain a small modicum of comfort from her, but Kristianna rejected her touch, pushing her hands away as she walked around the room. .

Her mind was working fast, trying to 'decode' the last few minutes. Now that 'could' be decisive... I hadn't thought of them killing Webb's family and taking the boy... very clever of them. She wondered around the room, her mind working through scenarios. 'Damn, I should have thought of that and done the same myself...' She thought. Again... she realised that one way or the other she had been out manoeuvred. Her mind worked quickly. How is our 'Webbley' going to handle this, I wonder?

"Did you... have something to do with all of this, Kristianna?" Gabriella screamed, launching a verbal tirade at her, pointing her finger. "If you did... I will tell Webbley... I promise I will and he'll kill you for it."

Kristianna leapt at her, snatching a handful of her hair and jolted her neck back, her other hand around Gabriella's throat choking the life out of her. Gabriella tried to scream, but the grip was too tight.

"If you say a word about any of this... little sister... to anyone, I'll send you packing as I did the other stupid little tart..." She forced Gabriella's head back further and further, digging her fingers into the soft flesh, throttling her windpipe. "Do you understand...?" she screamed at her, and then threw her to the floor. "We have come too far now to turn back... I will not lose what I have set up here... with or without you... Is that clear? If I find out that you have said anything, I'll kill you myself."

Gabriella nodded, struggling to her knees her fingers massaging her neck. All of her life she had been terrified of Kristianna. Even as children, whenever Gabriella made something, or did something creative, Kristianna would always destroy it, especially as they progressed through their teenage years. Gabriella could never hold onto a boyfriend or even an ordinary 'friend' for longer than a 'moment' before Kristianna took them away from her, just because she could. Every boy wanted to be with Kristianna.

She sat up on the sofa as Kristianna stormed from the room, shaking. What 'other little tart'? she thought. Surely not... no... not Anastasia! They said she had been... dismembered. Even Kristianna couldn't do that... could she?

Webb felt the pain in his legs and through his chest as he ran, holding his head up against the beating rain, the droplets stung his face but he was oblivious to the pain they were causing. He 'needed' to feel the pain, the grinding, deep pain that he hoped would cleanse him of his guilt, and fear. The rain added to the pain as it lashed his face, but it didn't matter, nothing seemed to matter anymore… nothing. He drove his feet into the ground, running faster and faster until he felt his lungs were about to burst but didn't stop until he had reached the top of the knoll and collapsed at the foot of the big oak. He could see the soft, innocent face of his daughter swirling in front of his eyes and felt the panic she must have gone through before they killed her… "Why… why all this?" He screamed at the oak tree. "The only thing she ever did wrong in her life was having me as a father. Greed… my fucking greed, that's what led us all to this…" He hated himself with a vengeance at that moment. Thoughts tortured him of his boy in the hands of those animals, knowing they weren't bluffing. Harrington had read out the ransom demand to him and he knew that the people holding the boy would do exactly what the note said…that a finger would be delivered to the local police station, every hour after eight this evening. The boy's captors had said Web was to leave his mobile switched on, from six o'clock so that instructions could be given. Tears of hate and frustration welled from his eyes…maybe, just maybe, he could do a deal with them…but he doubted it. Everything was far too late for that…he needed another solution…peace with them was not an option now…

***

"Well done, lad… damn, well done." Paul Kyso slapped Dick Cordon on the back. "I should have thought of that before, it's so simple. Now he'll damned well come to heal."

Dick smiled, he'd had secretly cleared the action with Alejandro first, but hadn't told Paul. "It'll cost us for the two policemen though, they'll never be able to work in England ever again. I promised them half a mill each…"

Paul smiled. "Worth every penny… where are they now?"

"Amsterdam, on their way to Spain, we can find work down there for them if they still 'want' to work."

"And the boy?"

"Don't worry, he's safe. I sent him down to Martha like you suggested she'll take good care of him until the hand over."

"Yeah, I want to go through that with you. Make sure nothing happens to that boy, nothing, not yet anyway. I want this bastard to suffer… and my God… he really 'will' suffer." The smile had left his face. "But don't touch the boy, Dick, unless I give specific orders, I want that bastard Pendelton alive… then afterwards you can do what you want with the boy… and I'll sort out Pendelton." Paul Kyso knew well enough Dick Cordon's 'sexual persuasion' for young boys, he had enough 'video evidence' to support that.' "You understand me…? We have to give the impression of 'a straight swap', at least." He pointed a finger, threateningly at him.

Dick Cordon smiled. "Don't worry, boss, it's all in hand."

"I want you to handle everything yourself. Only use the mobile… keep the call's short… and take Joseph and Domingo with you, they're bad bastards, but good at their jobs, nothing gets past them." He watched Dick's face closely. After this, as long as everything went to his plan he would be reinstated as head of The Met Corps and regain his true authority with Alejandro and have all his money returned, then… he would deal with Alejandro in his own way for putting him through this torture and anyone else he considered a threat... what ever happened he would make a 'clean sweep' of everyone he felt had been disloyal, even in the slightest way. But vengeance could wait for now, he needed to keep his mind secular. "You have my home number, phone me immediately after Pendleton's call…"

Cornwall:

"Get everything up together, we're out of here," Webb said coldly without emotion as he walked back into the lounge. He was soaked to the skin and his legs were covered in mud from the track, his face now old and drawn with pain. But a calmness had settled over him and his mind was functioning as it should in a crisis… calculating… cunning… and aggressive, ready to go on the attack. He sat for a moment in the old sofa, dried his hands on the throw and rolled a cigarette. "Where's Kristianna?"

"I think she went up to her room." Gabriella sat next to him, her hand on his shoulder. "What about you, Webbley, are you… okay?"

"Sure I am…" He leaned his head for a moment on her shoulder, taking some small comfort from her nearness and her warmth. "But there's a lot to do, we need to be on the road… now."

"But what about your son, darling?" She lit the cigarette for him from the lighter on the coffee table and then snuggled against his shoulder, her hands caressing his wet legs.

"They won't hand him back, you know they won't… it wouldn't be in their best interest, and they know by now that I would still come after them, anyway." He shrugged his shoulders, and touched her arm, affectionately. "Give Kristianna a call for me, Gabby, will you. I'll be in my bedroom, I need a shower and get everything packed away."

While she was away it gave him a little time to think. The main priority was of course the safety of the boy, but he knew he would need Kristianna's help, she had a better insight into the workings of the 'minds' inside of the Met Corps and how it worked and especially how to get to 'this' Kyso character than anyone else. They would need to go on the 'offensive', straight away not just wait for something to happen. But he knew that there was no way Kyso was going to hand the boy over… alive. Webb knew he had to bring them in 'closer'... so that he could deal with them on his own terms.

"Darling, how are you?" Kristianna 'floated in' giving her best 'affected performance'. She rushed over to him and knelt at his feet holding his knees affectionately. "I am so sorry..." She lifted his mud strewn hand and kissed it.

"Tell me about this Paul Kyso feller," he said, coldly.

Kristianna hid her smile behind her eyes. She wanted to scream to the world of her joy and her delight that it had all turned back into her favour. The second telephone call had been a Godsend, unbelievable luck... and she knew instinctively that it could only have been Paul Kyso who had carried out the attack. She wondered again about asking him to stay on as head of The Met Corps security, when she became the 'Director', but changed her mind in favour of her second choice... no, Herbert Tanner would be far better in that position, he held the same lack of morals and ruthlessness as she did.

It was just 'unbelievable pleasure' for her... she was the 'new mother' giving birth to her first child... 'the poor man winning the lottery', the 'cat that got the cream'... everything rolled into one pleasurable moment.

Gabriella looked suspiciously at her sister, desperate to warn Webb of her treachery, but fearful for her own life. 'Later', she promised herself, when they were alone she would find the courage to tell him... She sniffled again and rubbed her sore eyes with a tissue.

"What are you thinking, Webbley?" Kristianna, as usual answered a question with a question.

"I think we need to pay this 'little man' a visit." He drew deeply on his 'homemade' cigarette.

Kristianna controlled the excitement, wondering if he could actually feel her heart beating... to her, it was so loud. "Could I have one of those?" she asked, demurely.

Calmly he rolled her one, lit it and handed it to her. "Can you get me some P.E.?"

"Plastic explosive, of course." She coughed as she inhaled. "I can do better than that, if you want. How about Cemtex or C4? That gives a much louder 'bang'."

He smiled wryly. Wondering why he was so surprised, why shouldn't she be able to get stuff like that, she seemed to have a hand in most things that were unsavoury and didn't they sell it 'over the counter' at Tesco's? "Det. Cord... a couple of timers... and half a dozen... dets, and a small electricians tool wallet." He continued.

She nodded, smiling. "Is this what you did in the army?" Kristianna was frightened that he might feel her excitement.

"Part of it... I used to be quite good at it, at one time." He stubbed the butt out into the ashtray. "First we have to get out of here and find somewhere safe to hole up... they are going to call at eight, so we need to be ready for them and we need to get closer... this damned place is miles from anywhere."

"That's the best thing I've heard all day." It was the first time since his return that Gabriella had really spoken. "I hate this house. I just can't find anything nice to say about it."

"I was going to ask you to stay here, Gabby..." he could see by the look on her face that she had no intentions of staying. He held his hand up before she could speak. "You come with me then, show me where this feller Kyso lives and then I'll drop you off in the nearest hotel. Kristianna will have to go on ahead to pick up that stuff." He eased her away from his knees, having her that close gave him 'goosebumps.'

Gabriella smiled through her tears. "Thank you, I couldn't stay a moment longer here, not with these awful people."

In the gravelled driveway they heard the sound of a car, crunching to a stop and then the outside door slamming shut. No one took any notice, the house was a 'menagerie' of people coming and going all through the day…

Gabriella's scream was ear-splitting, deafening and startled the other two, from her position she was the only one with a full view of the doorway.

Webb watched the startling change on Kristianna's face, her eyes turning to huge, bulging 'saucers' as she looked over the back of the sofa… following Gabriella's eyes.

Webb turned, the automatic already in his hand, aiming at the figure in the doorway.

"Hi…" Simon said flatly. "Where is everyone?"

Chapter 37

Saturday evening:

"You are a very efficient chap, Dick." Paul Kyso snipped the end from a huge Cuban cigar and offered it to his deputy. "I'm thoroughly impressed. How long have you been with me now?" He lit the cigar in Dick's mouth and then handed him the lead crystal glass, half filled with his best, twelve years old malt.

"Eight years... almost nine." Dick puffed happily and sipped at the Scotch.

"Have a seat... please." He ushered him into the leather bound, handstitched 'Chabraise' armchair next to the fireplace. In the whole of Paul's extensive French antique collection, this chair was his absolute favourite. Since its restoration, two years ago, which had been carried out by a master craftsman from the original company, no one but him had ever sat in it... "Were there any problems?"

"No, none at all, it was unbelievably easy really." He shrugged, cockily puffing at the huge cigar. "I um... did let the fellers have their um... way with the girl first though, thought it might give them a little 'added bonus' for them, bit of an incentive and I thought it might make a better 'impression' on our 'client', show them that we weren't fucking about, mind you." He sniggered, puffing again on cigar, enjoying the attention. "That Joseph has a pretty healthy sexual appetite though… went through the girl 'and' the mother, almost without a break. He's 'hung' like a bloody donkey. It was strange though, the girl didn't even scream… she just allowed him to strip her off and fuck the arse off of her… didn't even make a murmur. Maybe she enjoyed it, although I doubt that very much. I think she must have just been paralyzed with fear, or something, she just didn't struggle or anything… he just manoeuvred her around like a rag doll, any position he wanted her in… weird… not a murmur, well… not until I cut her throat. Pity really, she was quite a looker."

Paul winced a little. "I don't need to know the details, Dick…please," he said quickly, feeling a little 'squeamish' at the thought of it all. "Why did you keep the boy and not the girl?" He knew he need not have asked, knowing full well Dick Cordon's sexual preferences.

Dick shrugged his shoulders but didn't answer…

"Well, like I said, it should flush him out, but we need to be careful with him… he's no fool, he's likely to come at us from any direction, so just be on your guard. Yeah, and Martha was good with it?"

"Sure. She ought to be, we pay her enough. That 'whorehouse' turns over more than any other six houses in the company and she's a genius with the customers… She's got the best looking girls 'and' boys' in the area, mainly Rumanian and Asian but they're all very pretty. I think it will be a 'first' for her to get an English lad. Do you ever get down there?" Dick sipped at his Scotch… one day… maybe… he would be able to afford to drink this… every night.

Paul shook his head vigorously. In his mind there was just 'something' horribly sickening about 'dirty, used women' that made his skin crawl. Not for him… he would always have 'the pick-of-the-bunch', long before anyone else touched them, while they were still untouched and virginal. 'His' latest 'aquisition' was still waiting for him in his bedroom, tied and gagged to the bedpost. She was fourteen years old and Swedish, a 'pure' blonde all the way through. Two days ago she had been 'unsullied' and virginal, by the end of the week he would be finished with her 'education' and she would be passed over to Martha for the 'trade' to use' and he would never want to see her again.

"We still make good money from it?" Paul's question was rhetorical and irrelevant... he knew the source of every penny that came into the Corps coffers and every facet that made the Corps 'tick'... it was his job to know... how else would he know about the 'scams'. Especially Martha's 'up-market' whorehouse, it turned over a phenomenal amount of money, due in the main to the very high quality of young women and boy's 'imported' from around the world and the 'very' exclusive, carefully selected clientele.

Paul glanced nonchalantly up at the very top row of his fabulous, hand-built bookcase, to the row upon row of DVDs. and discs he had collected over the many years with the Corps. Stored on these tapes was enough information to bring down 'several' governments. Judges, barristers of note, senior police officers and law makers... all were featured in ways that would bring about the downfall of their social and... or... political careers to an abrupt halt, if they were ever made public and the only other person in the world who knew about the cameras was Martha... and she would never disclose 'that' information to anyone... knowing that it would cost her, her life.

He sniggered inwardly. 'Why would these stupid people, make themselves so vulnerable, to allow themselves to be compromised in such a way?' he mused. On the rare occasion, when he was a little bored or tired, he would select one or two of the videos to watch. It never ceased to amuse him.

"Let me ask you something, Dick. Don't you feel… sometimes… that the company is getting a little… how should I put it? Let's say, tardy, overburdened with the power structure. Do you find that?" Paul Kyso edged around the question, cautiously.

Dick Cordon shrugged. "They've always been pretty good to me, boss… I can't complain. I do my job…" He raised his glass to his lips hiding his eyes, fearing a trap. "I'm a happy man, you know that."

"Mmm, the management is getting old, they have too many 'old' ideas. If we're not careful we'll be overtaken by the young, energetic 'gladiators' that are already showing their metal. Look how vulnerable we have become with this Pendleton chap… that would not have happened in the past and certainly wouldn't have happened 'now', if I had, had my way." He stood and walked across the room, his fingers touching the beautifully stained, antique walnut of his bookshelves from which he derived endless pleasures. "We need, well… people like you, Dick. People with a vision… people that get things done… do you see what I mean, Dick?"

"I'm not quite following this, boss. What is it you're suggesting?" He felt a little frightened, a little intimidated. His immediate 'boss', was talking 'treason', and would mean an immediate 'death sentence' if the wrong 'ears' had heard the exchange.

"A change…" He walked back over to face his deputy, feeling good, confident in his own ability again. "A change, Dick, kick out the 'old guard' and bring in the new… run the damn company ourselves… we already do, anyway… What do you say?"

"Wow… big step…" He swallowed the remainder of his malt. "Could I… have another one of those, d'ya think?"

"But we do. Don't we?" He refilled Dick's glass and handed it back, eager to get said what needed to be said. "We already run the company. Who knows more about the day-to-day running of it than people like us, not those stupid idiots that are up at the top now... they are just the 'pen-pushers', the 'accountants'... us!" He felt an excitement he hadn't felt in years surging through his veins. "We have enough 'loyal' people to do as we wish. Throughout history strong men have led the timid... it's our 'turn' now... don't you see that, Dick?"

Dick Cordon was young and ambitious, but he was no fool. He knew also that the situation he was in was what the American's would call... a rock or a hard place... If he said 'no', outright, then there would be little chance of him walking out of this office alive, to repeat the conversation to others. Since he had arrived he hadn't seen Bollo, Paul's personal bodyguard but knew that he was probably listening and watching close by with a very big gun pointed at Dick's head. If on the other hand he agreed, 'too' readily, he would probably face the same consequences. He thought about the possibilities of succeeding with Paul's scheme, to go against the most organised, most terrifying criminal organisation the world had ever seen... no, not a chance. It would be utter madness.

"I got a few reservations about it, Paul, but I like it..." Dick said, pretending enthusiastically. "Damn big job though. Do you think we could really pull it off, boss?"

"Damn right we can." Paul thrust his hand out and Dick took it. "Welcome aboard... partner."

"What the fuck!" Webb lowered the automatic and flicked the safety catch with his thumb. "What... how the fuck? The cops have just phoned... said you were dead..."

Gabriella had stopped screaming now but Kristianna's mouth was still wide open, in shock.

"Yes, I'm really sorry. It was just too dangerous to telephone, I didn't know if they had the house 'bugged', they seem to be pretty 'switched on', don't they." Simon apologised. "I got here as soon as I possibly could. Drove like a blessed lunatic..." He spoke calmly, as if nothing special, or out of the ordinary had happened.

Webb walked over to him, wondering whether he should smack him in the mouth or hug him, but did neither. "Go on then, for fuck sake... tell me how you got out of it and they didn't. How did that happen, and who were the two poor bastards that 'did' get killed?" He turned to look at Kristianna, she had said nothing, her mouth still open... appearing dumbstruck.

"They were my men...I sent them in as a 'recce' party, as I always would in this sort of situation, Webbley, regardless of where I was. It's was a perfectly normal procedure." He seemed a little shaken now. "I underestimated the people we were up against though, that was my fault and it won't happen again, I can assure you." He held the heavy briefcase out for Webb to take. "You told me that you and I and the policeman were the only ones who knew of the meeting, that was obviously not the case." He pushed past Webb and walked into the understairs den and poured himself a large Scotch, sank it in one swallow and poured another. Webb and the two women followed him in.

"I don't know whether that was an act of 'selfish' self-preservation or just pure bloody genius on your part, mate." Webb poured himself a gin and tonic and faced Simon. "Or whether there's some other agenda here... or whether I should just blow your fucking head off." In his hand was the big .45, pointing directly at Simon's head.

"Such as what, what ulterior motive could 'I' have, for goodness sake?" He didn't wait for an answer. "What are you saying, Webbley... that you don't trust 'me'?" He felt angry at the assumption. "Let me tell you, I'm damn good at what I do, Webbley, damn good, that's why I'm still alive. Those chaps were my men, they were colleagues and they were my friends... I know their families. So please don't remind me about losing people. What I did was perfectly normal for any 'commander in the field', otherwise we would have 'no' blessed commander's left at all, and please... take that damned thing out of my face..." He pushed the barrel of the gun away, scornfully.

Behind them, a wail from the doorway made them all turn. Pippa, distraught and frantic, framed by the doorway stood wringing her hands, her face distorted with pain and anguish... then suddenly, she collapsed to the floor.

Simon handed the briefcase to Webb and rushed over to her. "Poor thing... I don't normally 'bring my work home'...she's just not used to it." He picked her up in his arms as if she weighed nothing and kissed her face. "Give me a little time to settle her down and then I'll come back and join you all. I'm afraid it's been a little too much for her the past few days."

Webb looked at Kristianna and over to Gabriella and scratched his chin, neither spoke. He slumped down into the old ragged sofa. "Jesus! Get me another drink, Gabby, darlin'. I think we all need one. When's this all going to end? It's driving me fucking nuts... what I really don't understand is how they knew about the meeting?"

"I think I 'will' have one of those, Gabriella, if I may." Kristianna lowered herself onto the sofa to sit next to Webb, her hand tenuously on his arm, the 'swings and roundabouts' in her mind unsettling her normal equilibrium. "He's a clever man..." she said softly, speaking more to herself than for the 'consumption' of the others. It was the first time she had spoken since Simon's dramatic entrance and for once, she was 'rattled' and thoroughly depressed with it all, her plans array again.

For some time they sat in silence, each pondering their own thoughts. Gabriella sat facing them in the armchair, her elbows on her knees, her head resting in her hands, exhausted now. An awful silence seemed to have permeated the whole house. Way off in the distance they could hear the sounds of sheep and cows 'mooing' and the occasional bark of a dog, but other than that it was 'deadly' silent, as if the world was awaiting a major 'tragic event' to happen.

"I'd better phone Harrington..." Webb broke the silence, his mind working to clear the 'dross' from his head and concentrate on the job in hand... tonight was going to be extreme... even the 'plan' of 'attack' hadn't been finalised as yet, and that would mean talking to Kristianna... not a thought that he cherished, but knew it would be necessary.

Mechanically he dialled the number. The voice at the other end was female and very courteous and precise, telling him she would get Commissioner Harrington straight away.

"Webbley... you rang off, understandably of course. My deepest condolences, old chap. I'm so sorry for your loss." Roger Harrington sounded sincere. After a short silence he continued. "Be assured you will have my full cooperation in everything... whatever you want to do... as long as it is within the law, and I have the fall backing of the Home Office on this. We need to bring it all to a speedy ending, old chap and I think you would welcome that also."

"Well, that's what I called you for..." He briefed out the events of the past thirty minutes. Harrington was as surprised as they all were. "We still have the journals and I'll get them to you as soon as I can. Look, I'd like to handle this myself... getting the boy back, that is. Your hands would be too tied with the 'legal stuff' and damned negotiators and stuff, it's better that I handle it alone. Will you let me do that and keep your chaps out of it? I probably only need a day or so, win or lose you get the journals. What do you think?"

"I don't know whether that's wise, Webbley. Not at all..." There was deep concern in his voice. "There is a good chance the boy could be... killed. You know that don't you."

"Let's be honest here, Roger. These people don't work like that... they don't leave 'live bodies' around to testify against them, even if it is a child. The boy's dead anyway, if I don't do something." He forced his mind to think clearly... he was back in the jungles of Borneo... thinking like a soldier again... dealing with each problem as it presented itself... reasoning, rationally.

It took a while to convince him. "Are you... going to give them the journals?" Roger felt self-conscious and guilty for asking, a boy's life was at stake here... what did a few journals matter compared to that. But he knew without them, the Home Office would come down on him like a ton of bricks... if they didn't get what they wanted... there would be no deal and he would have to bear the full responsibility for all of it for failing.

"No, I'm not... like I said, you can have them tomorrow... if I'm still alive... they're yours. But whatever happens, I'll make sure that someone gets them to you. Is that fair?" It wasn't a thought he relished... dying, that is. "I... um... have some 'things' to do tonight, Roger, can I phone you later? If everything goes as planned... you'll have the journals by tomorrow evening, I'll make arrangements to get them handed over to you... personally. So what do you think, are you going to give me a free hand, or not?"

Again a long silence, before... "Unofficially yes... as far as I am concerned, this conversation never happened... but... If I don't hear from you before... say midday tomorrow, then I'll take my own appropriate action, as I see fit. Is that agreeable to you?"

Webb mumbled agreement as he replaced the receiver. "You'd better get going, Kristianna, there's a lot to do. I'll meet you somewhere near Kyso's house at nine o'clock. Where is 'prominent', we don't want to be chasing around all night looking for each other. Does that give you enough time?"

Gabriella suggested the old church in the village, three miles from Kyso's house and they agreed.

Kristianna fumed as she quickly packed her cases, occasionally pounding the bed with her fists and stomping her feet, hatefully on the carpet. 'Yes', she felt grateful that the journals were still there within reach for her to take rather than in the hands of the police where they would have been lost forever... but... damn it! She cursed her own stupidity for underestimating these people 'again'! That would not happen again, these 'friends' of Webbley Pendleton's were more adept at this than she had, at first given them credit for... especially Simon whom she had thought to be a little 'slow' and 'stupid'. She would take care of that later, wishing now that she hadn't wasted some of the shots she had taken when she shot the inspector and had shot Simon instead, it would have eased the burden she was saddled with now. But for now she would need to 'concentrate' her mind, this was the third time her plans had been thwarted. Slowly she controlled the rage... deal with Kyso first... get that idiots son back... and then she would have the journals and the rest of the cases... one way or the other.

She made a call to Herbert Tanner on the house 'phone, he would have the equipment ready for her on her arrival... On the long drive up, she would figure out other ways she could use him...

***

Webb 'gunned' the Range Rover for the last ten miles arriving at the old church with barely ten minutes before the time set on the kidnappers note, he stopped the car in the shade of a huge bushy Yew tree and settled his mind down to await the call. "Hope these bastards are on time, I want to get it done with," he mumbled glancing in his rearview mirror, checking that Simon had followed them without too much problem but a quick flash of his headlights told him that Simon was there. Webb watched him leave his car and wonder off into the darkness of the shadows, his back against the old rustic wall. Typical, he thought, admiring the craft of the ever cautious Simon. No one would ever catch 'him' napping.

"What was that, darling?" Gabriella released her seat belt and leaned on the arm rest, her hand in his lap.

He found her company had relaxed him, her voice soft and gentle, although he knew this wasn't any easier for her than it was for him it was that just sometimes she really did panic…at times. "Just 'chuntering' really. I don't want them playing 'silly-buggers' with me all night." He mumbled again. "I'm buggered if I'm, going to let them run me around all night on some silly bloody 'goose chase'."

Gabriella smiled at him. She could just make out the outline of his face in the moon light. "Sometimes you have the cutest expressions… I remember Kristianna asking you what 'chuntering' meant?"

He touched her neck, massaging it gently with his fingertips. "Pity this wasn't under better circumstances… isn't it." Slowly he eased her over to him and kissed her on the mouth. "This on its own has to be every man's dream, doesn't it… here I am with a beautiful, sexy woman… moonlit night. What more could a man want?"

She returned his kiss, passionately and touched his cheek. "Do you… think I am?"

"What?"

"Well…" She felt a little embarrassed. "What you said…"

"What, sexy and beautiful? Sure you are… you would certainly be my 'pick' to take to the ball, any night of the week, that's for sure." He leaned into her and 'pecked' her on the cheek, over the past week or so he had grown to like her…very much.

"Ooh…" She 'cooed' "That's so lovely, thank you for saying that…" Slowly she took his hand and placed it inside her blouse to touch her breast. "After this is over I am going to give you the best sex you have ever had in your entire life." She giggled. "I do so wish that we could just go, forget about the money and everything… just go."

"If 'wishes were horses, beggars would ride'." He quoted from one of his grandmother's sayings.

The mobile rang breaking the mood as he scrambled to open the case and press the on button. "Yeah?" he asked, simply.

"Mr. Pendleton, I hope you have taken my advice and are alone." The voice was distorted, warbling, as if the speaker was sending his message from the bottom of the ocean. One second the tone was high and then the next, dropping down to the bass tone, distorting the sound, hiding any identification of the talker, almost unidentifiable as a 'human voice'.

"Of course. Have you got the boy with you?" He felt his pulse rate rising quickly… with a little luck this could be over and done with, in minutes.

"No… do you have our goods with you?"

"No… I'm still in Cornwall at the moment, your 'goods' are three hundred miles from me. I can't get them until early tomorrow morning… the 'place' where I have them doesn't open this time of night." He had ran through this a 'thousand' times in his mind wondering how plausible it would sound.

"Don't play games with me, Mr. Pendleton. I told you, the first finger goes down to the police station at nine o'clock tonight." The distorted voice sounded angry and impatient.

"I'm not playing games, mister... and let me tell you this... if that boy is harmed, in any way the deal is off... 'plus', tomorrow morning I want 'proof of life', I want to see him and talk to him." He modulated his voice, trying to stay calm.

"You don't have any cards to play with, Mr. Pendleton."

"I have all of the cards, Mr. Dick Cordon... it is Dick Cordon, isn't it?" The silence confirmed what Kristianna had told him... that it would almost certainly be Dick Cordon who would call on Paul Kyso's behalf and Webb's disclosure seemed to have thrown him a little, to Webb's advantage.

A cream-coloured Porsche pulled up in front of them and flashed its brake lights twice. Webb placed his index finger to his mouth in the 'shush' position and signalled for Gabriella to quietly get out of the car and stop Kristianna charging in on them.

"Now let me tell you this, Mr. Cordon, if anything...anything at all happens to that boy, I will spend the rest of my life hunting you down and I'll give you a death that you could never even have imagine in your wildest nightmares." With a 'super-human' effort, he controlled his breathing and temper. "Now let me ask you again, is the boy with you or not?"

"No, he's not..." The voice didn't seem quite so confident now, sounding a little deflated even.

"Right, make your arrangements for tomorrow and please, make them sensible." He felt he had a modicum of control over the situation now.

For a long time there was no answer, only mumbled whispers in the background. "You are to join the M27 at junction ten, at exactly twelve o'clock and drive slowly until I call you. I will tell you where to turn off. What car are you driving?" The voice sounded a little uncertain.

"A black Range Rover." Webb gave him the licence plate number.

"Let's hope nothing goes wrong then... and, Mr. Pendleton, if I get even one tiny little inkling of a problem... I will hand the boy over to one of our 'agencies' as a 'jolly boy'. There are some really bent bastards who use our services... your son's rectum will look like 'Wookey Hole'. You understand?"

Webb gritted his teeth, if he could just reach down the telephone line and rip out this man's throat he would be happy. "And you remember, Cordon, I've given you a small taste of what I am capable of, and I will say it again... if you touch one hair on that boy's head, even a simple bruise, I will spend the rest of my life hunting you down and, Mr. Cordon... I can assure you I know more ways of making a dying man last for a week in unspeakably pain... than you can ever imagine, you will be begging me to kill you, but kill you I will and your 'mouth' and eye holes will look like 'Wookey Hole'." He pressed the off button, breathing slowly, at least now he had bought a little extra time for them. Gabriella and Kristianna were standing outside of the driver's door, so he wound the window down. "Right... get in... let's go and sort out 'a rat'!"

"I can bring in some of 'my' people if you like, Webbley." Kristianna had chosen to sit next to him as he drove. Gabriella and Simon had been relegated to the rear seats and sat quietly behind them.

"Your people, what's that mean... Kristianna... your people?" he said angrily. "This is a game to you, is it, a fuckin' game?"

"It was just a suggestion... that's all." She hated him with a vengeance, but somehow she needed to 'tolerate him' until she had the journals and the cases back. "I just thought it might help to have more people with us." She sulked, but forced herself to touch his thigh with her fingertips.

Dick Cordon removed the 'voice distorter' from the mouth piece of the handset and closed the door on the public telephone box. The conversation had not gone according 'his' plan... not at all. It was almost as if Pendleton didn't care what happened to the boy. He knew he would have to tread carefully, the basic plan had been Paul's, but the responsibility of carrying it through successfully was all his... and there was no other option 'but' success.

Slowly he dialled the number and waited until Paul Kyso answered. "He's eating out of our hands, boss..." He lied. "Hopefully this should all be over and done with tomorrow." He glanced at his watch and seeing that he was already late for his next 'appointment', hurried through the details. "He's still in Cornwall but our goods are up here, apparently. He sounded straight, boss."

"Well done, Dick... tomorrow you'll be 'King of the God damned castle'." Other than the delay it was exactly how he'd wanted it to go, but what the heck, they had all of the cards now... what would another night's delay be, nothing? He told him to go along with the new plan. "Set up another two cars after the motorway, that way he won't know 'who' is following him."

***

"You sure you don't want me to come in with you, boss?" Simon whispered, as Webb pulled off the road and tucked the Range Rover neatly against the long, red brick wall of Paul Kyso's estate.

"No, stay here, mate… take care of Gabriella for me, keep her safe, just give a couple of 'toots' if we have any visitors. Hopefully this won't take too long." He patted Simon on the shoulder as he left the car and shouldered the small backpack and then together with Kristianna, loped off, heading along the long high wall.

The wall around Paul Kyso's estate looked formidable, smooth Flemish brickwork topped with razor wire and interspersed with broken glass embedded in the concrete top. It appeared impregnable and almost impossible to climb over, but it didn't seem to phase Kristianna, at all. They quickly rounded the corner until she came to the side entrance where the branches of an old oak tree broached the top of the wall. Without hesitating she leapt the ten feet and swung herself into the lower branch, turned and looked back at him offering him her extended hand. On the second jump and with some difficulty and help from Kristianna he managed to grab the branch and swing himself into the tree, grunting loudly, and a little winded.

She shushed him to be quiet. "Stay close behind me… whatever happens don't get in front… tread where I tread," she whispered, hoarsely at him. They had run through the general plan at Hartness House and she had drawn him out a plan of the gardens and the interior of the house. She hoped that he had remembered it, hating working with amateurs, wishing now that she had done this by herself, or just with the help of Mr. Tanner it would have been far simpler for her to obtain the information he needed… solo.

"Look… there. Can you see the cameras? The one past the big oak tree is the one that doesn't work, but every individual camera covers the other cameras ark, so we need to wait for the camera right and left of the broken one to be moving away before we make a move. Whatever happens, don't touch the windows of the ground floor level, that will set off all the alarms… we need to use that drain pipe as a starting point to get around to the side door." She pointed at the grey line of the rainwater pipe in the corner of the house. "There are no alarms on the first floor, so as long as we can get up there safely, than we're home and dry."

As they ran she pointed out the CCTV cameras, occasionally stopping, waiting for the gap as the cameras traversed. Her 'source' had informed her that Paul's security had been pulled off by Alejandro, mainly as an act of 'spite', but also to teach him a lesson and to show others what happens when the 'trust' is lost. Kristianna also knew about Paul's money and how he had been made to forfeit it… all of it. That really appealed to her sense of humour.

"Look…" she whispered, pointing with her finger at an old grey door positioned just to the right of the drainpipe. "We'll go through the side door if we can, maybe he won't have bolted that yet," she whispered, pushing him back behind her as she followed the house wall around to a small, single door. From her jacket she produced a leather wallet containing a selection of lock picks. "Don't step on the matt… inside." She eased the door open and stared into the darkened room. "It has a pressure pad under it."

Webb stayed close to her and quietly closed the door behind him, stepping over the matt, adjusting his eyes. He felt her arm on his pulling him after her as they moved quickly into the house.

"The 'camera and radio room'…is there," she whispered, pointing at the door across the lighted hallway and put two fingers up, indicating she thought there ought to be two guards in there… "It's mainly the radio room, with a simple press of a button they can alert their people for miles around if necessary and of course the police.

They followed the wall around to the door of the camera room and she indicated for him to open it… slowly.

In her hands she held the big Colt .45, the black suppressor on the end making it look even bigger...

Webb swung the door open and charged in, two shots rang out over his head, even with the suppresser on Kristianna's Colt it was still loud and right next to his ear. A pall of smoke surrounded his head, burning his nostrils and stinging his eyes. Through the smoke he could see the two guards one slumped over his blood spattered TV screen, with most of his frontal head missing. The second man had taken the bullet through his throat and had fallen to his knees, his hands grasping at his windpipe, blood gushing through his fingers, gasping for air...

Kristianna pushed Webb to one side and fired a third shot, catching the second man high on his forehead, exploding gore and bone across the bench and wall. "Are you mad... I could have shot you?" Kristianna whispered hoarsely at him, her words meaning to hurt him. "I told you not to get in front of me... you idiot. I just told you to open the door... didn't I?"

"I thought you wanted me to..." He flicked the safety of his automatic back to 'off' and threw his arms up in the air feeling suitably chastised. "What the fuck am I explaining to you for?" His voice was a rasping, angry whisper, "... where next?"

She felt frustrated and annoyed, if the guards had been any good he would have been dead now... and then what... she would lose 'everything'. "Kitchen... three staff, all women... try not to shoot them, we'll just tie them up." She tapped the rucksack on her back. One of her favourites in the pack was the grey duct tape... she loved what it 'did' to people when they were bound, especially men... how totally helpless they were when they were bound up. "We need to watch for Bollo..." She had already warned him about 'Bollo', the huge Albania personal servant and body guard to Paul Kyso. "We can't do anything until we find him... he's too dangerous to ignore."

"Leave him…" Webb pointed to the lounge he remembered from the schematic she had drawn. "Get Kyso first… he can call Bollo in."

As they cleared each ground floor room, Webb was beginning to appreciate the danger he was in with his 'association' to Kristianna… he knew now, that she wasn't just some 'bimbo' that had once been an 'executive office worker' for The Met Corps. 'No'. This was a dangerous, ruthless fighting machine and he'd seen the efficiency of how she had dealt with the kitchen staff, it almost seemed as if she had merely 'touched them' on the neck, and yet each one, in turn, had fallen to the floor unconscious, as if struck by a bolt of lightning, without hardly a sound being uttered from any of them.

As they reached the landing of the first floor Kristianna pointed at the huge double doors… it was where the music was coming from. She still held the Smith and Wesson revolver at arms' length in front of her, acutely aware they still hadn't located Bolo… and it worried her greatly. The door was intricately carved with delicate oak panels and looked very solid. "That's his bedroom, be careful now… we still need to find Bollo," she whispered, softly… reminding him of the danger. She regulated and controlled her breathing, even though they had just run up two flights of stairs. "You go in first… but go to the right… I'll take the left." She tapped his shoulder. "Watch yourself…"

Webb turned the handle, slowly easing the door slightly. He knew immediately, that if it was locked and bolted, there would be no way on earth they would be able to break it down… not without half of the world hearing it, it would need a sledgehammer and an awful lot of noise to get through it. He nodded at Kristianna as the door opened a fraction and felt her tap on his shoulder… and then he rushed in, crouching low… his eyes everywhere. At the far end of the huge room on the bed was a naked, fat man, crouching on all fours. Webb stood slowly, his automatic pointing directly at the naked man.

Initially Webb didn't even feel the blow that grazed his neck and the back of his head. The pain came some seconds later as the strength in his legs suddenly wouldn't take the weight of his body and that he was falling quickly to the floor. In the fuzz of his dilemma, he hardly heard the two shots, followed almost immediately by a third and knew they must be gunshots from Kristianna's gun... nothing sounded that loud... and wondered if he was still alive... he hadn't felt any more pain, other than a huge weight pressing down on his body, pushing his head and body closer and closer into the woolly pile of the carpet... so that he could hardly breath.

"Stay where you are, Paul... exactly where you are, or I'll have to kill you here and now." Kristianna pointed the big gun at Paul Kyso and fired a shot into the headboard behind him. He was completely naked, straddled across the back of a woman that Kristianna couldn't properly see. Only the girl's legs and part of her upper body were visible. "I promise you... if you move from that position, you'll be dead."

Without taking her eyes from Kyso, she pushed and heaved at the body of Bolo until she could pull Webb from under him and dragged him to a sitting position. "Are you alright... Webb? Talk to me..." She slapped his face hard to shake him out of his daze, and then slapped him again until his eyes opened. "Webb... Webb... stand up, get hold of yourself, man..." her eyes still on the naked man on the bed... who seemed totally paralysed.

Slowly Webb pushed himself up to his knees, retrieving his automatic from the carpet and brushed the hair out of his eyes, his fingers touching the 'lump' at the back of his head. Glancing down he was amazed at the size of the man laying next to him... the pool of blood from his wounds spreading quickly along the carpet. "Jesus!" He felt for the bump on the back of his own head again and looked up at Kristianna. "That fuckin' well hurt..." He protested, indignantly, pushing her hand out of the way.

"I told you to keep your wits about you... how could you just walk into that? Didn't they teach you anything about clearing rooms in that so-called 'school of superman training' you went to?" Kristianna dragged him to his feet and walked him over to sit on the ottoman at the bottom of the bed.

"That's ridiculous... Jesus!" He was looking directly at the rear end of Paul Kyso, 'frozen' in the 'rear mounted position'. "Is this?"

"Mmm. It's my dear Paul." She tapped his buttock with the barrel, gouging the flesh. "Is that comfortable, Paul? It looks like it is... don't you think so, Webb, don't you think he looks comfortable like that?" She raised her eyebrows, smiling and sat on the edge of the bed, amazed at the strength of the young girl under him for supporting such a weight. "Dismount... slowly." She touched the side of his head with the barrel and waited until he had withdrawn himself from the girl and lay on his back, next to the girl, his genitals in full view, penis still erect, ejaculating seminal fluid onto his lower belly. "What a pathetic little man you are." She touched the gun barrel to the now deflating phallus, lifting it away from his ball sack.

He tried to cover himself with his hands, but a sharp tap from the barrel stopped him. "Kristianna... please..." He was shaking so violently that he could hardly speak.

Next to him the young girl hadn't moved from her position, fear freezing her as if she were a statue. She sobbed, her body trembling uncontrollably. For a second she looked over to Kristianna, but quickly looked away.

Webb stood, pushing Kristianna out of the way his hand touching the girl's arm. "It's okay... hey... its okay, come on. Get yourself covered." He eased her to the edge of the bed and handed her a dressing gown that had been loosely draped over the headboard and then led her over to an armchair, her back to the bed so that she didn't have to look at her assailant. "Sit there for a minute…" He touched her hand, hoping to console her, but she pulled away from him, terrified… drawing her knees up under her body and pulling the dressing gown tighter around her. "Okay…" He spoke softly to her understanding her fear, holding his hands away, hiding the automatic behind him, lest it frightened her any more than she already was.

"Forget her, Webb, get the door locked first, we don't want someone else barging in on us." Kristianna nodded at the still open door. "We don't want any more surprises tonight, do we?"

While he was attending to the door, she dragged Paul Kyso from the bed by the nape of his sparse hair and sat him on the ottoman at the foot of the bed, his body shaking, violently as if he was cold. "We need to talk… dear boy." Slowly she lifted his chin with the barrel of the big automatic. "This 'nice' man has some questions to ask you…" She held his head back and smiled at the tiny, limp penis. 'That', she hated the thought, had been inside 'her body', it had been her way of 'currying favour', years ago… when she had first joined Met Corps. "And he is not a patient man Paul, you will need to be very honest… and very quick with your answers." She grinned at Webb… as he returned. Everything now, had been worth it… everything single thing, all the trauma and the frustration had come down to this… just to be able to have Paul Kyso, exactly how he was right now. It was almost worth more than the journals and the money, put together. "He will know where your son is… Webb, and I'm sure he will tell you if you ask him nicely."

Webb replaced the automatic, carefully back into its holster and took a step forwards. "I told you I would come after you, didn't I… hum… you scumbag, did you think you were safe here, or did you think that I was just bullshitting?" In a fluid movement his boot arched upwards striking the limp ball sack, hitting it centre mass...

The scream was deafening as Kyso leapt into the air before collapsing onto the floor, writhing in agony, semi-conscious. Webb dragged him back up to the ottoman by his ears and sat him back into his original position. "Where's the boy... and I'll only ask you once?" He said simply. Behind them the girl had started screaming hysterically and wouldn't stop until Kristianna slapped her across the face several times.

"Please..." Paul Kyso screamed with the agonising pain wracking his body and raised a defensive hand, his right hand still cupping his scrotum. "It's... oh God, no more, please. It was Condon..." He gasped in mouthfuls of air, massaging himself, furiously around his groin. "Dick Condon. I told him not to touch your family... but he's an animal... animal."

Kristianna stepped back and stood in front of the girl draping her arms over the shoulders of the hapless, unmoving child and placed her hand onto the child's breasts, gently caressing her. "Tell him, Paul... or he will 'really' hurt you... really." She bent forwards a little, sliding her hand between the girl's legs, feeling the moistness of her flesh. "Quickly, Paul... quickly... now," she mumbled, excitedly. The child whimpered but hardly moved away from the probing fingers.

"Leave her be..." Webb pushed Kristianna away from the girl. "Fuck sake... what's up with you?"

"She doesn't mind at all... not after being with a 'slug' like that." Kristianna smiled, wanting him to touch 'her'... 'there'... as she had touched the girl.

"I don't care, leave her be..."

"They have taken him to Martha's house... that's all I know. I swear." The colour had drained from his face, completely now, leaving just a grey ashen skin. "I swear that is all I know... I swear." He cried, his eyes pleading with Webb, as the tears streamed down his face.

"Now we know that isn't quite true, Paul... don't we." Kristianna moved to the ottoman and draped a leg over towards the girl, but couldn't quite reach her with her toes, so she turned and rested her foot in Kyso's groin, pressing harder and harder until he squealed.

"Kristianna..." Webb shouted at her. "Leave the bloody kid alone... leave her alone." For the first time he noticed the television, flickering at the head of the bed. On the screen was an older man, performing sex with a young boy. "Jesus... this place, what is it with you people, you're all fuckin' bent." He leaned forwards and picked up the ceramic vase on the ottoman and heaved it at the screen, smashing it to pieces. The girl screamed, hysterically until Kristianna leapt at her covering her mouth with her hands until she collapsed in the chair, still whimpering.

"Dear God. How old is that kid?" It was the first time he had really looked at the girl's face. "She can't be any more than..." He swung his fist at Paul Kyso, connecting with his upper jaw, flinging him along the ottoman and then back onto the floor.

Webb dragged him back up again, forcing him to sit upright and then removed the penknife from his pocket and flipped open the long sharp blade, touching it to Kyso's scrotum. Webbley was a carpenter and carpenters 'knew' how to sharpen chisels and 'knives', this penknife was sharp enough to take the skin from a knat's ball bag without damaging any of the contents. "Details... I want the details," he shouted, inserting the blade into the outer skin of the scrotum.

"We should have brought the spikes and the hammer, Webb." Kristianna's excitement was almost overwhelming her, a dribble of spittle bubbled at the corner of her mouth.

She still had her right hand around the child's mouth and her left on the child's breast.

Webb shook his head, remembering that 'moment' of utter insanity and madness that he had gone through at Preston's house, knowing that he could never repeat it. He looked over at the half naked child in the chair, now huddling in closely to Kristianna... mistaking her lust for compassion. "No, no need for that... you'll tell me everything I need to know, mate... won't you?" Slowly he drove the blade into Kyso's ball sack and turned the blade around... over the next ten minutes... or so... had all the information he needed.

"We need to get that girl out of here, to somewhere safe, but I can't make any sense of what she is saying." For a long time Webb had spoken to her softly, trying to encourage her to speak to him but she was still totally incoherent with distress and fear of them. He had found her clothes and dressed her, but she could hardly walk.

"Just leave her here, someone will eventually find her." Kristianna shrugged and then checked the chamber on her revolver. "We can't let 'him' live, you know that, don't you." It was all part of her 'grand plan' for them all, anyway.

Webb made a face, not caring one way or the other as he walked over to Kyso's desk and picked up the briefcase. "Perfect... I have just the perfect job for this." He dragged Kyso over to the bureau and made him sit. "I need you to make a couple of calls for me and you need to make them very 'convincing'." He touched the knife to Kyso's throat and handed him the receiver...

They had been in the house for almost thirty minutes, much longer than he had planned for. "Come on, let's get out of here." Webb wrapped his arm around the hapless child, leading her away, his eyes watching Kristianna as she taped Kyso to the chair and then wrapped the tape tightly around his terrified mouth. It sickened him that she was enjoying herself so much. "Just kill the bastard, or leave him he can't harm us any more…"

Kyso frantically shook his head, his eyes begging Webb not to leave him alone with Kristianna.

"You know we can't leave him alive, Webb. He's the biggest danger to us in the whole of the organisation. Go… you go, I'll sort this trash out and catch up with you." She smiled sweetly, patting Kyso's face… almost affectionately. "Go…" she shooed him out of the door with a wave of her hand. "Paul and I go back a long way… don't we, Paul?" She slapped his face, almost gently.

Webb didn't look back, all this 'killing' was starting to sicken him again, and anyway, he had what he came for… that was all he needed. Later he would telephone Roger Harrington and get him to send someone to meet up with Simon and the girl, at least she would be safe with them. Behind him Kristianna was loading a pillowcase with videos, it didn't take too much imagination to know what type of 'material' the videos contained.

Back at the car, Simon appeared out of the shadows, in his hand he held a small Glock automatic and didn't lower it until he was certain it was Webb… "Where's Kristianna?" He was aware of everything around him, poised ready to instinctively act. "Is she alright?"

Webb nodded at the house as Gabriella rushed around and helped him with the girl, and then sat with her in the backseat of the car. "Alright…? That fucking bitch is always… 'alright'… it'd take a herd of stampeding buffalo's to kill that evil bloody cow…"

They heard a series of muffled shots from the house and then moments later saw Kristianna walking slowly, unconcerned towards them... her face a picture of pleasure and peace, over her shoulder was a bulging pillowcase so heavy that she had problems walking with it, but Webb refused to help her, out of some sort of misguided disgust.

"Jesus..." Webb cursed her silently, under his breath. What sort of 'womb' did that come from? The thought had occurred to him many times before... he knew that Kristianna was the epitome of everything that was evil.

"Somehow, you have to relax, darling, or you will make yourself ill." Naomi nestled down alongside her husband, on the long settee her hand linked through his. It was already eleven-thirty and yet the telephone call he had expected still hadn't come.

"It's like waiting for the dentist to pull a tooth." Roger Harrington wanted a large whiskey, it would settle his troubled tummy, but he knew he dare not, "...without anaesthetic."

"You said he seemed like an honest man, this Webbley Pendleton. I'm sure you're right, you're normally a very good judge of character." She leaned into him, hating to see him so stressed and kissed his cheek.

"I just don't understand it any more... none of it... and all in 'my ward', or at least most of it." He walked over to the cabinet and poured himself a drink, convincing himself that it would settle him down. As he put it to his lips, the telephone rang...

Slowly Naomi walked over and with shaking hands, picked up the receiver. "789685..." she said simply, and then nodded at Roger, with her hand covering the mouthpiece she whispered, "it's him..."

"Webbley... I've been at my wits end. Where are you?" Roger took a long sip, feeling the liquid burning his throat. "What about your son, is he safe, is he alright, old chap?"

"It's okay, Roger, the first part has gone well. I know where the boy is and I'm just on my way to pick him up, so hopefully we can clear up this part of the mess at least." He took a long, deep breath… saying it the way he had, had made it sound as if he was just going to pick the boy up from the train station after a day's outing. The shaking in his hands had subsided now and his stomach had settled down a little, and he felt a lot calmer. "I just need you to do some cleaning up for me… if you would."

"How… how do you mean, Webbley, you have the boy with you… how, I thought that they…?

"No…" He repeated that he was on his way to collect the boy. "They sort of 'capitulated' so to speak. About this 'cleaning up', Roger… and I just need you to keep it under wraps for a day, just until I get my boy back."

***

After the call from Police Commissioner Roger Harrington, Tracy Gould wasn't surprised at the carnage she found in Paul Kyso's house, not in the least… in fact it was what she had fully expected from any dealings which involved Webbley 'Bloody' Pendleton and she had hardened herself to it. After Alan's death, nothing seemed to matter very much anymore, anyway. This was the sort of destruction and devastation she had found at every scene of crime Pendleton had been involved in. The only difference in this scene was the 'senseless' killings of the kitchen staff… that didn't seem to make any sense, they were already bound hand and foot and would have posed no threat at all. It seemed strange because in his previous crimes all of his victims had been armed, or showed chemical traces of being previously armed… the three, female kitchen staff had been bound and gagged and then shot in the head, execution style… it seemed out of character with Pendleton.

That aside, the most disturbing aspect of the whole scene was an unexpected visit from a Chief Inspector Brian Richardson of the Met. Who had 'bullied' his way past her own police and barged into the bedroom as she was going through the scene with the forensics team, Tracy knew that Roger Harrington had not telephoned or even informed any other police agency of the crime, she had checked on that already and the only way she could get rid of Richardson, had been to call Harrington and put him onto the Met. man… every 'detective bone' in her body, instinctively told her that Richardson would definitely be on 'the list', in the journals that Pendleton carried, which made obtaining them even more imperative now.

"We can't back this sort of stuff up for much longer can we, governor, surely, aren't we just becoming as bad as them?" She had protested to Roger Harrington. "I know some of these are bad buggers, but Christ!"

The same thought had gone through his mind, a thousand times already. How close were 'they' to being part of this criminal conspiracy to murder and fraud and a multitude of other criminal activities? How far could they 'really' stretch the law? Did the end really ever justify the means, regardless of the consequence?

It went against everything he had sworn to up hold over the past three decades… and it worried him greatly. "At the moment, Tracy…" It was unheard of 'normally' for him to use 'first name terms' to any of his subordinates and yet the 'bond' that had 'necessarily' formed between them seemed to 'demand it'. "We are the pawns, we just need to ride along with it until we have those damned journals, otherwise the very structure of the force… the 'morale structure'… will be eroded to nothing but 'trash status'. Can you imagine the devastation we would all suffer if our respect as police officers… as guardians of society and the rule of law, in the eyes of the public was degraded to that of say, South America or North Korea… we just have too much at stake here. If we lose the trust of the people of Britain, we go back to being nothing but a 'police state'. Perish the thought. Just stick with me at the moment, Tracy, until I see the journals I dare not trust this to anyone else."

After the call, she cast everything else from her mind except this immediate situation. Later when she was home she would shower… twice… and try to wash all of this away. "It's a pity you can't do that with your mind," she mumbled to herself.

"What's that, inspector?" her deputy Sergeant Gordon Blake asked.

She hadn't realised she had spoken out loud. "Nothing…"

"Can you imagine what that poor bugger went through, boss." Her sergeant called her over to see the short fat man, bound to the chair. His genitalia had been cut off and stuffed in his mouth. The site was grotesque. "Jesus Christ…" Unknowingly, he was holding his own groin.

"And he was alive when they did that to him." A man from forensics walked over. "Look…" He pointed to the long strips of skin that had been severed from the man's neck and shoulders and then torn down to his waist, there were so many that it almost looked as if he was wearing some sort of bizarre skirt. "That must have been excruciating."

***

Dick Cordon waited nervously in the outer office of Alejandro De Los Santos. It was his first visit ever to such an 'exalted' location as the head of The Met Corps. He had met Alejandro del los Santos on several occasions but that was under very different circumstances, and had never met him alone…

"Mr. De los Santos will see you now... Mr. Cordon." The smartly dressed P.A. to Alejandro smiled, cordially and held the door for him, closing it behind both of them as they entered the office.

Alejandro was seated in a plush, comfortable armchair next to the imitation log fire, its 'flames' flickering against the glass, reinforced window. He had a heavy woollen shawl around his shoulders and looked cold and frail, behind him was his personal bodyguard Eduardo, a huge man well over six feet inches tall with a barrel chest and featureless face, he held his hands together in front of him, as a servant would. By the windows, just out of hearing range, were another two burly men. Dick felt the strength in his legs failing him and he coughed to clear the fear in his throat, the turmoil in his mind, wondering what madness had brought him to this.

"Mr. Cordon, take a seat... do you drink, smoke?" Alejandro's voice was flat and emotionless.

Dick Cordon cleared his throat and sat where Alejandro had indicated, opposite him in the matching armchair. "Um... yes, sir, I do. I shouldn't, but I do... not too good for my health." He stammered the words as Alejandro nodded at his P.A., who dutifully poured a glass of fine Scotch whiskey into a lead crystal glass and handed it to him, and then opening a box of cigars laid them on the small coffee table by his side before retreating to the end of the long settee.

"So, Mr. Cordon, what was so urgent that you needed to talk to me at this time of night?" He nodded towards the box of Cuban cigars, encouraging him to take one.

"I... let me first say, sir, how desperately sorry I am about your granddaughter... terrible tragedy. I had suggested to Paul that we double her protective custody, at least until this crisis was over." He hadn't, of course but hoped it would curry favour with Alejandro.

Alejandro winced, thanking him for his concern…

Dick waited until Eduardo had snipped the end from the cigar and handed it to him and then struck the lighter until he had successfully lit it. "I… this is a little crazy, sir. I feel like a traitor… in a way, but I just felt that I had to come to you with this, there was just no one else I could turn to, to talk about it." He drained the glass. The acrid, bitter taste helped to dissipate some of his nervousness. Eduardo immediately refilled it.

"Then it must be important… please, relax… proceed." A huge piece of grey, blue ash fell from Alejandro's cigar and landed in his lap but he paid no attention to it. "Please, go on."

Little by little, his confidence rising as he spoke, Dick told Alejandro of the conversation between himself and Paul Kyso, about taking over the Met Corps, embellishing some of the details in his own favour, taking full credit for the assault on Webbley Pendleton's family and the kidnap of his son. "I've spoken to him, sir… Pendleton, he wants to comply, so hopefully we should have your 'possessions' back by midday tomorrow. I'm sure of it."

"You seem to have done very well, sir." Alejandro's eyes were fixated on Dick's, holding them, unwavering. Some of the story, he knew to be true other parts of it he doubted the authenticity of… but that could wait. "And Mr. Pendleton… how did he sound?" The eyes were still holding Dick's.

"I… sort of got the impression that he was a 'beaten man'. We seemed to have worn him down. I definitely got the impression that he wanted it to all be over with. The clinching factor was when we took his son… I'm sure."

"And he will hand everything back over to us as soon as he has his son back?"

"Yes sir..." The second malt whiskey had settled him nicely and he leaned back into the armchair drawing deeply on the long cigar, completely relaxed now.

"Good, what time is the exchange?" Alejandro pulled the shawl closer, even with the fire roaring up the chimney and turned up to full, he was feeling the cold tonight.

Dick Cordon told him it was at midday and that he had arranged for an additional three cars with a total of twelve men to follow him after they had left the motorway they would follow him to the exchange location. "He won't get the better of us this time sir, that I can promise you."

Alejandro's eighty-four years were dragging on him tonight. "Good. As soon as you have made the exchange, I want you to check that everything is there, Miss Pentland will give you a full inventory before you leave." He nodded in the direction of his P.A. and she smiled back. "And then as soon as you are sure, I want you to kill both of them. Is that clear?"

Cordon nodded...

"I have an additional twenty men available if you think you need more. Use them after the 'event' if needs be. I want you then to take all of them to eliminate everyone that has had anything to do with this case... including the police chief..." He clicked his finger and thumb, the name had slipped his mind until Eduardo leaned over him and whispered in his ear. "Yes, of course, Harrington... and all of his family. We will have a complete new start to all of this as from tomorrow, just to be sure and for my own satisfaction, Eduardo will come with you to collect my property and then he will bring it all straight back here. As the new head of security, are you able to handle that, Mr. Cordon?"

Dick Cordon smiled broadly. "Yes, I am, sir... yes, sir."

"It's a bloody big house, Christ!" They could just make out the house at the top of a long gravel drive as they drove past the front, the gated entrance guarded by two men behind the tall steel gates. "How the fuck do we get in there?"

"Pull over there..." Kristianna indicated a grass verge she guessed couldn't be seen from the main gate.

"What?" He hated her being in his car, but he'd had to send Gabriella off in her car to get the child to a hospital.

"There, pull over..." Kristianna snapped at him sharply and waited until he had stopped and Simon had safely pulled in behind them, before she jumped out. She ruffled her hair quickly, and tore the front of her blouse open and then as soon as she was out of the car, grabbed a handful of wet soil and rubbed it around her face, smearing it around the front of her blouse and down the front of her slacks.

"Have you gone fucking nuts, or something?" Webb closed the door behind him as Simon joined them.

"We need a diversion. I'll take those two at the gate. You two stay behind me out of site until I clear the way. When we are in you had both better come with me. You take care of the back." She nodded at Simon and removed the big forty-five from her shoulder holster and screwed on the suppressor and then tucked it into the waistband at the small of her back before setting off at a brisk pace towards the gates.

Simon looked at Webb, shrugged his shoulders and smiled and then they both set off after her.

As she approached the gates, Kristianna screamed, falling onto the grass verge, clasping at her breasts and throat before tumbling into the gravelled driveway in front of the steel gates. "Help me... please." She staggered to her knees, the gravel cutting deep gashes in her hands and knees and stretched her arm out. "Help me..." she screamed again.

Twenty feet away, hugging the long wall and concealed by the ditch and high bushes, Webbley Pendleton almost rushed over to help her himself… she was so convincing. "That soddin' woman's a bloody genius…" he whispered quietly to Simon.

Behind the gate the two startled men rushed over to her. "Albert, call the house… looks like she's been attacked or something. Get them to phone for an ambulance, quick." The taller, rounder man spoke quickly, bending down to help the woman. Kristianna shot him in the face from almost point-blank range just above his eye and pushing him to one side raised the automatic and fired twice at the second man hitting him first in the back, and a second shot to the head as he fell.

"Get them out of the way, stuff their bodies somewhere that no one can find them, at least until we are done here." She was angry, bitter at the fact that they were even here, messing about wasting time trying to save a worthless child that was probably already dead anyway, instead of concentrating on the more pressing job of getting 'her' money back as they should be doing, and getting out of this damned country to safety where she could then plan her takeover of Met Corps.

"Do you have to keep doing that?" Webb said angrily as he dragged one of the dead men over to the side of the drive and threw his body behind the bushes. He brushed himself down and helped Simon with the second man and then came back to face her. "Do you? Why couldn't you just 'tap' him on the head, or something?"

"Really, don't be ridiculous." She almost ignored him, her eyes looking up the long drive to the dozen or so cars parked outside of the house. Alongside the cars were a number of men she assumed would be the chauffeurs. "This is going to give us a problem, get the Range Rover," she demanded whilst she attempted to straighten her clothes, tucking the torn blouse into her waistband and smoothing out her dishevelled hair.

For a reason he couldn't readily understand, Webb found himself, 'obeying' her. He chortled quietly as he started the car and reversed it towards them and waited until they were seated before driving slowly through the gates towards the house.

Kristianna looked at herself in the rearview mirror. "You had better make out that I'm your 'floozy', or whatever you call them. I'll pretend that I'm drunk... and for God's sake, make it convincing."

The rouse worked perfectly, no one even paid them the slightest attention as they walked... or in Kristianna's case... staggered into the house, her arm draped loosely over Simon's shoulder. They were met by a pretty receptionist heavily made up and dressed in the tiniest mini-dress Webb had ever seen... with most of her voluptuous body on display. She was polite but seemed a little 'tipsy' or even 'drunk' and a little unsteady on her feet, so she just leaned on the counter top, smiling.

"We need to see Martha." James smiled at her, his arm firmly around Kristianna's waist to prevent her from falling.

"Does she know you are coming, sir?" The receptionist smiled and leaned over the counter, revealing more of herself.

Webb shook his head and smiled back. "Yes, darling... this one's a 'special delivery' from Paul... Paul Kyso. Martha needs to take care of it herself, right away." He winked at her and smiled.

The girl dialled a number. "Yes... ma'am. They said it's from Mr. Kyso... mmm... I think you better." She replaced the receiver and leaned forwards onto the counter again. "She's on her way up..."

Martha Soberton was not what he would have expected at all from the madam of a brothel, but then he was no judge of brothels, never having visited one in his entire life. She was tall, discreetly dressed, elegant and very beautiful. Her face was lightly made up with just a touch of eye shadow and a thin, delicately applied line of red lipstick, and her light brown hair was short trimmed and tucked neatly behind her ears. She could have past as a top model with any fashion magazine. .

She looked at them immediately suspicioce. The girl they were holding was dishevelled and looked a mess, but she could see under the dirt splattered face and bloodied hands that she was very pretty, but she had never seen the two men before that were with her. "Paul sent you, gentlemen? That's odd, he doesn't normally do that. Why's he sent her here?" She smiled at Simon and then lifted Kristianna's head, looking into the half closed bleary eyes. "You work for Paul?"

Kristianna moaned…

"Yeah, long time." Webb took the chance that she didn't know all of Paul's men. "I understand he called earlier, didn't he?" It was one of the calls he had 'obliged' Paul to make for him.

"Yes, he did, but this is still a little… unusual'. Why did he send her here instead of going through Daniel?"

Webb shrugged his shoulder and hoisted Kristianna higher on his hip. "No idea, miss. We just do what we're told. Have you got an office we can go to… there's a few…" He 'wiggled' his fingers from side-to-side and shrugged his shoulders. "A few 'loose ends' that he wants me to tie up with you… I have to call him as soon as I'm through here just to confirm that I've handed this little 'trollop' over to your tender care." Webb flicked Kristianna's ear, spitefully and raised his eyebrows at Martha.

"Yes... I suppose so... um... come through, bring her into the office." Martha touched her cheek and brushed a stray hair from her blouse and then walked towards a door at the far end of the hallway, to the right of them. "This way, I still don't understand it though, why he's sent her here? I'll have to check on this you know." She closed the door behind them and indicated for the two men to be seated whilst she made the call.

"Well, you can speak to him when I call him." Webb shrugged, impressed by her efficiency.

Kristianna burst into life, her hand around Martha's throat forcing her backwards and then throwing her across the big desk, still holding her by the throat, tightening her grip. "You recently admitted a young boy, about twelve years old... where is he?"

Simon quickly backed away to the door behind them and stood guard, the Glock already in his hand.

Martha shook her head, her mind disjointed in turmoil. 'She' was protected by Paul Kyso... no one had ever done anything like this to her... ever. How could they...

"Let her speak... you're throttling the shit out of her." He watched Simon as he stood over to guard the door, pleased that his automatic was in his hand... "Let her speak..." Webb wrenched her hand away from Martha's throat. "He's my son... I need to know that he is here and is safe... where is he?"

Martha half sat, her hands around her throat, gasping for air, her eyes terrified. In the struggle her blouse had torn open at the front and she made an attempt to cover herself shaking her head, terrified. "I..."

Webb removed the knife from his pocket and flipped it open and then held it to her throat. "Be careful what you say next... if he is hurt in anyway, you're going to be very dead..."

She shook her head again and coughed, trying to clear the pain and soreness from her throat. "I... I just do what I'm told." She tried to back away from the knife but something on the desk was digging into her backside. "He's not hurt... I swear he's not. Paul said not to hurt him... and he hasn't been put onto the circuit yet..."

"Circuit?" Webb was horrified.

"The... it's what we call... well... with a client. I've personally looked after him, honestly I have, he's a sweet, nice boy. I promise you he hasn't been hurt." She coughed again. "He was just sent here... nothing has happened to him, I promise you... please don't hurt me."

Webb pushed her roughly from the desk into the swivel chair and then lifted the receiver, throwing it into her lap. "Get someone to bring the boy up here... and, miss, be very careful what you say." He pointed the knife at her. "Very careful."

Martha sucked in lungful's of air, almost hyperventilating in an effort to control her breathing. Slowly she dialled a series of numbers and spoke quietly into the handset. "Yes, dear... in my office now, they have come to collect the boy. Please make sure that his is properly dressed, Dawn. Yes... thank you." She tried to smile at Webb but the look on his face stopped her. "He's on his way up... sir." Her hands were shaking violently, her mind desperately seeking answers to this 'unusual' turn of events. She knew it couldn't possibly be a rival organisation none of them were as powerful as The Met Corps.

Some minutes later someone tapped the door, Webb tucked the knife alongside his thigh and motioned for Martha to answer it, pushing her towards the door, watching her carefully as she opened it and let the boy into the room. "It's alright, Dawn, thank you, you don't need to be here, thank you," and then closed the door on the girl...

"Dad!" The boy rushed over to Webb, throwing his arms around his waist, sobbing desperately.

Webb lifted him up and hugged him, tears gushing to his eyes, hardly able to speak. "Thank God for that, boy… you're safe now. Thank God." He kissed his face, their tears mixing together into a stream down their cheeks. "Look, son, we're not safe here, I need to get you out of this place. I just need you to be brave just for a little while longer, yeah?" He lowered him to the floor, wiping the tears away and knelt I front of the boy.

The boy staggered with his words. "They did things… Dad… to mum and…" He couldn't say his sister's name. "Awful things… I saw them."

Webb hugged him again. "I know, son, I know… we can talk about it when we're safe, right? But not here." He stood and held the boy's hand and then looked over at Martha. "Jesus! You people…" He wiped the tears from his face, flushed with hatred and anger, holding the boy's head against his leg and raised his automatic and fired once, hitting Martha just above her nose and without looking back, tucked the gun into his belt and walked out through the door…

As they drove away from the house the force of the guilt and of the relief at saving his son, almost overwhelmed him, so much so that he had to stop the car and ask Simon to drive and then got into the back of the car to sit with his son, holding him closely… allowing his tears to engulf them both. He knew that soon he would have to let him go again so that they would all be safe. He knew that the boy certainly wasn't safe around 'him' and that none of this was finished… yet. The only safe place at the moment would be at Simon's house, deep in the Welsh mountains surrounded by good, simple people. The tragedy of the past week had eliminated any possibility of leaving the boy with any close member of his own immediate family… most of them were now dead anyway, slaughtered by The Met Corp's thugs.

Thirty minutes later, after they had picked up Gabriella, he finally managed to control his shattered emotions. Webb called them all together in the car park of a transport café, as the boy slept in the back of the Range Rover.

"Gabby, I need you to go with Simon back to the house…" He held his hand up to her mouth, touching her gently and kissed her… stilling her protests. "It's not safe where I'm going, darlin'… please, go with Simon."

"Me? No, boss… I need to go with you…" Simon was indignant at being left out. "Why can't Gabriella drive the boy back to the house and I'll go with you? Doesn't that make more sense?"

"Nope… enough's enough. I need to end all this crap and finish with these people, one way or the other, or I'll be looking back over my shoulder for the rest of my days and so will he." He nodded at the Range Rover. "I need to do this Simon, find an end to it all, whatever that means." He patted his shoulder and then leaned over and kissed Gabriella on the mouth. "Go with Simon, darlin', please. With a bit of luck I'll see you sometime tomorrow. Oh, I'll need to keep the Range Rover, that's the car they are expecting… so you take the boy in your car, mate."

He waved at them as they drove off. Gabriella was still crying as she leaned out of the window to wave at him and wondered whether he would ever see any of them again.

"What now then?" Kristianna was still angry, and showed it. Hating the time they had wasted.

Webb despised her. If only he could just walk away from everything… right now, without recriminations… he would, but he knew 'they' would never leave him alone. "You offered me 'your men', is that offer still on?"

Her eyes lit up and she smiled at him, a surge of energy rushing through her excited body. "Oh course… how many do you want." She gently touched his arm feeling the juices already surging through her lower body, surprised at his renewed enthusiasm for 'the game'.

"Agh… I don't know, six… maybe. They need to be good shooters, long distance, if possible." He didn't move away from her touch, finding it strangely comforting now, it seemed as if she was his last 'allay'.

"Sure that's not a problem. What have you got in mind?" Her hand wandered down to his groin feeling for him against the hard cotton of his jeans.

"I'm going to take a bloody big gamble and chance my arm. They'll know about the boy when they go to pick him up tomorrow, but I'm wondering if they will think it was a rival organisation just out for some ransom money and no one saw us. Either way, I'll bet a 'pound to a pinch of shit' that, that bastard Cordon will turn up anyway and follow me. Think about it… he's probably made a 'million promises' to his masters about what he can deliver, how can he go back to them now and tell them that he's made a 'cock-up' of it. More than anything… he needs 'me'. And anyway, as soon as he sees me on that motorway he'll think I had nothing to do with it… he certainly wouldn't think I would turn up if I already 'had' the boy, would he."

Kristianna smiled and leaned into him, wrapping her arms around his waist and kissed his throat, her hands gently rubbing against his groin. She could follow the ridiculously crude, 'animal logic' of it… the sort of 'logic' that would easily fool someone like Dick Cordon. "You are a clever man… very, very clever. I like it." She looked at her watch, fanning it away from her so that the moonlight shone on the face. "One thirty… we need to find a motel so that I can make some calls, and you need to rest…get a couple of hours of sleep and a tidy up… and a good woman to hold you. 'Gladiators' to the slaughter', aye?"

Chapter 38

Sunday morning 10:45.

"Jesus! He doesn't know." Dick Cordon followed the black Range Rover onto the motorway, driving steadily at sixty-five miles per hour. He checked that the number plate matched and beamed superciliously when it did. At eight o'clock this morning when he had gone to pick up the boy, he thought that his whole world had ended. Police were swarming all over the house and grounds so he hadn't even tried to enter and had just driven past, parking in the grove a hundred yards or so away. Any enquiry he tried to make was just met by stony silence from people standing outside of the police cordon until he had spoken to one of the reporters at the gate who told him that it was a police raid on what they now knew to be a brothel.

"Can you imagine that?" the reporter had asked, enthusiastically, smiling. "A blessed 'whore house' in this area, no one ever knew it even existed before today, everyone just thought it belonged to some old eccentric millionaire or something. It's sure to drop the price of houses around here a few points, I would think, that'll really please the residents."

Dick Cordon looked in the rearview mirror as he drove, his eyes on the young boy seated between his two men in the rear passenger seats and smiled. It had taken him almost an hour to convince his sister to let him 'borrow' her son, just for a few hours. He'd told her that a film director friend was shooting a movie and that the usual stand-in boy had taken ill. "You alright there, Josh?" Dick smiled again smugly, pleased with himself. "Have you ever done any acting before?"

"Yes thanks, Uncle Dick I'm fine. But no I haven't really done any acting. I'm getting pretty excited though." The boy smiled back, his face beaming eager to begin his 'film career'.

"What about the acting then?" He encouraged him. "You think you can pull it off, what d'ya reckon?"

"I did a little bit at school, Uncle Dick. But only Nativity play stuff, nothing as big as this, not proper, real acting that is." The boy was excited and enthusiastic about his part. "Do I have to say any words, shouldn't we rehearse or something first?"

"No... it's just a walk on part really, but you never know what it could bring, mate. You could end up famous after this." Dick chuckled to himself, whistling a silent tune as he drove.

Eduardo, seated next to Dick, tapped his arm. "Concentrate on the Goddamned job." He cursed him. "And not the kid, look he's indicating to turn off... get ready." His eyes were carefully following the black Range Rover as it turned off the motorway. Eduardo hated even being here, his job was to protect Alejandro and normally that was his primary role, as it had been for the past twenty-five years... he considered this a 'demotion'... nobody could look after Alejandro like he could and in all those years as his bodyguard there had never been a serious incident that he couldn't handle.

"Right on bloody schedule, perfect." Dick Cordon's excitement was boundless. He looked briefly across at

Eduardo and nodded, not understanding fully why Alejandro had sent such an old man on a job like this which required fit young men only, men that could react quickly to any given set of changing circumstances at a moment's notice... not 'old men'. To Dick Cordon he considered that anyone over 'forty' was 'extremely' old.

Eduardo was a 'mere' fifty-three years old and still exceptionally fit and had always made a point of being very aware of 'everything' that was happening around him, constantly vigilant of every potential situation that could develop at any given moment. In his day, when he had first started working for Alejandro, no one could have bested him... ever, whether that was in physical strength, shooting or combat. But everything was so different then... in those days... people had respect, respect for their jobs and respect for those above them. Now, to the youngsters coming through it was just about the money and fast cars and even faster girls... they had little or no 'substance' to them, not loyalty or pride. Loyalty and respect... these were amongst the many values he had taught to his own children along with all the other 'family' values. He smiled to himself proudly 'puffing' out his chest. His two daughters had gone to university... the first in his family to do so. Both had gained their degrees in English and mathematics and now worked as accountants for The Met Corps in the office next to Alejandro where he could see them every day. Both had given him good strong and healthy grandchildren and would bring them over most weekends.

But his greatest pride was his son, he had stayed on at university to gain an honours degree in chemistry and biology and was now in his fifth year as a medical graduate houseman studying to be a heart surgeon... Eduardo sighed, relieved that none of his children would ever have to be involved in anything like 'this'...

As they left the motorway to join the slip road their other two cars followed in closely behind them.

"Another mile or so to the scrapyard and we'll have the bugger." Dick waved enthusiastically at them through the open window.

Webb felt relaxed as he entered the scrapyard, following the deeply rutted track around to the right as he had been instructed. The yard was strategically situated next to an old, disused railway shunting yard and looked like it hadn't been used for that purpose in years. Some of the crushed cars were stacked ten or twelve high and had been wired together ready to be transported, their rusting shells still dripping water after last night's heavy rains. He followed the lines of cars until he came to a large clearing in the centre that Dick Cordon had indicated for him to wait, but drove past it, looking for another way out of the yard, a rout that he could use, just in case everything went wrong. Over to the extreme right-hand side, the cars thinned into a sort of track with deep rutted furrows but he still couldn't see whether it offered a way out or not so he drove back into the clearing, stopped the car at the far end and waited... leaving the engine running, his back to the highest of the piled cars... at least they wouldn't be able to get to him from there, but it seemed a small consolation somehow. He looked at the big single barrelled, pump action shotgun on his lap that Kristianna had given him and rechecked the load. It held a charge of eight rounds of 'double O' buckshot... heavy enough to bring down an elephant and had another ten cartridges clipped neatly to the butt in separate pouches. He smiled... as long as they hadn't brought any high-powered 'long rifles' with them and as long as they were at least thirty yards away from him... he 'might'... just 'might' be okay, at least it would give him a slight edge. The shotgun would easily 'outreach' most hand guns and be far more accurate than the Uzis, that he'd seen them use when Inspector Dowling was shot, it seemed to be one of their favourite weapons. One thing he did know about was 'weapons'... and the Uzi would have been the perfect weapon for house clearing... not for this situation.

Slowly, he opened the door and stood behind it as the three cars drove into the yard, the two rear cars veered off to the right and left of the lead car in an attempt to flank him, but he stopped them with a shot in front of each car from completely surrounding him and put his hand in the air, pointing the shotgun at the lead vehicle...

"That's close enough... get them to pull alongside of you." He shouted over to the lead car taking steady aim at it until it came to a stop sixty feet in front of him. Now was the time he needed Kristianna to be here, but since their departure this morning he'd had no contact with her at all. "Damn..." he cursed her under his breath, wondering where the hell she could be... worrying about the little time she'd had to arrange for the extra people.

"Mr. Pendleton... it's good to meet you at last. You're quite an adversary we've turned the countryside upside down, looking for you." Dick shouted across the gap grinning cockily, waving his arms. "We don't need the 'heavy stuff', were just hear to do a quick swap. Did you bring the cases?"

Webb lowered the heavy gun to his waist, the barrel still pointing towards the cars and shouted back. "In the boot... where's the boy?" and was intrigued when a small boy about the age of his own son got out of the passenger door of the big Toyota Land Cruiser and stood next to Dick Condon. His hands were tied in front of him and he wore a hood over his head.

'Crafty buggers...' Webbley smiled at the connivance and craftiness of the scheme, it was quite brilliant. He watched as the men spilled from the two following cars and formed a rough semi-circle around Dick Cordon each side of his car, most had semi-automatic pistols but two had the dreaded, rapid firing Uzis... those men stood in the front, he knew those weapons would be fully cocked and loaded ready for use but breathed a sigh of relief that they hadn't brought any 'long-range' weapons with them. "Let the boy come into the centre, get him to walk towards me..."

"No... I need to see the 'stuff', first..." Dick Cordon pulled his automatic from the shoulder holster and held it loosely to the boy's head.

"No, I don't like that... send the boy over first. Christ! I'm not going anywhere am I?" Webb felt a comforting calmness surround him, he knew that this would be one of the last incidents he would probably have with these people... one way or the other. If he lived through this he would then be clear to get out of the country, tomorrow. In the past he had faced down worse situations in the Radfan where mobs of screaming, armed tribesmen had wanted to lynch him, or even in South America. The big difference was that in those days he had been so much younger, stronger and was a 'big-headed' lunatic full of youthful bravado and life or death never seemed to be as important as it was right now. For him, in those days it was only ever about the excitement and the adrenaline that it created, now... however, he actually 'wanted' to 'live' and was mortally concerned about the 'dying' bit of it. It wasn't his time yet... or at least he hoped it wasn't.

"I'll send over two of my people first, just to check. Yeah, is that fair? They won't be armed. Is that good with you?" He was determined that he wasn't going to bargain with this man... he... Dick Cordon... now Head of Security for The Met Corps was calling the shots here, no one else and certainly not this damned idiot 'amateur'. More than anything else he needed it to be a success and over with quickly, this was his first major 'solo' event and he needed it to be dramatic... and above all successful.

He had thought many times since leaving Alejandro's office of the bright, 'powerful' life he would lead after he returned all of the suitcases back to Alejandro... intact, where he would be welcomed in as 'the conquering hero'... the 'single-handed savour' of The Met Corps Corporation, and in everyone's eyes he would be 'The Man'... the only 'man'.

Webb smiled, waving his hand accepting the offer, glancing down briefly at his hands he could see they were steady, with no visible shaking, pleased at the calmness he felt and the sense of the 'inevitable'. "You think I'm some sort of a 'twat', don't you?" he mumbled to himself, waiting patiently as the two approached cautiously to within twenty feet, their hands out to their sides. But as they took another step forwards, he quickly raised the shotgun to his shoulder and shot them both in the chest, from that range, the destructive power of the big gun was devastating. On the first man, the man closest to him and to his right, Webb could actually see a hole, right through the man's chest the size of a dinner plate. But he had readjusted his aim to quickly for the second man and the shot had hit him in the face, there was almost nothing left of his head and even though still writhing on the floor, would have been dead long before he hit the ground.

He smiled as the bodies writhed and kicked at the muddy soil around them, in the throes of death. As the second man rolled over and over, just the dying nerves of his body causing the violent spasms, a 45mm handgun which had been tucked into the small of his back fell from his belt into the mud. Webb had rightly guessed that they wouldn't chance coming over unarmed.

Webb walked back to the open door of his car and stood behind it, the barrel of the shotgun pointing through the open window, surprised that the others hadn't charged straight in or opened fire yet, but they were all just looking nervously at their 'leader' waiting to see what he wanted them to do, unwilling to risk their own lives against a man with the big twelve gauge shotgun.

"Now don't take me for a cunt, send the boy over." He shouted over to them, pleased that his 'shock tactic' had worked so well and was fascinated to see what Cordon's reaction would be now, still surprised that no one had fired back, or acted on their own initiative to make a move towards him, but then, at the back of his mind... he knew they wouldn't... it takes a certain, 'single-minded' type of courage to make the first move knowing full well that it might cost you your life.

He knew that if Dick Cordon had been any good and had thought out this 'exercise' with a little more detail attached to it he would have put in a couple of high-powered rifles... from way back at the entrance to the scrap yard... if he had, the situation would have been very much different for him now and that he would have been lying face down in the mud, like the other two men. He watched as his adversary placed the gun to the boy's head again.

"Jesus... you fucking wanker. Right, I'll give you to a count of three and then I'll blow the boy's fucking head off. One..." He pushed the gun harder against the boy's temple, his thumb cocking back the hammer, just for effect. "Two..."

Webb chuckled to himself...

"Three..." Cordon looked over at him. "Three, you bastard... didn't you hear me I said 'three'." He was beginning to panic now, all of his options were gone, so he fired two wild shots at Webb, but they merely hit the mud ten feet in front of him.

"You haven't got the bollocks, mate..." Webbley cupped his hand to his mouth and shouted back.

"Shit... shit... shit..." He fired another two shots, this time aiming higher... but they were wild, not even hitting Webb's car. White hot panic swept across the face of Dick

Cordon. He felt nauseous and his hands were clammy and shaking so badly that he nearly dropped the automatic. In his befuddled mind, he couldn't think of one single thing to restore the situation… not one thought…

A single shot rang out to Dick's left and slightly to his rear and he watched in horror as the boy's head exploded in his hands, gore and brain tissue splattering his face and the front of his new grey suit. As the bullet exited from the boy's forehead it tore through Dick Cordon's hand, ripping off several fingers and part of his lower arm was ripped to shreds, tearing through bone and tissue. He collapsed screaming and fell to the ground, still desperately clinging to the remaining parts of the boy's head in the shattered strands of his own hand.

On the ground he cradling the boy's decapitated head in his lap trying desperately to stem the impossible blood flow with his useable hand and to still the desperate death throws of the boy. "Josh… Josh…" He screamed at the top of his lungs, manic desperate tears pouring from his eyes seemingly oblivious till now of his own wound, screaming louder and louder as the realisation of what was happening to him dawned. Still unable to imagine where the shot had come from.

Eduardo pointed his smoking gun at the standing men around them, fanning the barrel in their faces as they began to back away. "Now get over there and get that bastard…" He screamed at them, firing twice more, over their heads until they apprehensively moved slowly forwards, firing wildly at the man standing across the void from them. One man threw down his weapon and ran trying to make a break for it… stooping, running behind the cars, ducking and weaving as he went… but Eduardo steadied his aim and checked his breathing and fired just once, hitting the man in the back, just above his waistband and dropped him like a stone, still screaming as he held his hands over the massive exit wound in his stomach. "Go... go, or I'll kill all of you myself or anyone that turns back... go! Get that bastard."

"Shit... shit." Webb raised the barrel and fired twice as they rushed him, dropping two of the leading men, but the others were running fast now and only had a bare forty feet to run. Two of their rounds hit the front of the car and ricocheted off harmlessly into the mud, but a third tore through Webb's coat just below his chest... but there wasn't any time to think about that now, he knew he couldn't get all of them, not from that distance, they were running too fast now, closing the gap on him. He fired again but the empty case jammed in the chamber, unsure through the smoke whether he had hit anyone... or not, so he quickly threw the shotgun to one side and drew his automatic firing randomly, steadily as the shapes came through the smoke, desperately faster as each shape appeared, and then behind him and to his right, a massive volley of fire opened up, almost deafening him and through the clouds of dust and smoke he watched as each man in front of him fell, writhing and screaming to the floor... the last of them dropping almost at his feet.

"Are you alright, Webbley?" Kristianna shouted from behind the barricade of stacked cars.

"Ha... I fuckin' well am now." He laughed, waving at her, clearing the smoke around him with his hand and then quickly reloaded the automatic with a full clip and re-cocked the gun.

"There's still one left... it's Eduardo, he's Alejandro's personal bodyguard. Good lord, they must be getting pretty desperate to send him out here, that's really unusual. Shall I shoot him from here, do you think?" She was pleased with herself as she jumped down from the rusty hulks of cars. She knew she had killed four of them, maybe more but cursed herself, that she had left the big Mannliker rifle at Simon's house, or she could have shot another two may be even three of them, maybe even more.

Webb raised his hand and smiled. She looked like something from a cheap 'spaghetti movie' with two automatic's in her double shoulder holster and a long barrelled rifle in her hands. Even though the weather was still quite cold, she had stripped off her coat showing her bare arms and smiling like a demented lunatic as she approached him.

"No, leave him I need to have a word with him... anyway." He crooked the rifle across his arm and threw it back into the car, later he would sort out the blockage.

"Webbley... you're a demon." She threw her hand around his neck and kissed him hard on the mouth, pulling his head into her. "Look... look what you do to me..." She grabbed his hand roughly and forced it under the tiny mini skirt into her groin. "You see that, Webbley, how wet I am... that's what you do to me. We ought to get in the back of your car now... take me now, Webbley, whilst I'm this hot." Her eyes looked demented and weird.

He smiled, pulling away from her and shook his head, not really believing what she had just said, the situation was just too ridiculous to even contemplate having sex with 'anyone' and anyway he was so 'pumped-up' with adrenaline that he doubted whether he could even manage an erection at this point. "That, Kristianna, could only come from you, couldn't it... Jesus?"

"But didn't it excite you... didn't it bring your blood to the boil, wasn't there just something about it." She felt his groin for the 'hardness' that wasn't there. "Nothing... nothing at all?"

"I don't derive any pleasure from killing anyone, Kristianna. Regardless of 'who' they might be." But he knew he had 'lied'... at the back of his mind it had brought back the old memories... tracking down the Indonesian Rangers that had just ambushed them and killed his 'partner'... and then tracking them for four days in the jungle until he had finally 'executed' every one of them... He shrugged... best not think on that now, he thought.

Slowly they walked over to the cars, Kristianna following slowly behind him sulking a little, a cast of bitter disappointment on her face, unable to understand his reluctance to make love to her... no man had ever done that to her in her entire life.

Dick Cordon was still sprawled in the mud, blood and gore caked his lower body and arms... crying hysterically, cradling the dead boy's head in his lap, his eyes pleading with Webb as he stood over him screaming out for someone to help them. "He had nothing to do with this... nothing."

"Well, not until you brought the poor little sod into it...that is." Webb leaned over to see if there was any chance for the boy, but grimaced at the extent of his injuries. "Who is he... yours?"

But Dick Cordon didn't hear or have the faintest idea what was going on around him.

"Webb kicked the gun out of his reach and walked over to Eduardo who was kneeling, his hands across his stomach holding back the blood from the tiny entry wound, completely oblivious that he was losing far more blood from his back where the high velocity, heavy calibre round of Kristianna's long rifle had exited. Webb kicked him in the face, forcing him onto his back and poked the barrel of his automatic into his open mouth.

"Well... well... well, old man, I understand you're the 'man-of-the-man', then. I bet when you got up this morning you never dreamt that you'd be lying in a heap of wet soaking, shitty mud and a pool of your own blood with half your guts blown out. Did you?" Webb stood to one side the smile gone from his face. "There but for the hand of God... go I." He mumbled... more to himself than to Eduardo.

Eduardo tried to smile but the muscles of his cheeks had frozen. To him it wasn't the 'dying'... not at all, but Alejandro... he would think badly of him now... and who would be there to look after him... and what of his children and grandchildren... this weekend there would be an empty chair and it would be a very empty, sad house without him.

Kristianna came up behind them, accompanied by the ugliest, most gaunt man Webbley had ever seen... he carried a huge 'long-rifle' and an automatic in a shoulder holster and wore all black including a ridiculously small bowler hat which barely covered the top of his head. Strands of long, wispy grey hair protruded around the sides of the hat, partly obscuring his face, the hair reaching almost to his shoulders. His face was white... no... not white, it was grey... ashen grey, making it look as if he was wearing some bizarre 'Halloween' make-up, and yet his teeth were almost pure white. The flesh of his face seemed to be transparent and to be barely covering the jutting bones of his jaw and cheeks, the skin was drawn so tightly that it looked thin and glassy like ice on a pond, like greaseproof paper.

"This is my dear friend, Herbert Tanner," Kristianna said simply, wishing that Webb wasn't staring so much at her friend she knew how sensitive Herbert got when people did that.

"Just the two of you?" Webb forced his eyes away from the gaunt man to look at her.

"Was it enough?" She smiled. "Short notice I'm afraid." She nodded at Dick Condon and then at Eduardo. "Should I finish them off?"

"No point... 'He' might live." Webb looked over at Dick Cordon. "But only 'till his bosses find out what a cock-up he's made of this. I hope the kid doesn't belong to one of them, that'll really make his day." He walked over to the now prone Eduardo. "And this feller... he'll be well dead in an hour, that's for 'dead' sure, there's more of his guts hanging out of his back than in where it should be, I reckon."

Chapter 39

Sunday 12:40. Heathrow airport was not a good place to be at the end of August, what with last-minute holiday makers and package tours desperate to be away from the worst, wettest summer England had suffered in more than fifty years and the usual delays at this time of the year had been accelerated with almost double the numbers of people wanting to get away to the sun.

The departure lounge was beginning to overspill into the main thoroughfare of the check-in desks and long queues had already started to form, some stretching back almost to the entrance doors of the airport, causing major security problems and tempers were already frayed with the backlog and delays.

It was almost midday and the congestion had been building all morning. Thirty flights had already been cancelled due to the recent French air traffic controllers' strike and other planes were delayed by as much as two or three hours, some even longer. Most of the planes were not even where they should be.

Howard Robertson-Wainsburgh collected his passport from the customs officer without smiling and walked through the last gate of 'Arrivals' into the midst of the chaos looking expectantly for the sign beyond the barrier that should have had his name on it. He would have expected it to have been held high enough for him to see... but there was nothing.

A rather plump woman and a pale, white-faced man dressed in baggy, multi-coloured shorts and 'towing' three large suitcases, ushering two noisy children pushed roughly past him, forcing their way to departures, oblivious that they had almost knocked him from his feet. Gradually he edged over to the wall, away from the crowds and placed his suitcases next to him and waited for his two colleagues to come through.

He was a small man, barely five feet four inches and wore thick-rimmed, dark glasses and a grey, weathered raincoat and yet there was an immediate air of 'bearing' and 'confidence' about him that spoke of dignity and charm. Those who knew him had learned quickly to fear and respect him. His position as the head of The Met Corps, American division had warranted that fear over the eighteen years he had been at the head of the Corporation. In the early days he had been ruthless about increasing the efficiency and the 'legality' of The Corps, so much so that now his authority was never challenged.

At the moment he was feeling a little 'vulnerable', and wished that he had taken the flight, 'first class' instead of just business class, but his relatively, poverty ridden childhood and his accountancy background disdained the waste of money on such an extravagance.

It wasn't his first visit to London on the contrary he had been here on numerous occasions but had never seen it quite as chaotic as it was now. Under any normal situation he would never be alone like this... unguarded and unprotected... exposed and alone... normally his two 'colleagues' would always be with him, wherever he was whether that was at his home, in the office or even in his bathroom...

From the corner of his eye he spotted a burly man in an ill-fitting suit standing next to the roped off barrier of the arrivals exit. The man had half-heartedly raised a hand written sign that looked like it had been torn from the side of a dirty cardboard box, on it was his name. It annoyed him very much that the man was barely holding it as high as his chest.

Howard Robertson-Wainsburgh looked down at the bulk of his suitcases against the wall and then at the crush of people around the exit and fretted. Hating the thought of dragging the cases back through that mêlée, he tucked them in tighter to the wall and fighting his way through the crowds of people, barged his way over to the man with the sign.

"You are late, damn it..." Wainsburgh grumbled, dragging the sign from him. The man towered over him.

"Mr. Wainsburgh, sorry... the traffic was awful and we have a bit of a problem on at the moment." He apologised, looking down on the small, bespeckled man. "I was told there would be three of you, sir."

"If we ever get through this Goddamned place, there will be." He looked back over to where he had left the suitcases as two armed policemen approached them. "I'm there bring the other two over as they come through." He grumbled irritably and he fought his way back to the wall.

"Are these yours, sir?" the policeman asked. He had a small sub-machinegun slung loosely across his chest, his hand on the stock.

"Yes... yes they are, I'm sorry. Is there a problem, officer?" He felt like a fish out of water, everything in this country was so different and he always hated coming here anyway.

"D'ya see that sign up there?" The second officer looked about ten years old and pointed at the long, easily read sign hanging from the ceiling which read 'All baggage must be attended to at all times.' "Can you read... or don't they have that skill in America yet?"

He covered his mouth and coughed, nervously. "Yes we do, officer, and I am very sorry. It won't happen again, I'm sorry." Wainsburgh was angry but tried not to show it.

"We have a lot of I.R.A. stuff going on at the moment and that..." He pointed at the cases. "Is bad news to us, yeah?" the first officer said, a little more kindly. "Can I see your passport, sir?"

Wainsburgh fumbled around in his pocket dropping the contents of his shoulderbag on the floor and handed the document over, still with his boarding pass inside. "I can only apologise again for the trouble I have caused you gentlemen, I'm sorry."

The officer made a note of the name and warned him that if it ever happened again the bags would automatically be taken into the customs house and confiscated.

After they left, Wainsburgh cursed. He pulled his overcoat tighter around his body and waited…

***

"What happens now, Webbley?" It was three o'clock and they were alone again in the motel, she had showered and dressed a little more 'appropriately' and she was pleased about that.

"We wait… I've arranged to meet Simon." He had cleaned the guns and cleared the stoppage on the shotgun and had then showered and changed into a clean pair of jeans, a white T-shirt and a heavy woollen pullover… and yet he still felt so cold.

"For?" She sat next to him on the bed, her fingers toying with his woolly pullover.

Webb looked at her face, still hating her. Last night they had 'made love', although there had not been a shred of 'love' attached to the act. It had been brutal and dispassionate, just a desperate need on both of their parts to satisfy some 'archaic, prehistoric, animal lust' of savagery after the 'battle'.

Most of all he still couldn't trust her… wouldn't trust her. There was no proof that he could find of her involvement in the deaths of Inspector Dowling or the other's for that matter but he just somehow knew that she 'had' been involved. "We need to get the journals back to Harrington…" He saw a tiny muscle in her face twitch, involuntarily… and smiled to himself. "I agreed with him to hand them over and that's the end of it."

"Oh…" she said simply, smiling. "When?"

"Tomorrow… I hope." It was 'another' lie but he had made his mind up that he wouldn't let her out of his sight until the journals were safely in Harrington's hands. "Look… it's our ticket out of here, for God's sake and I'm really so not into any of your mad brained schemes. Anyway, he's agreed to turn his back on us until we are out of the country, we just need to get this done, the motor yacht is all ready to go and the tides look good for tomorrow, early evening. Harrington's given us 'free passage', with verification from the Home Office, we can't expect better than that, can we."

"No, I agree, it's a good deal." She forced a smile and leaned on his shoulder so that he couldn't see the torment in her eyes. "What about the cases, Webbley?" She purred close to his ear.

"They'll be on the yacht tomorrow morning, before we get there." It was a lie again, this was one part of the overall scheme he hadn't quite figured out yet, how to pick up the cases and get them on board without her seeing them and bring them down to the yacht… or did it really matter if she saw them. 'Bugger it', maybe it would come to him later.

"Why don't we just divide everything up here, wouldn't that be much simpler?" She ran her hand down the front of his pullover and rested it on his groin. "Just a thought... I was just wondering, that's all, darling."

"No, I don't want to do that and it would break my agreement with Harrington." He knew that if she had her share here she would be even more lethal than she was now. "Wait until we get to La Coruna, we can sort it out there without the fear of having our arses shot off again and no worry about the cops, either. What will you do with yours, where do you think you will go?" He edged away from her, preferring her at arm's length, or better still... not even in the same room.

"Back to South Africa, I suppose. I can disappear there, easily." She smiled, sweetly. She had absolutely no intention of going back there... none at all... why should she when she had an 'Empire' here to run. His movement away from her hadn't gone unnoticed, but she persevered. "And you, what will you do... why don't you come with me to Africa?" It seemed to add a level of credence to her story.

He shook his head... after this he hoped their paths would never cross again. "I don't know... I haven't figured that bit out yet, just disappear for a while I suppose." He knew 'exactly' where he was going and with Gabriella along, he knew he would enjoy the rest of his days with her.

Chapter 39

Sunday evening 11:30pm.

"What happens from here, Steve?" Jack Jaeger took the line he'd been thrown and made it fast to the cleat. "Do we know?"

Steve McGillicuddy shrugged and looked over at his wife, Sue. "Not a bloody clue, mate, he just told me to dock up here and wait. Apparently he's going to be here at ten, so we'll find out then." The crossing from Cork to Dartmouth hadn't been Steve and Sue's easiest sail, even so they had thoroughly enjoyed it, it had been their first 'proper sail' together in years. "I'm sure the 'bogger' has something planned out."

The Irish Sea was notorious for short choppy waves and nasty, bitterly cold winds and on this trip it had lived up to its reputation, even Sue had felt a little queasy as well as the other lad Jason, who Peter Copping had sent down. In fact Jason had been 'bunk-bound' for ninety percent of the crossing and was still in the 'heads' praying to the 'God's' of 'puke'.

"You got the stern line, Sue?" She raised her thumb from the end of the pontoon, but he could barely see her in the half-darkness as some of the lights on the hammer head had either been turned off or were just faulty. "Right, let's get down below get out of this soddin' weather and get dried. Cup of cocoa and me and thee 'old girl' are off to bed." He helped Sue back on board and put his arm around her.

"You known him long, Steve?" Jack asked as they stowed their heavy, waterproof Henry Lloyds in the wet locker and dried off their wet hair. "He seems an 'alright sort of feller'."

Steve looked over at Sue and smiled. "Who Webbley? Yeah, known the 'bogger' donkey's years, we were in The Regiment together, but he stayed on longer than me. Basically he's a decent sort of bloke we bin mates forever it seems. It's just that he's such a bloody 'nutter' at times, like now. I've never know a human being that could get himself into so much shit as him. Trouble is, anyone that's stood around him gets covered in shit as well," he chuntered to himself. "Ain't that right, Sue, aye?"

"Oh, Steve, he's a good lad really, you know he is. His hearts in the right place, you know it is, 'e don't mean no 'arm." Sue defended Webb, as she always did. "It's just that... well things seem to 'appen to him. Somehow he can't ever stay out of trouble like you says, can he, but he's like a little puppy-dog really. Thas' all."

"Puppy-dog my arse, more like 'The Hound of the bloody Baskervilles'. From what Peter Copping was saying, there's people gettin' killed all over the place and that bloody Webbley seems to be at the heart of it all. Never figure out 'ow 'e does it."

Chapter 40

Sunday evening:

"We don't have the necessary skills for this type of operation, sir, not even our S.W.A.T. teams, you know that. This is just out and out 'terrorism' and we need outside help... damn it." It was unusual for Roger Harrington to lose his temper, especially to someone as senior as the Home Secretary, but he felt it called for it just to get some sort of positive 'feedback' and a little more 'action' and commitment from him. He had placed the call to the Home Secretary two hours ago and the call had only just been returned.

"What is it you are asking for, Roger?" He knew he wasn't going to like the answer.

"We need the Special Air Service, sir... nothing else will do." Roger paced around the room, glad now that he had put the call over to 'speaker' knowing that he couldn't sit down for long when he was so agitated. With him were Inspector Tracy Gould and George Dobson, his own sergeant. "Just a troop, eight or nine men, at least it will give us a slight edge... they don't have to be dressed in full combat gear waving around big machineguns or the like, hopefully just their presence will be enough to deter the bad buggers." He hated politicians even more now than he did before. "What do you think, sir, we just can't do this on our own?"

"I can't authorise that on my own, I would need to get the P.Ms. authority and probable half of the damned cabinet as well."

"How long?" Roger tapped his foot, irritatingly on the side of his desk. "Sir… how long?"

"It's nine o'clock at night, Roger… I… I don't know. It will mean calling the P.M. now." He had never been a man who could make decisions easily, not without the full backing of his security team.

"Then, sir…" He bit his lip. "I would suggest that you call him 'now'. I have a meeting with Mr. Pendleton tomorrow afternoon at two o'clock and I would prefer not to go there and get bloody shot or lose any more of my people. Can you understand 'that'… sir?"

"Where's the meeting, Roger?"

"I don't know, sir, Pendleton is going to let me know where and when an hour before the meeting so it must be fairly close to here."

"Damn… look, give me a couple of hours and I 'will' get back to you, bad business… very bad."

***

Monday morning: 9:35 am.

"This came in first thing this morning, sir, delivered by taxi cab. It's Mr. Kyso's briefcase, apparently he telephoned last night to say that he was ill and wouldn't be in today." The security guard handed the briefcase to the C.F.O. as he was about to enter the boardroom.

He thanked the guard and closed the door behind him, finding the exchange odd and very unusual but didn't query it. Most of the executive board members were already seated at the long table, chatting aimlessly, the topic of conversation of course was about Webbley Pendleton, which had effected all of them in some way or the other... followed closely by the visit of Howard Robertson-Wainsburgh and his team from America, all of the members knew the officious little man well and even though none liked him, all admired his efficiency and ruthlessness in getting 'work' to 'progress' rapidly and in good order and knew he'd been more than just instrumental in the massive turn-around in the fortunes of Met Corps America over the last several years.

"What's that, Walter? It looks familiar." Edward Stouridge, the Chief Executive from the Cumbrian branch asked lightly, indicating the briefcase. "Good lord, old chap, is that...?"

Walter Denham placed the case at the head of the table where Alejandro de los Santos would sit. "Yes... its Kyso's briefcase, he's phoned in sick last night, apparently, I would count that as a bonus for all of us, wouldn't you aye? I can't stand the wretched, awful man."

"I thought it looked familiar." Stouridge stood up and walked to the head of the table, fingering the lock of the case. "Good lord, I think it's open... I'd love to see what's in there, very unlike him to leave this around, especially as it's unlocked... normally he doesn't let it out of his sight. I wonder if I ought to just take a peak..."

"You'll get more than a peak if Alejandro walks in, Edward." Walter refastened the clasp and turned it to face Alejandro's chair.

"The three gentlemen from America are here, sir." Sara Pentland smiled and escorted them in. "I'll organise some coffee, shall I."

Everyone stood as Howard Robertson-Wainsburgh and his two companions entered. Suddenly the room was full of smiles and 'cordiality' and embraces for some, for others just a handshake, eventually the conversation circulated around to the 'problems' being caused by 'Webbley

Pendleton'... but ceased as Alejandro de los Santos entered.

"It's good to see you again, old friend." Wainsburgh shook his hand and then wrapped his arms around Alejandro's shoulder, kissing him on both cheeks. "I'm sorry about your troubles, maybe we can help... but there is of course the problem with the shipment, somehow it all has to be paid for 'old friend', you know that." A slight hint of a 'threat' pervaded the conversation.

Alejandro nodded glumly. He had always hated his American counterpart with a vengeance. He walked over to his chair and sat, signalling for Wainsburgh to sit next to him. "I know, my friend. Hopefully it will be sorted out soon, I should know within the next few hours." He thanked Sara Pentland as she placed the cup of steaming coffee in front of him... and then retreated to the rear of the room with her pen and notepad. Alejandro's coffee was black and strong with no sugar, as he always took it. "What's this?" He pulled the briefcase closer. "Is that Mr. Kyso's?" His fingers flipped open the first catch. "What's it doing here... where is that damned man now?" The coffee burnt his lip and he cursed, leaning closer to the table before he flipped the second catch and opened the lid...

***

A dark, onerous cloud passed over the motel, threatening rain. Webb stood and moved over to switch on the television idly flipping through the channels, anything to be away from the reach of Kristianna really. Fortunately she was showering again and would be out of the way for a while, at least he hoped she would be. His body or his mind, for that matter couldn't take on another 'love-making session' like last night... He had put his big coat over the heavy pullover and still the motel chalet felt cold.

"...and they believe the explosion was caused by a gas leak on the fourteenth floor. Apparently the blast could be heard all over the city and showered adjacent streets and buildings with debris." The moving, 'Breaking News bar' at the bottom of the screen flashed a yellow warning, the screen showing the devastated building, still partly ablaze with fire and police still covering the site. " so Just to repeat that breaking news. Twenty-four people were killed and multiple numbers seriously injured when a gas explosion ripped out most of the top floor of an office block in Southampton some of the dead haven't been identified as yet and police will not release any names until such times as the relatives have been informed. We understand that most of the high- rise block is occupied by an international trading company called 'The Met Corps' which is an import/export company, by all accounts…"

"Fuck it…" He turned the television off, disgusted with himself for allowing his hatred and anger to make him carry out such a brutal act of murder. "Jesus, now I wish I hadn't done that, it was a bastard thing to do, damn it. I'm no better than them now. I'm just a fucking murderer. Fuck… I was so bloody angry at the time… damn."

"What's that, Webbley..?" She came through the door naked, dripping water across the floor, a large bath towel in her hands, around her head she had tied a small hand towel, dabbing the water from her breast she approached the screen.

Her eyes took in the scene immediately and she smiled. "Don't put recriminations on yourself, darling, they deserved it."

"Fuck off, that…" He pointed at the devastation, wincing. "There were women in that damned blast. I'm no better than they are." He held his head racking his fingers through his hair in despair and then quickly switched the television off, hiding from the scene. "No bloody better than them… damn it."

Kristianna walked over and touched his hand, lifting it to her breast, gently rubbing his fingers along her erect nipples. "It was very clever, darling... very," her lips kissing his throat. "You said that was what you used to do when you were in the army, darling, this is no different is it?"

"Explosives? Yeah, that was part of the job, but not like this, I never did anything like this before. Christ... I've turned into a bloody 'terrorist'... a murderous bloody 'terrorist'."

Three hundred miles west in the mountains of Wales, Pippa fretted as Simon came through the door to the lounge. "Where's Webbley, Simon?" Pippa rushed over to him as soon as he entered, her hands touching his face affectionately. "Is he alright, why isn't he with you? Are you alright, darling?" She wrapped her arms around him and kissed him.

Simon pecked her on the cheek and then hugged her, and his mother... ignoring her question. "This little chap is Webbley's son and we need to take very good care of him, just for a while." He eased the boy forward, away from Gabriella. "He's had a pretty rough time of it lately, haven't you, old chap." He stroked the nape of the boy's neck. "I wonder if you could look after him for a while, Mum, just while I have a quick word with Pippa."

"Of course..." Rowan knelt in front of the frightened boy, her hand brushing the hair from his face and gave him a big hug and then taking his hand gently, she led him away. "Let's see if we can't find the girls. I wonder what they are up to." She spoke softly to him, folding her arm around his shoulders.

"Have you done with it all now, darling, finished with that awful man?" Pippa touched his arm, her face a mass of worry and fear.

"We'll talk about it later, shall we, darling?" He glanced furtively over at Gabriella, and made a face. "I need a long hot shower and so does Gabriella, and something to eat, we're worn out." He felt tense and a little angry at her for reacting so strongly.

"Beth Westward's here. She came back down after they released her from the hospital." Pippa looked exhausted and the bags under her eyes showed the pain she had been suffering. "She looks well, still has a sling on but she's fine. I've put her in one of the suits."

Simon hugged her again, wrapping his arms right around her, wishing that she was a little stronger. "I'm so glad. Later I'll pop up and see her... but how are you, truly?"

"How long is this going to go on, darling, I've been frantic with worry, waiting for you. Couldn't you have at least telephoned?" She wiped her face with the tips of her fingers, patting the tears away from her eyes, finding it difficult to catch her breath.

Simon shook his head. "Later... we'll talk later, aye?"

Gabriella walked over to the wine cabinet at the far end of the lounge and poured herself a large gin and tonic. She liked it, now that Webbley had introduced her to the taste. She glanced over her shoulder at the 'loving couple', wanting to slap Pippa's face for her stupidity and her weakness, wishing that Webbley was here, hoping... praying that he was safe. She had surprised herself over this past week on how 'practical' and 'pragmatic' she had become, putting her strength down to the courage and love she had been given by Webbley, it gave her a strange feeling of 'belonging' and of caring. It had been so long since anyone had shown her such attention. She wasn't a religious person, not in the true sense of the word but tonight, for the first time and for as long as she could remember... she would say a prayer for their safety and for the safety of everyone around her that they could come through this safely. Webbley had said they would sail tomorrow and she believed him... he was the 'hero' and the man she had always dreamed about... and he was 'hers'. This time Kristianna wouldn't be able to take him away from her... ever. More than anything... it was so important to her that he preferred 'her' over Kristianna. Finely 'she' Gabriella Van Ouden, the 'Nothing woman' had won over her older sister at last. She raised the glass up to the fading light and gave a silent toast.

Simon touched Pippa's cheek. "One way or the other this all ends tomorrow, the motor yachts' ready to go and they will all be on board by tomorrow evening and out of our lives." He whispered pulling her to him, whispering so that Gabriella couldn't hear him. "Do you understand? Everything will be finished tomorrow, but... I have to take the journals back up to Webbley, first thing in the morning... then everything will be finalised completely, do you understand? Don't you see, darling, everything will be over tomorrow. I promise you there is no danger now."

"Truly? It was those blessed journals that nearly got you killed last time. Send someone else, darling, please. It doesn't have to be you, surely does it?" She cupped his face in her hands and gently kissed his mouth, her tears wetting his face.

He shook his head. "I gave my word, I really must get them up to him... please, please there will not be any trouble this time... I'm sure of it.

"We'd better get moving, there's a lot to do today." Webb packed the last of his clothes into the holdall and zipped it up. Earlier they'd, had breakfast, in silence and he'd paid the bill for their stay.

"Do I get to know what the plan is for today, Webbley... or not?" She smiled to herself and touched his shoulder. Last night she had 'made him,' have sex with her, but she could feel that he was distracted and the sex had been boring and 'tame'. Not like their previous encounters.

"No... you don't," he answered simply. "Today I have to keep a clear head. All you need to know is that we are meeting with Simon and that you will go back with him to his place and wait for me there. I ran through this last night with you. Just pick up Gabriella and go down to the boat and wait."

"What about the cases?"

"Damn it, I said I'd deal with the cases... leave that to me, please." He felt badly irritated as he closed the door behind them and threw his bag onto the back seat of the Range Rover.

"You still don't trust me, Webbley, do you?" Kristianna fastened her seat belt and watched his face.

He shrugged...

"Why? After all we have been through, you still don't trust me?" In a way she didn't really care... it wouldn't alter her own plans, not one jot, but she did worry a little about him picking up the cases by himself... what was there to stop him just disappearing with them? 'No'. She smiled, knowing full well that he wouldn't do that... whatever happened... he wouldn't leave Gabriella behind and that he would 'dutifully' take her with him wherever he went from now on. She scoffed at his weakness. People made themselves so vulnerable. Smiling to herself unable to comprehend any of that, it was a 'luxury emotion' that she had never allowed herself to be burdened by. "Are you sure you don't want me to go with you?"

"Just stick to the bloody plan, Kristianna. That way, hopefully nothing will go wrong... this time."

He was really starting to miss Gabriella...

Chapter 40

Tuesday 10:15 am.

In a peaceful spot in the New Forest, Roger Harrington watched anxiously as the helicopter landed in the empty field in the meadow, the field that Naomi would normally pen her horses, and disgorged its passengers... eight in all... most were dressed in civilian clothes, heavy coats and jeans. Some wore 'city' clothes as if they were on a business trip, most were clean shaven with the exception of two heavyset men, dressed in scruffy jeans and jackets, their long lank hair and beards looked like they hadn't washed for an absolute age... but all looked fit and muscular... capable. Nothing could disguise that.

"I was starting to panic." Roger held out his hand to the man in front. He was tall with a thickset jaw, looking like a rugby fullback rather than a business man or a captain with The Special Air Service.

"Sorry about that, old chap. We'd initially only been given a sort of 'sketchy brief' on this, but we only got 'the go' two hours ago and came straight here from Hereford." He shook Roger's hand, smiling. "Tommy Symes... perhaps you could fill me in on the rest of it. I understand this chap Pendleton used to be one of 'ours'. Gone 'rogue' has he?"

"I hope not, but he's a clever devil. Look, bring your chaps in, we can't do anything at the moment until he telephones." Roger ushered them all into the house, Naomi had already put the kettle on and was serving tea and coffee and platefuls of sandwiches. "He's not going to call until an hour before the meeting, so it won't give us any time to get set up around the location. That's what I mean about being a clever chap, he always seems to be one step in front of us, most of the time."

He introduced them to Tracy Gould and for the next thirty minutes briefed everyone on the entire situation, as far as he knew it, but including only what he felt was relevant. "So… now it's just a case of waiting, I'm afraid…" No sooner had the words left his mouth than the telephone rang.

Naomi held the receiver up above her head and nodded. "It's… Mr. Pendleton, darling…" Her heart raced and she wished that she could just replace the receiver and pretend it had been someone else… or pretend it was anyone rather than 'this' caller.

***

"Why can't I go with you, Webbley?" Kristianna pouted. She was beginning to worry now, the radio beacon she had attached to his Range Rover only had a range of five miles and she knew that if he got too far away Herbert Tanner might actually lose contact with him.

"Because I fucking said so, go with Simon…"

He had asked Simon to meet them at the crossroads outside of Lymington town centre and he was already waiting as they drove up. Webb put his arm on Simon's elbow and eased him off to one side, out of earshot of Kristianna. "Take that bitch with you, mate, but for fuck sakes watch yourself, she's like a pit full of rampant vipers," he whispered and tapped the left-hand side of Simon's chest. "You carrying?"

Simon shook his head, feeling anxious now. "No, I thought we were all done with it."

"Shit… you want to fuckin' die, or something or you just playing 'pussy, silly buggers'?" He turned his back on Kristianna and pulled out the spare automatic from his waistband and handed it to Simon. "Take it… that bloody woman there, has more guns with her than an armoury and she won't trouble herself at all putting you away." He raised his eyebrows and shoved the gun into Simon's hand. "I'll make her put all of her bags in the boot, including her handbag, but you still need to watch her, right?" He looked over at the almost new Mercedes Sprinter van that he'd asked Simon to hire. "Great, you couldn't have picked a better motor, at least it's got a decent turn of speed to it."

"You really want to do this on your own, Webbley? Wouldn't it be better if I came with you?" Simon was concerned.

"Yes, it's better that I do it alone... and no… I don't want to do this, not at all, I'd sooner just fuck off somewhere else and hide 'til it's all over and done with, I'm sick to death of the whole bloody 'shootin' match'." He clicked his teeth feeling agitated and bad-tempered already. "The main reason is that I need you to keep an eye on 'her', keep her out of my way, otherwise I'll be looking behind me all day fully expecting her to turn up and shoot me in the damned back, or something. Whatever happens don't let her out of your sight or I'll have her back up my arse again and that really frightens the shit out of me. Look, I'm going to pick up the rest of the stuff and then go on to see Steve McGillicuddy. He's got two of Peter's chaps with him, so I'll take them with me to see Harrington." He tapped Simon's shoulder. "Get 'her' and Gabriella onto the boat 'today' even if you have to tie her up and gag her, just get them on the boat, then you're finished, mate. Look, I'll come down to see you as soon as I'm done here. I need to see the boy before I go, anyway. You just stay alive, mate, and keep your wits about you." He tapped him again, hating himself for getting people like this involved.

"You don't have to worry about me, boss." He nodded his head in the direction of the car parked a hundred yards away in a side street. "I've got two of my own men with me…"

Webb smiled, feeling more at ease. "When I come down, I'll sort out all the money for you and the chaps, yeah. If… something 'untoward' happens to me, there's enough in the suitcase in the bedroom I was in at your place, under the bed, just make sure everyone gets paid off in full. Take care now." He walked back to Kristianna and threw the keys to his Range Rover at her. "You drive…"he said simply as he opened the door of the big Mercedes Sprinter, and drove off.

Webb walked up to the lounge bar of the pub and leaned against the counter. "Are you the landlord? I need to reserve a table." He spoke quickly to the barrel-bellied man behind the bar counter dressed in a smart grey suit and white shirt with an 'over-the-top' pink and bright yellow tie.

"Yes, I am, sir…" The man smiled politely. "It's Monday, so there shouldn't be any need to book a table really, we won't be too crowded, not today, unless we get a coach load in, but I'd doubt that somehow."

"I'd still like to reserve one, please." Webb took out his wallet and looked around the lounge, already it was reasonably crowded with people milling about, as he had hoped it would be. He mentally estimated at least twenty. "That one, over by the window…" He knew it would afford him an unobstructed view of the lounge and part of the car park outside. He counted out ten fifty pound notes from the wallet and passed them across the bar. "I've got some guests coming in a minute, could you make sure that I'm looked after, please and not disturbed."

The manager looked around him and smiled again, expecting a trick but collected the money from the bar anyway. "I should think we could look after you, 'very well', sir."

"Gin and tonic, please... a large one." Webb knew it was madness to drink now, but needed it to settle his nerves... he felt calm, in himself, but still a little anxious and anyway it could well be the last gin and tonic he would ever drink if things didn't go to plan. "Have you got a phone I can use?"

"Use the one at the end of the bar, sir... no charge." He slipped the notes into his pocket, crinkling them between his finger and thumb smiling, no one else needed to know about the money, or the fact that he had just made over a month's wages without even raising a finger...

After the call Webb sat at the far end of the table, his back to the wall and tucked the briefcase alongside his leg... he lightly tapped his left breast pocket, knowing that the automatic was there, he'd already checked it a dozen times before he'd even entered the pub, and had put 'one up the spout', dangerous, but at least the safety catch was on... not wanting to blow his foot of if he had to pull it out quickly... but it gave him a strange comfort to touch it. As he sipped his gin and tonic he suddenly felt very tired... exhausted with it all... the past week had worn him down greatly.

The dye had been cast now and wheels set in motion so that it couldn't be stopped and he knew there was no going back. If everything went well in the next hour, or so, he could walk away a free man, but whatever happened the next hour would determine his future on whether he could pull this off or be carried out of here in a body-bag. In less than thirty minutes Harrington would be here and from then on things would start to move, very fast.

After leaving Simon and Kristianna he had collected the remainder of the suitcases and driven on down to see Steve and Sue McGillicuddy. Persuading Steve to go along with the rest of his plan had been the hardest thing he had ever had to do in his life.

"I can't protect you here, mate..." he had pleaded with Steve. "This way you and Sue will be safe... just do this last thing for me, please. Hate me now as much as you want but please... just do this for me. Afterwards, you can live any normal life that you want, they won't come after you I swear they won't... they'll just be too busy looking for me... and Inspector Harrington has guaranteed that he will put men with you for at least a year. Or just bugger off... if you want, start up a new life, you have enough money now."

It had taken almost an hour, and with the help of Sue, Steve agreed. But Webb still worried for them...

He watched as the two men entered the pub, and walk over to the bar, they ordered their drinks and took a table at the entrance, facing him... as he had asked them to do. Both were armed. Beneath their heavy jackets they carried the highly efficient Glock 9mm automatics and in the tool bag between them were the two Uzi machineguns he had 'confiscated' from Dick Cordon's men. Both men were smiling and jovial and seemed to be enjoying their beers that they had hardly touched.

A tall, frail looking man in his early fifties came over to Webb's table and placed a hand on the end chair. "Would you mind very much, if I took one of these chairs, old chap?"

"No... fuck off." Webb felt angry with himself afterwards.

"Where's Webbley!" Gabriella almost screamed at Simon as he came through the door with Kristianna. "Simon, where is he?"

"He's probably dead by now..." Kristianna said, hatefully as she pushed past her sister and Pippa, Simon's wife... as she took the stairs two at a time, on her way to the bedroom she had occupied to collect the remainder of her clothes. "And it serves him right, too." She hated being outsmarted, especially by a man. Her instructions to Herbert Tanner was for him to stay out of sight and simply follow the radio signal... now he would have followed 'her' to this God forsaken place and was now many miles out of place for what she wanted him to do...

"Simon...?" Gabriella was distraught.

"He's alright, Gabriella. Don't take any notice of her. He wants you to get your things up together and go down to the motor yacht." He touched Pippa's fingers and pulled her closer, kissing her lightly on the cheek, winking at her. "I'm done..." He whispered close to her ear. "I just need to check on something, give me a moment, darling, please."

Gabriella beamed. "Are you sure, really... are you positive?" She clasped her hands to her mouth, stilling her tears. "Where is he... is he following you, Simon?"

"No, he's not, darling, but he'll be along later." He touched her face lightly, feeling elated. His work with these people was done with now and with a tiny slice of luck he would earn more out of this job than anything he had made in the past two... or three years. In fact he would make 'jolly well certain' that he did... "I just need to go up and check on something, darling." He pecked Pippa again on the cheek, waiting until Gabriella had left. "Good... now look, darling, you really don't have to worry about this anymore. Everything is finished now... completely, do you understand that? My contract with them is finished, done with. From tonight they will all be gone and I promise you I will never bring a client into this house ever again." He tried to reassure her. For the last few days he had been formulating his own plans for their future... their very 'lucrative' future.

In the bedroom Webbley had occupied, Simon scrambled under the bed and pulled out the huge suitcase and flipped the lid open. He had been expecting to see more of the bearer bonds but instead there were just stack upon stack of polythene wrapped bank notes. He made a quick calculation. They were stacked in sealed bundles of a thousand pounds to a bundle. Carefully he lifted out a single stack to see how deep they went... ten, and forty along the front row and fifteen deep. He was disappointed... a quick mental calculation told him that there was just over four million pounds... not enough. He cursed. 'There's not enough for what I wanted.' He wondered where Webb had hidden the bearer bonds. 'They' were what he needed if his plan was to succeed. "Damn it..." He cursed out loud, not caring if he was heard or not.

Webb watched each person carefully as they entered. Young couples holding hands and laughing, two older men in sports jackets and neat golf type trousers followed soon after by what he assumed would be their wives as they chatted and made their way over to a table and sat with the men. It amused him to think that there was at least some 'normality' in this crazy world... he had created for himself, after all. Somewhere in this weird, twisted world people were out playing golf or going to the cinema or doing the everyday things that made it all work, giving it all a sense of 'cohesion' for them.

For him, he had surrounded himself with good men and women that he had put in harm's way and now he had 'murdered' multiple numbers of people with the bombing. Looking around him it was good to feel that some people could actually just come out for a pleasant drink and bite to eat with the people they felt the closest to. There had been a time when 'his' life had been somewhat like that... maybe never quite 'normal', not in the true sense of the word... but just 'normal'.

His focus of attention was attracted by the two burly set men with long hair and scruffy-looking beards. They were wearing untidy clothes and their boots were splashed with mud, as if they were farm workers. One wore a simple cloth cap and the bottoms of his trouser were stained with the same splashes of mud. Both were heavily bearded and seemed to saunter as they walked over to a table at the far end of the bar. Webb smiled to himself... it amused him to think that one of the greatest 'failings' of The Special Air Service... if it could be termed as a 'failing.' He doubted it was a failing... was that they trained their men and now, their women to the highest physical and mental degree of any specialised force in the world to be super fit, super active and super intelligent... able to take care of themselves in any given actively changing situation... and to act on their own initiative and yet they then expected these same people to 'appear normal' in this type of scenario. He knew from his own experience in Northern Ireland that 'undercover work' as such for these sort of people was not possible... it wasn't their 'primary role' to be 'disguised' and look like 'ordinary people'.

He'd picked out the two burly men, instantly as members of The Regiment, even though they had 'slouched', and sauntered and actually 'looked' like farm workers, but their very bearing... the confident walk... the 'strut' and the way their eyes took in their surroundings in an instant, making assessments of every single person in the lounge. To their trained eye... they would know exactly who 'he' was. Their very professionalism gave them away, instantly. He wondered where the most likely threat would come from and where the easiest escape routes were, what backup would they have if trouble started? He chuckled again, if he had gone over right now, to the table those men were seated at and gave them a sheet of paper and pen and then asked them to write down the clothing that everyone in the lounge was wearing…without even a second glance… he knew they would get nine out of ten right…

The waitress placed the glass in front of him and smiled as she removed his empty glass. "Is there anything else I can get you, sir, something to eat maybe? We have a very good special today."

"Yeah, I'll tell you what, luv. I could quite fancy a big plate of those battered prawns the couple over there have and maybe a little salad with it." He smiled back. "They look great." He watched as another three men, smartly dressed in suits and wearing neat business waistcoats and ties entered. They settled into a table ten feet to his left, seemingly oblivious of everything around them except their own conversation. 'Harrington's done well for himself. He's really brought in the cavalry'. Webb felt like walking over to their table and introducing himself to them. "Thanks…" He smiled again at her and lifting his glass, taking a small sip, watched them over the rim.

His hand shook a little as Roger Harrington came through the entrance, flanked by two smartly dressed men, one of them much taller even than Roger. Webb knew that if his 'bravado' or courage failed him now, it would be the end of everything, maybe even his life… his mind flashed back to just a week ago when he was just a simple, ordinary 'chippy'… was that 'really' just a week ago? He looked over at his own men noticing that they somehow seemed a little agitated. He knew they must have identified the 'opposition' as 'he' had, but couldn't understand why they were so trouble by it.

"Roger, good to see you again." He stood and offered his hand, nodding at the other two men, but Roger didn't take the hand offered, instead... "... pity it wasn't under better circumstances, aye?"

"I need to know straight away, Webbley, whether you had anything to do with that 'Southampton business', the bombing, before we can discuss anything further." Roger's face was dispassionate and stern, his lips hardly moving as he spoke.

"No... no, I didn't." He didn't lie easily, but forced his eyes to hold Rogers, unwavering... not a muscle in his face told Harrington anything different. "Desperate business, I saw it on the television... bloody awful, but they said it was a gas leak. No?"

Roger shook his head and pulled out the chair in front of him and sat down, staring at Webb's eyes. "That's what we've had to give to the press. If I find out later that, that is not true... I will hunt you down and any arrangement we make here today will be null and void. Is that understood?"

Webb nodded. "Very..."

"What about the scrap metal yard, was that you're doing?"

"Yes, it was... they wanted to kill me, and I didn't really fancy dying, not right there and then." Webb was as dispassionate as Harrington.

"By yourself...?"

"Does it matter, Roger, really?" He looked at the two men, still standing. "Please, gentlemen... sit down."

The taller of the two men reached over to touch Webb's coat, intending to search him. "I just need to..."

Webb slapped his hand away, watching his face. "You don't need to do anything... matey."

"Sit down, gentlemen, please," Roger insisted, irritably, eager to have done with it.

"Will your guests be dining as well, sir?" The waitress interrupted them as she placed Webb's plate of steaming battered prawns and the salad in front of him. He thought her voice sounded a little high pitched, squeaky almost.

"I expect so, luv, but a little later." Webb chuckled, the scenario seemed ridiculous. "Gentlemen, please..." He waved at the two vacant seats and wasn't satisfied until they were seated. "Now, can I get you something to drink?"

Roger said he would have a soda water, but the other two declined...

"They'll have something later, luv... thanks." Webb nibbled at a prawn as she left, but his eyes were focused on one of the bearded men that had left his seat and was now propping himself on the bar, the man had unbuttoned his long coat all the way down the front and Webb knew he was being watched through the mirrors behind the bar. "Mob handed then Roger... full troop by the looks of it. I can see... what two... five and these two, seven. Where's the eighth man... outside, I suppose?" He bit into another prawn. "You ought to try these... they are absolutely delicious."

"Have you got anyone else with you, Mr. Pendleton?" the Captain asked. Dourly... a little shaken by Webb's attitude.

Webb shrugged and raised his eyebrows...

It was the first time the more 'elegant' man of the two men of Harrington's 'close cover' had spoken...

"You're the troop leader... you tell me. What did your 'recce' group say?" He watched, a little dismayed as his own two men got up from their seats and walked towards him. For a second it threw him out of kilter. He had given them strict instruction not to do 'anything' unless someone started shooting or he gave them the 'nod'.

"Look, sorry, boss." Jack Jaeger nodded at Webbley and then glanced over at Captain Tommy Symes, sitting on Harrington's left and grunted. "Hiya, Tommy... Look, boss, we can't go up against these fellers... they're part of our old troop. I thought we were up against some bad buggers, not these fellers." He reached across Roger Harrington and shook Tommy Symes's hand. "Sorry, mate... you know how it is."

"No worries, Jack." Tommy smiled, he had seen both men as he walked in... feeling a little 'puffed up', with himself now.

Webb laughed and leaned back in his seat, wiping his hand on the serviette.

"Well there ya go then... is that me fucked, or what?" Webb smiled and nodded at Jack Jaeger. "No, it's alright, Jack, no problem. I wouldn't have expected you to pull on chaps like this. I didn't even know they were going to be involved, believe me I was as surprised as you were. It's fine... you want to wait in the car, I'll be out in a minute... well, I hope I will." He raised his eyebrows at Harrington. "I wasn't expecting these chaps, either."

He looked cautiously over at Harrington and then back to Tommy Symes, wondering if he had just simply walked into a trap. "Gentlemen, I'm just going to reach down for my briefcase... yeah? Don't start getting all bloody twitchy and 'cock-happy', now."

He leaned one hand on the table and lifted the case up... slowly, with the other hand and looked back at Roger Harrington. "We had a deal, Roger, remember you gave me your word on it, and I've kept my end of it." He opened the briefcase and took out the five journals, passing them across the table. "Bedtime reading, but it might give you a few nightmares when you look through some of those names. It looks like half of your senior police officers are involved in some way."

Tommy Symes reached over the table and collected up the journals. "I'll take those, Chief." He passed them over to his aid, standing next to him.

"But I need to..." Roger knew he had been outsmarted but that at this moment there was nothing he could do about it.

Whilst Tommy Symes was turning, Webb winked at Roger, shrugged his shoulder and mouthed the words 'Don't worry'... He'd wondered from the outset if something like this might happen. What government, regardless of political persuasion or alliances could allow the disclosure of so many of its 'incorruptible, highly respected' citizens of public office and law enforcement to be disclosed to an innocent public that respected and trust these people. He knew and understood how these people in authority worked and what they could... and in some cases, 'needed' to hide from the general public. No, the main 'high rankers', named in the journals would be asked to quietly retire, their fat pensions still intact, their extravagant lifestyles untouched by any scandal... and they would still be holding their respectable positions in society. But he was determined that, that... would not happen.

Webb finished most of his battered prawns and took two fifties from his wallet, tucking it under the plate and stood up. "Are we done here?" He threw the serviette on the plate, straightening his jacket easing the pain of his leg, his eyes watching Tommy Symes carefully.

Captain Tommy Symes stood up, almost at the same time as Roger. He had already read through the highly confidential military file of this man Webbley Pendleton, from start to finish. In a strange, unconcerned way he sympathised with him. In the past he himself had been on operations with M16 and M15 or their covert 'Out Source' departments and had noted some of the underhand, dirty 'tricks' they employed, 'tricks' that would never be excepted by standard military personnel. But 'hey' what the hell… what would the general public care anyway about such matters, until a suicide bomber or a Jihadi terrorist rocked their own community… or blew up a train they were on, they cared more about their next pay rise or that their council house rent had been raised by another two pounds per week. "I am…" he said simply.

"Where do they go now?" Roger looked at the journals tucked into Tommy Symes's arm. He felt bitterly angry at the ruse he'd had pulled on him. Angry at how the whole operation had been kept a secret and angry at himself for not seeing it coming.

Tommy Symes shrugged. "I have no idea, I just pass them on, sir…"

Outside in the car park Webb turned and held his hand out to Roger Harrington. "Sorry it turned out that way, Roger."

Harrington smiled. A thin, aggrieved smile and returned the handshake, warmly. "Where do you go now, Webbley?" He couldn't think who was the worst offender, this man or his own incompetent government.

"I'm out of the country tonight…"

"You know you can never return, don't you." He was looking into the face of a man that in the past week had, had all of his immediate family… murdered. "What about your son?"

Webb shrugged. "He's safe, I'll make arrangements for him, I hope. I obviously can't take him with me. It'd be far too dangerous and I'll need to keep moving for a while. Too many of the bad bastards still left out there, I'm afraid, and you, what will you do now?"

This time the smile was genuine. "I'm going to do what my wife has been trying to get me to do for the past ten years, and retire… maybe do a little fishing or buy a small boat. Who knows? Perhaps I'll even help her out with her pottery business… if she'll let me."

No one even saw the small, almost diminutive figure of Inspector Tracy Gould as she leapt from the car that had been parked immediately outside of the pub. She crashed through the semi-circle of surprised Special Forces men and fired one single shot before they could close in around her, tackling her to the ground, dragging the gun from her hand.

"Oh God… don't hurt her… don't hurt her. Please." Harrington screamed at the top of his lungs flinging himself in front of the men, covering Tracy Gould's body with his own.

Suddenly, everyone seemed to be armed… automatics and Uzis were in their hands the men, forming a defensive perimeter around the Chief Constable and Webbley Pendleton. A woman in the background scream and retreated quickly back into the pub… as did many others. People seemed initially paralysed with shock and fear… and then desperately panicked, rushing around like headless chickens, seeking shelter and protection anyway they could find it, as long as they weren't in the close proximity of the assault… or near to the men with the guns.

"Don't hurt her… please." Roger covered her body with his hands, pushing two of the men out of the way, and gently touched her face. "Tracy, Tracy, Tracy… it's alright, please, everything is alright now."

The anguish on her face was evident. She kicked and fought against the man holding her legs down and against Roger's touch. "You can't let that bastard live… you can't. He killed Alan, sir."

"Tracy, no… you said yourself he didn't." He brushed the hair away from her face, gently running his hand down her cheek. "Tracy, listen to me please… please."

"But he caused it, the bastard caused it…" She wept quietly, responding to his touch. "He caused it…"

"Shush… now, shush. It's alright. Tracy, it's alright." He knew that whatever happened nothing untoward must happen to her she had suffered far too much already.

"Your man's down, Commissioner…" A single voice behind him said softly, touching Roger on the shoulder.

Roger looked back at the prone unmoving figure of Webbley Pendleton… a single trail of blood already pooling around his head.

***

Tuesday 3:40 pm.

Kristianna dumped her cases at the foot of the stairs and called over one of the house maids. "You!" she shouted demanding immediate attention. "Get that into my car…" and then stormed off into the lounge to find her sister. "Gabriella!!!" she screamed. Nothing in the past few days had gone right for her and she was livid with the recent turn around in her 'fortunes'. Earlier she had made her telephone calls to Mr. Herbert Tanner, directing him back up to where they had just come from and to update him on the situation, adding that they would need to quickly 'revise' their plans as the situation had become too fluid and that they needed to plan further ahead now, but she was determined she 'would' have all of 'her' money returned to her, regardless of what that might cost…

"What?" Gabriella appeared behind her, followed by Simon. She had already put her cases reluctantly into the car.

"We need to go." Kristianna unzipped the front of her ski jacket and felt for the big .45, slung under her left armpit.

"I want to wait for, Webbley." Gabriella sobbed.

"Just get in the damned car, please." Simon spat the words at Kristianna and then gently touched Gabriella's arm. "This is what he wanted you to do, Gabriella. From what I understand from him, you are sailing as soon as everyone is on board, tonight." He glanced over at the doorway where his wife was standing, anxious also to be rid of these people.

"But I'm so worried, what if he doesn't come?" Gabriella held his arm, still not wanting to leave.

"He'll come. I know he will." Simon wondered where Webb could have hidden the remainder of the bearer bonds. He knew they were with him when he first came here, but there were a million places in this house that anything could easily be hidden and never found. As soon as these 'damned awful' people were out of it... he would start his search for them again... tear the place apart to find them, if necessary.

Kristianna felt cold. It was a thought that hadn't actually occurred to her. If something happened to that damned man Webbley Pendleton, they would all be back to the starting point they were in a week ago... no... worse. "I'm leaving... do what you want," and then stormed out of the room.

"Wait..." Gabriella chased after her.

"What time we casting off, Steve?" Sue McGillicuddy fussed around the galley. Today, because things were a little more 'settled' she had made her special Cornish pasties with chopped swede and carrots and diced potatoes she knew it was his favourite.

"Give it another hour, or so... tide'll be right up by then." He checked his charts again, going over his figures for a last time, just to be sure.

"You reckon that 'lad's' alright?"

"Who?" He knew exactly who she meant.

"Webbley, I always worry so much about him, you know I do, I just can't get it out of my mind, the thought of him being hurt somewhere." She poured the hot soup into the flasks, ready for the night watch. This time she was really looking forwards to the sail as it would be just her and Steve, rather than have to reckon with feeding and worrying about a crew. "That 'big tough feller', Peter sent down, 'e weren't so tough on 'ere, were 'e." She chuckled to herself remembering how long the S.A.S. 'boy' had spent with his head between his legs or over the lavatory bowl.

"Agh, it don't suit everyone, sailing don't." He looked around the massive, beautifully designed saloon. "Lucky bugger that Webbley having a boat like this ya know... right lucky bugger."

"Ain't that so true lad." Sue clicked her teeth. Years ago, when Steve had first left the army they had intending buying themselves a yacht... perhaps not as 'grandiose' as this of course, but something that would get them safely and comfortably around the world. She often wondered where those dreams had gone... or had it all just been complacency?

Since their return from Ireland, the sail across had rekindled his enthusiasm in sailing. He rubbed the growing 'barrel' of his tummy, it hadn't been there when he was sailing full-time, or when he had first come out of The Regiment. "Maybe we ought to do the same, gal, get us something like this, ya know... go awf, do a bit of sailing ourselves... jus' like we always promised 'ar' selves we'd do, aye, gal?"

Sue chuckled again. "Mmmm I'd like that, lad." Their minds were like the minds of 'twins', always somehow thinking along the same lines, most of the time he always knew exactly what she was thinking or about to say.

This was the easiest yacht he had ever sailed. Everything had been designed for ease of handling. "You could sail this beauty around the world single-handed without any problems at all, ya know." He ran his fingers, lovingly down the silky softness of the vanished fiddles surrounding the navigation table. "Yeah, I reckon you could." If he could have picked out his 'absolute dream yacht'… this would have been 'it'.

"Do you think he's alright though, Steve?" She glanced over at him, repeating her question.

"Him? You don't 'ave to worry so much about that bugger, darlin', he's a survivor and anyway, shit don't stick to a 'turd' do it, only to everyone around him. Course he's 'awlright'… he's a crafty bugger." Steve clicked his teeth, remembering some of the situations they had both been in when they were in The Regiment… even 'that' patrol where the M16 agent had gotten himself killed… but Webb still 'slid out' from under it, he always did… well… until the 'business' with the scraggy cat that is…

"I was wondering if I should call my sister, she'll be getting a bit worried by now. What d'ya think?"

"You could phone her, but for Christ sakes don't tell her where we are, or where were awf to. If this damned mad brained scheme of his goes 'tit's–up', then we'll all end up at the bottom of the sea, in 'Davie Jones's' bloody locker." He looked across to Sue, whatever happens he had to take care of her if anything at all looked out of order… or he felt they were in any kind of danger he would pull out of it all together… and be done with Webbley 'bloody' Pendleton.

"I asked her look after the house whilst we were goorn."

"Who?" His mind was elsewhere…

"Martha, my sister… she gonna look after the place just 'till we gets back… is all." She put the big Cornish pasty onto his plate, carefully and the tomato ketchup next to it. "Best get this inside of you, lad, it'll oil the linin's in yor belly, so it will."

"We gotta be a bit careful with this 'ere business though, darlin', I'm getting a really bad feeling about it." He went over to the galley and wrapped his big arms around her waist and hugged her, kissing the back of her plump neck and laid his head on her shoulder. He had often wondered how different life would have been if they had been able to have children of their own... they had tried for years and eventually they'd gone to the doctors, but after so many tests on both of them it was discovered that Sue had a 'miss-placed womb' and that child birth would never be possible. Over the years she had replaced the absence of children with taking care of her 'lad'... determined that their loss would not impede the massive love she felt for him.

He leaned his head gently onto her neck, touching the soft skin with his lips. "We do alright, old girl... don't we, I always done my best for you, haven't I, d'ya think?"

Slowly Sue turned around and kissed his mouth, her arms draped loosely over his shoulders. "Yor the best man I could have ever found, lad. None better, you won't hear me ever complaining, not ever." She lowered her head onto his chest so that he couldn't see her tears as she wiped her face. "Yor a good man..." She sniffled and held him tighter "There... look now, you got me all 'motional again, you devil."

"You are a very lucky man." The Medic had sewn up the deep gash to Webb's face and covered it with a lint, moist plaster and was wrapping the bandages around his head and chin. He smiled kindly. "Another half inch to the left and she'd have taken the whole of your head off."

"Lucky my arse." His head was splitting and his face was already swelling up tightening the stitches the medic had put in. "Look, get that fucking bandage off of me and just tape over the bad bits. I look like father bloody Christmas with that lot strapped around me head." He tugged at the bandages until they were off and looked at himself in the mirror. "Christ, what a bloody mess... it looks like 'Scarface'.

The bullet had grazed his cheekbone, and gone through the side of his ear taking most of the bottom half of his earlobe with it.

"I only put that on to keep the bleeding away from your clothes, but whatever." The police medic shrugged not really caring, at least none of his own men had been hurt.

"You sure you don't want to spend the night in hospital, Webbley?" Roger was more concerned.

"No, thanks." He waited until the medic was out of earshot. "I've got a complete copy of those journals for you," he whispered, cautiously glancing around him. "I'll give them to Simon... he'll get them up to you." He touched Roger's arm and looked over at Tracy Gould huddled in a big blanket in the back of the ambulance. "What happens with Tracy, she's a damned good copper you know, and over these next few months you're going to need all the 'good coppers' you can get your hands on."

Harrington smiled and nodded, his hands furiously shaking Webb's. "I know, but don't worry about her... I can promise you that I'll take very good care of her, be sure of that. Are you sure you are going to be alright? It looks awful."

"Yeah sure. Right, I need to get off anyway... I'm badly late and I've got a long drive in front of me." He watched Roger's eyes. "Am I going to be clear... with you?"

"With me? Yes... but I'm not so sure about these people." He indicated towards Tommy Symes and his men, silently watching them in the background. "I don't know what their orders are, you have upset so many people that I don't think they are going to let you live, Webbley."

He smiled. "Yeah, I'd already pre-thought that situation, don't worry 'they' won't catch me..."

"Did you tell him?" Kristianna leaned on the door jamb as Gabriella unpacked her cases onto the huge double bed of the yacht's stateroom.

"About what?" Gabriella didn't look up.

"Anastasia..."

Gabriella shook her head. "No..."

"I hope not..." She removed the big .45 from its shoulder holster under her arm and cocked it... looking into the chamber before she released the slide to take a round into the chamber.

"Kristianna... please, please don't hurt him." She touched the tears already forming in her eyes. "He is doing everything you asked him to do, what more do you want?"

"It is 'my' money..."

"All of it?" Most of her life she had 'disliked' her sister... now however... she hated her. "Even with 'your share', you will be one of the richest women in the world. Isn't that enough?"

"Enough?" she said venomously, tucking the automatic back into its holster. "Money is never 'enough', it is what can be done with it. Do you really think that he loves you, honestly? You have known him for just over one week... that's all, you stupid girl."

"You would never understand..." Gabriella screamed at her, but her outburst couldn't hide the desperate fear she felt.

Kristianna smiled. "You are so stupid, he'll dump you as soon as he gets fed up with you, can't you see that?"

"No... no he won't, I can feel it... I can feel it here..." She touched her hand to her heart, forcing back the tears.

"Tell me something about this 'love thing'. Do you understand it... really, honestly?" she said spitefully.

"I know something about it now... with Webbley."

"Love! It can be bought or sold... and he certainly bought you..." She smiled. "He loves you so much that he made love to me, last night... passionately... and he told me that he loved me, too."

"That's a lie, I know it is." But she knew the powers of her sister as far as men were concerned... especially Gabriella's 'men'. "You will never, never, never, never understand that, Kristianna, because all you ever were was Daddy's little...whore."

Gabriella remembered her sister's 'charge' at her... but never felt the blow to the side of her face that had knocked her unconscious. Some hours later she woke and staggered to the bathroom, dabbing cold water on the bruise that was already swelling on her cheekbone. When she felt a little better she covered the bruise with a thin coat of foundation working it gently into her skin. Whatever happened she mustn't let Webbley see it... it would just cause too many problems and he might kill Kristianna...

She staggered back into the cabin and opened her clutch bag and removed the tiny .38 snub-nosed revolver and checked the load. "That is the last time, Kristianna..." She whispered a silent promise to herself. "The very, very last time... now, the 'mouse' has turned into the 'rat'...

***

Tuesday: 5:35 pm.

Webb pulled into the motel car park and parked close to the red Range Rover. It wouldn't have been his ideal choice of colour, but it was fairly new and all that Simon could come up with at a moment's notice.

The trip to the motel had taken over an hour, even though the distance from the pub was barely ten miles, but he had spent the time... and used all of his skills to shake off any car that might have been tailing him... even if they had put 'ten cars' on his tail they wouldn't have tracked him... not the amount of times he had turned five rights... four lefts... and then repeated the process, several times over, constantly stopping and checking his mirrors.

He ran his fingers over the front right tire until he found the keys and opened the door, quickly transferring the cases to the Range Rover and drove away at a nice easy, steady pace... it was done. He touched his sore face and winced as his finger caught one of the stitches beneath the gauze and plaster and looked at himself in the rearview mirror. "Christ, what a bloody mess."

He didn't blame Tracy Gould, not at all. Hadn't he done worse, far worse with the bombing of the Met Corps building? He felt himself cringe at the thought of the carnage he had caused and all the unnecessary deaths, killing all of those innocent people? And he hated himself for it as a senseless act of misplaced hatred and revenge.

Forget it... just get the fuck out of here... He shook the thought from his head. Before he got to Simon's house, there was a call that he just had to make... it would finish it all... for good, he hoped.

"Good God! What happened?" Simon was shocked at the blue, green bruises still forming around Webb's face from under the mass of plaster. "What in God's name happened?"

"My ex caught up with me…" He tried to smile but it hurt too much so he casually brushed the hair from his face. With an extreme effort, he smiled. "Have you got any codeine or something?"

"Your ex?"

"I'm just kidding… really." But he didn't give any further explanation. "Codeine… maybe?"

"Yeah sure… of course, old chap." Simon rushed out of the room coming back several minutes later with a glass of water and a pack of Paracetamol. "Here… try these."

Webb walked through to the 'den' opening the pack as he went swallowing three of the tablets, Simon trailing behind. "Forget the water…" Webb poured himself a large gin and tonic and dropped in a couple of ice cubes and sunk most of it in one swig. "Christ, I needed that…" and then walked over to the large, tall locker against the wall, opened the doors and brought out all of the bearer bonds, neatly tied in a huge bundle.

Simon cursed, inwardly. He had almost torn the house apart looking for those damned things and here they were… hidden in plain sight, where he would never have dreamt to look for them… not in 'his own' den… He almost spoke out loud, but managed to hold his surprise back.

"Here… I roughly worked it out that there must be about two hundred and fifty million there." He threw the whole pack onto Simon's desk. "Get your banker friends to set up a trust for the house and for my boy… and especially for Beth. She told me she had always wanted a farm. I'll trust you to be fair with her and everyone else." He watched Simon's eyes, looking for anything untoward, but having seen nothing, continued. "Get Peter Copping and his men paid off for anything that's outstanding. Will you do that for me, Simon?"

He nodded dumbstruck, hardly moving his head, overwhelmed with the guilt of his own betrayal. "Of course…Yes, yes, I will… anything, Webbley."

Webb took the two passports out of his bag and handed them to Simon. "Take the details off of these and set up an account in each of them for me. Twenty million in each, that'll do me. Make sure that it will be good anywhere in the world will you?"

Simon nodded… his eyes still fixated on the bearer bonds as he shakily scribbled down the details. "Sure… yes, yes I will."

"One other thing…" Webb shrugged, feeling uneasy… wanting to be out of here before any other catastrophe hit them all. "The boy… would you consider, adopting him for me, taking care of him as if he was your own?"

Simon's mouth fell open. "Of course I would, old chap, yes. I would deem it an honour, an absolute honour, old chap. The girls love him already and I think he already feels at home here." It was such a small thing to ask, for so much. For one terrible moment he had thought Webb was going to ask him to accompany him on the yacht. Relief swept over him in clouds and he felt drained.

"Great…" Webb tapped his shoulder. "I'll just go up and see the boy and Beth… then I'm off."

"Webbley…" He hardly dare ask. "Do you… mean that I can… um spend this on the Hartness?"

"Yeah… is that enough?" Webb grinned.

As soon as Webbley had left, Simon collapsed into the chair, desperately holding his head in his hands, his eyes filling with tears at the 'miracle' that had just happened to him… swept by his own terrible guilt, again…

He could just make out the big motor yacht from the hill overlooking Dartmouth harbour, but didn't want to go down there yet... not until he had settled the turmoil raging through his emotions.

"Fuck..." He wiped the tears from his face and his eyes and blew his nose into the handful of tissues. The meeting with his son had been more traumatic than he could ever have imagined and it had almost ripped the heart out of him. He knew that he had always been such a lousy father... and now this. Just when the boy needed him the most, he was running off again, but Harrington had made it quite clear...the 'deal' was for him to leave the country... forever... with no return. He had explained the situation as best he could to his son, but it had still seemed pathetic and weak... and feeble and seemed to lack any sort of credence or understanding, or clarity. Worst of all... was that the boy didn't really understand any of it.

Afterwards, saying goodbye to Beth had been almost as bad. "Why don't I come with you? You still need looking after, boss." She'd held his arm, affectionately, wanting him to stay. "Or you could stay and help me 'muck-out' the horses... or something." Normally she wouldn't get emotional, but couldn't stop the tears, this time.

He'd hugged her. She was one of the few people in the world that he would trust... implicitly and yet he had known her for such a short time. "No, mate... you get on and get that farm of yours sorted out. I've left the money with Simon take as much of it as you need. Anyway... I've got Jack Jaeger and his mate to look after me." He shrugged feeling his own emotions would erupt. "Anyway..." He sniffled and forced himself to laugh. "Sometimes I think I'm bloody-well cursed, ya know."

He had handed her the old hessian sack containing the diamonds. "Use these as well, but get rid of them very slowly or someone will pick you up." It was his 'gift' to her for her service to him. At the back of his mind he wished they could have met under different circumstances... she would have been his 'perfect woman', without a doubt.

She had hugged him. "When you are settled, get in touch with me, Webb... you can always reach me through Simon." She had held his hand, tears welling in her eyes. "Would you do that, Webb... please?"

Slowly he fanned across the deck with the binoculars. The captain and a crew member and what appeared to be Kristianna were in the big wheel house, easily identifiable from his vantage point at the top of the hill overlooking the bay.

The figures of Jack Jaeger and Edward Brindley were clearly visible on the foredeck. They both seemed happy enough and both were smoking. Peter Copping's 'lads' always seemed 'good humoured'. It gave him some modicum of comfort to know that they were already on board.

But he could see no sign of Gabrielle. 'Surely she would have come down with Kristianna'. At least he hoped she had...

A car entered the car park to his right and hooted, once. Webb waved his hand indicating for the occupant to join him.

"I asked you to come alone." There was a second man in the car. Webb watched amused, as the hugely fat man, struggling to get into the Range Rover, eventually succeeding, carefully shuffling his backside around to make himself more comfortable.

"After your very intriguing call, they were a little concerned about my safety." He fidgeted again. Adam Bilton was the Chief International Correspondent for the B.B.C. News and well-known throughout the industry as being fair and honest. "I was covering a feature in Reading when they asked me to come down here, it's a three-hour drive you know, so I hope it is worth it." He fidgeted again, still not comfortable. "They told me that you had said, 'you have the biggest story since Christine Keeler and Profumo, the minister of defence scandal'. Is that true?"

"It knocks that into a cocked hat… mate."

Bilton smiled, how many times over the years had he heard that line. "I'm intrigued, why did you telephone The B.B.C.?"

"You were my second choose actually, I couldn't get through to anyone on C.N.N. which is who I really wanted to speak to." Webb fiddled with the thick buff file in his lap, wanting to be rid of it. It contained the photocopies he had printed out from the journals.

"Oh…" Bilton smiled, a little embarrassed. "That doesn't really say too much for us then, does it?"

"Yeah, not a lot, mate." His head was starting to hurt again and he'd run out of Paracetamol.

Bilton touched his arm, concerned. "Are you alright, old chap, you look absolutely awful?"

Webb nodded trying to ease the pain in his face, dabbing it with the tissue. Over at the car Bilton had arrived in, a big, fit-looking man was getting out of the driver's seat and had started walking towards them. The last thing he wanted was a physical confrontation with anyone. In his present condition even if it had been a 'Barbie doll' it would have beaten the shit out of him, very easily.

"Hey." He pointed his thumb at the approaching man. "Call your 'dog' off. I'm no threat."

Bilton waved his security man away…

"Yeah, I think your news channel is just shit actually, but I haven't got the time to piss around with anyone else at the moment. They are especially bad in the mornings. You do ten minutes of very brief, sometimes irrelevant news coverage, ten minutes of sport and then you just repeat the same boring process of 'boring old crap' for the next few hours…"

"Oh dear, you really do have a very high opinion of us then?" He looked over at Webb. "What's this all about, old chap, do I get your name?"

"No, you don't." Webb briefed him on the events of the past week, covering only the parts he wanted him to know about... never giving him any of the names that had worked for him, simply emphasising the police corruption and the corruption of certain members of the judiciary and avoiding anything that would implicate himself...

"The only straight copper I have come across in all of this is Commissioner Roger Harrington and his deputy Inspector Tracy Gould. I've written a footnote about them so that you won't get them mixed up with the bad bastards." He explained the situation in the pub with the members of the Special Forces and how Harrington had, had to relinquish these same files that he assumed would now be handed over to the Home Secretary or some other likeminded body who would make them 'disappear' forever.

"And you have proof of all this?"

He handed Bilton the buff file and waited for him to read through a few of the relative items Webb had put to the front of the pile, before handing him a set of keys.

"What are these?" Bolton was still flipping through the pages, quickly speed reading the main details. "Good lord, is this really true... all of these people? It can't be surely."

"These are the keys to a motel room I stayed in last night." He gave him the motel name and the directions. "In there you will find two bags of videos that I 'confiscated'... I think you will find them 'very' interesting."

"And you, who are you, what's your involvement in all of this?" Bilton tried to insist.

"You don't need to know that..."

"This is unbelievable." He was making notes alongside the margins of the files. "If 'any' of this 'is' true, it'll bring the blessed government down."

"You'd better get ready for an election then…" Webb shrugged. "Right, I need to go…"

"Look wait, please, I just need to talk to you, just for a short while… there is so much 'stuff' here."

"No… that's enough for me, the rest is up to you lot." He flicked his head for Bilton to leave. "And Bilton…" He called after him as the reporter waddled back to his car. "Lose some weight you're a bloody walking dead man…"

Chapter 41

Final departure: 6:35 pm.

Webb called over to Jack Jaeger and Edward Bindley as he boarded the motor yacht, asking them to get the cases out of the Sprinter, later Simon would collect it and take it back to the rental agency. "Stick them in my cabin. I need one of you stay with them at all times, and, chaps... don't let anyone near them, I mean it no one at all." He walked over to the wheelhouse where the captain and one other crew member were, and shook their hands. "You can get under way as soon as you want skipper, sooner the better."

"Right then, fine... ten minutes, sir." The captain looked pleased, understanding how quickly men and boats 'rotted' when they were ashore. He nodded at his second in command to make the necessary arrangements for a speedy, smart departure.

"Webbley!!!" Gabriella screamed, rushing headlong at him along the side deck and was about to jump up and fling her arms around him when she saw his face. "Oh my God," she screeched. "What's that, whatever happened to your face, you poor thing?" She clasped her hands around her mouth, fretting and held his hand.

He kissed her on the mouth, hoping she wouldn't want to hug him around the neck like she usually did. "Its fine, I'm okay. I'll tell you about it later, look let's get down below, I'm feeling as rough as a bears bollocks at the moment." He threw his arm around her shoulder hugging her to him. It was really so... so good to see her again. He had missed her jaunty charm and cheerful face so much.

...On the way down, he past Jack Jaeger. "Jack, find Kristianna and bring her down to my cabin. Please... and Jack, watch yourself with her." He raised his eyebrows as a warning, even though he had thoroughly briefed both of the men about how dangerous she was, they still seemed to be treating her as if she was a 'harmless, silly woman.'

The owner's suit was truly enormous. Even for a motor yacht as big as this one, it was big. The yacht itself was a hundred and twenty feet overall and thirty feet in the beam and was of steel construction. She had been specially built for a Dutch owner for his retirement who had then unfortunately died before he could take his first trip. The widow had little or no interest in the yacht and as a consequence had put it up for sale, but in the meantime it would be put out to luxury charter hire, and at three thousand pounds a day, it wasn't cheap but it suited Webb's needs perfectly.

"Gimme your guns, Kristianna." He snapped at her before she could utter a word, holding his own automatic loosely by his side as she entered the state room, escorted by Jack Jaeger.

"Webbley?" She smiled her very 'best', childlike innocent smile, touching his shoulder, her eyes hatefully fixed on Gabriella.

"Guns..." He ripped open her coat and took her .45mm from its holster. "And the other one..."

Her brows furrowed. "The other one... darling?"

Webb handed his automatic to Jack Jaeger. "Watch her..." and violently thrust his hand between her legs, feeling around her groin and tummy. "That one..." He could feel the hard metal of the tiny automatic strapped across her belly. He guessed that was where she would keep it as he had seen the tiny panty holster, one time when she was dressing.

Slowly Kristianna slipped her hand into her pocket holster and removed the lethal little firearm and handed it to him with the barrel pointing down. "Who is going to protect me now, Webbley?" She purred, hating him with every fibre that existed in her body. "And please, take care of that, it was a present from my father and I want it back as soon as we dock... please, darling."

"If I catch you with a gun on this trip, Kristianna, I'll shoot myself..." He frowned, unable to understand how she could just put on that innocent, childlike look she wore on her face in times of crisis. It wasn't the first time he had seen it, either.

"We have an overnight trip... one night." He pointed a finger at her. "That's all. As soon as we get to La Corunna, you'll get your money and we'll split up, then I never want to see you again, is that clear. One night... so please be patient 'til then. If you fuck me about, in any way... I'll have you locked in your cabin for the bloody duration... yeah?"

"What a waste..." Jack Jaeger grinned. What he wouldn't give to be inside her panties, right now. She was definitely the most beautiful woman he had ever seen... this close.

Kristianna turned slowly into him and smiled, her tummy resting on the barrel of his automatic and touched his cheek tenderly, and then slowly lowered her hand to his groin gently taking him 'in hand'. "Mmm..." she purred close to his ear as if she was really enjoying herself. "Just as I thought… that tiny little thing would simple never do… not at all, 'sonny Jim'. I need a real man, one that would at least stand a minimal chance of satisfying me." She smiled, pushing past him, slamming the door behind her.

"What a bitch." Jack scowled as she left.

"I told you, mate…" Webb took his gun back and tapped Jack's chest. "Don't fuck about with her, I told you she's dangerous."

Jack scoffed, feeling desperately humbled and embarrassed as much as he had ever been in his life. He needed to ease the 'disturbance' in his groin but was embarrassed and unable to do so in the present company.

"Stay away from her, I'm not kidding. If you think you're good… I can tell you now, she's better, and why aren't you 'tooled up'?" Webb clicked his teeth. "Get Edward and go over to her cabin and collect any other weapons she might have, by force if necessary. I don't want that evil bitch armed in any way on this whole trip."

"You reckon it's necessary for us to be armed on the yacht… I thought?" He shrugged, raising his arms, symbolically. "Okay… man, you're the boss."

When he had left, Webb slumped down on the bed holding his head in his hands, it was really hurting badly now. "God… I'll be so glad when this damned night is over and done with. I don't ever want to see her again as long as I live… man, I'm tired. See if there's any codeine, or something in the medicine cabinet for me darlin'. Please."

When she returned from the bathroom she sat next to him, gently soothing the nape of his neck. "I was petrified with worry, Webbley… petrified. I thought you were… dead." She handed him the packet of codeine and a glass of water and wrapped her arms around his shoulders, sobbing quietly. "What happened to your poor face?"

The big yacht lurched a little, straining at its spring line as it left the dock. In the background they could just hear faint voices of the crew taking in the lines and a soft, quiet thrusting of the engines coming from deep in the bilges as the propellers bit into the water.

He explained the circumstances of how he was shot, not elaborating on too many of the graphic details, just giving her a general outline of what had happened. "I felt so sorry for the poor girl really."

"She tried to kill you…"

"Yeah I know sounds a bit crazy really but she was upset… she really liked Alan Dowling, a lot. He was like a father figure to her. It must have been a terrible loss."

"That doesn't make any difference, surely. You were there to help them," she protested, trying to hold back the tears.

"Yeah, but Christ… how many people ever get to see someone they love, die right in front of them?" He shivered just the thought of it now turned his stomach over. "And that poor bugger virtually had his head blown off, and she saw it." He could still recount every detail of it… with Tracy Gould trying to collect bits of Alan's head, trying to put it back together. "Christ, she'll have that with her for the rest of her days, regardless of how long it is."

"We still have to be very careful, Webbley. I'm still so frightened with Kristianna on board." She cuddled into him.

"I know…"

"I was hoping that…" She didn't finish.

"What?"

"Oh… nothing…"

"Go on, silly. What were you going to say?" He touched her cheek and kissed her on the mouth.

"Just that…" She shrugged. "It sounds so awful… but I was hoping she would have been… killed."

"I know what you mean…" He nodded.

Gabriella kissed the 'good side' of his face. "I've… never loved anyone like I love you, Webbley… ever. Do you… think that maybe you could learn to love me back… just a little, someday?"

He gently pulled her back onto the bed and leaned over her, kissing her mouth. "I think I do now, mate."

"Really… do you really?" Her face beamed.

He nodded and kissed her on the mouth again. "Yeah…I think I can honestly say that I do."

"Webbley…" She wriggled out from under him, her face full of concern.

"Mmmm?"

"I… think that Kristianna really 'did' kill Anastasia…"

"Why…how?" He sat back away from her, horrified.

"Just… something she said. She threatened to kill me if I told you. Something about, 'killing me like she had killed the other 'stupid bitch'." She touched her hands to her mouth and nodded.

"I knew it… in the back of my mind I knew it, all along…" He pummelled his hand into the mattress. "I knew it. Damn, I should have killed her when I had the chance."

"What do we do?"

"Nothing… not yet… I'll have to think of something…"

Dartmouth inner basin: 8:34 pm.

Sue cast the last spring line off and pulled the live end through the cleat and gave Steve the 'thumbs-up' to say that it was all clear. He gently powered up the engine and eased the big yacht away from the dock. Their departure had gone unnoticed, as they edged through the last of the channel entrance out of Dartmouth harbour basin. As soon as she came into the wheelhouse, they swapped positions and Sue took the wheel and Steve raised the main sail. When he was satisfied that it was perfectly set with just one reef, he returned to the cockpit and let out the big self furling headsail, gently steering the yacht until both sails had filled.

"There ya go my lovely, she's away." The yacht heeled slightly, her bows easily nudging the waves to one side, 'a bone between her teeth', so to speak. "What a beautiful baby this is. Of all the yachts I've ever sailed, I've never felt as comfortable or safe in my life as on this boat."

Sue hardened up the sheet with the power winch, 'tweaking' it a little until she was satisfied with the set, just a touch and then put her hand over his, leaning her head on his shoulder. "Why did we ever stop sailing? We always wanted to sail all around the world... why didn't we ever do it, Steve?"

"Things... just things. Ya know, things that always seemed to be in the way... life 'things', like trying to make a living, starting up a business, an' all that 'silly' rubbish." He kissed the side of her cheek. "We could never in a million years afford something like this though, could we?" He eased the yacht over a little to starboard to avoid and oncoming ferry, blasting its way into the port. He reached down and turned the engine off. This was always the highlight of any 'good' yachtsman's sail, when finally the engine was silenced and the yacht was under her own silent power, driving them towards the destination. "What a bloody boat, aye?"

"We made excuses really though, Steve. Didn't we? About giving up on our dreams of sailing, we should have used the money from the house and the bit you got from the army and just bought a boat and gone off..." She huddled in closer, running an arm around his waist, beneath the warm sailing jacket.

Inside the wheel house it was warm and snug and they were sheltered from the rain steadily beating against the wheel house roof. The light had just started to fail but the channel was well illuminated and they both knew it well. Once they were out of the English Channel and heading around towards Biscay they would have to keep a close watch, they both knew well enough how busy the sea traffic was at any time of the day or night in those areas.

"We could do it now though, Steve... with the money Webbley gave us." His skin felt warm and welcoming.

"Yeah, true... you still want that then, what about the house?" They still had another fifteen years to go with the mortgage, which at times had been so difficult to find, when business had been slack.

"Well, we could pay off the mortgage... first and Martha would be more than happy to rent it, her and Tom can't afford to buy their own, not with two kids and another on the way." Martha was her older sister and for a short time had lived with them, but the situation had become too 'difficult' for Steve with so many people in a three bedroom cottage.

"Yeah true, I'd go for that, let them rent it a bit cheap like, that way they will be able to afford to keep up the maintenance whilst we'em gorn , so long as it covered the expenses. I'd be happy with that, it'd be alright I 'spose." He returned her affection with a kiss.

"What do you think he has in mind?"

"Tom?"

"No, Webbley."

Steve scratched his chin. "I don't know old girl, damned if I do."

Tuesday evening:

"Do you have everything you need, sir?" The captain popped his head around the door of the main saloon. He was smartly dressed in a pressed white uniform and held a braided cap in the crook of his arm.

Webb thought the uniform a little 'over the top'. Somehow it seemed to be more suited to the Royal Navy. "It's excellent, captain, thank you and please thank your crew for me, especially the chef, they have done an absolutely excellent job." The dinner had been of five-star restaurant quality, no one could have ever imagined that they were out at sea on a yacht other than the occasional wave that was slightly higher than the others that had made the 'ride' a little more 'bumpy'.

"I've put the stabilisers out until you have finished dinner. It slows us down a touch, but as soon as you are through we'll pull them in and get up to speed," the captain added, deferentially.

Webb smiled, never in his life... regardless of how many miles he had sailed had he ever... 'dined' at sea. Whenever he had 'eaten at sea' it had always come straight out of a can, quickly heated in a pan and 'dumped' into a deep bowl with a spoon and 'golloped down' before the next tack had to be put in. "Thank you, captain, oh, captain, do you think I could have a look over the boat later... I'd be really interested in seeing the engine room... must be some pretty big motors pushing this along."

"I'd be happy to, sir..."

"How long have we got on this damned ship, captain?" Kristianna grumbled, she had barely been aboard for three hours.

"As long as we don't hit any weather, madam, I expect to dock at La Corunna at around eight o'clock tomorrow evening." The captain was courteous and polite. He had dealt with 'this sort of client' on many, many occasions… it was part of the job, he didn't like it much, but one day when he was retired on his farm he would happily relate these stories to his guests. And fortunately not all of his 'guests' had bad attitudes. Some were even quite nice and pleasant.

"Stop moaning, Kristianna. From tomorrow, you won't ever have to get onto another yacht as long as you live, if you don't want to. Life will be a bed of roses for you and you can do exactly what you want." Webb scolded her, lightly.

Gabriella giggled, she had taken three glasses of Champagne and was already feeling a little light-headed. "I like it…" She ran her hand onto Webb's lap and edged towards his groin. "Why don't we just go to bed, Webb?" She hiccupped and put her hand over her mouth. For once in her life she felt 'superior' to her older sister.

"You want to take something down to your mate Jack, and relieve him, he must be starving." Webb nodded at him. He was certainly not the best 'dinner companion' Webb had ever sat with. Jack had spent the whole of the dinner, sniping at Kristianna and it was beginning to get tedious.

***

Tuesday 11:48 pm.

Timothy Alderton-Morehead removed his glasses and laid them carefully on his desk and then slumped back into the comfortable, softness of the swivel chair. To his very closest friends he was known simply as Tam…the 'nickname' was derived by picking out the first three letters of his names.

His wife had bought the chair for him at an auction, two days after he had been selected for the position of Home Secretary and it had cost her a small fortune having it restored but she had kindly told him that he was worth it.

He often laughed about the title of 'Home Secretary', when he was a young man at university his own father had teased him constantly about his inability to stick to and persevere with, one simple task at a time, rather than 'faffing' around... as he called it... constantly changing direction. "The way you are going, lad, you'll only ever end up in the back office as some ones secretary... that's all you'll ever amount to." It had been a source of 'merriment' for his father but from his part, it had only ever been a source of constant pain and derision and had reinforced his own insecurity in his desperate search to find employment that really would satisfy his father...

'It's such a pity that the old fool wasn't still alive to see what I have achieved,' he mused.

"Well, I don't know, Home Secretary. What in God's name is all this about... have you checked out the facts yet... can all this possibly be true? One would certainly hope not." He coughed, clearing his throat before continuing. "And what do you intend doing about it, we certainly can't allow this to go public surely... can we?" Admiral Moresley grumbled, he was the Chief of The General Staff, with them was the head of MI 5 David Brainswood and MI 6 Chief Donald 'Duck' Downberry and the Chief Police Commissioner for England and Wales, Martin Snowden, in the background was Walter Smyth, personal secretary and senior adviser to the Home Secretary.

Timothy Alderton-Moorhead leaned forward and lowered his head into his hands. He had been in the job for less than a year and was now stuck with this problem. "I don't know, damn it... I don't know."

The journals had been delivered to him, personally by Captain Tommy Symes, and so far, as far as he knew, no other 'eyes' had viewed them until this meeting.

As Home Secretary, he had asked for an emergency meeting of the cabinet, for eight-thirty tomorrow morning, barely eight hours away and after deliberating over the journals for more than two hours already, they still hadn't formulated any definite conclusion or made a satisfactory decision about what they should do about them.

"It would be disastrous, absolutely disastrous. My God, this would bring the government down," David Brainswood added. "Without a shadow of a doubt, it would."

"Well thankfully none of my people are involved in this mess." The Admiral scoffed. "You damned 'cloak-and-dagger' people. I've said for years you all ought to be kicked out onto the streets, the whole lot of you... you cause more damned trouble that you're worth, most of the time." Even though the Admiral was barely sixty years old, an extremely young age for the position he held, he stuck religiously to the 'old ways' of honour and integrity in all things, especially when it came to handling 'policy', or his subordinates.

"Those sorts of comments don't really help this situation, Admiral," Donald 'Duck' Downberry retaliated. "When my department was handling Pendleton, I was barely out of university, for God's sake. Am I to be held responsible for 'the sins of the father's'?"

"Look..." The Home Secretary slammed his hand on the desk, stopping the budding row. "Let's not start bickering, gentlemen, please... it gets us absolutely nowhere. I need to know what we put in front of the P.M. and the cabinet tomorrow."

"Well how 'can' we go public with it?" David Brainswood asked. "The P.M's. rating is already at the lowest ebb ever, for any past P.M. What's this going to do for his rating if we jolly well release it? I doubt whether 'Joe public' will stand for it, anyway."

"What I need to know is what we are going to do with this fellow, Pendleton?" MI 6 came back. "Are we just going to let him walk away from everything, 'Scott free'… again?"

"That is not for debate here, arrangements have already been made with Pendleton, that can't be changed. I gave my oath on it." The Home Secretary sighed and pushed the few sparse strands of hair he had left on his head over to one side. Tonight had been his wedding anniversary and his wife had booked a table at the Savoy with just a few of their closest friends, he had been looking forwards to it for weeks… as had his wife. "Can we go public with it, I doubt it really. Truly I do?"

The Admiral grunted. "Count me out I won't be party to this sort of 'cover-up', it's disgraceful to say the least. This will end up as a blessed 'Pendleton Gate', mark my words it will."

"Look, few people actually know about this, if we just give a 'no comment' it will arouse suspicion, as it always does. If it all 'does' come to the public attention, why don't we just get the P.M. to make a 'noncommittal' statement to say that the matter is being investigated thoroughly… maybe even suggest a public enquiry, that would take years. In the mean time we can shuffle the main offenders off to one side until the pressure dies down and the public moves on to something new…" 'Duck' Downberry was starting to panic a little, as most of the responsibility would fall on his shoulders.

"Gentlemen… can I just interject something here?" The calm, softly spoken voice of Walter Smyth came from behind them. He was The Home Secretary's person adviser. Interrupting them… gave him a great deal of pleasure. All heads turned in his direction.

"Go on, Walter..." The H.S. sighed, desperate to have it all done with so that he could at least get 'some' sleep before meeting with the cabinet.

"I think we should go the opposite way, altogether. We declare everything 'now', beat the pundits to the post and disclose everything we know about this matter. Why don't we get the P.M. to make a statement to the effect that this matter has just recently come to his notice and that a full in-depth inquiry will take place, immediately, and that he declares no prior knowledge of this... which is true of course. Please, don't let's hide anything we have here from the public because one way or the other it 'will' all come out in the end."

"Rubbish... rubbish." MI6 and MI5 spoke almost at the same time.

Motor Yacht: Capallia Tuesday 8 pm.

"The Captain asked me to pop in, sir. He said you would like to be shown over the yacht." The fresh face young man was the second in command and Chief Engineer. He was dressed as smartly as the captain had been in white, neatly pressed trousers and a brass buttoned jacket and held his hat neatly tucked under his arm.

"Yeah, love to." Webb stood and touched Gabriella's shoulder. "You want to come, mate?"

She shook her head, smiling and stood next to him, whispering close to his ear. "I'm going to have a lovely hot shower and get myself ready for you, so don't be long... please. You remember what you said?"

Webb raised his eyes, not understanding...

She leaned in closer and stood on her tiptoes, whispering. "You said you were going to 'rip my draws off with your teeth'... and you never did." She giggled again, loving the opportunity to flirt with him.

"Right… I'd better be quick then."

Docklands: London 8:35 pm.

"Well where is the bastard then?" Peter stormed into the handset. "At the moment I've got coppers all over me, two dozen of them…" This time they had come with the correct warrants and paperwork and even his call to Timothy Shrimpton, his barrister in London hadn't managed to call them off. He snatched the framed photograph of his wife and children from the hands of a Detective Inspector who was about to remove the outer casing to inspect the inside of the frame. "Get yor fucking hands off of that, you shit. You think I have secret bloody 'micro-dots' behind the fucking glass or something?"

Simon smiled to himself and tucked the handset between his jaw and shoulder. At this moment he was in a meeting with his two banker 'friends' discussing the future of his 'Empire' and the investment of such a very large sum of money, and was the happiest man on the planet. "I don't know, Peter, and what's more I don't give a monkey's left tit." It was unusual for him to swear, but today was a very special day and he really 'didn't' care.

It would be the first time in over four hundred years that Hartness House and all of its grounds and lands would be free from debt… 'and' that soon it would be 'fully' restored to its most magnificent original grandeur.

"But I thought he was supposed to be staying with you…"

"He was…" Simon touched Pippa on the shoulder and kissed her cheek. "But now… I'm very glad to say, he's gone…"

"Where?"

"I don't know… I've already told you that, you chump. He got onto his big boat with all of his incredibly awful friends, oh and your two chaps, and sailed off into the 'wild blue yonder'. I hope. More than anything, I'm extremely glad to be rid of him... thank God."

"Is he coming back?"

"I don't know," he said irritably, his voice raising an octave.

Beth came into the den, her face looking like thunder. She had overheard most of the conversation. "You didn't think like that when he was here, Simon, when you spent most of the day, kissing his arse... did you."

The smile left his face, she was leaving today... with her money and it would be the last he ever wanted to of see her. "Hi, Beth..." He pointed to the telephone in his hand. "It's Peter... you want to say 'hello', or something?"

Beth turned on her heels and walked into the Great Hall, without looking back. The butler and his staff had put the last of her cases into her car. It would be a long, slow drive up to Sussex to meet with the land and property agents, but she didn't mind... the air outside of this house smelt much fresher, much cleaner anyway...

"As I said, Peter, I don't know. The last thing he said to me was to sort out your money and that your two chaps would be back with you next week. That's all, old chap." He wrapped his arm around Pippa's shoulder and pulled her closer. "Look... got to dash, old chap... tons to do."

Wednesday morning: 1:30 am.

"What's that land over there, Stevie, Brest?" Sue pointed at the barely visible lights on their port side.

"No, my lovely, that ain't Brest, its Ushant Island. Because of all this traffic I decided to go right round the outside, instead of using the Raz de Seine in between Brest and Ushant Island… to blessed dangerous in there this time of the year, so it is."

Steve smiled. He was awed at the amount of shipping traffic that was rounding the Cape or heading off into Brest harbour. "Second busiest shipping lane in the world this is, the only one that beats it is The Dover Straights. Thank God some bright bugger put in shipping lanes and separation zones around these places or it would be a blessed free-for-all."

"How long do you think then, before we get there?" She didn't mind really, they were in the wheelhouse, safe against the weather and the big yacht was being steered quite happily by the automatic self-steering wind vane. It always fascinated her to see the wheel moving… 'on its own'… making slight corrections every few seconds.

"Why don't you pop down below and get some kip, lovely… I got this." He rested his hand lightly on her shoulder, tickling the underside of her earlobe with his fingertips. "I'll wake you in a couple of hours, if 'n you likes." It was the happiest most content moment he had felt in years.

The young, fresh-faced engineer was proud of being first mate on the beautiful yacht 'Capallia. "And this, sir, is the engine room."

Webb was amazed at the size of it, the two big green, Volvo Penta engines were sited ten feet apart and looked enormous, dominating the whole area, even walking very close to them they could hardly be heard, shrouded in their sound proofed enclosures. Throughout the engine room there was full, six foot headroom and only a tall man would have to duck his head.

"Christ, it's so big…" He steadied himself as the boat heeled slightly, although down here the movement was far less than in the main saloon. "What size are they, they look enormous."

"Six hundred and fifty horsepower each, sir," the Chief Engineer said proudly and was really pleased that someone had wanted to visit 'his' little domain. The whole of the engine room was so spotless that he never worried about coming in here in his full 'whites', as he was now. "Together they give us a cruising speed of about twenty-two knots, but she will do thirty-five at full tilt." He smiled. "That burns an awful lot of fuel… though, this way we only burn about ten gallons an hour…"

"Each engine?" Webb was horrified at the engines consumption and the cost of the diesel. His experience of sailing had been purely 'sailing' where the motor was only ever used when entering or leaving port.

The boy nodded… seemingly unconcerned. "This is your 'escape hatch, sir." He walked over to the far right-hand side and pointed at the ceiling hatch. "It actually comes out in your heads… um bathroom, sorry. It's under the mat as you step into the bath… and that…" He pointed to door in the furthest bulkhead. "Leads to the after pontoon deck, or what we call the 'toy room'."

Webb followed him through to the 'toy room', as it was affectionately called, which held the high- speed rib, secured to the floor by lashings through big welded iron rings. It had an eighty horsepower Johnson out board attached to the transom. Alongside the rib where two jet skis and around the outer walls a mass of scuba diving gear and several huge inflated rings and a yellow banana that guests could ride on, when they were being towed behind the rib.

To Webb, it was a completely different sailing world that he had ever experienced even when he compared it to the occasional times he had crewed for owners of much bigger yachts than his... there was still no comparison to this Leviathan.

"A service tunnel runs the whole length of the boat." He pointed at the round watertight hatch in the forward bulkhead. "Because it runs the whole length of the ship, it comes out in the anchor locker, but it's very tight in there and you need a strong stomach to go through it, especially at sea."

"I thought you were never coming back, darling." Gabriella smiled. She was propped against the pillow on the huge bed, lying seductively on her side, wearing only a simple sheer, white silk dressing gown and a tiny pair of delicate white panties that, although the waistband was at her 'waist', the material covering her lower body was so fine as to be almost nonexistent.

"Jesus!" He knelt down beside her, his feet on the carpet and gently touched her thigh. "That is truly a sight to behold, 'madam'." He lowered his head to her tummy, following the soft contours to the meeting of her thighs with his lips as she purred and rolled slowly onto her back, surrendering herself to him... overpowered by her own, desperate emotions.

"I've been waiting so long for this, so very, very long..." She touched his neck, urging him into her.

"God... and me. Just to be alone with you and have a bit of peace to ourselves... without the damned worry of it all."

"Did you see the silly 'engine room'?" She giggled as he nibbled the soft flesh inside her thighs, feeling the heat of his tongue.

"Bugger the engine room..." He slowly lifted his face to her tummy, kissing the softness of her skin and then buried his head into her groin again, gripping the delicate material between his teeth and tore them from her. "Just give me two minutes to have a shower and then I'm going to devour you... all of you in one go..." Webb eased himself away from her and stood.

"Tell me where we're going, darling... is it somewhere 'exotic'?" She rolled onto her back, stretching her arms out... opening her legs wider so that he could see more of her and then slowly moved her hands to her thighs, sliding her fingers under the delicate torn material.

"I'm so bloody 'paranoid' at the moment that I don't even want to say it out loud. All this business has really screwed with my head."

"Whisper it to me..." She purred, moving her hands slowly inside the tiny remains of the gusset. "Whisper it..."

"Bugger the shower." He ripped off the remainder of his clothes throwing them haphazardly to the floor and leapt back onto the bed to lay beside her, his lips gently touching hers, his fingers wandering softly across the gentle curves of her body. "Later..." he whispered, close to her ear. "I'll tell you later..."

Kristianna pulled the heavy coat over her shoulders and then stepped out of her trousers, tearing off the rest of the clothes she was wearing angrily throwing them onto the floor and kicked them under the bed before going into the bathroom to shower.

She knew, above all she would need to make this very 'special'... as 'special' as she had ever made herself look for anyone...

Resting her foot on the edge of the lavatory bowl, she spread her legs as wide as she could, her fingers searching for the cord between her legs and with a gently tug removed the long leather sheath... washing it carefully before unscrewing the cap and removing the slender folded knife from inside, touching it lovingly she unfolded the blade and locked it into position, glaring at herself naked in front of the long mirror, posing with the long blade in her hand. Silently she thanked her father for all the skills he had taught her.

She knew that even another 'female', full body searcher would be reluctant to carry out a full 'body search'… of her down 'there'. Often she wondered what her father would think of her now… but knew that he would approve and would have been so proud of her.

The cold shower water stung her body as she washed herself but it didn't matter, it would make her skin lustrous and pink and 'pure' again. It would bring out more 'tone' and colour and make it shine even more. She agitated the skin briskly with the long handled louffer wand all over, making her feel alive and fit…

Afterwards she applied the same rough treatment to her skin as she dried, making sure that she used the roughest towel from her case… afterwards she sat on her bed and did her breathing exercises until she felt relaxed and calm and then removed the folding stiletto from the leather case opening the blade and touched the flat of it to her tongue running it along the whole length, without cutting herself… loving the feel of the sharp steel against her skin.

The last time she had used it was to dismember Anastasia before 'packing' her off to her parents. The act had been carried out without hatred or malice and without any emotion at all. To her it had been no different than skinning and gutting the antelopes or deer they had just shot in the bush on the hunting trips with her father. He had taught her how to skilfully separate the meat from the bone without damaging the flesh and to carry this out with just a simple, long bladed knife required extraordinary skills.

Always after their kills they would make love and it would be a passion that she had never felt with any other man since her father. The 'morality' of it had never been a concern to either of them… just looked on as the reward to the 'hunters' after the kill.

The fact that Pendleton's men had ruthlessly searched through her cases and taken all of her weapons made little or no difference to her now or to her plans for them.

Carefully she tucked the long bladed stiletto under the pillow and smoothed out the creases and then walked over to the tall wardrobe and selected the tiniest black dressing robe she could find and folded it delicately around her body, easing the neckline almost to her waist exposing a little more of her breasts, running her fingers over the nipples to excite them to hardness.

"Perfect…" She flicked her head back, pinching more colour into her already soft delicate cheeks with the tips of her fingers. This is how she would project herself. What man wouldn't want to touch 'this body'…? It wasn't a question… just a simple statement of 'fact'… Kristianna 'knew' how beautiful she was. Already the passion inside her was rising to fever pitch at the thought of her plan… already she was physically and mentally prepared for the excitement and intrigue that lay ahead. "Guide me 'Daddy', steady my hand if I should falter." It was a prayer she used for such occasions.

Over the next thirty minutes she prepared herself, physically and mentally for the task ahead, touching delicate, fragrant perfume to her body in the places where she knew it would count for the most… and then teasing her hair into place, turning the tiny blonde flicks behind her ears, constantly checking herself in the mirror to make sure she was completely satisfied with each minute detail. When she 'was' satisfied she opened the biggest of her suitcases and took out a black box marked 'cosmetics' in gold plated lettering and slid the inner secret lid to one side revelling the hidden contents of the radio.

She smiled. "If 'I' had carried out the search, I would have found 'this' without any problem. These people are such fools."

Slowly she turned the switch to 'on' and a silent, single red light bleeped twice before settling into a steady rhythmic beat, sending one flash every ten seconds or so. When she was satisfied that it was working perfectly she placed it back in the case and closed the lid and returned it to the case. She knew the radio beacon had a range of about thirty miles… but it didn't matter, she knew that was easily far enough for her purpose.

Kristianna looked at her watch on the bedside table… thirty minutes to go… before things would start to change back in her favour. Earlier she had made a mental note of the time the two guards changed shift and knew that they had stuck 'religiously' to doing their watches in two hourly shifts. She smiled again wondering what sort of stupid, idiotic training they taught at these 'Special Forces' schools… one of the very first things her father had taught her, and had insisted on… was 'never' to be predictable… 'in anything'.

Now, in less than thirty minutes she would go out into the passageway were the 'guards' had stationed themselves and meet her 'friend' again… the man she had humiliated by touching his small, limp penis in Pendleton's cabin… and she would apologise to him… and humble herself… and of course, make things right with him again…

Peter Copping stormed out to the front door of his office complex close on the heels of Chief Inspector Richard Brian Richardson. "What am I supposed to do without my fucking computers… you arsehole? My whole bloody company is computer based."

"You'll get them back in due course, sir, undamaged." Richardson kept his distance, from the big man.

It was almost eleven o'clock in the evening and the police had been searching his offices for almost twelve hours interviewing every member of staff, until everyone was completely exhausted. They had taken every computer and every hard drive in the entire building with them.

"Fuck you…" He was still ranting as they drove off.

Richardson fidgeted and adjusted his overcoat, still a little shaken and very tired. "Pull over…" He gave instructions to his driver. "Damn, man…" He had been a little 'rattled' all day.

They had driven for about five miles and he felt a little more confident now that he was at a safe distance from the big, aggressive black man. A glance at his mobile confirmed that he had good reception so he dialled the number and pressed 'send'.

"Yes…" The voice was cold and singularly direct, and obviously well-educated.

"Nothing, sir… absolutely nothing at all." Richardson fiddled with his fingers, drumming silently on the dashboard. "I have confiscated all of his computers and we are now on the way back…the 'tech lads' can go through them, thoroughly tonight, maybe they can come up with something."

"What in God's name are you doing calling me on an unsecure line, you fool." The voice was sharp and irritable. "Get back to the office and call me from there, damn you."

Richardson slowly returned the aerial into the body of the mobile feeling suitably chastised and closed the lid, cursing… everything was starting to quickly unravel and he was fearful about being left 'holding the baby'…

Sixty miles away in the sleepy outskirts of a small Sussex village called West Palbourne, Lord Marlborough replaced the receiver and paced slowly around his magnificent library. He felt justifiably angry, after all the time and resources which had been used in the past week, this damned Webbley Pendleton 'character', still hadn't been located.

Lord Marlborough was the, Thirteen Earl of Kent and for many years had been a senior member of the Government Select Committee. He was also a judge advocate and senior adviser to the Prime Minister. He also held the parliamentary seat for Westminster East, as his family had for the past three generations. All of his 'standing', wealth and numerous executive positions had been handed down to him by the generations before, as were most of his titles.

Unfortunately, Lord Marlborough had two very serious weaknesses which in order of priority were 'women' and 'gambling'. The former hadn't ever caused 'too' much of a problem and his long suffering wife had learned over the years to just grin and bear his 'indiscretions' and to turn a blind eye to his shenanigans, but the gambling had held far more serious consequences and had almost led to his downfall. Fortunately ten years ago, in his 'roll' as 'Chair of the Board of Finance and Commerce', he had been introduced to Alejandro de los Santos... who had 'kindly' agreed to offer him a possible, 'satisfactory' solution...

"Darling... it's awfully late, aren't you coming to bed?" Baroness Cressida Altringham came into the lounge and touched his shoulder. She was a 'handsome' woman, tall and very elegant and a woman of genuine 'quality'. "You have a very busy day tomorrow, you know." They had been married for almost thirty-five years and for most of it, it had simply been a duty. "What time is the meeting with The Select Committee?"

"Ten-thirty…" He winced, for some hours now he had been trying very hard to forget it.

"Have they said what it's about?"

He shook his head… knowing 'exactly' why he would be appearing in front of the committee.

"That's odd…"

Edward Marlborough smiled and touched her hand, affectionately. "Thank you, darling, I'll be up in a moment, just a few loose ends to go through." He sat up, allowing her to kiss his cheek. Deep inside his tummy a small dull pain had already erupted… two days ago he had been told of the existence of the journals and that he might well be implicated in the crisis that was now engulfing The Met Corps. It had occurred to him after he'd read about the awful explosion and murders at The Met Corps headquarters that he might have been 'forgotten' in all the 'who-ha' that had followed and yet now… everything seemed to be imploding all around him.

The mind is the most difficult 'muscle' in the human body to fully understand. Under certain circumstances it can be 'trained' to become used to almost anything… pain… boredom… routine. In a noisy situation, such as a motor yacht where noise, in general, is a constant... the brain can be woken up from a deep sleep by sudden silence… conversely a regular, rhythmic steady noise that could eventually lull a body into deep sleep can reawaken the brain when an additional 'out of rhythm' sound is added to interrupt the noise and then manages to break through that 'noisy' rhythm…

It was such a situation that brought Webb to an immediate wakefulness in the semi-darkness of his bedroom suit. It hadn't been the steady thump… thump of the engines or the occasional squeaking of a loose spar or rope… or a cupboard door that might have opened against a loose catch... the noise had been 'different', loudly out of tune and time with every other general noise a vessel at sea might make, and it seemed contrary to anything else he had heard since he'd drifted off to sleep or since boarding.

It occurred to him also, that the yacht had 'stopped' and yet the engines were still quietly 'ticking over', idling. He knew that because he could feel the slight vibration through the floor. Slowly he pulled the cover over and swung his legs out of bed, gradually adjusting his eyes, peering through the faint light of the emergency red cabin lights into the gloom of the cabin.

He craned his ears, cranking his head from side-to-side trying to identify the 'additional' sound and then walked over to the port light, cupping his hands against the glass staring into the mist and fog that surrounded them. Far off... far out to sea he could hear another, much larger boat sounding it's fog horn, eerie and solemn... and yet, he knew that, that was not the sound which had woken him.

"What is it, darling?" Gabriella yawned, sleepily and sat up in bed.

"Don't know... just... something, different, we seemed to have stopped for some reason." He looked back at her for a brief second, deeply worried. "Stay in bed, mate... I'm just going to take a look outside." He quickly pulled on a pair of jeans he'd discarded by the bed the night before and smiled at her. She seemed to be shrouded in a halo of red light, naked above the waist... a picture of serenity and beauty.

Cautiously he unlocked the door, listening for the sound again and tip-toed into the companion way, cautiously making his way towards the other cabins. Nothing seemed out of place or untoward until he came to Kristianna's cabin, the last cabin on this level and he was surprised to see that the door was slightly ajar, the bolt tap tapping against the keep plate closing and opening... tapping against the door jamb.

It worried him greatly that neither Jack Jaeger nor Edward Brindley were at their station even though the chair they had used was still at the end of the passageway.

"Kristianna?" he whispered, his hand on the door preventing it from banging again, wondering if this was the noise that had woken him. He eased it slightly open and peered inside. "Kristianna?"

Through the dim night light he could just make out a figure on the bed. "Kristianna?" As he entered he stubbed his toe on something hard, metallic on the floor and winced at the pain as the sharp metal cut through the soft flesh of his foot. "Shit..." His curse was louder than he wanted it to be. "Kristianna..." Cautiously he bent and picked up the empty magazine from the carpet, still failing to make a connection with the noise.

He reached out and touched the foot on the bed, knowing instinctively that it was the foot a 'man'. "Jesus..." and then rushed back to the bulkhead at the entrance to the cabin, stubbing his toe on another metal object again and cursed, his fingers searching for the light switch.

"Fuck..." He looked back at the bed as the light flooded the cabin, and squinting his eyes against the glare, could clearly see the half-naked, blood-soaked body of Jack Jaeger. "Jesus... You silly... silly bastard." A deep cut around Jack's throat had almost severed his head... "You silly bastard..."

In a fit of panic Webb rushed back to his cabin and slammed the door behind him, turning the lock...

"Webbley?" Gabriella was out of bed in an instant, touching his arm...fear written across her terrified face.

"Get dressed, quick, darlin'." He scrambled around the floor trying to find his shirt and jacket, the white light of

Kristianna's cabin had ruined his night vision... but he could only find the jacket. His mind racing, for now it would have to do.

"What is it, Webbley?"

"Trouble... Kristianna kind of trouble."

"But."

"Quickly, darlin'... get your clothes on, find something warm..." He swept his hand under the pillow and found his automatic and checked its load, his mind thinking fast... hardly coming up with a suitable answer. "She's murdered Jack Jaeger... and God knows who else."

"Oh God, not all this again... I thought we..." Gabriella scrambled for her clothes, tears welling in her eyes as the fear returned.

The 'different' sound that had woken him from sleep, sounded again, this time he recognised the unmistakable sound of another boat bumping against the side of the yacht...

"Fuck... I wondered why we'd stopped..." He tried to remember where he had put his additional magazines, cursing himself for being such a fool... for relaxing his guard, but for the moment his mind had gone blank.

"Webbley..." Kristianna's voice came from behind the locked door, from the companionway. "I want my cases..."

Gabriella touched her mouth with her fingers, terrified. "Oh God... Webbley." She quickly pulled the heavy coat over shoulders and fastened the zip of her jeans and touched his arm.

"Doesn't that fucking bitch ever give up?" He pulled Gabriella away from the door and whispered close to her ear. "Gabby, go into the bathroom, darlin', quick."

"No... please, I want to stay with you..." Her hands were shaking violently, fear written across her face.

"Gabby... please, you'll be safer in there." He touched her face gently and kissed her mouth. "Go..." His mind was starting to clear a little. This was 'his' punishment... the punishment of 'old age'... of being so much out of 'practice' that he could no longer 'elevate problems and 'pre-think' them before they happened. Last night he had relaxed when he should have been at his most vigilant, especially with Kristianna so close to them. Years ago, nobody would have caught him out like this, not when he was younger... damn it.

"Webbley... I know you are in there... please answer me." Her voice was calm, almost reasonable and it seemed to be 'smiling' at him.

He knew he should have killed her last night and just dumped her body over the side. "What the hell is it you want now, Kristianna?" He stood to the side of the door, the big .45 held low in both hands.

"My money..."

"We agreed to split it all in Corunna, why change that now?"

"Because it is mine, all of it... I earned it."

"So did we, damn it..."

"You were just the 'vultures' who picked around the 'corpse' I created. It was my plan... my long, long plan."

He could hear whispered voices behind her... just faintly. "How much can you spend, Kristianna?" He knew it would be pointless trying to bargain with her, but he needed time.

Webb rushed over to Gabriella in the bathroom. "The floor... under the carpet," he whispered close to her ear. "Quickly, my darling... go down into the engine room, there's a door at the back that leads into the after bay... wait there for me."

"Oh, Webbley… no." She started to cry, touching his arm… fearing to be away from him. "I'm so frightened." She held the snub-nosed .38 nervously in her tiny hand. "What… what are you going to do? She'll kill you…"

"Maybe not…" He rushed back to the door. "What do I get out of it, Kristianna… anything… nothing?"

"Your life… Webbley."

He could hear her laughing…

"Give her the cases, Webbley…" Gabriella was standing behind him, tugging at his arm.

"Give me a second…" He shouted at the door and ran his fingers along the softness of Gabriella's face, feeling her fear, knowing that she was not going to leave without him, pulling her into him he whispered. "Just pull the carpet back and open the hatch… underneath, there's a good girl, can you do that for me, darling, and wait for me in there, mate."

"Just give her the cases, Webbley… please." Her face was tormented with fear. "Just give her the cases, please."

Webb shook his head, he knew Kristianna well enough by now to know that she couldn't afford to let them live, not after this. The 'birth' of a small idea was beginning to form in his brain. "I… can't."

"I… why?" Gabriella clung to his arm.

"I'm getting them out, Kristianna…" He shouted at the door again and walked over to the bed, pulling out the first of the red suitcases… these cursed cases that had caused so much death and destruction and that had ruined so many lives… because of 'him'. Slowly he lifted the lid… to show Gabriella the two filled sandbags and the reams of torn up newspapers… he had stuffed the cases with just enough to fill up the inside of the case and the weight had been made up with small bags of sand to assimilate the approximate weight of the originals.

"Oh God!" Gabriella fell against him. "How?"

He shook his head. It didn't matter now and pulled out the second of the cases containing the four million pounds. "This might just give us a little time it's the only one with any money in it." He shrugged, wishing now that he had tried harder to convince her to go on ahead with Steve and Sue McGillicuddy... where he had transferred the contents of the cases into the big Henry Lloyd bags. She would have been so much safer with them.

"I'm going to open the door, Kristianna. Get your people to the end of the companion way... I'll put the cases outside, if I see anyone but you there I'll blow everything up... then you won't get a penny of it." He knew it was rubbish, but it would 'possibly' make her think. "You understand?"

"Agreed..."

Cautiously he dragged the case over and opened the cabin door. "You are such a bent... greedy, psychopathic bitch, Kristianna. How much can you spend for God's sake? What's the difference between ten million and twenty million... or maybe thirty million... what the hell's the difference?"

"Everything..." Her hands were resting, easily on her hips below the holstered automatics under each armpit. She was dressed in the same ridiculously short-sleeved black blouse, open at the front to her waist and the thigh length miniskirt she had worn during the scrapyard attack.

"Are you 'wet' again, Kristianna, is this that what turns you on... not just the killing?"

Slowly she lifted the miniskirt, showing him her naked, unshaven groin. "Always, Webbley, always, my darling. Didn't I tell you that you had chosen the wrong sister... you should have stayed with me."

"You're a fuckin' lunatic..."

Kristianna shook her head, laughing and ran her tongue around her lips. "I could have made you into something, Webbley... you were a little bit 'special' but you chose the wrong sister."

"You don't love me anymore then?" He smiled as he eased the case in front of his feet.

"I'm disappointed in you, Webbley... You failed me..."

"How's that?"

"You became weak and sentimental... you allowed your emotions to take control...now you've lost everything."

"No, I became 'practical'... we have enough... can't you see that?" He dared not look behind him to see if Gabriella had gone through the hatch... but prayed she had.

"Enough is never enough..."

"Madness... absolute bloody madness..."

Webb shook his head, as he lifted the case, chest high and heaved it as far as he could in her direction... spilling its contents as it hit the floor at her feet.

Gabriella came behind him dragging the remainder of the cases in front of him... his heart sank, and then she stood back as he stacked them neatly in front of the door. "What have you done with the rest of the people on board, Kristianna, the crew and my men?" It was a question he feared to ask her... but already knew the answer.

She scoffed at him, cursing under her breath. "You don't have to worry about them, Webbley..."

"But I do."

"They're resting peacefully now... no pain will ever touch 'them' again." She edged a little closer, treading over the scattered stacks of the polythene wrapped money.

"Jesus…" He could only think of the fresh-faced young engineer… who had been so very eager to please. "Everyone…?"

Kristianna smiled and nodded. "You know I am always 'thorough', Webbley… don't you."

"What happens now… to us?" He could see Herbert Tanner at the end of the corridor and two other men with semi-automatic Uzis… the perfect weapon 'now' for this type of engagement.

"Can you sail a yacht this large by yourselves, Webbley?" She smiled at him, her eyes on the pile of money in front of her.

Webb nodded. "Will we be given the chance too?"

"Kristianna, we need to go, there are too many ships in this area." Herbert Tanner shouted from behind her.

Kristianna smiled, disregarding him. "Of course you can go, my darling, I'm not totally heartless and after all… Gabriella 'is' my sister."

Webb closed the door behind him and locked it. "We have maybe a couple of minutes before they open the other cases." He grabbed Gabriella by the arm and rushed her through to the bathroom, ripping up the hatch. "Maybe they won't even open the other cases." He knew that was rubbish even as he spoke the words but it gave them a little comfort, just for a moment.

"What if they do?"

"Then we're in the shit… deep, deep shit. He tried to smile as he dropped down into the engine room and then helped her down. "Then we'll have to try something else…"

He knew that the rib offered them a tiny, minute glimmer of hope, as long as he could free the lashings in time… open the stern hatch… 'and' that it would start… although earlier as the idea had formed in his mind, an awful thought at the back of his mind occurred to him just briefly that for safety reasons the captain might just have had the tanks drained... only to be refilled 'outside' of the yacht. "Damn..."

"What?"

"Nothing..."

Above them, Kristianna's screams could be heard all over the yacht followed by volleys of shots being fired into his cabin door and the sound of rushing feet above them... and then further shots as they entered the cabin. He knew immediately that she had already opened the other cases... but then, he knew they would... Kristianna was far too smart not too.

"Webbley!" She screamed down at him, firing randomly into the engine room, over the open bathroom hatch.

Webb fired three times at a man's head framed in the hatch next to Kristianna, hitting his target twice in the shoulder and neck... his third round ricocheting harmlessly around the steel bulkhead of the engine room. He still hadn't found his magazines in the turmoil and cursed himself for his own inefficiency knowing that there were only nine rounds left in this one...

"Where is the rest of my money... Webbley, what have you done with it?" she screamed at the top of her lungs.

He quickly opened the door to the after bulkhead leading to the 'toy room' and pushed Gabriella through as Herbert Tanner and another man dropped through the hatch, firing rapidly in his direction... bullets ricocheted around the bulkheads.

"Don't shoot in here, you fucking lunatics, you'll blow us all to bloody hell and back." But he fired back quickly, twice... missing Herbert, but hitting the second man in the chest, his aim distracted as Kristianna dropped down and hid behind one of the big engines, firing rapidly in his direction until her clip was empty.

Two of Kristianna's ricochets hit the gas bottles that were stored neatly in the steel, ventilated cages on the far bulkhead and bounced harmlessly off but the third smashed into the regulator sending a fine, misty spray of 'jet propelled' gas around the engine room.

"Fuck..." Webb dived for the 'toy room' bulkhead door, just as a rogue wave healed the big yacht over slamming the bulkhead door into Gabriella, trapping her hands.

For a brief second her screams stopped the shooting...

"Where to now, Webbley?" Kristianna shouted. Her voice manic, firing randomly in his direction until her clip was empty again.

Gabriella's screams cut his heart apart as he rushed over, ripping the big steel door open to free her smashed hands and held her to him as she started to fall. "Oh God, no..." He cradled her in his arms, trying to lower her gently to the engine room floor as she screamed again, thrashing her arms in front of him. "Gabby..." The tears overwhelming him.

Kristianna slowly stood and ejected the empty clip and reloaded with a new one, there was no need for hurry now, she had him exactly where she wanted him... and then taking careful aim at his head... fired once.

Gabriella screamed again, flinging herself forwards, covering his body with hers. "Nooooo..." and threw herself in front of him, pushing him to one side as the bullet tore through her chest...

Webbley staggered to his knees and crawled over to her, cradling her on his lap. "Why?" he screamed at Kristianna, his tears mixing with the blood gushing from Gabriella's chest. "Why? She was harmless... harmless. She just... wanted someone to love her... some compassion, that's all... she wanted nothing more than that..." His grief overtook him as he pulled her up closer to his chest, spittle and blood dribbling from his mouth. "Why?" He dragged her bloody, damaged hands over and cradled them on his lap, shaking his head wildly, her blood soaking his legs.

Gabriella turned her head towards him and smiled weakly, her lips moving slowly into a thin smile... whispering. "I... I do love you, Webbley. We... could have... " and then she was gone.

For a brief moment, even Kristianna seemed shocked... and lowered her automatic, but behind her Herbert Tanner took careful aim... at Webbley. This had all gone on far too long and had become far too complicated... it all need to be ended... now, so that he could get on with his life, and take up his new position as head of The Met Corps Security...

Slowly... precisely... almost without thought, Webb sat up and reached into his pocket and took out his favourite, battered old Zippo lighter and struck the wheel... once, already feeling the fumes of gas stinging his nostrils.

"Fuck you... all of you... and fuck the money." And then threw the lighter at the nearest, punctured gas bottle...

Roger Harrington closed the door behind him and walked back into his study. In the huge buff folder he carried were the photo copies of the journals Webbley Pendleton had promised and delivered by Simon de la Croix.

"Is that what you have been waiting for, darling?" Naomi came in and touched his arm. "I saw the car leave and thought it might be."

"Yes..." He returned her touch, sliding his arm around her waist. "I think Mr. Pendleton might well be right though... I'm not sure now that I actually 'want' to read through them," and pecked her on the cheek, his fingers fiddling with the buff folder.

"You must, of course... I suppose? They have caused so much trouble and so many deaths, haven't they?"

"Mmmm... is Tracy up yet?"

"I think so... I'll check..."

Since the shooting at the pub, and as soon as the doctors had checked her over, and given her a clean bill of health, Roger had insisted she stay with them at least until she felt well enough to return to duty...

He had submitted a full report on the events as they had happened on that day to the Home Secretary, with a strong recommendation that Sergeant Tracy Gould be exonerated and given the full substantive rank of Detective Inspector and that her action had been purely 'defensive'. For which the Home Secretary had been in full accord...

"Could you ask her to come in, darling? I think it only fair for her to be here when I open these. Don't you?"

"Is it possible that all of this is true?" The Director General of the B.B.C. News paced around the long table. "Is it?" In his hand he held a huge, unlit cigar...

Crammed around the table were fourteen of his senior editors, company lawyers and a splattering of senior journalists. At the head of the table was Adam Bilton... grinning from 'ear to ear'.

"Seems like it..." Bilton smiled again. It really was the biggest story he... or anyone else for that matter had ever come through with.

"If you are absolutely sure, we'll break it tonight, on the early evening news. But you had better be absolutely sure, Bilton." He stopped pacing. "Who do we give it to? Anna?" He answered his own question. "Give it to Anna

Betting..." Anna Betting was a very senior reporter that had covered the 'Congo' massacres over a number of years and was a household name.

"But it's my story, boss... it has to be me." The smile left Bilton's face and he was angry at the suggestion that someone else would use his story.

The D.G. scratched his head and looked around the table. He had been in the 'news business' all of his adult life and knew it inside out and 'backwards', how could a young 'cub' reporter break something like this?

"Alright... alright. But if you fuck it up... you'll never work again for me or anyone else. Is that clear?" He directed the cigar at the smiling Bilton. "Run through everything with our legal people and let me see the final cut before you go on air. Damn."

"Senor... you are awake, that is very good."

Through a hazy cloud he could barely make out the features of her face, cloudy and indiscriminate. As he moved, a deep cutting pain stabbed through his lower body and he screamed out in agony. Something that he couldn't see or determine was restricting his movements and he felt a cold numbness in his legs and lower body, but further down there... there was no feeling... or pain just a damp cold sensation.

"Senor?" She spoke softly, her voice kind and encouraging. Gently she separated the mass of wax bandages around his face and touched his lips, wiping them softly with a sterile swab cleaning away the mucus. "This is good, senor... you have awakened... this is very good. You must try to drink something now..."

He felt the straw in his dry, sore mouth and tried to suck on it, but there was little strength in him.

Slowly she withdrew the straw and wetted his lips with a little water again, with her fingers, gently touching the inside of his mouth, feeding liquid around his tongue and the insides of his cheeks until he responded, sucking greedily at the finger.

"This is good now..." She fed the straw back into his mouth, carefully and smiled as he sucked, dragging the liquid around his mouth and down his throat. "Slowly now, senor... slowly." For a second she withdrew the straw until she was sure he had swallowed properly and then reinserted it back into his mouth, monitoring his intake carefully until the flask was empty. "Good..." She wiped the access from his mouth, watching his sparkling green eye... the only eye that wasn't covered with bandages... it was the only eye he would ever be able to see out of from now on.

"Can you understand me, senor?"

The softness of her voice, stirred him a little. Slowly he moved lips but no sound came through and a desperate panic touched him. He 'directed' his body to turn to face her but again, nothing happened and the pain and panic tore into his body and mind... he could hear guttural, animal sounds... that seemed to be coming from him... his throat said they were 'his' sounds... but he knew they couldn't be coming from him... could they?

"Shush now... you must rest, I will call the doctor here for you, señor... shush now..." She gently touched his head, soothing him to be calm, feeling the heat of him through the bandages. She gently touched her fingers to the one single spot just below his chin that wasn't covered with the waxed bandages on the whole of his body, trying to calm him. "My name is Antonia Vargas... can you hear that, senor?"

He blinked his eye... once, unsure of where he was or how he had got here... flashes of memory briefly returning and then as suddenly as they came... disappeared again.

Two weeks before this, he had been rescued by fisherman out at sea, they had seen the explosion on the big yacht and were close enough to render assistance and he had been brought into the hospital, barely alive with terrible burns and injuries. Even after several emergency operations and a major blood transfusion, no one had thought that he would have survived the night... except Antonia Vargas who had seen that glimmer... and the strength in his sparkling green eyes.

"It don't look too good, my lovely, not good at all." Steve gave her a hug as he stepped back onto the yacht from the dingy, his eyes watching the long, streaky Syrus clouds racing across the sky.

"Did you find anything out, Stevie?" Sue took the paynter and made it fast to a cleat on the after end of the yacht.

"I'm not sure." He had just returned from a very long taxi ride into La Coruna, north of them and about forty miles distance. He touched her shoulder and 'pecked' her on the cheek. "Like I says it don't look good. I managed to find a fisherman that spoke a little English and he told me about a big British registered motor yacht that exploded out to sea, twenty miles out. From the description it sounded like 'our' yacht, so it did." His face was shrouded in a cloud of worry.

"What about the people on board... did 'er sink, lad?"

"I gotta go back tomorrow, that fisherman, feller... he's going to find out what he can fer me. Better do... I gave him enough money to keep his family in sardines for a few years, I'd think." He shrugged. "We can't stay here too long though, gal, this 'ere coast is too damned treacherous."

Three days ago they had sailed into the 'picture postcard' mooring of Laxa and Corma, twenty miles south of Cape Finisterre on the northern most tip of Spain. To their immediate north, some forty miles by road was the large commercial port of La Coruna.

To seasoned fisherman this extreme Northern coast of Spain was known as 'El Muerte'... the 'Coast of Death'... and for good reason. Every year fishermen were killed here... last year alone it had accounted for twelve, four of which were members of the same family.

They had fully expected Webbley to be waiting for them on the end of the new pontoon here, smiling and full of himself... as usual. The new pontoon at Corma had been erected and paid for by the whole village and everyone in the area had contributed something to the cost, even if that was just their labour in an effort to attract passing yachtsmen to stop off in their pretty village, and to spend a little money with them instead of by-passing them for safer moorings further along the coast.

The entrance to Corma was at the entrance to the Rio de Arrosa and was dangerous enough in calm weather, mainly because of the usual Westerly Atlantic swell that dominated these areas and was flanked by the villages of Muros and Sol, which provided no safe anchorage. To Steve it had been the most difficult entrance to a channel he had ever had to make, with high, rugged cliffs each side of the narrow entrance and waves that crashed constantly against them. If that wasn't bad enough the channel itself was strew with outcrops of jagged, pointed rocks which were, 'occasionally' marked with tall floating 'withy's', but even then they were barely visible to the naked eye.

For six hours, before making their approach they had been forced to 'stand-off' outside of the entrance and suffer being battered by the long troublesome swells of the Atlantic to wait for daylight before entering... the 'pilot' book clearly stated, in no uncertain terms, that... 'This entrance should not be used when the weather has anything of a 'Westerly' in it'... and... '...should only be entered in daylight hours.'

"Why didn't he get us to go to Vigo, Stevie... it's only another thirty miles down the coast?"

"The bugger wanted somewhere to hide, 'duks'... Vigo is too big, too public." Steve shrugged. "No, I can see why he wanted us here, it's perfect... look who the hell would risk their lives at this time of the year to attempt that damned channel?" He pointed at the pretty village. "We bin 'ere all this time and I ain't even seen a policeman yet."

Sue nodded, knowing enough about the weather and the sea to know that the mooring here wasn't safe enough to stay for too long, even this far up the river they could still feel the effects of the Atlantic swell. "What dy'a think then, lad, we stayin', or what?"

Steve scratched his head, looking up at the sky again. "I'll go back into La Coruna, early tomorrow mornin'... see wot 'e's found, but after that were out of here early afternoon, that's for sure."

"Excuse me, my Lord, my Lady, but there is a gentleman who would like to see you, my Lord," the housekeeper said, deferentially. "I have put him in your study, sir. He says he is the Chief Constable for Hampshire, a Mr. Roger Harrington."

"Darling?" Cressida Altringham looked across the breakfast table at her husband, a little concerned and bewildered.

Lord Marlborough removed the doily from his lap and stood up, slowly. The pains in his stomach had returned with a vengeance. "Thank you, Mrs. Brown, could you tell the gentleman that I will be there presently."

"Is this something to do with the Select Committee, darling, and why would a senior policeman be coming here, at this time in the morning?" She knew that her husband had been acting very strange of late and yet she could never get him to give her a satisfactory answer for his behaviour. "Is it, James?"

"Do be quiet, just for a moment, Cressida. Please," he snapped back at her, unkindly.

"Are you in some sort of trouble?"

He shrugged his shoulders and dabbed at his lips with a tissue. "Possibly... I don't know."

"You are, I can see it in your face you've gone quite white. What is it?" She stood and stretched a hand out to him, but he simply pushed it away.

"Oh for God's sake, woman... will you please desist, just for a moment I'm trying to think." He pushed his chair back so quickly that it toppled over, but he took little notice of it as he stomped out towards his study...

Sue could see the dingy quite easily now from where she stood on the foredeck. Steve was rowing towards her at a nice steady pace. As he came closer she waved and readied herself to take the line.

"Don't worry about that, love, swing the boom over and we'll winch her up... get her roped back down to the after deck."

"We're awf then, lad?" The look on his face made her worried.

"I reckon so..." He waited for the line on the boom to come over the dingy and made it fast, ready to be hoisted. "Bout an hour..."

After the dingy had been secured she made a pot of tea and they sat quietly in the wheel house. The weather now had settled to a steady fifteen knots, North Easter. She hadn't liked the look on his face from the minute he'd stepped back on board after his second trip into La Coruna, but she was patient and didn't press him... knowing him well enough to know that he would tell her everything as soon as he'd sorted it all out in his own mind.

"Looks like 'eem be ded, gal." He was somber.

"Webbly? Oh dear." She touched her hand to her mouth, fearing the worst.

"Aye... I reckon." He leaned over the table and touched her hand, patting it gently. "That feller... the fishin' man. From what 'e wos sayin', it 'were' our boat, fer some reason that they can't figure out, it blew up... twenty odd miles out and it don't look like there were any survivors, my Lord... what a mess." He sipped slowly at the hot, strong tea.

"No one?"

Steve shook his head. "Another smaller motor boat that was close by went over to help them apparently and got caught up in the blast. There were two survivors from that boat but they haven't managed to identify either one of them yet... cos they was so badly burnt."

"What happens now then, Steve, to us?" Sue sat a little closer to him, her arm on his.

He shrugged. "Damned if I knows, gal."

"That silly boy... 'e weren't so lucky this time then?" She shook her head and touched Steve's hand, not sure whether she should cry or not... but held her tears back.

"Anyway, we need to get further south, somewhere safer before this weather blows up on us. I don' as much fancy going north again, not across that Bay. We'll go down to Figuiere de Foz in Portugal, it's an all year round safe mooring and we need to take a bit off time to think this through." He finished his tea and washed the cup in the sink and then tucked it safely back into its wrack in the overhead cupboard. "I got this bad feeling that it ain't safe right now, to go back to Cornwall."

Two hours later as they sailed steadily south helped along by a pleasant North Easter, Sue came over and sat with him at the helm…

"Wot you bin up to then?" He grinned at her and tickled her around the ribs, nuzzling in closer to her.

"Stevie?"

"You got that look about you… wot?"

Sue fiddled with her hands in her lap and partly hid her head from him. "When you wos ashore I… um… went through those Henry Lloyd bags that Webbley left…"

"And?"

"Well…" She fidgeted restlessly, flicking her fingers on her leg. "There's an awful lot of money in them… an awful lot… like 'millions' and blinking 'millions'. I couldn't even count it, there was so much."

"Should you a dun that, d'ya think?"

"I were jus'… curious, that's all." She felt guilty now as if she had spied on him.

"It don't hardly seem right really, going through someone's sea bags, somehow. Do it?"

Sue shrugged and made a face. "Weren't you just a little bit curious then, lad?"

"No, not at all…"

"Why?" She felt supremely guilty now.

"Cos I'd already gone through them the first night out of Dartmouth, when you was asleep…" He smiled and leaned into her, pecking her on the cheek.

"You devil… you." She slapped him, playfully across the shoulder and then snuggled into him.

"But I dumped a big bag of 'white stuff', powder over the side. Don't like things like that on any boat I sails."

"Well then, lad, where we awf to?"

Steve smiled, leaning his head into the warmth of her shoulder. "Somewhere warm I reckons..." He cuddled her closer, from this day on...he would never let her out of his site, for as long as they lived.

And they didn't stop laughing for almost an hour...

"Senor?" Antonia Vargas touched the tiny patch of bare flesh at his throat so as not to startle him. "Can you hear me, senor?

Webbley opened his eye and turned his head slightly so that he could see her, but the pain was excruciating, so he just blinked his eye... once.

"Good... that is so good. This is your surgeon Doctor Jose Gill, he did all of your operations. He speak perfect English, jus' like me." Antonia stood back from the bed to allow the surgeon closer.

"Senor, how are you feeling... you look so much better this morning?" He touched his finger to Webb's forehead and checked the pulse in his neck. "Mmmm... 'so' much better, but it will be a while yet before you can sit up I'm afraid. You still have some nasty burns and your body has suffered much, these must be treated of course."

Webb managed to nod his head and blink his eye again. The pain down his back was almost unbearable and his right leg was hurting, dreadfully.

"Do you understand what I am saying, senor?"

Webbley nodded, relieved that he now had 'some' movement in his head and neck.

"We have a very nice surprise for you... senor... a very big surprise." He could just see the doctor's beaming smile.

For a second Webbley lost sight of the doctor as he moved away...

"This, senor... your wife has been waiting for you to awaken for so long, she has been so very worried, so very, very worried. I know that you will be so relieved she has survived, also..."

"Darling..." Kristianna moved slowly, painfully over to the bed and sat close to his shoulder, precariously leaning into his face and smiled. "Darling... I'm so glad that you are alive. I thought you had been killed out there in that awful boat..." Most of the surface skin of her face and her hair had been blown off in the blast and the remainder of her body had been severely burnt... and yet she had sustained no broken bones, only severe bruising.

"You can't believe how much I have waited for this moment to come... darling..." She touched the waxed bandages covering his cheek, almost tenderly just below his eye, poking a boney, broken fingernail... stroking the sharp edge along his lower eye lid. "But now we can make up for everything, darling... can't we?"

As the panic tore through his body he tried to scream but managed only throaty gurgling sounds as his chest swelled to bursting point inside the broken rib cage causing unbelievable pain... and then the tears came, flooding from him in spasms... wretched waves of pain as the memories flooded back to him, the tears unsuccessfully failing to cleanse his soul.

Epilogue

In the long years that followed, many things had changed. After the downfall of the government the newly elected government was swept to power on an 'anti-corruption'... manifesto in a landslide victory that would give them the biggest majority of any previously elected body in the history of the British Government. It would oversee the rapid demise of The Met Corps which had been mortally weakened by the many deaths at all levels they had suffered, and bring to an end the reign of many other powerful criminal organisations. Most of the Met Corps business would be taken over by similar, 'Corporations' assimilating it into their own crime syndicate, but they would never again have the power or authority The Met Corps had once wielded... soon the names of people like Alejandro de los Santos and Paul Kyso and many, many other key players would be cast into the 'criminal bin' of history and forgotten, recognised only as 'a bad period' in the country's history when gangsters were permitted to rule with police consent and a period that England had suffered for far too long, but had endured.

The shipment from America was brought into Plymouth harbour in the dead of night as the town slept.

For some months afterwards, international lawyers battled through the courts claiming that the ship had been apprehended in International Waters, although the Special Air Service team, combined with an M16 and C.I.A. field unit, strongly denied the claim, declaring that the ship was apprehended three miles inside British territorial waters. The Captain however, with a secret 'inducement' from the British Authorities... clearing gave his position as being... 'ten miles' inside British waters... and any opposition was immediately dropped.

The shipment turned out to be the largest single drug haul Europe had ever seen, with an estimated street value of over four billion dollars. Governments throughout Europe praised the action of the joint 'police' action and commendations were recommended for all those who had taken part in the operation.

On behalf of the Special Air Service and M16, the British government respectfully declined the offer... but the C.I.A. 'humbly' accepted.

Simon de la Croix fulfilled his lifelong ambitions and those of his many ancestors' before him by completely renovating Hartness House and its twelve thousand acres, restoring it back to a more magnificent stature than it hadn't ever seen before... even when it had been first erected. He also made provisions for all of his tenant farmers to have free rent for the next ten years and for the free education of their children.

He carried out his promise to Webbley Pendleton by formally adopting David Pendleton as his son... who in later years would become the tenth Earle of Breconshire... superseding his two stepsisters as the only male heir.

Beth Westward bought a six hundred acre farm in the Cotswolds where she had been born and had always loved the tranquil, peaceful life the area and the people imbued in their surroundings and their culture. She set the farm up as a donkey sanctuary and a retirement home for ex-race horses. Eventually she married a man that everyone who had known Webbley Pendleton commented on the similarity of looks and personality between the two men. But on her own wishes, they remained childless… not wanting to bring another human being into the turmoil of this disturbing, unsettled world and she would die peacefully in her bed at the age of eighty-six.

Retirement suited Roger Harrington but suited his wife Naomi far more. In the interim, before retirement he had been selected by the new Home Secretary as head of the Special Investigation Branch to bring to trial all of the perpetrators listed in the journals and had delayed his retirement only long enough to finish with his immediate business of fulfilling that task.

His deepest regret was that Lord Marlborough was never brought to trial, for after the initial hearing Marlborough had been granted bail on security of a two million pound bond, but on a sunny Sunday morning he had retired to his exquisite library, smoked a long cigar and then tucked a shotgun under his chin and blown his head off.

If Roger had known some years earlier how much he could enjoy pottery, he would have retired long ago…

Peter Copping was shot dead whilst attending a meeting of the International Security Conference Forum in Lagos, Africa by an unknown assassin. His three sons took over the company but they had never been in the armed forces and knew little about the security business, consequently they squabbled so much that eventually they fell out and the company was liquidated with losses that would be later calculated in the millions of dollars. Peter's wife and his youngest daughter went up to help Beth

Westwood out on the donkey farm and lived in one of her farm cottages…

Sue McGillicuddy had always wanted children of her own, but her loss was fulfilled after they had sailed around the world… twice, eventually settling in the tiny island of Apia in Western Samoa in the South Pacific. The island had a population of barely three thousand inhabitants and for centuries the rest of the world had seemed to ignore the desperate plight of the tiny poverty-stricken nation… until the arrival of Sue and Steve McGillicuddy.

In time they would have two hundred 'adopted' orphans and would love every one of them as if they were their own… and together with a little assistance they would bring in teachers and educators and set up schools and hospitals throughout all of the islands with free tuition, and for those clever enough to go to university to become the future doctors and educators of the Islander's, their university fees would be covered completely.

As for Kristianna Van Ouden, after her recovery she had stayed in Galicia, Northern Spain for a further three months, until her patience and 'endurance' ran out, harassing the life out of Webbley Pendleton constantly as he recovered but she had eventually given up trying to 'extract' the information from him… throughout the whole of that time he had never spoken a word to her and had appeared demented and lost.

Three years later she went back to Africa and married a white, ivory poacher who had shown similarities to her own father. On one particularly profitable hunt, she was gored and trampled to death by a charging bull elephant when the big Mannliker rifle jammed on her.

Tracy Gould would become the police Commissioner of Serious Crimes throughout England and Wales and be awarded the M.B.E. by Prince Charles, for her services to law and order… but she would never marry… and would spend the whole of her working life devoted to keeping the law and making sure that 'bent coppers' were not allowed to ever prevail again…

Chief Inspector Richard Brian Richardson was convicted of assisting in the murder of Peter Copping and of serious fraud and a multitude of other crimes, as were three of his senior detectives. Richardson would be sentenced to twenty-five years in jail without the possibility of parole and was put into the same prison as some of the convicts he had helped to convict… most of them were from rival cartels. His three colleagues would be sentence to fifteen years each, again without parole.

Webbley Pendleton, would live for a further twenty-six years after he had been rescued from the burning motor yacht and would be paralysed from the waist down for the rest of his days, he never fully regained the power of speech, but his mind, although badly tormented with guilt for the first years and the pain he suffered, was as sharp as it had always been. To Antonia Vargas, his disabilities never seemed to matter very much to her anyway. In him, she saw a gentleness and softness that she would eventually come to love.

Many, many times he wondered about the miracle that had brought her to him on that fateful day and why she had stuck with him and cared for him all these years, and in thanks for her care and devotion he had named her as his sole beneficiary.

In an odd way, he had become deeply 'religious', deeply 'spiritual', not in the true sense of the word but in an inner sanctity of his soul it provided a secure 'temple' within his tormented mind from which he could occasionally retreat, to find a small modicum of peace within, helping him towards reconciling himself for his selfish greed and all the wasteful deaths he had caused.

Three years ago he had contacted Beth Westwood on the 'new-fangled' Internet that Antonia had taught him to master and he had persuaded Beth to smuggle him back into England to see his son David being appointed to the 'Bar' as a Queens Counsellor. It had been the proudest day of his life and yet, in some ways… the saddest.

No one other than Beth and Antonia Vargas knew who the old man in the wheelchair was… seated at the very back of the auditorium and no one seemed to wonder about it either… as he had wished it to be. He would have like to have introduced himself to the boy, and also to have thanked Simon de la Croix and his family for their time and energy educating and bringing the boy up to such high moral standards, but that would only have ruined everything… he knew it was far better that they assumed he had died in the fire… along with everyone else.

On a bitterly cold August evening, at the exact coordinates she had visited for the past thirteen years, Antonia Vargas leaned over the ship's rail and crossed herself, and then carefully unscrewed the cap of the brass urn. Waiting for the right moment for the wind to ease a little, she emptied the contents into the sea and crossed herself again… whispering a prayer for 'him' and whoever was down there waiting.

She knew now that he would be at peace and that he would never again suffer the terrible pains he had so stoically suffered without complaint over these past years… she was satisfied now in the knowledge that she had completed her penance for the child she had betrayed... so long ago.